ROBERT HUDSON

The Dazzle

VINTAGE BOOKS
London

Published by Vintage 2014

2 4 6 8 10 9 7 5 3 1

First published in Great Britain in 2013 by
Jonathan Cape

Vintage
Random House, 20 Vauxhall Bridge Road,
London SW1V 2SA

www.vintage-books.co.uk

Addresses for companies within The Random House Group Limited
can be found at: www.randomhouse.co.uk/offices.htm

The Random House Group Limited Reg. No. 954009

A CIP catalogue record for this book
is available from the British Library

ISBN 9780099575887

The Random House Group Limited supports The Forest Stewardship
Council® (FSC®), the leading international forest-certification organisation.
Our books carrying the FSC label are printed on FSC®-certified paper.
FSC is the only forest-certification scheme supported by the leading
environmental organisations, including Greenpeace. Our
paper procurement policy can be found at
www.randomhouse.co.uk/environment

Typeset by Palimpsest Book Production Limited, Falkirk, Stirlingshire

Printed and bound in Great Britain by Clays Ltd, St Ives plc

dazzle [ˈdæzˀl]

vb

1. (*usually tr.*) to blind or be blinded partially and temporarily by sudden excessive light
2. to amaze, as with brilliance *she was dazzled by his wit, she dazzles in this film*

n.

1. bright light that dazzles
2. bewilderment caused by glamour, brilliance, etc. *the dazzle of fame*
3. (*also known as razzle dazzle or dazzle painting*) a camouflage paint scheme consisting of geometric shapes in contrasting colours, interrupting and intersecting each other

For Jane

Foreword

Scarborough was mostly, but not exactly, as I portray it during the tunny-craze of the early Thirties, and so was Send Manor. Zane Grey, Lorenzo Mitchell-Henry, Mike Mitchell-Hedges, Martha Gellhorn, Joe Carstairs and various minor characters in this book were real people, and I have tried as best I can to capture their voices and characters. John Fastolf and his circle are invented, but draw heavily on the real lives of the interwar fast set. The contest I describe can be inserted, more or less, into the biographies of the real people involved, but Grey never visited England and he never competed with Mitchell-Henry.

At various points I have had to choose between truth and invention. My guiding principle was: what makes for the book I would most enjoy reading? This is not a work of history.

1934

August 1934

Prologue

Martha Gellhorn is strapped to a chair on the deck of a motor launch called *Harlequin* on a calm, bright summer's day and she is in terrible pain. Standing over her is Johnny Fastolf, Earl of Caister, a tall man with a shock of white-blond hair. Behind him, elfin and watchful, is Henny Rosefield. Martha grits her teeth.

Harlequin belongs to Fastolf and she is painted in jagged, multi-coloured stripes. In the harbour this looks insane, but out here on the glittering sea, from even quite a small distance, her outline shifts and wavers. It is not entirely clear whether she is coming towards you or heading away.

Harlequin is just for day trips. She spends each evening back in Scarborough under the lee of her big sister, *Dazzle*. Where *Harlequin* is garish pinks and greens, *Dazzle* is striped in sombre blacks and blues, but the stripes have much the same effect. *Harlequin* and *Dazzle* have plenty of company. Scarborough these past few summers has become a minor sort of Monte Carlo as movie stars and aristocrats have yachted north to hunt the mighty tunny.

That is why Martha, Johnny and Henny are here. They are hand-maidens to a contest between two titans of the tuna, a best-selling American author called Zane Grey and a crusty English gent by the unlikely name of Lorenzo Mitchell-Henry. It is a gaudy stage of gaudy players and Martha has seen enough gaudy stages these past few years to know that the contest is not the real story.

'Hold tight,' says Johnny. Her shoulders are burning. Something about Johnny has changed this week.

She met him a month ago on another gaudy stage. After careful consideration, she has decided that he is not the wicked dissolute of popular fame, and that behind this distortion lies a man at the pivot of his life, and that a little weight upon the scales might tip the balance for good or ill. Johnny took Martha to bed when they met, but he has made it clear that he won't do so again.

Martha looks across at Henny, who stands effortlessly still as the horizon rocks behind her. Henny came to England as 'secretary' to Zane Grey, and Martha knew at once that there was something dangerous about her. Henny might not be a bad person, she might not know that Johnny is vulnerable, you cannot blame the iceberg for being an iceberg, but Henny might destroy Johnny all the same. Or maybe Martha is just jealous.

That's the thing. Martha does honestly believe that Johnny is hiding something, that he faces some kind of crisis that he will not acknowledge, but she also understands that she is stuck on him and that this will inevitably skew her judgement, and so she must be careful. However hard one tries to focus on the bigger picture, on what is important, on what is really happening, one is always distracted by one's own petty concerns, by the six feet in front of one's face. When one finally sees the tiger, or the iceberg, or the crash, it is already too late.

'Now!' says Johnny. Under his instruction, Martha leans back, uncertainly at first, the rod bending until she is sure it must snap. Then, finally, the great unseen mass inches towards her and she quickly drops her hands and reels in the slack line.

After twenty minutes of painful heaving she catches sight of a faint pale flicker in the depths and someone mutters, 'Well done!' Almost immediately, as if the fish can see them too, the rod begins to vibrate, gathering energy. Martha's next effort doesn't move the tuna, and after a few seconds of shivering tension it plunges away again. The fight has already lasted an hour. Martha will have this creature if it kills her.

What is it about these bloody fish? This was not supposed to be about the fish.

11.52 p.m., Tuesday 14th August

Rudderick Drake – Send Manor, Surrey

Molly's girl was perfect apart from the heroin scars. Drake let her cuff and gag him. He was nearly forty and she was eighteen. He should never have let himself be persuaded into this mess. He should be disgusted with himself. He couldn't remember her name.

She offered him cocaine from the silver sugar bowl on the bedside table. He shook his head. What was he doing here? He was not this kind of person. She giggled and spooned an uneven line onto his chest.

Afterwards, wanting her own release, the girl took a syringe from the soft calfskin case which had been set out next to the sugar bowl. Again she offered, again Drake declined. She pulled a strip of velvet tight around her left bicep and injected into the vein below the elbow.

Immediately, she started shaking. Within seconds, it seemed, her neck had started to spasm, and then her arms and legs, and then she collapsed, eyes wide.

Drake struggled to free his wrists and ankles, but he could not. He tried to shout through his gag, but the band was still playing downstairs.

Drake heard something. The door handle was turning. Drake knew this was coming, but he still tried vainly to free himself.

Kim Waring stepped smartly into the room and closed the door quietly behind him. He raised his eyebrow. 'Oh, Ruddy,' he said. 'This is embarrassing.'

Drake tried to be sensible, to resign himself to the situation, to do whatever Kim Waring wanted.

After a moment's consideration, Waring donned his evening gloves and switched on the central light. The girl was on the floor. Waring lifted her onto Drake. She was warm but clammy. Drake recoiled and shook her off and Waring slapped him. 'Don't do that again. I can make this much worse for you.' Drake believed him. He was terrified.

Waring slipped a Leica from his inside pocket and took two pictures. 'I blackmail chaps sometimes,' he said. 'I always carry it. Just in case.' Then he stood back and cocked his head. 'This does look bad, but I'd prefer it if you were still excited. Maybe I could give you a hand?' The door opened again.

Enter Johnny Caister, impeccable. 'Well, I never,' he said, but he was already lifting up the girl, laying her on the floor, checking her pulse. 'Ah well.' He stood. 'A brief life, but a merry one.' He removed Drake's gag. 'How long?'

'Five minutes,' said Drake. 'Ten. I don't know.'

Caister turned to Waring. 'Get Molly,' he said.

Waring bridled. 'I'm not your—'

'She'll want to tidy this up without troubling the staff.' Caister was already untying Drake. Over his shoulder, before he left, Waring caught Drake's eye and patted his camera pocket.

Earlier That Day

John Fastolf, Earl of Caister –
Send Manor

John Scrope California Fastolf, Caister that is, Waterlands that will be, six feet two inches tall, useful sort of body, comical face and comical hair, beautifully dressed, scarred. Johnny Fastolf. Johnny Caister. Caister. He doesn't mind which, and he's called them all.

He's one of the richest men in the Empire. Or his father is, but his father stays in Norfolk, so his father doesn't count. Johnny goes everywhere. Surprisingly, he hasn't lost the family fortune, gambled it away or anything. Don't forget that.

How did they get so rich? They own a lot of London. They still have a gold mine near Sacramento. They invested well and they got out before the Crash. They have lucky blood. Don't forget that, either.

In a few days' time Johnny will take delivery of *Harlequin*, a twin-engined motor launch. For three summers London society has been agog with tales of giant tunny. It was time Johnny got in on the act, and it would have disappointed his public if he hadn't done it in style. He had *Harlequin* manufactured after a design by Zane Grey, the world's champion deep-sea angler, and he'll send her up to Scarborough for the end of the month. Johnny finds it helps to do what people expect, to hide in plain sight. It stops them asking personal questions.

He swings round the long drive into Send Manor – rather a small house to be called a manor, truth be told, but the outbuildings make up for it, and Stewart is an excellent host – and skids to a halt in a cloud of dust and gravel. It's only mid-afternoon, but at least a score of guests have already arrived.

A tiny, dark girl with huge eyes and a striking, unfashionable Eton crop is the first to try her luck. 'My name's June Smith,' she says. 'Isn't that the most awful thing you ever heard? I should absolutely change it, but Pa would have a cadenza.' She's very young. She says, 'I'm not one of Molly's "actresses", by the way, I'm legit. Gracie brought me down, darling thing that she is.'

They talk. She thinks Send is marvellous fun. He prefers them harder. She's the sort of girl who might get upset after one night. He could do it anyway, to teach her a lesson about the world.

Then Caro joins them. Caro is Johnny's ex-wife. '"June" is it?' she says. 'Don't do it. You'll get burnt.'

'I don't want anything from him,' says June. 'I don't expect anything.'

'You'll still get burnt.'

'To touch the fire is a sensation,' says June. 'Only sensation matters. Only sensation is real.'

Caro laughs. 'Oh, my dear!' she says. 'If it's reality you want, you've come to the wrong party. Johnny unmoored from that a long time ago. He's empty inside, bottomlessly bloody empty, like the rest of them here – anyone who was in the bloody war. He has no sensations left, have you, Johnny? No idea what it is to feel anything?' Johnny doesn't react. Caro turns her dark eyes back to June and says, 'It's the ice that burns you deepest, darling, not the fire.'

After dinner Johnny notices Rudderick Drake's bumbling exit with one of Molly's girls and shortly afterwards he sneaks away to follow them. Ruddy is an innocent, basically, and he's an old friend. When he finds them, the girl is dead. Johnny is not surprised to discover Kim Waring in attendance.

He dispatches Kim, and Ruddy starts to explain the scene as best he can, but he is ashen and shivering. Johnny pats his shoulder and says, 'Calm down, old lozenge. This is the kind of thing that happens. Now we have to get everyone cleaned up and out of here.'

'Will you take me back to London?'

'Probably for the best. Grab your clothes and dash back to your room. I'll be there as soon as I've dealt with Molly.' Johnny turns. Ruddy is fumbling for his wallet. 'Don't worry about that, old chap. I think it would be fruity of her to expect payment when the girl expired courtesy of her Chinese chum's rotten dope. I'll sort everything out.'

Ruddy puts on a robe, bundles up his dinner suit and scuttles off, peeking furtively left and right from the door as if he were in a movie.

Johnny lifts the girl onto the bed. Her shingled hair looks almost grey in the electric light.

Five minutes later, Kim returns with Molly Parker. She takes in the scene. Kim and Johnny are standing at opposite ends of the room like bad cats. 'Oh, for God's sake,' says Molly. 'I can't think with you two glaring.' Kim leaves with exceeding ill grace.

Molly locks the door. She turns to Johnny with a breathy 'Darling!' and they kiss. She's a more or less standard bombshell, with wavy chestnut hair and full lips. She's thirty-three and she's been given the use of two bedrooms for the duration of the house party. Her girls are not cheap, not by any means, but they are the subsidiary of an altogether larger affair, hence her access to dope and cocaine.

'What were you doing here?' she asks.

'I was looking for you.'

'Darling!' They kiss again. 'I thought you were going to gobble up the little actress.'

Johnny breaks away. He gestures to the girl. He says, 'I told you this kind of thing would happen. It's the Sphinx's dope, but you're the one who'll swing for it.'

'What can I do? I'm not his partner. He owns me.' Molly smoothes her hands down the front of her dress. 'Will you help, darling?'

'It's hardly in my interest.'

'Darling!'

He makes a show of thinking about it. 'All right,' he says. 'I'll deal with Ruddy.'

'Thank you, darling. I'll get the boys. What should I do? Wrap her in a rug?'

'Just get her away from here. People won't remember her. I'll drive Ruddy home.'

'Will you be back tomorrow?'

'Probably. Go. I'll guard the room till you get back.'

Molly throws her arms about him in pathetic gratitude and runs to find her boys. Johnny looks as if he is helping her, but that's not really what is happening. He's here because he doesn't want Ruddy getting sucked deeper into the great and awful game that his own life has become.

He looks back down at the girl. She'll disappear without a ripple, as if she had never been.

He stands. He goes to the window for a moment, then wanders around the bed, inspects the sugar bowl. The syringe is still on the floor. He picks it up.

For all the things he *has* done, Johnny has never touched drugs. The reason he gives, to himself as well as to others, is that he doesn't want anything to cloud his relationship with the world. This is absurd on various levels. First, he drinks. Second, he has often wanted nothing more than to cloud his relationship with the world. Third, if Caro is right about him, if he is ice, then he has no worthwhile relationship with the world anyway.

He stares at the girl, willing himself to be moved. When nothing comes, when she continues to lie there in the abstract, he turns away and sits on the edge of the bed with his back to her. He has seen too much senseless death perhaps.

The syringe is still half-full. Johnny turns his left hand palm-down and tenses his fingers several times. He rubs the needle along one of the veins that emerge. He's held loaded guns before, on his own, several times. He's stood at the edge of railway platforms. The reason he's never followed through is that suicide would betray all the chaps who didn't make it out of the trenches. It's another absurdly simplified reason, just the thing he's decided to tell himself to explain the fact that every time he's considered it, on balance he's decided against, and so onwards he trots, trots, trots, waiting for the sun to set. God knows, his life is probably more of a betrayal than his death would be. He lets the needle scratch his skin, but it goes no further. He is just playing at being a soul in torment, like he's playing at everything else.

'Bottomless,' Caro called him. No bottom, no heft. He quite likes that. Molly returns and he goes to find Ruddy.

Saturday 18th August

Mike Mitchell-Hedges – New York

Battles with Sea Monsters
By F.A. Mitchell-Hedges

[Note to self: *Battles with Sea Monsters* is a good title – double meaning too. This is a first bash at a prologue. Might need to change it when I actually go to Scarborough but best to get ahead of the game!]

I stared at the edge of the world, as powerless before its bleak and pitiless majesty as any woad-spattered Celt. I have wandered our teeming globe for half my life and more, one of those curious creatures whose curse it is that they may find peace only on the wildest ocean or in the most Hellish jungle. How had I blundered into Scarborough, brilliant with princelings and bright-lit pleasure yachts? And how was it that, far from being sickened by the stench of civilisation in all its degenerate decay, I found myself dreaming that there might yet be hope for the soul of modern man?

I was on board Earl Caister's fabulous *Dazzle* and alongside me, ready to lock their souls in primal struggle, two strong men stood face-to-face: Lorenzo Mitchell-Henry, the tweed-clad English gentleman-warrior and Zane Grey, the expert mountain man of the Wild West. They were preparing to duel on the high seas, and I was the foolish character who had brought them together!

It would be a death-battle, but the deaths would not be their own. Mitchell-Henry owned the world's record for giant tunny long held by Grey, and Grey desperately wanted it back. The Yorkshire coast, running thick with nutritious herring, is home to the world's greatest tunny, and my experience in the wild oceans told me that if puny man had landed fish of ten feet in length and weighing a half ton, then leviathans of fifteen feet and a full ton would most assuredly lurk in wait. I was with the very men to haul them out. I would try my own luck, of course, but for the pure joy of it, not for any fleeting glory!

If I scorn the records mania, the dull dream of catching the fatter fish rather than the better one, then do not imagine I scorn the sport, for there is no challenge finer than this hunting for sea monsters. Nowhere does a man connect so directly with his ancient foe. He does not send in dogs to do his work, or shoot cold lead from a cosy hide. But nor, to my surprise, as I stood observing the principals in this contest, did I scorn the urge which had brought these two proud champions to this duel, to best each other at all costs. In the endurance of this urge lies the very soul of man.

[QUERY: *Does it indeed? A good thought. Use it more. Is 'The Soul of Men' a possible subtitle?*]

Behind Grey and Mitchell-Henry stood *Dazzle's* celebrated owner, our host and judge. I first met John Fastolf, Earl of Caister, some years ago on a trip to Germany, which I had undertaken for reasons which must remain forever obscure. I had been prepared to despise him, for I presumed him a debased, luxurious sort of creature, famous merely for his fame. But on shaking those fine hands, I felt a hidden hardness, and I searched his pale eyes for that spark of fellow-feeling in which I have never known myself mistaken, the sense that one has met a man who must live in civilisation, but who is not part of it. I saw then that he had the indestructible steel core of the sportsman and soldier, a core that our degenerating world has not quite managed to breed out of the English race, the core you may find in dukes and yeomen, the core which, so long as it is preserved, means Britons never, ever will be slaves.

[NOTE: *Caister's probably a bounder, but he's a bloody rich one. Butter him up. If I ever meet him!*]

Rounding out our gallant company was Grey's beautiful and eager new secretary, a cloistered child of the city looking eagerly forward to seeing the great fisherman at his work.

I have written extensively about the malevolent savagery of the deeps. No prehistorical forest holds terrors more horrible than those I have seen in tropic seas. The doors of death never swing outward, though ghastly and varied are the ways in which many enter. I have not previously described these bitter Northern waters, but it is not because I do not know their rips and subtle traps, their secret coves and the awful risks that may be run. I have reasons for my silence and I shall never break it, or perhaps it is better to declare I shall never be allowed to!

So let me say merely that my personal doom has lain more southerly and anyway – I am not ashamed to admit it – I am happier when I am hot! Also, men of my stamp do not necessarily like to return to civilisation in the evenings.

But make no mistake, these are savage seas, lair of the whale-killer and the great kraken.* Miss Rosefield wanted to see the crack fisherman at his work, but she could scarcely imagine what lay in store for her. The mountainous grey waters of the North are as rude and primeval as any rocky wasteland. They are the wilderness all Britons inherit, our glory and our birthright. We have fed our sea for a thousand years and she calls us still unfed, and how few of those pompous praters demanding massiver Dreadnoughts and stealthier submarines ever pad from their sleepy offices to gaze upon this precious legacy?

I do not despise the Surrey office sloth – civilisation needs him, I suppose – but he will not lift his eyes to his inheritance. He pootles around his garden and rhapsodises about his hedgy hills and never comprehends the hard and fearful wastelands scant miles from his burrow. Even if he manages to totter to Cromer, does he gaze in wonder at the distant deep? No. He stares at fat red children and poseurs in bathing suits. It drives one to despair.

Or to the jungle! The civilised world isn't fit to live in. Everything

---

* What Mitchell-Hedges calls a 'whale-killer' is what we would call a killer whale. There is no such thing as a kraken.

is prostituted to Mammon, nations are destroying one another with the greed that always brings destruction. I firmly believe I shall live to see London and New York a bloody shambles, a heap of ruins. Man's lust for power and money will destroy him in the end. I prefer the tropics where man speaks fair unto man or stabs him in the heart, but never the back. Life is clean and simple there. Nowhere else shall I ever find peace.

And yet in all my tropic exploration I have seldom seen a sight so wondrous and so raw as the sea the evening we arrived in a Scarborough scrubbed clean by a summer storm.

[NOTE: *Can probably just say this, but pay some attention to prevailing conditions, in case they turn out to be unusual.*]

The sun beat hard from crystal blue on the retreating purple clouds which filled the sky from a few miles in front of us and out to the distant horizon. The heavy surf beneath that roiling range still lashed with rain, and then, in a slow moment, the vista filled with crimson gold, the waters aflame, the heavens glorious, as if with a weary gesture some divine Turner had drawn his brush at random over the scene, leaving behind a painted hazard of the richest colours on his palette, merging each with each almost imperceptibly.

The glorious gold and red that evening were a reminder that our North Sea can have a weird, unearthly beauty, but I have never been seduced by mere beauty. It is wildness I love, and truth be told I prefer it in its honest daily garb. The slate grey waves and pale iron sky of the calm dawn, the low sun which turns it flittering and flinty, the angry metal greens and whipping white crests that we seamen know spell danger. I have seen enough deep water to know that even in the summer softness, the ocean can gulp and gather whole civilisations to her salty bosom. Either one is prepared or one is not.

Dazzle, with her neatly scrubbed decks, polished chrome, damask sheets and Parisian kitchen was a hundred worlds away from the dear old *Amigo*, sweating her way to Panama and crewed by the most dangerous men in the Americas. It was the sheerest chance I was here at all, and once again I found myself grinning at the perverse sprite that leads me to all four corners of the world, into the glorious adventures I have written about and the deadly scrapes which must never be revealed.

I had left England that August after three months concluding the sad business of my father's affairs, and I arrived in New York ready to head south with urgent instructions from the British Museum to return to my study of unknown civilisations.

My first evening in that great labyrinth of concrete canyons, so well-remembered from my misspent, money-gathering youth, I found myself invited to a cocktail party given by my old friend Stoat Ledger, editor of *The Wolf*, America's most venerable and prestigious sporting magazine. I need hardly say that I had no desire to subject myself to a room of twittering females, but I did not wish to offend Ledger, and I freely own that some part of me was drawn by curiosity concerning the double life of Zane Grey, in whose honour the party was given.

In one incarnation, Grey is his nation's darling, the celebrated author whose picturesque tales of honour and romance in the Wild West have made him an unimaginable fortune. But in addition, he is the towering figure of the American wilderness, the outdoorsman and hunter who has done more than any other writer to bring alive the thrill of fishing for giants.

Tunny-fever is not so pronounced in New York as it is in London, but every man present knew that an Englishman called Lorenzo Mitchell-Henry now held Grey's most precious record – poor Colonel Peel's brief tenure as world's champion was rather forgotten since he, unlike Mitchell-Henry, had chosen not to bicker with Grey in the letters pages of *The Wolf*, among other familiar journals! Disconcertingly for a man whose name has once been widely known, I found myself explaining over and again the difference between a Mitchell-Henry and a Mitchell-Hedges! 'They both hunt giant fish,' I declared, 'but they do not both hunt records.'

I swiftly perceived that Grey, standing at the eye of the gossiping storm, was the lone individual less comfortable at his party than I. But when he heard my name, he sprang suddenly alert. The very man with most reason to mistakenly hear the words 'Mitchell-Henry' was the first man to make no mistake. 'Mr Mitchell-Hedges!' he said. 'Can it really be you? I'm darned pleased to make your acquaintance.'

Incredible to relate, the great author was an avid reader of my own poor works! He cared nothing for my scholarly labours amongst the tribesmen or on behalf of our proudest museums, but he recalled with instant detail every moment of my battle with a giant sawfish in '27, and was keen to press me on the knotty topic of rays. The party melted away for us. We were lost in the brotherhood of the fish.

By the most curious coincidence, Grey told me that he had recently received a challenge from Captain Mitchell-Henry. 'You'll have to take him up on it, of course!' I said. 'It will be capital sport!'

'I'd be darned pleased,' he replied, with a hint of distant danger in those quiet eyes, a look I've seen before in careful men you would not wish to rouse to anger, 'but I shouldn't like to travel to some strange town on the far side of the world without an honest broker. I don't suppose you'd turn yourself around and be my second?'

I laughed heartily. 'Between you and me, Mr Grey,' I said, 'I've never been one for regulations. I'll do it if you want, and I'll travel with you anyway because I wouldn't miss the sport for worlds, but there's only one man alive I'd pick to referee this duel: my dear friend Johnny Caister.'

The Pierre, NY
But Scarborough-bound, incredibly
18th August

Dear Jane,*

As you'll have noticed, young feller, I was not waiting at the Chelsea Piers to greet you. Long story short: I am heading back to

---

* Jane Harvey Houlson (b. 1899) was Mike Mitchell-Hedges's devoted girl Friday between 1924 and 1934, accompanying him on adventures to Honduras and the like. She was following Mitchell-Hedges to England, having tarried a while with 'Joe', one of the most dangerous men in Central America. She planned to find someone to marry in her native Devon.

England only two days after arriving in New York. I shall be parlaying my unimpeachable credentials as a big-fish man – whatever they say about the rest, I can show them pictures of the bloody fish – into some form of quasi-official role, as yet undefined, within a party heading for Scarborough to hunt giant tunny.

At this moment it's nine in the morning and, powered by some of the Pierre's thickest and most nightmarish Abyssinian brew, sticky with life-giving sugar, I have spent an hour clacking away at the old typo and producing a stirring tissue of lies to give myself a head-start on the oppo when it comes to getting said adventure into the hands of whichever miserly publisher can resist it least.

I should really have made hay in Scarborough before now. England has gone completely tunny – tunny records, tunny society, tunny train timetables, probably tunny-tooth jewellery if you look hard enough. Some bold souls even eat the things. I have explained that the flesh is perfectly well if it's all you can get, but it's hardly marlin or tiger shark.

I've only avoided Scarbie because it costs so damn much and Hardy's bound to be around, demanding to be paid for his bloody rods. But it's been an unexploited opportunity and now I'm going to exploit it. I've helped provoke an unwilling Zane Grey into battling the pesky near-namesake M-Henry, and Grey will also be thinking this is worth a yarn, but I'll have written most of mine before we even get to Scarborough. It's going· to be English Gent duelling Western Cowboy on the wild Northern seas, the last English wilderness, a manly prophylaxis against sissifying civilisation, and so on. Sounds good, doesn't it? Hardly need to go there to write it, but better safe than sorry.

Everything else is fine or fine enough. I'll get back to this letter later, but the fingers are starting to seize up.

I sailed back to America in a high sweat, I'll admit. I hadn't expected a fortune from the old man, but I hadn't thought to be cut off. He was hit by the Crash, of course. I'd hoped for a year of carefree sailing, but Alfred got the lot. Alfred isn't a bad hat, though, and little Dicky adores me. Alf's wife, on the other hand— She and my father never forgave me for the trial. Either trial, actually.*

Anyway, Alfred slipped me a couple of rather good delfts, which more than covered my expenses for the trip, along with something for Dolly. So, not exactly on my uppers, but not enough to put me at my ease. Nothing changes.

Is everyone talking about *Anthony Adverse* in Honduras? If they're not, it's the only bloody place. London and the ship were full of it, and so was the cocktail party where I met Grey last night. It's a great brick of a book. Lady authoress on the *Empress* pointed out that if you listen when people talk about it, you notice how obvious it is that no one's actually read it. It's true, and I couldn't believe I hadn't spotted it myself. Everyone has an opinion of the moral and asks other people's, but no one talks about what actually happens. Sharp woman, and damned funny. Didn't get anywhere with her. Thought to myself that I should read the book, however glum. Bluff explorer turns out to be well read, puts people on the back foot, man of substance, and so on.

That's why a tunny-book would be so bloody useful just now, especially if I could break the world's record. Or if one of the others breaks it, but better if it's me. Memory's shorter than humbug, that's part of The Way, but it's not short enough for my taste and it's not just my harridan of a sister-in-law who remembers that blasted trial. Even the *Mail* won't touch me. I need an honest coup to hurry matters along.

'Honest' in relative terms, of course! This is how the thing came off:

The buyer I found for Alfred's delfts was a big-faced Irish bugger who's been bitten by the tarpon bug, and via tarpon trips he knows Stoat Ledger of *The Wolf*. The Irishman introduced us at his club. Ledger misheard my name as Mitchell-Henry, of course, and he practically fell over his beard at the thought of Grey's reaction. He

---

* Mitchell-Hedges refers to the divorce trial of his earlier travelling companion, Lady Mabel Richmond-Brown, in which he was named as co-respondent, as well as to the libel trial where a scheme he had participated in to publicise an easily traceable form of luggage, involving a fake car-jacking among other things, had gone badly wrong.

could hardly back down when he realised the truth, and he covered it well enough. He dredged up some memory of my jungle broadcasts, and even *The Wolf*'s review of *Giant Fish*. I told him to look out for *Blue Blaze* and I think he will.

I mummed the he-man horrified at the thought of small talk in a roomful of females, but not so much as to run the risk of his not taking me along. One never knows what use can be made of someone like Grey, but I hardly thought the banana would ripen so quickly!

Nice party. Stoat can do it in style, like all the blessed, and he introduced me to Grey. I played the modest adventurer for all I was worth, said I was an explorer naturalist more than a sporting man, and certainly not a record-breaker, though I'd broken some records, incidentally.

If you think I can talk for hours about killing a shark – and I know you do – you have never met anything like Grey. The man will tackle-gab for an hour, not because he wants a free reel, but because he's genuinely interested. It boggles the mind.

And he is *obsessed* with records. He ranted for damn near twenty minutes about a marlin which couldn't be ratified because it was incomplete, even though it was still record weight after losing 200 lbs to sharks.

I think it may actually have been to stop his flow that I threw in the jab that led to this whole business. Like I say, the homeland is tunny-mad, and half the noise comes from M-Henry, who seems a prosy sort of ass and who is hell-bent on making all possible capital out of his record. Can't criticise the man for that, of course, but he does it with such shocking style. If it were me, and God knows I hope it is soon, I'd pretend it was a happy accident. I'll make bloody sure I stick to the rules so that anything I catch counts, but I'll pretend I'm fighting the manly battle for the fun of the thing, and so on. And if I hit the jackpot, I'll say how little I care about it and I'll do so everywhere that printing presses can be bought or be found. If you draw aces, play them like they're fours. That's what the truth-tellers never understand.

Similarly, when some bugger inevitably caught a bigger tuna, I'd pretend I hadn't heard for as long as possible and then I'd be damned pleased for them. There's no point looking like you're chewing a bee every time someone brings it up; it just encourages beggars like me.

Grey: he's small, and he's not young, but he isn't soft. He says he's spent his life in wild places, and even if they are not so wild as he pretends, and even if he talks a lot of horseradish about the spirits, I will say he seems an outdoorsman.

Unlike me, he's not comfortable in a suit, or cannot look comfortable in one anyway. One of the advantages of being raised an English gentleman.

He was squiring a stunner of the classic, dark-haired, butter-wouldn't-melt variety. I assumed she was his daughter until Stoat put me right. Apparently, Grey is always accompanied by at least one beautiful secretary and he'd just picked up this new one. When I jibed him about the tunny, he looked sick, but she leapt in. 'Zane won't go to England. Captain Mitchell-Henry challenged him, but he won't go.'

'Bit rum.' That was all I said, but you can imagine the tone of voice.

'I'm not interested.'

'I understand,' I said. 'Champion sportsman won't rise to the fly, that sort of beeswax? Interesting tale. Sure I could sell it here and there.' Then I watched the bugger twist.

'It would be an adventure, Zane,' said the girl. 'You said you need an adventure!'

'I want virgin seas, not a provincial town,' he said, or something like it.

'The North Sea is not less wild than your precious Atlantic,' says me. 'I've seen things no white man has seen, looked the native in his jungle eye, but the North Sea is as fierce a place as fish ever swam, and there are tunny there to freeze your blood. They've burst my rod. If I hadn't had to come here for business, I'd be in Scarborough now.' It was practically broadcast-quality. I almost believed myself.

Grey obviously hated the whole idea, but the best he could come up with was, 'It's his water. His boats.'

'But Zane is the greatest fisherman, isn't he?' the girl implored me. There was something odd about her tone and I thought 'Hang on!' It sounded like hero-worship, but it wasn't. She wanted something that Grey didn't want. A game was afoot, and I was happy to play. I told him that I could make the contest happen. The girl said they could do that without me. I said they needed an honest broker.

She laughed! I knew right then that the prim little baggage had seen straight through me, but I'm fast on my feet. 'Not me, of course. I'm an explorer, not a sportsman. But I know the country and I know the man you need.'

'Who?' she said. I didn't know what she wanted, and she was trying to queer my pitch, but I didn't dislike her for it, curiously. She's got style. Still, she needed to know her place.

'Who would you suggest?' I asked.

'Well, I don't—'

'Where are you from?'

'Wiscasset, Maine.'

It was a lie. I said, 'Really?' and she knew I knew too. Interesting girl. Quick. Cold eyes, though.

'So,' she said, 'who is your honest broker?'

'My old chum Johnny Fastolf, Earl of Caister,' I said. That got her attention, which means she's a society chit, or wants to be. 'You know him, Mr Grey?' I asked.

'I know of him,' he said. 'But—' He started sounding off about the primitive Scarborough style, which he has outdated with his various motor launches. I was waiting for this. One of the advantages of the tunny-frenzy is that all London knows that Caister has built just such a motor launch for the present season, and he cites Grey's boats as his model. The local tunny aficionados are unhappy about it, but there's nothing against it in the rules. They've spilt so much ink proclaiming that their way is best – because they don't have the money to build motorboats – that they can hardly cry 'foul'.

And so, 'This is exactly why I suggested Caister!' said I. 'I presumed you realised. He's built a launch on the Grey pattern!' He was stuck now, and the girl egged the pudding, saying he would surely triumph, especially with his own methods.

Ledger's paying our fares and *The Wolf* will publish reports by both Grey and yours truly. The only problem will be getting Caister to play ball. I'm popping out now to gin up a couple of cables pretending that he's thrilled about the whole affair. Once I've got Grey in England, the *alea est jacta*, even if Caister runs a mile.

Better go and face a telegram. Pip pip.

Done, courtesy of an easily bribed little German fellow at the Western Union. 'Mine' implies that Caister is a chum. His 'reply' says simply DAZZLE AT YOUR DISPOSAL SOUNDS CAPITAL SPORT MY CLUB THURS NEXT CAISTER.

The more I think about Grey and his enigmatic houri, the harder I find it to pair on our Humbug Scale. I got another good squizz at them when I tottered over to *The Wolf* to make travel arrangements.

On the one hand, Grey's whole life is a lie: he has a wife, but he spends his time running around with these young women (his wife is another 'Dolly', remarkably! I'll see what he says when I raise *that* coincidence). On the other hand, there's a puritan naïvety to him. He refuses to accept he's a humbug at all. He wants everything to happen for his benefit, but he also wants it all to be true. He doesn't just want to hold the world's record; he wants it to be because he actually has caught the biggest fish. You and I think right and wrong are nonsense made by civilised men. Grey thinks right and wrong are as he defines them.

The girl – Miss Rosefield – is trickier. She knows she's a humbug, at least. Until I know what she wants, it is impossible to say what kind. She could simply want to climb the greasy ladder, but why is she so keen on this trip? Because she's after an earl? American girls are stupid about European princes, but I don't think that's it. Could be that she is new to The Way of the Humbug and she's flexing her muscles. Most likely is that she wants as much as she can get and has some devil in her. I shall keep a weather eye.

So, in short, young feller, I'm not here, but at least the Pierre is expecting you. I've left enough money to keep you for a while. It's practically ruined me, but you deserve every cent.

It will have been hell for you to leave Joe, but you knew he was a final savage passion before returning to civ, an itch you had to scratch. You have been a damned fine companion these last years, in everything!

I'll say again: you will be happy as an English wife, and I shall enjoy having a respectable house to visit on my trips home. And I am sure a demure little Devonshire matron will be a role you could play to useful perfection at galleries in want of small pieces of unimpeachable silver. Whichever of the boys wins your hand, I hope he never wins quite all of your heart, and I would wager that he is in for a couple of surprises he will not regret! Only an ass would regret that kind of surprise, and you are not likely to choose an ass.

I wax sentimental. Unforgivable. I may be back here before you are, in which case this letter is all just wasted words! If I am not, I hope you will wait for a final (unforgivably sentimental) farewell,

Your Chief

Henny Rosefield –
Various Times and Places

The girl born Margaret Hartshorne read everything she could find about Zane Grey. There was nothing about his women, which was good. It meant fewer people would have had her idea.

She was still resident at Mount Hope Asylum, over the bay from Halifax, and she decided to familiarise herself with certain physical acts. Grey's previous choices suggested that he might not demand expertise, but she must at least be unafraid. 'Modern' perhaps was the word, although Grey would probably say 'natural'. It was possible he preferred virgins, but he certainly did not insist.

She discussed the matter with Cecilia, who did not approve, but was prepared to help her. Margaret settled on Captain Haugesund, a melancholic patient in his mid-forties.

Margaret apprised Captain Haugesund of the situation – of the need for her to gain experience and learn what was normal – and he enquired as to whether she might not prefer someone of her own age? She said she would, but felt that an older man might have fewer expectations of her. She did not tell him that he had been chosen because, as a sailor and a European, it was felt his morals would be flexible.

Captain Haugesund was bearded and portly. He removed his trousers and aroused himself manually before putting on the prophylactic procured by Cecilia. He split it, and apologised that he was not used to the new latex varieties. He was talkative, probably out of nerves. Margaret gave him another. While he put it on, he said that on the next occasion she should arouse him, since that was more usual, but he thought he should do it this first time and he hoped she didn't mind. She said she didn't. When Margaret had undressed, Captain Haugesund kissed her mouth, which he opened with his lips and flicked with his tongue. She recoiled. He said, 'Do not be scared, it is normal.' His tongue was chilly and slippery. Then he kissed her breasts hard, which aroused her slightly, and then he placed his hands between her legs. They were small hands, but there they felt large. His fingers were hot where his tongue had been cold. He pushed and poked for some time while his bristly mouth worked upon her breast. Eventually, with surprising suddenness, her cleft slid open and he mounted her, and with much grunting succeeded in gaining access. There was a sharp pain, but not a great one.

Afterwards Captain Haugesund said, 'I should not have done that. It was wrong.'

She asked, 'Why? Was it not normal?'

He said, 'It was normal, but—' He turned to her, and she could see he was crying. 'You do not need to do this.'

'You know nothing about me.'

'I have asked. I know why you are here.'

'No, you don't.'

'I know why you want to run away.'

'I don't want to "run away"! I have an object.'

'If you must do this to achieve your "object", then it is a "bad object". It is immoral. It will destroy you.'

'I don't care.'

'If you don't care, then it will also destroy others.'

'I don't care.'

Afterwards Cecilia was waiting nervously in Margaret's room. Margaret told her that she would not be returning to Captain Haugesund, that she had already tarried too long at Mount Hope and that she was pleased to have achieved her womanhood in this efficient fashion. She did not discuss her decision to achieve further comfort with the act elsewhere and to confirm that Captain Haugesund was as other men were.

Cecilia moved to embrace her. Margaret stepped back. Cecilia said, 'Whatever happens, wherever you are, please know that I will help you, if I can. Please write to me.' Margaret said she would. It was easy to lie to Cecilia.

Some days later she was travelling under the name Alice Toogood. She found a carriage with a single, male occupant. He was quite handsome. She ascertained that he did not have a wife and asked that he kiss her. He was very surprised, but after the request was repeated he did so.

On arriving in Buffalo, she accompanied him to his hotel. She planned to arouse him as Captain Haugesund had aroused himself, but he was already in that state. When it became clear that he did not have a prophylactic, she went to her travelling case and fetched one from the package that Cecilia had provided.

This second coitus was considerably more energetic than the first, and quicker.

Later she did arouse him manually, learning to achieve which had been one of her aims. When she stopped, awaiting further coitus, he requested that she continue. She went with her hand, and he said, 'With your mouth, if you will.' She had presented herself as a certain kind of person. Her sister had described this thing to her. She steeled herself to the shock of his emission, but still a small part went down the wrong way and she coughed. The man was apologetic and said she was wonderful, like a dream. She dressed. He asked if he would ever see her again. She said no. He appeared relieved.

From Grey's novels, she built up a vision of his ideal woman. She chose various names before settling on 'Henrietta Rosefield'. She selected a home town safely distant from the sea and a family history not unlike her own. She would come from the suffocating oppression of provincial gentility. She did not bother to change her appearance – her hair was very different now – but she improved her wardrobe, selling a stolen necklace to do so. She looked like a sheltered Eastern sophisticate who had never seen the wild places.

She extended her experience over the subsequent month as she travelled to California. Once there, she learned that Grey's current girl, Brownella Baker, was nothing like Henrietta Rosefield. Baker was what people described as pagan, intellectual and free-spirited. Henny assimilated this information.

She found two of Grey's previous lovers and told them of her admiration for him. They were guarded, but they spoke tenderly of him rather than in anger. Both were, like her, slender and dark-haired. Their lack of hostility was interesting, in anthropological terms. They asked why she was so fascinated by Grey, and she was evasive. She had similar conversations with others from his retinue.

She learned that Grey, in spite of his unparalleled sales, had squandered the vast part of his fortune. This was a disaster for her plan. She continued with it, however.

Grey's finances were kept afloat by his wife's good management, even though the couple led separate lives. Dolly arranged that Grey, against his will, undertook public engagements at the behest of his remaining publishers. At one such engagement in San Francisco, Henny met Grey for the first time since August 1927.

Brownella Baker was present. She looked scornful of the conventional, unfashionable throng. Henny spoke to a publisher's agent, who said that a number of the crowd had been dragooned at the last moment when it became clear the event would be meagrely attended.

Henny watched for some time. She caught Grey's eye, and Baker's. She waited until the pair were considering their exit.

Henny remembered what her mother had taught her about the vanity of men, panted twenty times very fast to flush her face and hurried over to the author. Baker laughed. 'Here she is at last!' Henny pretended not to understand. 'He knows you've been sneaking around,' Baker said. 'You're not unusual.'

'I wasn't trying to be unusual.'

'Why have you been asking questions about me?' said Grey.

Henny stood stock-still for a moment, as if she needed to gather herself. While doing so, she forced air into the top of her palate to squeeze her eyes to the edge of tears. Then, in a quiet voice that appeared to be cracking, she said she was very sorry, and she did not know what it was in his books that ravished her so utterly, since she had spent a cloistered life in a big house in a small town, but when she read them she felt she was standing beneath a strange, peculiar sky. She said that his descriptions of the eternal wildness of man, of his hunger and his need for redemption at the hands of woman, tore bleeding strips from her soul. She needed to know the West herself.

'You travelled through the West to get here,' said Baker.

'Yes,' Henny said. 'But very quickly. I was running away.'

'What from?' asked Grey.

Henny said that she must sound like a terrible ninny, and of course Grey's books were just books, but books could be the truest things in the world. Some people today were too clever to see that, but that was their loss.

Baker laughed that this was enough horseshit to float a battleship.

'What were you running away from?' asked Grey again. 'Are you safe?'

Henny started to sob. Grey took her hand. Baker said, 'For God's sake, Z.G., the girl's ridiculous.'

Henny gulped, 'I'll go,' and she made to leave.

Grey said, 'Stop.'

Baker said, 'Good grief! If—'

'Brownie!' Grey said. 'I just want to know that she's all right.'

'For God's sake, Z., she's—'

'I will not be crossed in public,' said Grey. After a murderous look, Baker left. 'She's—'

'I know,' said Henny. 'Please don't worry. I knew girls like that back in— Oh, I nearly said! They thought I was very old-fashioned, and they were all smoking and dancing, and somehow it started to feel as if the whole world was out of joint for me and the only place I could find any peace was in your books. I didn't want to cause trouble. I just wanted to thank you.'

'It's a long way to come to say thank you. Are you sure that was all?'

'Yes. No. Not all. But I can't talk about— Sorry.'

Grey took Henny to dinner to help her calm down. Over the subsequent week she let him chip away at her history: the quiet girl with a vile socialite mother and a beautiful, arrogant sister; the drunk, defeated father and the cruel years of being sent to the sanatorium to 'rest' whenever she showed a fragment of independence; the terrible things that had been done to her there. Frequently her eyes glistened.

Brownella Baker attended the second dinner. She snorted when Henny told Grey he was a wonderful listener.

During the third dinner Grey announced that he had fought with Baker, terminally. Henny placed her hand on his. Afterwards, rather formally, Grey took her to bed. He asked if she was comfortable and he showed her his prophylactic and explained its use. It was a reusable one made of rubber, and it had been painted to resemble a small totem pole. He said that the images gave it a queer, inexplicable vitality. She nodded solemnly, biting the inside of her cheeks to keep herself from laughing. Then he said that her terrible past experiences of the act must not discourage her.

Henny's various preparations did not prepare her for congress with Grey. 'Don't worry,' Grey reassured her afterwards. 'That was normal.'

Grey travelled to New York for another engagement arranged by his wife, this time in partnership with Stoat Ledger of *The Wolf*. Grey took Henny, pointing out landmarks on the journey and explaining where they would stop on the long, slow trip home.

Brownella Baker travelled with them, to Grey's annoyance. She already had her ticket, she said, and it would be foolish to waste it. She intended to stay in New York afterwards.

Grey told Henny that she had nothing to fear from Baker. He said he had no patience with jealousy – that, indeed, was why his marriage had been so successful. He said he was disappointed with Baker, who clearly could not see that his feelings for Henny were something new and strange in his life, something paradisiacal and unique. He said his poor words could not capture one-thousandth part of the strength and splendour of this emotion, that she made him young again. She replied that there was nothing poor about his words.

Over the subsequent days she continued to explore for a weak point. She asked Grey why he didn't win back his world record for tuna. He said it was not that simple. The Englishman Mitchell-Henry had got lucky. Some fisherman are lucky and some are unlucky. He himself was unlucky to an unparalleled degree. In his vexation, he let slip that Mitchell-Henry had challenged him to a contest.

Immediately, with shocking clarity, Henny was overwhelmed with a yearning for England. She could not explain it to herself, but felt an absolute desperation to escape, to swap this continent for one where she might be renewed.

That very night, they went to the reception which *The Wolf* was hosting in Grey's honour. Grey did not enjoy the party. He only lit up when Ledger introduced a tall Englishman, Mike Mitchell-Hedges. At first Henny heard this as Mitchell-Henry, but Grey made no such mistake. The Englishman talked disparagingly of records and said he'd just as happily hook a marlin on a rope as on a rod and reel. He could enjoy the sport as a sport, sometimes, when he was at leisure, but he wasn't often at leisure. He was a rather archaic human being, he supposed. He still saw fishing as a way of catching food.

He and Grey entered into a long discussion of tackle. Mitchell-Hedges's face glazed over, but he grew animated when Grey began to berate some 'Hardy', a reel-maker who used Grey's name on his products, by licence, but overcharged for his goods and wouldn't take back unused items. Mitchell-Hedges claimed to have had a similar experience with Hardy, on a smaller scale, of course. He said it reminded him why he didn't get mixed up in commercial affairs. He said he'd had his fill of such matters as a young man. He hinted that he understood more than most people about the practices that had brought down the banks. He said this with his eye on Henny, and finished by asking her whether she'd like them to stop talking about fish. What did she know of high finance, for instance?

'Nothing,' said Grey, and returned to reels and lines. Mitchell-Hedges listened with increasingly obvious impatience. Grey said that it was crazy to hunt big fish without a motor launch. Mitchell-Hedges said, 'Oh yes. I've heard your theory. Damn persuasive. Not what they say in the old country. The place is tunny-mad.'

'Is it?' said Grey. He rocked back slightly. 'Anyway—'

'Everyone wants to beat Mitchell-Henry's record, you know.' Grey rocked again, and Mitchell-Hedges grinned. Henny seized her opportunity. She told Mitchell-Hedges about Mitchell-Henry's challenge. The big Englishman said it was a capital idea and between them they overrode Grey's objections.

It had taken less than half a day between conceiving this urgent need to flee America and having a concrete plan for so doing. Henry was exhilerated.

Mitchell-Hedges said, 'I fancy Ledger will pay for it, too. He'll want more than one view of the great battle. You in the thick of it, me the impartial observer, and so on? I'll go shanghai the bugger.'

Ledger agreed immediately. Grey said morosely that he was delighted.

They travelled to England on the *Majestic*. Ledger bought them first-class tickets. Henny spent most of the journey in Grey's cabin. Once, with difficulty, she pretended to be bored and unaroused and Grey grew frantic.

Henny, Grey and Mitchell-Hedges dined together in the evenings. The men got on warily. Grey muttered that he was glad finally to have forced Mitchell-Henry into an honest contest. Neither Henny nor Mitchell-Hedges contradicted him.

There were several American heiresses on the boat heading for Europe to find husbands. Henny spoke to them about their plans. They cursed the Great War, because so many of the eligible had died. On the other hand, they giggled, since the Depression there were fewer heiresses, so maybe it evened out! Deep down, they knew they were going on an old-fashioned Grand Tour, and if they struck lucky, then all well and good. More than one was fixated on Caister. More than one said that they were being accompanied by a frustrated mother who had never had the chance to hook a prince herself and was secretly on the lookout for a widowed baron.

Henry wondered what she might do with a widowed baron. Or a castle.

Wednesday 1st–Monday 20th August

Zane and Dolly Grey – Altadena / NY

East Mariposa Street
August 1st

Dear Dolly,

I am sick and tired of life. You seem to think I have become a madman who will buy a yacht if he is not snooped on every hour. Sometimes, I feel I *am* mad.

Brownie harries me until I could throw her over a cliff. You are right that she is not like Wanda, that Wanda was more 'suitable'. Brownie is not suitable, but she makes me feel alive at least. You of all people know I am not a normal man. I cannot bear the thought of dying slowly by inches, cooped up like this, imprisoned. Most people could bear it. For most people, it would be nothing. They are like trees and they do not change. They look back on their lives and grow roots. But I am not a normal man, and I have no roots. I change always. I am not ordinary in any sense. I am a collection of supple branches, tied together from many different trees, and the sap is seeping out of me. If I do not constantly weather and renew myself, I shall snap and perish.

Oh, Dolly, I need to believe in the future or there is no point! I have lived my life in anticipation, always looking forward to this trip or planning that one. I have an insatiate belief that happiness is forever just moments beyond the horizon.

Fisherman II is a dead dream, I know that. That yacht would have been my glory if you had not let me be so badly cheated. For the amount of money I lost on her, I could have built her equal from scratch. But I will not blame you for it.

There must be something! *Frangipani* is still mine. Even if Tahiti has rotted and festered, at least it is not Australia. Why are you so determined that I fish from a city, surrounded by a crowd? You know it would be unbearable to me. It is as if you revel in my torture, at seeing me brought low.

Even so, I do your bidding. I see my face on the Camel advertisement and I quake at what I will allow for $1,000. I gird my loins to motor down to Los Angeles and face the small public that still cares for my name, even while the movie theaters are fat with crowds who do not realize that nine-tenths of everything they watch is feebly faked from words I sweated out, every one of those words a truth that I alone could have put onto a page, every passage a distillation of some thing or place I have seen and known as intimately as I know my heart.

Have you really had no reply from Hemingway's agent? Can it be that the man is too jealous to fish with me, to make a film where my precedence and his debt to me are clear? If that is what has happened, I will finally make public what I feel about his slavish imitations. But I cannot do so until he gives a clear reply, while there remains a chance that his rudeness is simply a miscommunication. If only we could travel perhaps as comrades, as teacher and pupil! We would not have to go cap in hand to Ledger to print it – it would be the greatest fishing story ever told. We could publish wherever we wanted. I will not give this up. Hemingway will see it too, in the end.

I have seen pictures of his *Pilar*. It is pretty enough, but it is not the *Frangipani*.

I hope you are enjoying New York. Yes, yes, I will go to Ledger's party. If *The Wolf* is all that is left to me, then I suppose I must. Brownie is delighted, of course.

Brownie reads Hemingway's books at the breakfast table. She pretends she likes them, but it is clearly to torment me. I am racked this way and that, but I cannot give her up and never shall be able to. She is all that keeps me from being kindling.

Los Angeles tomorrow, New York at the month's end. I will

never forgive the thieves and parasites that have brought me to this pass.

Your,

Doc

24 Prospect Park West
August 4th

Doc Dearest,

The Farrells hope you are well. I passed along your good wishes in return, although you managed somehow to omit said good wishes from your latest letter, overflowing as ever you were with tender queries as to my wellbeing.

I too am sorry that you must scrimp and scurry. I too am sorry that you squandered your fortune on a ruinous ship and kept squandering it long after the ship should have been scuttled. You will notice I took down the pictures of *Fisherman* during my last stay in Altadena. I could not bear to see her hanging there so beautiful and so perfect for all you dream of doing and cannot do. I fell in love with you because you would never rest, that you had to keep running up the mountain, and so I must not complain that you threw her away, but all the same.

Frangipani is in Tahiti, but where do you want to take her? You could barely afford the fuel to get her anywhere else (in fact, you could not afford it) and she will be impounded as soon she docks anywhere else in the South Seas. You have, if I may say, 'burned a lot of boats'.

Hemingway will not fish with you. He does not need to. You are right about his reasons, of course. He thinks he invented the whole thing and will not bear a rival. But neither will you, my love. You have never climbed into a boat with a man you even dreamed might be your equal. That is why you won't take Mitchell-Henry's challenge, and he knows it, which is why he made it. I don't say you should – England would be miserable for you. So please, please, go to Australia! You need to, and they want you, and there is nowhere else.

I suppose you have heard by now that there is a new flitterbug? She has seen Dot and Lillian,* and she has been asking questions about you in Altadena. Dot is worried, she says that there's something not right about her. We both know Dot is not a jealous creature, so be careful.

You know very well what I think about Brownie. The best I will say for her is that she is better than Mildred. I understand you, Doc, better than you will ever understand yourself, and I know you only depart from your normal sort of girl when things are at their blackest. Brownie's a devil to you, but she's too proud and too vain to suck you dry like Mildred did. She'll batter you, no doubt, but it will be a tempest, not a long, hard winter.

Be resolute. I hope Los Angeles was bearable. Ledger, who is a good friend to you, will give you a wonderful party here, which should remind people who you are. I know, Doc – they should not need reminding! I at least have never lost faith in you or your writing. You have endured a vast deal and if you will only let yourself learn from it, if you will only give yourself the time and space to express that learning, I truly believe that you could write your very greatest books.

It is painful for me to say this, but you will never achieve this if you do not gird yourself to the task. *Horse Heaven Hill* is a weak effort – you complain at my revisions, but I would never dare revise a story that I felt had received your full attention. Would I touch a word you write about fishing? You know I would not. You must think very carefully about what it is you wish to produce. I cannot sell *Twin Sombreros* for anything like you are worth, because the world is full of your stories, and ones into which you have put your soul. We both know that you have not done that for some time.

Take what you have learned, Doc, and use it! Go to Australia.

*Dot (Dorothy Ackerman) and Lillian (Wilhelm) were two of Grey's former girlfriends. They remained on good terms with him and his wife.

Leave Brownie behind. You will write a thousand times better about fish than you have done lately about the West, because you have stopped caring about the West. And while you write about fish, while the ink flows from your pen, remember what it is like to care and what it is you care about.

This adjustment has been a long and painful one, but you have emerged triumphant before, and you will again. My love and faith are with you.

Will we meet in New York, briefly? I should like to. I don't suppose Brownie would be pleased, but I am your wife and she is not. I will not be too demanding.

Go to Australia. Say you agree and I will organize everything.

Love,

Dolly

Altadena
August 12th

Dolly,

It has been a momentous week, a great week!

As you know, I was at the last of my tether with Brownie and had decided that you were right and I must be free of her. By a miraculous coincidence, that very evening of my last letter, when I went so unwillingly to Los Angeles to what was a very poor reception, I met the 'flitterbug', as you call her. She is nothing like the others. She is no fortune-hunting painted girl with bright lips and waved hair. I was transfixed by her long before she realized who I was – I have seen the red beauties of the savage West and the proud olive beauties of Spain, but here was a different kind of wilderness, something the Creator had molded purely for me, a quiet and graceful beauty, like a dappled green day on the Rogue, the clear brown stream trilling golden in the sun, a late-evening beauty of solace and perfection, the wilderness that civilization cannot respect or comprehend because it seems so gentle that civilization thinks it is civilized. But behind those eyes, in the deep pools of that trilling stream, there lie dangers and miracles that will not be known until the rude and rugged mountain fastness has crumbled into dust. I saw at once that she was a creature at bay, that something in the world wanted to own her or contain her, to deny her her own true nature. I swore to myself an unbreakable oath to protect her.

She is remarkably sensible, that is the thing you must know, from a good family in a town out east, by which I mean a terrible family with a good name. She hates them, but refuses to tell me more for fear of shaming them. So you see that loyalty runs very deep in her, the quality I prize above all others.

I dismissed Brownie. She raged and stormed, but I kept your soothing words in my mind – the tempest, not the long, hard winter – and I was able to win through to clear water.

The girl's name is Henrietta Rosefield. She understood nothing of the special nature of our marriage – she knew me from my books alone, and found in them something that was missing in her life, and from those books she knew me better than Brownie or any of the others ever have. I feared that she would be shocked to learn the truth, but she is an utterly natural creature, a faun escaped from a forest, untaught, but also unafraid. It is as if I have been wandering blind in a cave, and now a white living flame has come to guide me.

I know a little of myself by now, and of how love and inspiration are synonymous in any faculty of creative labor. You say I have grown in experience of pain and wisdom, and that is true, but if I do not write with a boy's passion and romance, then I hardly can be said to write at all. That is what has sterilized the labors of these last years, but the dark days are over now.

We travel to New York in two days. I shall be delighted to see you, and Henny will as well. Brownie has insisted on traveling at the same time. I said she could pick any other train, but she is clearly distraught. In this state I see how piteous she is, and how her tantrums were a carapace to protect her vulnerability. She was afraid of me, of what would happen when I cast her aside as one casts aside all unsuitable things. I should perhaps have been kinder, and so I relented on the matter of the train. She is bitter about Henny, which Henny, sweet creature that she is, does not even notice.

Of course I saw that you had taken down the pictures of *Fisherman*. I do not mind. She was a wonderful boat for me in her way, and added immeasurably to my experience, but she was vulnerable to storms and I had grown out of her. I need something durable if I am to battle my way to the free and open waters, to the last best place. The right boat for me must be out there. It is a dream I will not let die, for when hope is gone, nothing is left.

And, today, I am filled with hope! I have always guarded the truths of fishing jealously to myself, and I have only ever written of that which was true, but what you say is right. If I am to sear readers as once I did, then I must write again from the red hot center of things. The West is used up now. The last frontier is the sea. I have an idea forming in my mind, a tale of Catalina* and the genesis of great sea fishing. It will rock Hemingway to his feet! I might even have a version of him appear near the end, a doltish latecomer!

Of course, I can only do this when I know, *when I know for certain*, that he will not fish with me. You say you are sure, but I must have a piece of paper to prove it.

Your ever-questing Doc

24 Prospect Park West
August 16th

Doc Dearest,

You are an impossible man!

If I had a hundred dollars for every girl that was 'unlike all the other girls', we wouldn't be in this fix. What do you think the

*Santa Catalina, an island twenty-two miles southwest of Los Angeles, was the birth-place of big game sport fishing. The Tuna Club on Catalina was established in 1898.

flitterbugs talk to Dot and Lillian about, if it is not the 'special nature of our marriage'? Don't worry. I'm not trying to change you. I know what you need to believe in order to write, and I have no idea that you will listen to me this time anymore than all the other times. You live in a world of make-believe, and you need to clothe your affairs in the shining garb of romance, and then when these are rent and smirched you look around anew.

But you must force yourself to remember: some of these girls are dangerous. Dot has sent me another letter about this Henny. She is very worried about her. She says Henny is like an iceberg, that she is cold and that although she pretends to be naïve, there is something fearful underneath the surface. Dot is a sensible girl, and I take her qualms seriously.

Remember, please, that a 'faun from a farm' (a mixed metaphor, my dear romantic old Doc) would not have found you where she did. Please be careful.

And do not be too sorry for Brownie. The girls know perfectly well what they are doing. No woman is ethical, can possibly be, in the position you place them. You have to ignore that part & get what is worthwhile to you out of your personal contact with them. Of course you idealize them all – you idealized me once and I still remember how wonderful it was – but you make them into something to fit your momentary need. You do not grasp *at all* their real characters or their relation to the world. As soon as that reality impinges on your dream, the trouble begins.

I fear that Brownie will revert, now she is challenged, to the 'female of the species', and she will react to Henny and use her claws, and if Henny is worth anything she will claw her back. The fighting spirit in mankind demands a hurt for a hurt. The Christlike turning of the cheek never manifests in a battle of woman against woman for a man! That's where nature does her deadly work.

Of course, you will say, *I* am not like this. And I will say, I am not like this *anymore*. You pretend the girls aren't jealous, but they only aren't jealous when they never cared or when they are burnt out. So beware, and that is all I have to say about that.

A story about Catalina sounds like a new departure that might just be what you need. I mentioned it to Ledger and he was thrilled.

You did not give any kind of answer about Australia, which I pray you to think about before we meet, during which meeting I expect to talk as little as possible and kifoozle as much, despite my advanced age.

Your continued solicitude re the Farrells, passed on by me with eloquence, touches them greatly.

To repeat, you are impossible, but we are one flesh, for good, ill or whatever lies in limbo.

And my love for you persists, whatever that means,

Dolly

20/08/1934

DOLLY STOP SAILING TO ENGLAND FOR TUNA STOP LEDGER PAYING STOP LAST ADVENTURE STOP LETTER WILL FOLLOW AND EXPLAIN STOP DOC

20/8/1934

DOC STOP RECALL VIVIDLY YOU SAYING ENGLAND OVER YOUR DEAD BODY AND MINE STOP MY BODY NOT DEAD STOP PRESUME YOURS NOT ALSO STOP LAST ADVENTURE GOOD TITLE STOP THIS WONT BE LAST ADVENTURE STOP GOOD LUCK STOP DOLLY

Algonquin Hotel
August 20th

Dolly,

You had my telegram, here is the explanation.

First, please do not be obtuse! I have longed to battle Mitchell-Henry, but he was too cowardly to come out here like a man and do it my way. The difference now is that it will finally be possible to do it my way in Scarborough. If they broke my record from a rowboat, think what I could do from the *Frangipani*! It won't be the *Frangipani*, of course, but I will be fishing from a motor launch. England is in the grip of a tuna-fever, it seems, much beyond what we have here, and anglers are as famous as movie stars. Any Briton with a yacht goes to Scarborough to hunt. Until now, they did it from rowboats, but the Earl of Caister has joined the frenzy. The biggest news in all of England is that he has commissioned a fishing launch based on my designs to pair with his horrific *Dazzle*.

Caister's decadent sort of fame hardly breeds confidence, but my fears were allayed by the fellow who secured Caister's participation, an English fish man called Mike Mitchell-Hedges. Why are there so many fishing Mitchells in my life?

Mike says that Caister is a sportsman, and I trust Mike. I can see that Henny is suspicious of him, but Henny is not an angler. Mike has written a fine book about his catches in tropical waters, and is particularly good on sharks. Also, he has a rather special and familiar kind of marriage, and his wife's name is Dolly! What do you think of that!

Caister will pay for everything in England, once we get to his boat. Ledger is paying other expenses. It will make a splendid book, do you not think? The New World pioneer, the self-made and restless innovator, returns to blast the tired Old World out of its own water!

I will be interested to see *Dazzle*, even if it is only to gape at the money Caister has wasted on silver goblets and other falipperies. For sheer scale it is one of the few that might have challenged *Fisherman II* and I must know its measure, if I am to exceed it. If you wish to write me, I am sure that addressing care of Earl Caister in Scarborough will punch the ticket.

Henny is extremely keen on this adventure. She had never until recently left her small northeastern town, and now she is to travel overseas! She also wants me alone and away from Brownie, and I revel in the thought of our Atlantic passage. She is learning about herself and her enthusiasm is enchanting.

You may put aside Dot's ridiculous fears. They would have made me angry if they didn't make me laugh. Henny came to me not 'pure', but unspoilt. If only you could have met her in New York, as she wanted to meet you, I am sure you would have understood the way I feel. She went to Dot and Lillian not out of any hope or even thought of snaring me, but out of a simple, childlike yearning to learn more about a man she idolized. She says she wanted to glimpse me one time, and that would have been enough. She thinks that what we have now is like a dream and she has never been more terrified of anything than that she might awake. I start to feel something like the same. You say you have heard it before, but you cannot have done. I have never felt this cleansing freshness, as if all the scum and scarred accretions that have built up around my too-much-tender heart have been washed free by soft and luminous waters. There is no violence, but simple, irresistible innocence.

It is therefore ridiculous for you to suggest that she wants something from me. As you have said so often, I do not have anything to give. I have not bought her jewels, as once I bought girls jewels. She has asked for nothing and she has got nothing.

Again you give no clear answer with respect to Hemingway! I wish you would because I have filled a notebook with ideas for the Catalina story and must know whether I am to lampoon him or no. My only concern is lest I get these two great works – for the works will be great – confused in my mind. I keep leaning towards an English villain in Catalina, with Mitchell-Henry's foolish views, but that will never do. *The Last Adventure* will tell that story, the tale of two mature lions in death-battle. *Catalina* will be about the birth of this noble sport I have given the world. My enemies on the island will be Pygmies refusing to let an elephant rise from the ground, jabbing it with sticks until finally, enraged, it stampedes. There will be a hard New Yorker and his wife being ferried to the fishing grounds and fished for, and a record ill-won and claimed as fair. A battery of little men that never saw a big fish will want to catch giants with tiny, silly rods and reels. The hero will disappear into the open sea, alone apart from a beautiful stowaway. They will find solace in each other, such solace as no two people ever found, on some wild, untouched island, peopled by an unknown race. They will return with pictures of fish that will stagger Catalina to its knees, and skeletons of astonishing dimension. The hero, on his final approach to America, will do battle for the marlin of his life. They will nearly break each other. The battle will endure for days, not hours. He will break the marlin's heart, and, as the fish rests dying by the side of his boat and looks him in the eye, he will know the marlin's soul. Is *Soul of the Marlin* a good title?

It is time. I am off again, adventuring on another ship of fools. I will soon start dreaming of the home I always dream of leaving. The things you said in New York, your patient faith in me, the compact we have signed in tears and time and understanding, they make up a love that is perfect in its way, a love as true and long and remarkable and unbreakable as any voyager ever endured.

Your Odysseus,

Doc

Wednesday 15th August

John Fastolf, Earl of Caister – Send Manor

Johnny motors back to Send. Red house, blue sky, yellow drive. Colourful guests strutting against green, green grass. Gordon Stewart, the restless host, always within sight of the drive to welcome a newcomer, drags a somnolent dog over to greet him.

Johnny talks briskly with Stewart who is a good man if effortful, apologises for dashing off ('a secret mission, old thing'), and then strolls inside. He tracks down Molly and reassures her that Ruddy is not going to do anything stupid.

'He mustn't say anything to anyone,' Molly says. 'I offer people discretion and safety. He mustn't say anything at all.'

'He won't. What about the girl?'

'She's gone, everything is cleaned up. And she was no one, she's got no people.'

'That's good.'

'Yes. Thank you, darling, you are my knight in shining armour.'

Johnny laughs at that.

At tea, Caro cannot stay away from him. Kim Waring trails a step behind. 'You had an adventure, I hear,' she says. 'Ruddy is going to get away with murder.'

'Don't say that, Caroline. Not in public.'

'Don't worry, darling. He'll never hang for it. Nothing touches the gilded.'

'It was an accident. He wasn't doing anything wrong—'

'Oh, really? Shall I tell his wife or shall you?'

'Ta-ra!' says Kim. 'A palpable hit.'

'You need professional help, darling. All of you poor men need help. You need to sit on a sofa and talk to a clever Austrian about your mummies and the bloody war.'

'I'm fine,' says Johnny.

'Oh, gracious!' says Caro. 'Look at yourself, darling! Look at your friends! Have you wondered why Ruddy let himself be tied to a bed by a drug-addled whore?'

They are taking tea on the terrace. Johnny is facing the sun. Doubtless he looks washed even paler than usual. Caro is dark and fine. Johnny says, 'Ruddy is a chum, he has a rather important job, and this wasn't his fault. I'm sorry the girl died, but she knew what she was doing. She was a dope-fiend, and it killed her.' He looks significantly at Kim.

'Dear me!' says Kim. 'Not fair. I pass a little cocaine to my friends now and then, but I'm hardly a peddler.'

The other members of the house party can't hear them. Johnny leans languidly back. 'There was nothing I could do for the girl, so I did what I could for Ruddy.'

'And for Molly.'

'I don't mind Molly.'

'You're a hypocrite, darling,' says Caro. 'You rant about Kim sharing a little cocaine, but you help this woman who's in league with the Sphinx.'

'Ruddy didn't touch the drugs,' is all Johnny can say to that.

The Sweenys have brought a new American girl with them, Martha Gellhorn. She is one of Schiaparelli's society mannequins and she is very striking, unusual. Over cocktails, Kim and Kiki Preston make a beeline for her. Johnny knows what they'll be doing and he steps in. Gellhorn doesn't know enough to be grateful. She probably thinks he is trying to seduce her.

Kim and Kiki flounce off. They're quickly surrounded by syco-phants. Johnny hands Martha back to Charles Sweeny, who should be a safe-enough pair of hands.

'That was gallantly done,' says his host, sidling up to him. 'I'm sorry they have to be here. One can't cut people like them without making a scene.'

'I quite understand,' says Johnny. He's not sure he was being gallant. Maybe he can't prevent himself from competing with Kim, whatever the arena. It's all very stags and antlers, but it's often been useful.

His host says he'll be seated with relaxing old friends at dinner, but when Johnny approaches the table he sees Martha Gellhorn switching her place-card with his neighbour's. He is momentarily annoyed, but she is composed and interesting throughout the meal. She has targeted him, but she doesn't seem fragile or foolish. He takes her to bed. It will keep her away from Kim.

It is an unusual experience. She is extremely eager to please, but doesn't seem to care about being pleased. Eventually, he pleases her. She is surprised by this. He thinks that she must have been unlucky in her previous lovers. He is pleased to have pleased her.

She says, 'It can be surprisingly wonderful, can't it, for something so meaningless!'

'That's rather hurtful.'

'I only meant it's meaningless in the grand scheme,' she hastens. 'A crude sort of holdover from our bestial ancestors. But it's not *important*.'

'Yes, it is.'

'Well, of course we need to propagate, and so forth. I just mean it's not the centre of things, is it? Even of relationships? One mustn't worry too much about it.' She is trying to say she won't get obsessed with him. He likes her for that.

The next day features all the usual activities. He has seen it before and takes himself away for periods. During one of these, Martha tells him later, Kim tries to seduce her again and Kiki offers her cocaine. She is wide-eyed as she describes Kiki injecting herself casually with heroin while everyone else drinks tea.

Kim hovers around Martha again over dinner. Johnny would normally be careful about taking someone to bed twice in two nights, but because of Kim he does so. It is a mistake.

In his room, she asks why Kim doesn't like him. He says, 'Kim can't bear that I'm happy.'

She says, 'He seems very close to your ex-wife.'

'She was vulnerable,' Johnny says.

Martha has read Caro's books. She has read, therefore, that Johnny is a hollow man, and that his faithlessness ruined Caro's youthful dreams. In the books, Caro blames the war for all this.

Martha cautiously re-raises the subject of sex. She asks if it can be a big enough thing to drive two people apart – if that's what he meant last night when he said it was important? And if it went wrong for him and Caro, was it the *fons et origo*, as it were, or merely a symptom? Johnny can see that she is speaking about something that has happened to herself. He asks her what it is.

'Sorry,' she says. 'Was I being obvious?' Apologetically at first, but then with increasing animation, she explains that she was married, in all but name, to a Frenchman. That the physical side was marvellous, initially, or at least it was marvellous that he was her lover. Her body had demanded intimacy for a time, but then it stopped demanding it, which is natural, isn't it? In savage societies, women die very young and there was no point evolving the desire or capacity for pleasure beyond a certain age. It was important that young women felt the urge and some pleasure, to surmount their fear of the act. In civilised societies, we live more or less for ever and so we pass this youthful period almost before we realise. She said she was pleased to learn last night that she retained some capacity for thrill, but that the fire in her body was more or less gone out.

'Do you really believe that?' asks Johnny.

She says she doesn't just believe it, she knows it. She explains that Bertrand sent her to various doctors and there was nothing abnormal about her physically, merely the inability to take pleasure.

'You don't think it can have been something mental?' he asks. 'Or—'

'Bertrand was splendid. I know about my body.' She doesn't sound convinced by herself.

He says, 'It's terrible guff that there's only one person in the world for each of us. But the problem is that we only have one heart, and if it's smashed we can never get it back in order. There are dozens of people you might trust with your heart, but the heart only gets one chance.'

'Gosh,' says Martha. 'That's good.'

'Yes,' says Johnny. 'I almost believe it myself. Be that as it may, the capacity for thrill is a separate matter and I don't think it is a capacity one exhausts. Very much the opposite, in fact.' She holds him tightly at this point. He feels her opening up to him, whatever she says or pretends to herself, and he is wary. He changes the subject. 'What were you doing in France?' he asks.

'Oh God, I want to be a writer, but . . . Well, I've written a novel and I wrote for Bertrand's magazine, but I want to write something *real*.'

'Wasn't what you wrote in Paris real?'

'I thought it was. The people I knew there were all so serious and idealistic, and we went on visits to Germany, which was awfully well organised but rather horrible, but Bertrand thought that we could perhaps take their organisation and use it on the left, and then we all wrote about that and the economics conference, except I couldn't concentrate on it, partly because the women were all wearing such extraordinary hats, and partly because it was all so abstruse and convoluted, and partly because a year earlier I had been driving through the dustbowl.'

'So?'

'So there I sat looking at all these rich, lucky people and I thought to myself that they were always going to be distant observers looking at real life through their microscopes, and running in smaller and smaller circles shutting themselves off from everything that really matters. Sorry, I've been thinking about all this for a long time. It just blurted out.'

'Indeed it did.'

'Sorry, I—'

'Don't apologise. It's bracing. I will say this, though: don't think your life is unreal, just because you have been lucky. Poor people are not realer than rich people.'

'No, but there are more of them.'

'Yes, there are,' says Johnny.

'Bertrand thinks that if you understand part of reality, then you understand it all. That it's all one system.'

'He sounds fun,' says Johnny, and Martha laughs. She's serious, but she isn't glum. He continues: 'The world isn't a "system". It's a chaos and we're all lost, just doing one thing after another. You can't possibly understand what you're doing when you do it, and often it's the toss of a coin one way or the other, and then a few years later there you are, and it's all real, however much you bungled the choices that got you there. You'll never be happy if you think your own life isn't real.' He is extremely aware of the irony of these words. And he's tired. He says, 'My advice is very banal. I think you are a fine person. You are struggling to find your place because you want to commit to it absolutely. You are whole-hearted.'

'I think so.'

'I admire you for it, old fruitbat,' he says. 'But I'm not like that, not any more. I'm half-hearted, at most.'

'Oh, good golly!' she says. 'I'm sure you're right, but you almost sound as if you're not a terribly desirable earl in bed with an eager, if equine, young woman! Things could be worse!'

'Yes, yes,' he says. 'You are very American. But don't try to rescue me. I don't need it.'

'I know.'

'I mean it. Nothing is going to come of this. You know that? We won't do it again.'

'I know,' she says. Her cheek is warm on his chest.

Martha leaves for a fortnight in Gloucester, at the end of which she calls Johnny to say that she is going home to America shortly and to ask if they might have a farewell lunch in London. He is happy to do that.

She's lucky to have caught him. His boatmen Andy and Saul have already piloted *Harlequin* and *Dazzle* up to Scarborough and, in a day or two, Johnny will be joining them and heading out to the tunny-grounds. Johnny grins. Something happened this morning that might make his trip north more interesting. In Johnny's inside jacket pocket is a telegram from a mildly famous fraud and raconteur by the name of Mike Mitchell-Hedges, which reads: AS PER PREV COMMS RE TUNNY CONTEST SHALL BE YOUR CLUB SEVEN PIP EMMA TOMORROW STOP MITCHELL HEDGES STOP.

There have been no 'prev comms'. Johnny told Patterson to find out what is going on and it transpires that the explorer manqué has arrived in England with Zane Grey in tow. He has clearly heard about *Harlequin* and he's embarked on a hare-brained scheme that depends on claiming Johnny's acquaintance. Well, Johnny doesn't mind. Hosting Zane Grey on a boat of Grey's own design will be entertaining, and it will give the papers something to write about other than Johnny. It's not the risk-free option, but it will let him get on with his own thing. Hiding in plain sight.

He sends Mitchell-Hedges a confirmatory note, suggests dinner afterwards at Kitty in the City, dresses and walks down from Mayfair to the Royal Foresters' Club.

Thursday 30th August

Martha Gellhorn – London

August 30th, 1934
Lanesborough
London

G. Campbell, dearie,*

Thirty-six hours have passed since I last wrote to you, and I have continued the process of gathering myself together. I think that with those latest two letters, dreadful screeds that they were, I have finally worked out the last poison from my system remaining from the wasted years I spent with B—. What a fool I was! Never again.

I am sorry that you had to endure the dreary working through of all those thoughts, but you were the only one who knew about B—, you were the one who tried to persuade my dear, sweet, sensible parents to accept him, and I have needed *someone* to unburden myself to. Is that dreadfully self-absorbed? It sounds is if it might be.

In my becalmed state, I worry that you might think I am a crazy person after those last letters. I claimed I was finally clear of B—, but I did not explain why I am so certain. I do not want you to think I am a crazy person (I am terribly vain in that way!) and so I must tell you the rest of the story.

I mentioned that I was half in love with an impossible earl. Well,

---

* G. Campbell Beckett, a lawyer friend of Martha's, with whom she had once travelled to Tunisia. He knew the details of her drawn-out relationship with Bertrand de Jouvenel, recently ended, having tried to explain the legal situation to both her and her parents. Because of this, she used him in this brief period as a sounding board in a series of intimate and soul-searching letters.

he's impossible in spades, redoubled, because he's Johnny Fastolf, Earl of Caister, of whom even you must have heard! Please, please don't think me under any illusions! Johnny is merely a charming, aristocratic millionaire with a bad reputation and a castle, who makes me laugh. He has made it absolutely plain that I have more chance of marrying the Maharajah of Indore. I am breathless with gratitude for his charity and his clarity. B——'s great crime was that he refused to let me go, and my great crime was that I let him, and so the wound festered for long, painful years. I will not sink myself into another doomed dream – but twice would be carelessness.

I met Johnny at a house party two weeks ago, immediately before I went to Gloucestershire and wrote you those agonized letters.

Oh, G. Campbell. I sometimes feel I do not exist if I do not write, and you have been this year's victim. I must skewer my life to a page to understand it, and I simply cannot do so in a diary. I need to be speaking to someone. The ghastly irony is that forcing myself on you like this is the world enough and time more self-indulgent than writing into the vacuum. You may always tell me to stop, and if you do, I might. If I don't, simply burn the letters as they flutter through your weary door. I shall quite understand.

The house party: well, we think Boston has impenetrable social layers, but it is a sheet of glass compared to England. One gets a terribly good view as an American because one doesn't exactly fit, or at least there is enough doubt that people can pretend you are acceptable if they like your dress and legs. When I squirmed my way out from B——'s coils last month, I started flapping around London like a moth in a field of flames trying to sell anything anyone would let me write, eating bits of moldy air during the day and stocking up on champagne and caviar in the evenings as I paraded my darrrrling baaack wherever Schiap's little helpers thought it would display her wonderful wares to their best advantage.

It's easy enough to say that this is not 'real life' but, as Johnny said, it happens to be the life I live, and what can be more real than that? What a clever and important thing to have realized so late in one's existence. It is real life I am interested in, darling, and I must be able to observe it pitilessly and freshly wherever it is and whoever is living it. Everything is real – it is simply patronizing to say that Johnny is not as real as some poor farmer's wife in Idaho – but the thing is that I do not care equally about all the different things. I don't think B— and his friends are very interesting. Johnny said I must work out what I care about, and what I think is important, and then I will know my place in the world. I claim I want to live in a cottage in the countryside and write, write, write, but will I go mad from the belief that I have run away from the harder types of reality? Do I want to feed soup to starving children, or will this be foolishness if I could improve their lives much more by writing about them while incidentally living in bliss with an earl or similar? It is a very difficult subject to be tackling with one's morning coffee, and one wants to joke about it, but of course it is exactly the thing I must work out. It may take me some time!

Back to the country-house party. I was invited to it by the most darling American boy, who is exactly the kind of clean-limbed society creature I have made it my life's work to detest. He's Charlie Sweeny, his wife Maggie is more beautiful than ten suns, and they are both heirs to fortunes, so there is no scandal there, except that she was previously engaged to an earl and her father would have preferred that, even though he was not a rich earl like Johnny, but just any old earl. The magazines, as you might imagine, follow them everywhere they go.

I met Charlie in London, and he chatted with me and danced divinely, and we told lies about mutually distant friends and acquaintances, and when I said I was practically on the boat home he insisted I visit Send Manor to complete my education in the ways of the English.

Send is quite astonishing. The house party was graced by the most glamorous beings imaginable, but the manor's *raison d'être* is dogs. The owner, who is rich enough to be eccentric rather than mad, made his money in cars, and he got it into his head sometime in the dim and distant past – probably about five years ago, but you know how the English are with 'tradition' – to become the world's champion breeder of Great Danes. In a kennel complex as splendid as a hospital for Brahmin grandees, dozens of maids in aprons fluster around these giant mutts, teaching them to jump through hoops and peering nervously at their teeth. It is rather obscene, if you think about it, but I am trying not to turn cynic in my advanced years and there is something so earnest about the operation, almost Quixotic, and everyone is so delighted and committed to it, that I found it impossible to hate. Anyway, how do you hate a house party when you are shown around the exotic bird lofts by an indiscreet Gracie Fields?

I have, I fancy, some poise, and I have wandered through Paris with highly superior and influential personages, but there is a difference between that and meeting people with popular fame. My Parisian set was not the subject of public gossip. I certainly never spent ten minutes in an underground train listening to people bemoan the morals of Colette (which are quite bemoanable), but here one can sit gogglemouthed in the Tube and listen while your fellows earnestly debate which eighteen-year-old should be 'Deb of the Year', or speculate about which Hons these debs will marry and which ones they *should*, and which ones have retained their virtue, and whether it will do them any good in the long run. It is grotesque, but one gets sucked in. One simply cannot avoid knowing who these people are, it's a human zoo. Maggie Sweeny's wedding dress stopped half of London.

Gracie told me about our fellow guests in a fashion that made me shudder that she might ever learn anything about me – it was wonderful! Prince George was at Send, and he has just got engaged to Princess Marina of Greece, but Marina's going to be terribly disappointed, because Georgie's list of conquests includes Noël Coward, the Kaiser's grandson and an Argentinian playboy! I believe that my eyes did not quite pop out of my head – the de Jouvenels were a useful education in the ways of decaying Europe – but it is intoxicating to be told a prince's secrets by a movie star and I would distrust anyone who said differently, especially if they were telling the truth.

There was also a lesbian speedboat-racer called Joe Carstairs; a dishy bear of a man called James Justice, who is factotum or some such to Whitney Straight, the racing driver, who was also there, draped in beauties and very nearly as dashing as Charlie Sweeny, whose wife I did not take to incidentally, or perhaps it was vice versa; and there was a hilarious woman called Lady Yule, who talked loudly about hunting bears and wants to make 'proper, British' movies; and Binnie Barnes and Malcolm Campbell and a dozen others you'll know of, if you have utterly transformed your reading habits and now follow the trashy papers. It's like living in a magazine or comic opera, and that was before we started blibbering about Johnny.

I asked Gracie if he was as wicked as people say and Gracie said she wished she could tell me, if I knew what she meant (her tone of voice was not oblique). What she *did* know was that Johnny was about to be a sensational divorce co-respondent, even though he had never slept with the woman – he's doing it as a favor to her because her beastly husband won't free her if the world knows she's really leaving him for someone called Mavis, and there's a music-hall skit about it, although music hall is deader than a dodo, and Gracie knows the dear boy singing in the skit, who absolutely should be in better things, and, back to Johnny— Boy, can Gracie talk! Well, the rest of the scoop about Johnny was that his Derby winner, Little Pony, has been entered for the Arc de Triomphe and that he has built the most wonderful new sort of boat for tuna-fishing. Neither of us could quite imagine what kind of a boat it is, but the papers describe it as the most technological marvel this side of a space rocket, which seems unfair on the tuna. He was apparently lying low (lying low!) at Send to escape the enormous daughter of a Swedish shipping tycoon.

My eyes were like plates when we gathered for cocktails – thank God I am Schiap's mannequin or I would have looked like a scarecrow. I waited until well after the appointed hour, but I was still shamefully early. Almost immediately, I was pounced on by Kiki Preston.

Kiki's notorious from New York to Paris, but I don't suppose you've bumped into her. She's spurned hundreds of the people you meet, and slept with the rest, including Prince George, who likes them manlier, as I said. In fact, I shouldn't be at all surprised if she's slept with you at some point, maybe without you even noticing. Though, if she did, you would probably be on dope by now. Herr Preston died earlier this year, I don't know quite of what, but she was apparently wild as a squirrel even before then.

She's a famous dope-fiend, as I say. England appears to be under awful threat from a network of dopers. They are led by a Chinaman who has enslaved simply dozens of young actresses and dispatched them to do his sinister bidding, leading to murder and degradation on all sides. I confess that I am quite shaken every time I read this, but I have not run across more dope-fiends here than I did in Paris, and it is hard to imagine Kiki is in thrall to anyone, Chinese or not.

I dare say she gets away with it because she looks divine, floating like an airy sprite through the room. I was new, so she grabbed my arm and asked me if I needed cocaine to get me through the beastly evening. I was trying to gather my wits when Kim Waring arrived and said he'd come to seduce me.

Everyone knows about Johnny – you do, don't you, or I'm being an awful bore! – but Waring has a more exclusive celebrity. Johnny is written about; Kim is whispered about. Everyone says Johnny is the wickedest man in the Empire, but there's a kind of open-heartedness to his devilry. Well, I say there is, but what I mean is that his wickedness is so public that it isn't frightening. The private man is terribly nice and there is something lost about him as well. I'm getting ahead of myself.

Waring is supposed to be truly wicked, though. I've heard stories of boys committing suicide at his behest and girls committing murder. They can't be true, but you get his measure from them. As we looked out over the evening grass, covered in ducks and little parrots of some variety and the inevitable dogs, he asked silky questions that I couldn't help answering. He is a terribly beautiful man, and I choose 'terribly' with care.

I don't know how long we talked, but I was mesmerized, as if by a snake, and then Johnny joined us. *He* came over to *me*! He said he had a private message for me. Kim Waring and he stared at each other, then Waring left, taking Kiki. Johnny introduced himself and said he was sorry for interfering. He wouldn't do it again, but he felt it important to give me a warning, in case I didn't know about Waring. He said that Waring was dangerous. I said that Johnny was supposed to be dangerous too. Johnny said, 'Only if people want me to be. That's the difference,' and then off he went, like some modern species of knight errant. I was rather breathless.

By an odd coincidence, Johnny and I were sat next to each other at dinner.

I succumbed to his charms. Why? I think it is because I was curious about him. Also, I am already damaged goods, so it could hardly ruin my reputation. I had drunk champagne as well. I only tell you because you are a creature of maddening discretion and would rather be drawn and quartered before revealing it.

Johnny was very nice, or at least he seemed nice, and seeming nice can be as nice as being nice, if it is only for a short time, which it clearly was.

After all the horrors of B— and the months of po-faced physicians and self-blame, and the sense that I no longer was the same person as my body, I remembered how warm it can make you, and how whole. I had so firmly decided that I should never feel like that again that I was unprepared, and it put me into a state of combined thrill and confusion of which I was very aware. I tried desperately to stop myself from babbling and humiliating myself. I tried to be careless about the whole business, to show him that it might happily happen again without my pursuing him about the place like a giant Swedish heiress. I must have succeeded, because he came to my room again the next night!

But before then, there was another long day of dog-worship and soul-searching. We started with a highly cerebral post-breakfast contest, stood around in an enormous barn clutching gin fizz or champagne according to taste while an unfathomable pantomime unfolded before us. Eventually, I pieced together the following idea of what was happening, but who knows if I am right because I was too embarrassed to ask: the barn floor was painted in squares, and dice were thrown by each of six dog-handlers in turn, and then the handler had to move his specific dog the indicated number of squares, via a series of shouts and whistles. There are so many dogs that, in order to keep the commands individual, some of them are not fit for a lady to hear, let alone repeat, but no one seemed to mind.

The gambling was frightening. The Prince keeps Great Danes at Send, and his prize hound, who looked the same as all the others, competed in this titanic battle of skill and science, as a result of which the Prince lost £2,000 in a quarter-hour. Johnny wagered with me and Gracie, no stake higher than a farthing. He said his father wouldn't approve of any wilder extravagance.

Then we lunched and attended the Send Races, which featured more of the dogs – they are the size of ponies – running around a track and leaping little fences, each accompanied by its kennel-nurse. Watching the girls barrel after their giant charges would mend a splintered heart, I swear, and I wish I'd seen it when I had one.

I was not thinking about the dogs, primarily. I was trying to quieten my reawakened body.

Afternoon tea was a pause for collecting ourselves, but I had barely sat down when Kim Waring pounced on me again. I think I might have been susceptible to him once upon a time, but his is exactly the type of beauty I got used to in Paris. It made me wonder again that I wasted so much time on B—.

He said my gowns were wonderful, and I thanked him. Then he said that if I came to his room, he would show me things Caister couldn't dream of.

You are shocked, I know you are, and this was very poor form even at a decadent house party. I've heard worse, though seldom on a glorious afternoon over cucumber sandwiches, but his voice was so soft that somehow I didn't react as I felt I should or wanted to. Then he laughed as if he had been making a joke about the ducks.

He asked if I would like some cocaine, or perhaps heroin. I said I didn't take dope. He said I should try, especially if my view of the world was so shuttered that I didn't find Caister impossibly dull.

I demurred. Maybe I was composed, maybe I was not.

'You think me bad?' he said. I didn't reply and I didn't leave, even though I wanted to. 'Well, I am bad. But it's only because I understand that civilization is a foolish bauble we've knocked together between bouts of fighting and fucking, and that all we can do is make the most of what little it has to offer us in what little time it gives. Caister understands it too, by the way, but he'll never say it out loud. He wants to play the bigger man, but he'd eat your beating heart for another hour of living.'

'I don't believe—'

'Not yet, but you'll think about it. Really, you're too young and pretty to be a bore. Let Johnny fuck you to sleep, and then dream about me. We'll meet again.' He spoke just like that. The fluency quite distracted me from what he was saying and intensified it at the same time. I can't really explain how that worked. He circled me at dinner and after, but Johnny stayed near. It was exhilarating for me, I cannot deny.

Later, in my room, returned by Johnny to my unwise state of thrill, I asked about Kim Waring. Johnny said that Kim doesn't like to see him happy because Kim is Caro's bosom friend, which I found surprising, since Caroline, from her books, seems rather a prude. Then I told him about B— and he said that it's stupid to think there's only one person in the world for us, but that's not the point about true love. The point is that we only get one heart, and when it's smashed, that's that.

It's another rather brilliant thought, and he spoke gaily, but you never heard anything so tragic in your life. When he said, 'You only get to trust one person with your heart', or some such, I almost wept.

I felt sure he was speaking about himself, but everyone who has read Caroline's books knows that she was the one who was desperately in love and that Johnny was a brute to her. Certainly she still seems to be obsessed with him. I wish I knew more about him, but he seemed terribly vulnerable.

Also, however brilliant he sounded at the time, I think that he is wrong. I smashed my heart utterly into B—, and I did the most foolish things long after I had ceased even much to like him, and I have put everything back together! Maybe I am harder-hearted than Johnny. They wouldn't believe that in the gossip papers.

We talked about physical love also. I told him my theories about how we use up our sexual capacity, about how it is only important to women when we are young. I told him about the doctors, and he immediately asked whether the hindrance might be mental.

As well you know, I long ago rejected this obvious explanation because it would have meant that my subconscious was trying to reject B—

Naturally, I couldn't admit this to Johnny. I repeated for the millionth time the self-constructed self-defence I have worn as a shield to persuade myself I was not clinging hopelessly to B— out of a prideful inability to admit that I had been a fool, and romantic, and young, and a fool, and young. It has been a useful fiction, but it is so absurd when I examine it that I can barely bear to type the words. Johnny didn't laugh at me. He said that of course he could not be sure, and humans are many and variegated, but he would be surprised if it were a physical capacity one used up. Maybe he is right. I don't ever want to take the risk, though. The thrill is thrilling, but it's not a fair price to pay for freedom.

(A question suggests itself: is sexual love a price that the lower orders happily pay for their freedom? Is it the opium of the masses? Is it what makes their chains endurable? Am I being clever or unforgivably glib, G. Campbell? I rely on you to tell me.)

Anyway, I do not want to lose my freedom, so if I ever feel I am going down that path, I suppose I must just watch out!

But I am not in danger from Johnny, as I said. Before he left, he looked at me seriously in that way a good man will when he has bad news to impart, and which B— never did. He said that he thought I was a fine person – he said 'fine' in an old-fashioned way that made me feel honored – and that it would be hard for me to be less than absolute in anything.

He said he admired me for it, in many ways, and that it was a brave course of action, but he himself is not an absolute sort of person, and it would be better for both of us not to be entangled. Did I agree? I said I did. I do.

'Better for *both* of us,' he said – did you notice? I certainly did.

There was so obviously much more on his mind than he could say. I think, *I truly believe* (and do not dare laugh at me, on pain of excommunication from my highly sought-after inner circle), that Johnny may be at a vulnerable moment in his life. If so, he might be nervous of anything that could destabilize him, even me.

Yes, yes, I am a little in love with Johnny, and he knows it, but he will not let me be a fool and I will not let myself be a fool. I have other things to do with my existence, more important things. I shall not be a slave to my baser self.

All the same, I like and admire him. I think there is more to him than meets the eye, and I want to know what it is. He seems so said. I am back in London from Gloucestershire, and I am having lunch with him today. And by today, I mean now. Toodle-pip.

Well, that was interesting! I hoped I might try to cheer Johnny up, but he was already in high spirits because of a telegram from a famous English rogue called Mitchell-Hedges. This Mitchell-Hedges made a splash some years ago as a manly jungle explorer, but it turned out he was a fraud and he got himself into some legal scrape or other, and his absurdity became public property. Well, this Mitchell-Hedges has apparently claimed Johnny's acquaintance and embarked on a screwball scheme to get Johnny to sponsor a tuna-hunting competition between an Englishman called Mitchell-Henry (no relation to Mitchell-Hedges) and Zane Grey! (Have you ever read Grey's books? I have not.) Johnny is meeting these fellows this evening, and I am allowed to join them afterwards and find out what has happened.

After lunch I hawked my tawdry wares to the usual places and to little avail. As I trudged disconsolately down the stairs at *The Illustrated London News*, I heard someone calling my name. Well, old son, *The Illustrated London News* has a ghastly cousin, like the rest of us, and it is called *The Illustrated Sporting and Dramatic News*, and one of the bright young things wasting time in its office before marrying someone suitable had been at Send with me. Her name is Penelope-but-everyone-calls-me-Pippin, and she had heard me railing at some poor fellow guest about the awfulness out West, and she tugged me into the editor's office – he's her uncle, of course – and described me as a combination of Hemingway and Farmer, which he found as interesting as a plate of rice.

He was a mournful-looking soul, who I realized several hours later had been extremely droll in a manner beyond my limping comprehension. Sadly, he said, arriviste Home Counties matrons buying *The Illustrated* on the pretext that their charladies adored it were not interested in depressing stories about the dustbowl, and he regretted that even Schiap was done to death. He sent me on my way with a sad glare at Pippin, who fibbed about how much he had liked me as she showed me the stairs. She asked what I would do now, and I told her about Johnny's telegram. She squealed at me like I was a mentally deficient species of owl. She grabbed my hand and returned me to her uncle. At the magic words 'tunny' and 'Caister' he said the magic words, 'That might not be uninteresting', which in a British editor is the most passionate conceivable statement of effusion. The British public might weary of Elsa Schiaparelli, the toast of Paris and the greatest designer of her age, but earls and giant fish – never. Upshot: I am the newly minted tunny correspondent for *The Illustrated Whatsit*.

Momentarily, I shall change into the ever tattier halcyon with the flounces, which is the only one I really like that Johnny hasn't seen before, and twirl my fingers until his Negro butler appears to drive me to the nightclub. (Yes, Johnny has a Negro butler. This initially seemed recherché, but like everything else it has settled quickly into normalcy.) I know I have no chance with him, and I shall mainly attempt to demonstrate how cool and realistic I am capable of being, but I am young and he is so different from B—, and, well, there it is! I shall post this tomorrow.

Friday 31st August

Henny Rosefield – London

The Royal Foresters' Club didn't admit women, so Henny had to wait at the hotel until the anglers were ready to dine. She tried gently to open the satchel in which Grey kept his precious notebooks, but she didn't want to damage the lock.

Earl Caister was tall and not particularly handsome. He had excellent manners. His clothes were beautiful. Everyone treated him with the respect due to his wealth. Or maybe it was just that Henny knew he was rich. Grey would be sensitive to that, which might be useful. She let Caister charm her, without getting too close to him, without being too obvious, not yet.

There was another girl there, an American, Martha Gellhorn, clearly enraptured by Caister. She might be a problem, she might not. Henny was interested to meet Mitchell-Henry, but he had gone directly home.

They had been sitting for twenty uncomfortable minutes when a loud party arrived in the nightclub and slid across to join them. They were led by a dark-haired, pale-faced man called Kim Waring. One of the women was Caroline, Caister's ex-wife. She was slender, also dark, wearing plum. Henny observed her closely. The rest of Waring's party took the next table, but Waring and Caro joined the anglers. Caister grinned. Not a wolfish, dangerous grin, just a grin.

Waring sat next to Martha Gellhorn. He seemed to know her. He covered her hand with his and said, loudly enough for everyone to hear, 'Caro heard he was going to be here. There was nothing I could do to keep her away. Everyone knows how the poor bitch feels about him.' Caroline laughed, in a way.

As soon as Waring put his hand on Martha's, Caister started edging towards the pair of them. That was worth noting.

Caro said, 'So you're Zane Grey?'

Grey said, 'Yes.'

'No one in England reads your books. Are they any good?' Grey didn't know what to say. 'You've sold millions of them, haven't you?'

'Yes.'

'And they're just westerns? How bizarre. Do you know,' she said to Kim, 'I think I'll struggle through one for *Time & Tide*. Wouldn't that be funny, darling?'

'Priceless,' said Kim.

'These people are my guests, Caroline,' said Caister.

'Of course, darling. Of course. But we have to get to know them, because we're coming fishing too!' She jutted her chin. There was no reaction.

'Caro inveigled an invite out of Joe Carstairs,' said Kim. 'Couldn't bear the thought of being away from you. Or maybe she's finally going over to Sappho.'

'Joe's in Scarborough now,' said Caro. 'We'll be there in a couple of days.' She turned to Henny and said, 'So, darling, who are you? Where did you find that hilarious old dress?'

'Who is Joe Carstairs?' Henny replied.

'You *are* from out of town, darling! Joe's a wonderful bull lesbian. You know what a lesbian is?'

Henny said, 'No.'

'Oh, darling. A lesbian is a woman who—' Caroline stopped. 'I believe you are teasing me. Aren't you the little mouse that could? Joe will like you. She has a marvellous yacht, rather decadent and spiritual, quite different from Johnny's vulgar mechanism.'

'It's new, isn't it, Johnny's yacht?'

'You have been doing your research. Don't worry, he's used to that. He built the *Dazzle* when he finally let me divorce him. Rather an obvious piece of sublimation, don't you think?'

Henny saw Martha free her hand of Waring's and shuffle towards rising. Henny stood also and said that she needed to powder her nose. As soon as they were out of earshot, Henny said, 'How far could we get before they miss us?' It might be helpful to have Martha on her side, or at least not hostile.

As they finished in the bathroom, Caro Fastolf arrived. She was swaying slightly. She looked Henny up and down very slowly and drawled, 'Sorry, darling, I didn't realise you were Grey's whore. I presumed you were both Johnny's. Well, well. I suppose Grey *is* an old, rich man.' She swept through the door.

Martha was stunned.

Henny stood for a moment, calibrating. Then she said, 'I don't like her much.' She took Martha's hand and walked them back to the group. She directed Martha towards Caister's side of the table and took the space next to Kim Waring.

The conversation had turned to fish. The conversation always did. Waring whispered to her, 'Trying to make friends with horse-face? Sensible girl.' He patted her hand. 'You have to get close to people if you want to gut them.' Henny said nothing, didn't move her hand. In fact, she squeezed his. He was beautiful. He wasn't surprised. He said, 'I see you.' He probably did.

Caro returned, more energetic, but still moving erratically. She was soon bored by the fish. She said to Martha, 'So, you're my husband's American whore?'

Caister said, 'Caroline!' She was looking at him, not at Martha, her eyes flashing. Waring was delighted.

Before anyone could continue, Henny said to Caro, as if she were changing the subject, 'It's interesting that you hold your cigarette the way Kim holds his, and your glass. And you part your hair in the same way, too, and you stand alike, and you look at him all the time, as if there is a terribly deep bond between you. What could that be? An unacknowledged sibling? I've heard about English families. Perhaps that's it?'

Caro went white. Waring's grin wasn't what it had been, but it was more that he had become wary than that he wasn't enjoying himself. He was still holding Henny's hand, and he stroked her palm with his middle finger. Henny caught it in hers. Caister looked at Henny differently. She returned his look.

Soon after, Grey escorted Henny back to the hotel. As they left, Caister said to her, as expected, 'Beware of Kim Waring.'

Caister's tone, his attitude, was not predatory. She had thought it might be, but Grey was his guest and Caister's manners were impeccable. At least, they were in public. She wondered what he would be like when they were alone and she had made it clear she was no longer interested in Grey.

She was nice to Grey in the hotel one last time. Grey could always thrill her, but tonight she was already excited.

Friday 31st August

Martha Gellhorn – London

Letter to G. Campbell Beckett, ctd.

Good morning, darling. Apols if this letter is a disarray, but my head is like a drum made of cymbals. If I avoided eternal humiliation last night, it was not for want of trying. I think I have done something foolish. I shall find out just how foolish later today when I try to sneak onto Johnny's yacht.

The tuna party met at Johnny's club and then moved on to Kitty in the City, which is *the* place to be seen. Mitchell-Hedges – 'Call me Mike' – is a lantern-jawed English gent and was doing his best to look insouciant. Mitchell-Henry is a stocky, dapper, bristling fellow – Captain Lorenzo M.-H. if you please – who must be in his fifties or even sixties. He left almost immediately. Zane Grey is a little man, about the same age, very fine-featured.

Also present, in a highly significant paragraph of her own, was Grey's secretary, 'Henny' Rosefield. She's my age, I dare say, a dark slip of a thing, strategically designed to appeal to all those many people who think I look like the latest Derby winner. Mike Mitchell-Hedges hissed delightedly to me that Rosefield and Grey are an item and that she practically forced him into this whole fandango to get him away from some other nubile girlfriend. She is quieter and more mysterious than you would imagine from this description.

But, you ask, what is this whole fandango? Let me tell you a story, best beloved: a small eon ago, Grey caught the biggest tuna ever seen. Last year Mitchell-Henry caught a bigger one. He challenged Grey to a contest. Grey didn't want to come, but Mitchell-Hedges and the girl baited him into it. Mike claims he only got involved to see how things turned out, but he's desperate to be here so he can write about it for *The Wolf*, which is still a going concern, remarkably. So he proffered Johnny's boat as an inducement and you can see that he's rather surprised that it's all come off so smoothly.

It was the oddest evening. We were sat around in edgy mood – elderly adventurers are not natural nightclub-goers – when Kim Waring arrived with a train of squawking creatures including Caro Fastolf, who was a vision in purple. I noticed them before Johnny did, and I turned quickly to see his reaction. I swear, G. Campbell, that his face shifted and, when it did, I saw behind the calm, and there was a man at the very end of his last resources. It was only a moment, but it confirmed everything I thought at Send.

Anyway, Caroline and Waring caromed over to us and Waring introduced everyone as if he were the host. It was breathtaking in its way – the shape of manners, but rude in almost every detail.

Waring caressed me in his creepy fashion, and Johnny couldn't get close enough to stop it. Eventually, I had to escape to the little girls' room. I did so at the exact moment Henny ran away from Caro. I was uncomfortable about that, but Henny asked, 'How far could we go before they notice?' It doesn't sound like much, but it made me warm to her, just for a moment.

Caro followed us. She asked Henny if she were 'Grey's whore'. She was drunk, but it's no excuse – these people are awful. I say she was drunk, but I think it was cocaine. I've been a mannequin long enough to recognize the signs, and I checked her nose when she returned. I'm almost sure I saw some. Maybe there really is a Chinese mastermind behind every marble pillar.

When we got back to the table, the men talked about fish, and Caro was bored and swaying all over the table. Eventually she asked loudly if I was 'Johnny's whore' – she clearly enjoys saying it – and Henny piped up in a sparkling little voice. She said it was very interesting how Caro's words and gestures were so similar to Waring's, as if there were some special, unspeakable bond between them, and had anyone noticed?

Caro was crushed and Waring laughed darkly and said he'd better get Caro home before she fucked a waiter. As we stood and milled about, he said to me quietly that Henny was a dangerous one, that she was going to set her cap at Johnny and that he wouldn't be in Grey's shoes for all money. Waring is horrible, but he's not stupid. They left, with their gang.

I was stuck standing by myself, feeling as inconspicuous as a salmon in a cup of tea. And I still hadn't dared tell Johnny about *The Illustrated So-and-So*. The perils of being around him were quite apparent to me in my champagnified state, but nothing will ever come of it, he will not allow it, so I needn't be afraid.

All the same, I just know Waring is right. Henny is going to set her cap at him, and there is something really rather frightening about the way she dealt with Caro. If Johnny *is* at a vulnerable moment in his life, then he is in particular peril of anyone he might trust with his heart. Even if Henny doesn't intend anything particularly wicked, even if she is just a common adventuress, she might do him terrible harm. Last night as I stood there, I got quite frantic with worry about this, and I decided that I desperately wanted to go to Scarborough.

And so, brave girl that I am, I sauntered up to Johnny and explained about *The Illustrated*. I said they were practically relying on me, and might I join him for the fishing, just as a friend, as I had been tonight, to cover the contest?

He didn't look surprised. He said it would be much the most enjoyable thing, but on the whole he thought better not, and didn't I agree?

I was altogether deflated. That was that, I thought. But while Johnny was off organizing the cabs to take us home, Mike said he wouldn't mind having a secretary for the trip. I stared at him. 'You don't want to miss the fun?' he said. 'You don't want to see him fall prey to the mysterious Miss Rosefield? Come as my secretary and write it up for *The Illustrated Doodah* while I wax lyrical for *The Wolf*. I'd like to see Caister's face when you arrive!' Mike can't resist poking lions with sticks, I see that now.

I said that Johnny wouldn't allow me on board, but Mike was

having none of it. He said that Johnny was too well bred for that. Anyway, he added, I was a bright girl, and he and I had the same nose, didn't we? The nose for something interesting, something that makes life worth living? He was tipsy too.

And so, G. Campbell old bean, here I am in my jolly old hotel room, packed and ready to go, and typing furiously to finish this letter before Mike arrives, so it seems I really must be going to send it to you. I might dispatch it this evening, when Johnny has refused to countenance my presence on his precious yacht and I am returning home with my tail between my legs. I could stay in Scarborough, of course, and do *The Illustrated*'s bidding from the safety of dry land, but I don't think I could bear that.

All I want to do at this moment is sit in a tiny house on the edge of the wild and wasteful ocean and gaze at the waves from my bed, in blissful instants of contemplation between reading from a giant pile of books. But here I am running again to somewhere I do not know why I want to be, and at I do not know what cost. What has come over me? I used to be tolerably sane.

Evening, same day, Scarborough

I've arrived in Scarborough as Mike's 'Girl Friday' (his expression) and all is well. Mike traveled in a shorts-suit whose left sleeve bears a stain which leaves one praying that it is merely blood. He was reading *Anthony Adverse* – actually reading it, my dear, not just talking about it like everyone else – on the train, though I don't know where he produced it from, because he arrived carrying a typewriter in one hand and a tiny trunk in the other, in which trunk there can scarcely be two pairs of spare— Well, let's leave such thoughts where they are, but suffice to say that the whole effect is calculated to enhance his tarnished exploring credentials.

Johnny motored up from London in the reddest car ever painted and he met us at the station. Mike – he wouldn't thank me for telling you this – was nervous. It was one thing to tease Johnny by inviting me last night when we were several glasses to the wind in a nightclub, but he is here on Johnny's whim.

I was nervous too. I so utterly don't want Johnny to get the wrong idea. But when he saw me, he was marvelous. He didn't skip a beat, looked at me and said, 'New secretary, I presume?' Mike nodded gratefully. And then when Johnny took my bag, he said quietly, 'Don't look so worried – it's all right. It's a big boat. We'll have fun.'

I am not certain exactly what he meant, but I was reassured. And it is a big boat! Johnny is practically Rockefeller, but he somehow makes you forget that and then, suddenly, you see the *Dazzle*. She looks like a junior sort of ocean liner, except that she is painted in the most extraordinary diagonal stripes. Johnny claims it is a kind of camouflage, and I dare say it would be very effective if you were trying to hide a giant ship in a roomful of zebras dressed by Schiap and Dalí.

We're about to zoom off, so I am throwing this in the postbox. I don't know when you'll get another. Maybe I'll be eaten by a tunny. If so, remember that you were always my dearest and most reliable darling, and burn every self-indulgent soliloquy I've ever written you.

A life on the ocean wave,

Marty

Friday 31st August

John Fastolf, Earl of Caister
– Scarborough

There's a hint of drizzle, but Johnny de-roofs the Type 90 all the same. He drives to Scarborough alone. He needs to think. Patterson takes the Hispano-Suiza via Caister Castle and various other eastern points. It's going to be a long day for Patterson.

Johnny pops very briefly in to see Ruddy Drake, to check that there have been no unexpected hitches since the party. Ruddy is still very upset about what happened to Molly's girl, but Johnny explains that there is nothing to be done. The girl is gone for good and ever, and Ruddy must look out for himself. One barely has time to deal with the quick; the dead can go to the Devil.

Johnny considers the events of last night. He knew that Joe Carstairs was going to be in Scarborough with the *Berania*, and it is entirely unsurprising that Kiki Preston will be on board, gliding destructively through whatever transpires. He hadn't been certain Kim and Caro would come too, but he had hoped. If Johnny's private dream of escaping the mess he's in is ever going to come to anything, he needs them to be there.

The tunny contest is a good idea – it means he won't have to select which of the excited locals to fish with or where – but he didn't properly consider the ramifications of having to arbitrate between two prickly sexagenarians. He will play things scrupulously fair, but he hopes that Laurie will emerge with the laurels. The Captain's a tetchy old bugger, but he's had a tough time and he's an old family friend.

Johnny didn't get a handle on Zane Grey at all last evening. Johnny respects success. You don't sell millions of books by accident; you have to have something going for you. Patterson will be picking up a couple for Johnny to read, in case that helps. Grey's girl was— Well, Grey's girls were another thing Patterson and Miss Pink had already found out about. All the same, Grey isn't what he anticipated and neither is the girl. They don't seem like a millionaire and his doxy.

The girl worries him, in fact. She must know that Grey has squandered his fortune, so she either likes him or she's after something else. Johnny assumes the latter – she flirted with him after all – but people flirt for all kinds of reasons. If you flirt with someone, they don't usually notice what else you're doing. He gets the feeling that he will have to pay close attention to her.

So, in conclusion, the contest will take more of Johnny's time than he originally planned. Grey and Mitchell-Henry have agreed to daily meetings at a neutral venue. Neither can entirely recall why this is. They certainly don't realise it is Johnny giving himself an excuse to make landfall.

Mike's not a problem. He'll enjoy the grub and write a rollicking collection of lies. He is better company than Johnny expected. It's easier to talk to a man who knows he's a knave than one who believes his own bluster.

Johnny stops for lunch near Cambridge and takes tea near Gainsborough. It's brighter the further north he drives, and his cheeks feel scrubbed.

He ferries his bag to the harbour. Kiki Preston, apparently, is already on board *Berania*, which is standing a few hundred yards further out than *Dazzle*. Alongside the jetty, *Harlequin* looms over a series of rowing boats.

He meets Mike at the station. Mike has brought Martha Gellhorn and he looks like a man who knows he's blundered. Johnny isn't happy, but there's nothing he can do that would fit his persona. He says, 'New secretary, I presume?' and reassures Martha that everything will be all right. It's best that Martha believes that.

He's waited a long time to deal with Kim. It'll be the right thing for Caro, but she won't thank him for it.

Saturday 1st September

Martha Gellhorn – The North Sea

September 1st 1934
Harlequin
Somewhere off Scarborough

G. Campbell, oh my days,

I am on board the *Harlequin*, which is Johnny's fishing boat. It's
sharp like a sword and shines like jewelry, and when I climbed into
it yesterday evening it felt like the front edge of a place beyond the
future. Three hours into today and it feels like home. Grey says it's
bigger than it needs to be, but he is just jealous. It's painted in the
same screwy stripes as the *Dazzle*.

Why am I writing to you yet again? Well, darling, I suppose it's
become rather a habit this month. And anyway, I have to scratch
down notes for *The Illustrated Thingamajig*, and I see no reason not
to do it like this. I'll type them up for myself later and giggle, as I
do so, at the harm my marine scrawl must be doing to your charming
eyes.

It is nine o'clock in the morning, but we clambered aboard at six.
As soon as we left the harbor, I had to go downstairs and lie in one
of the cabins. Looking across the sea, which is like a particularly flat
variety of millpond, I can hardly believe in the weakness of my
stomach, but there it is.

It was extraordinarily cold. Mike's tiny bags were dashing, but
now he is wearing Johnny's clothes. I myself am outfitted not by
Schiaparelli, but by *Dazzle*'s first officer, a luscious creature of perhaps
twenty-four summers called Miss Scarlett. The shoulders are rather
tight, but I am grateful beyond words. I am wearing thick woolen

stockings, flannel trousers, rubber boots, undershirt, shirt, pullover, mackintosh golf jacket, thick sweater, woolen scarf and oilskin jacket. I have not, because it is 'mild' and no one else has put theirs on, donned oilskin trousers. I look preposterous. In the same garb, Miss Scarlett looks look like a princess.

Grey says it is balmy compared to Nova Scotia.

Harlequin is dwarfed by the mother ship, of course. I don't know how to measure the *Dazzle* and it seems vulgar to ask, but she is sixty-six strides from stern to bow (I know which is which, too!). Johnny, Mike, Grey, Henny and I are in different cabins, which leaves as many free, and there's a crew of eight as well, not including Johnny's Negro, who is called Patterson and seems able to do almost anything. They all look terrifically capable and efficient, and they are more like a gang of debs and desperadoes than a collection of servants. Whatever they are, they are not above polishing, because absolutely every surface gleams. There is a fabulous saloon with a cocktail bar, a grand piano and an awful lot of silver metal (chrome perhaps? what exactly is chrome?). Mounted with ceremony on the otherwise bare main wall is a stickleback, perhaps three inches long. This is supposed to be funny, and it is.

The ship's captain (or is *Dazzle* a yacht? I don't quite know. Nor do I know whether she is '*Dazzle*' or 'the *Dazzle*' and my crewmates seem very undisciplined in this matter) is Miss Pink, who is in her fifties at least, and Scots and regal. Miss Pink and Miss Scarlett: exactly what you are thinking. I do not know any more about them at present, but I am agog. There is a rather nice play-battle between Patterson and Miss Scarlett for tertiary eminence behind Johnny and Miss Pink. Miss Scarlett has no chance of victory, and the practiced routine is that she flirts outrageously with Patterson, pretends he is blushing – as indeed he might be – and then flounces off to Miss Pink in triumph. If Miss Pink were to battle Johnny for primary eminence, I am not sure I know how the matter would turn out.

Surprisingly, Miss Pink has hit it off with Mike. They are playing a backgammon tournament for stakes they insist are in the millions of pounds.

It is all too easy to see why someone might say this world isn't real. It has so few people in it, and they do not have the same concerns as the mass of humanity, but this perhaps gives them ('us', darling, I must say 'us') more time to worry about deeper matters: who we are and what we want and so forth, and civilized varieties of love, and what people should do when they are not bothered by the brute concerns of nature. Perhaps this is a laboratory for a sort of advanced humanity. It is real, but in a special way, like a fairyland in a story, which has parables and morals even though it is not like the world that almost everyone must endure. I have not properly thought this through, but I rather like the idea and favored Grey with it, in an attempt to stop him from talking about rods and reels for five minutes. The attempt failed.

This is how the fishing works: one spends an hour and more scooting from the safety of the harbor out to the fishing grounds (if one is one, one spends that period greenly on a bunk). Once there, one emerges blinking into the sunlight to be greeted by a small flotilla of actual, proper fishing boats and a lot of shouting. Because we are futuristic sybarites, we sped to sea in the same boat we will fish from, but the tunny-polloi trudge out in dirty old wooden affairs dragging (or carrying) the little rowboats from which they will cast their lines. The dirty old wooden affairs, you will be thrilled to learn, might be called cobles or they might be called keelboats. I thought at first that these were two words for the same thing, but I am now almost certain they are not. That is as far as my investigation has proceeded. I think I will have ample time to resolve the issue.

Anyway, the actual fishing boats are hunting for herrings, and shoals of tunny gather around them. I have seen no evidence of this, G. Campbell, but sometimes in this world we must rely on faith. Some bold anglers haunt bigger fishing boats called drifters, which means getting up at two in the morning and being in position by four or five. This approach, according to the Captain (as we have all taken to calling Mitchell-Henry), is favored by people of masochistic tendency who assume that the value of something is proportional to its difficulty and is by no means scientific. We were all eager to agree with him.

Most of the herring trawlers are stubby, two-masted affairs with a little cabin perched precariously about two-thirds of the way back, and a tall, thin smokestack. Somewhere over half of the ones I saw had a bizarre, upward-poking prow. I will see if this is normal or a piece of local ship-design. Anyway, we didn't approach one of these. We made for a 'Dutch herringer' called the *Verloren Hoop*, which was much larger than the English boats, slenderer to the water and more antique-looking.

Miss Scarlett darted the *Harlequin* under its lee and started yabbering away in the native tongue. We sent over a bottle of good Scotch and they sent us back a bucket of living mackerel, which seemed like no kind of a deal.

Then, while they cast out their herring nets – which possibly differ from other nets in ways I am unqualified to judge – Johnny and Grey set up our rods. The ploy is that one hangs around a likely trawler waiting for action. As the fishermen heave in their catch, the sea is a boiling frenzy of fishes, hopefully including tunny, which have for some reason evaded the nets (and which are picking up scraps, I presume). If some other trawler sees tunny, then it sounds a horn – the skippers are very game, apparently, and get tips if the toffs succeed – then everyone dashes across to it, because only the first tunny-fishers to arrive on each side of the trawler can cast a hook, or else lines will cross, fish will be lost and all kinds of catastrophe and bad blood will ensue. Since we are in a mighty motor launch while our competitors are in little rowboats, which have to be cast off from their labouring parents, I suspect we shall have an advantage on this front.

The tunny we are hunting are giants, G. Campbell, quite six feet long and fat as you like. I assumed one must haul them in with steel poles or some form of industrial crane, and I confess I was rather disappointed in the rods, which look like fishing rods always look. I said so, and Grey said I had surely never seen rods of such a size before! I said I might not have done, but I had seen very few fishing rods and these seemed much of a sort with the others. He looked crestfallen.

What about the reels? he wheedled. Well, there I suppose I was impressed. They were shining great things, something like the size of the saucepan you used to heat milk in when you were making us cocoa. Here Grey went into a dense technical explanation of the differences between his reels and the Captain's. I am not sure what these differences are, but I managed to divine that the key aspect of them is something called 'braking' and that, in Grey's opinion, the differences favor Grey's reels.

I always assumed that 'wetting the line' was part of the poetry of fishing and really meant throwing your hook overboard, but it's a thing you actually do. There's a piece of wire on the end of the line that a tunny can't bite through (I presume that must be it) and then what seem like a hundred miles of cord. When the fish 'strikes', it dashes away like a runaway train and you have to let it (this seems defeatist, but everybody nodded wisely and I did too). If your line is dry, then for some inexplicable reason it doesn't run evenly, but jumps about in spastic jerks that imperil rod, reel and fingers. Thus, Grey thoroughly wetted the lines and rewound them. He let me help. I was glad of the experience, but I wouldn't want to do it every day.

As we did this, he favored me with an inexpressibly involved description of what I might expect when he hooked a fish. I listened carefully, thinking all the while how astonishingly dull it all would be to readers of The Illustrated Doodah. They need have no fear. It went in one ear, looked around the blank interior walls and hopped straight out the other, except in the most general terms, which are: this is a thrilling, high-stakes sport, a duel to the death and so forth, and one must be primed and ready for action at any moment. It will be wait, wait, wait, wait, wait, and then, suddenly, mayhem! Instruction lasted an hour, I dare say. Mike chirped up from time to time for the show of the thing. Johnny sat quiet. The only instruction that truly sank in was that one must buckle into one's harness prior to dropping bait over the edge of the boat, because if tunny are around, they might strike immediately, and if one isn't buckled in, one might lose one's entire rig or, if one isn't quick enough, be dragged overboard. Why the smooth, wet line doesn't simply run off the reel while you hold the rod with sedate and insolent calm was not clearly explained.

The harness is attached to a 'fighting chair', which is not unlike a dentist's chair on a swivel with a set of straps and buckles. Johnny's boat contains two of these. Grey pointed out that only one person could fight a fish at any time, but having two chairs doubled *Harlequin*'s chances of a strike. Does it, though? I can see how two rods would, but why two chairs? Oh, never mind, it's all so boring. No, wait, I have worked it out! Two people can strap in this way, and then if one hooks, the other reels in their line and waits. Clever Martha.

Anyway, Grey has strapped in. Mike grunted that if it were him he'd just throw a rope over the side with a steak on a huge hook, tie it to the boat and go to sleep.

It's mid-afternoon now. When somebody tells you how thrilling something is going to be, you must always be terribly wary. For seven hours we have watched the sickening horizon gently roll. We have raced to the side of several herring boats and seen the Captain jump into his rowboat on a number of occasions, but nothing has come of it. Grey has the dubious advantage of being able to fish constantly, since we never have to switch vessel. It doesn't seem to make him happy. Periodically he repeats how dramatic things will become when a fish strikes. The fifth time he said this, Henny caught my eye. I stifled laughter and then I thought, 'What is she up to?' She's supposed to be on Grey's side. I am right to worry about her, I know I am.

The only wild excitement came in hour the third when Grey suggested a kite on his line. The kite is just that, G. Campbell. Without it, the bait – a poor living mackerel, by the way, hook stabbed through its back and squirming on the line – wiggles around somewhere under the water, but this kite drags it up and and keeps him skipping along the wavetops. Grey says that it is because tunny prefer to hunt at the surface. Johnny says that tunny are caught high and low, and he rather believes that the kite's main purpose is to give the helpless angler, mute before the omnipotent void, some sense of his own agency. Or to save him from dying of boredom.

This is probably why poor old Herman M. went so overboard describing every rope and jagged whaling knife – he was stuck on a ship for however many months and you have to concentrate on such nonsense or you simply lose your mind. Maybe if I were out here every day I would learn what 50-lb line means (do you know?) or create some complicated allegorical scheme involving man's relationship with the tuna. Or maybe I wouldn't, because that kind of guff has all been done to death already. Our generation is jaded. We can't do anything like that – we are constantly looking over our own shoulders, thinking how ridiculous we're being. A tuna is a tuna, and if I make him a metaphor it is only because I lack the rigor to describe the world clearly. I don't want to editorialize, G. Campbell, I want to describe. I want to be a camera.

We are heading home, tunnyless. The 'good news' is that the Captain had no better luck than we did.

The day has not been without incident, however. Johnny, Miss Scarlett and I each attempted to draw out Henny. A total failure in my case. In fact, I felt she was measuring and analyzing me as if I were some kind of experimental dog. And then, after Grey had packed up his rod, he went to speak to her. I thought nothing of it at first, but suddenly their voices rose, or Henny's did anyway. She said, very distinctly, that she didn't let him into her cabin last night because she was tired. And, she said, she'll be tired again tonight. Then he said something. Then she said, 'I'm not your creature, Zane Grey. You will never enter my cabin again.' She knew we could hear her, and Grey knew we could hear, however much we pretended to look at our shoes. So Henny has cast Grey over, just like that. I think we all know what she's going to do next! She makes me shiver.

We had to go to the harbor so Grey and the Captain could have their daily meeting – the Captain won't set foot in Scarborough and is based in Whitby, the next town up the coast. I stayed in Scarb. and I watched excitedly as Lady Broughton weighed her catch of the day. If I told you the details of her life you would be scandalized, but marriage really doesn't seem to mean very much to these people. Her tunny was a 'handsome fellow' and 'fair-sized, but not a giant'. I was told this by a lanky, pipe-wielding Englishman called Taylor. From what I could tell as he buzzed around the dock, he is a sort of local fishing eminence. He is certainly very excited by tuna, and by the appearance of Grey to do battle with the Captain, but he seems untouched and even faintly amused by the general rancor. He explained the fishing process in so concise a fashion that I understood it more clearly in ten minutes than I had after three hours of Grey's painstaking instruction, and I noted it all down hastily for *The Illustrated Doodah*, who I hope will be very grateful.

While we were talking, another, slightly larger tunny was brought ashore. I wondered what we were doing wrong. Taylor replied, 'The sea is nothing but luck. Everything we do is at its sufferance.' He's rather a poet.

Johnny and Grey returned. Grey was rude to the locals who had turned out to greet him and boarded the *Harlequin*. I apologized to Taylor. He grinned that he was used to that kind of thing.

Dazzle on the starboard bow. I can, all of a sudden, barely keep my eyes open. The routine appears to be that we take a restorative snooze before dinner. I'm all for it.

Friday 31st August–Saturday 1st September

Henny Rosefield – The North Sea

The *Dazzle* was bigger than Henny expected. She was not surprised to see Martha Gellhorn.

The first night on board, everyone went to their cabins at ten-thirty in expectation of the early departure. Grey said he would wait for Henny to join him. She locked her door and went to bed. Eventually, Grey knocked. She did not answer. He knocked harder. She let him.

On Saturday morning he complained. She said that she had been tired. She did not say she had been asleep.

Aboard *Harlequin*, Grey sat for hours in his harness. He'd brought his satchel with him – he always did – but while Martha and even Mike scribbled away, he didn't touch his notebooks. Henny ignored him. The others noticed. Johnny Caister asked if she was all right.

'I'm—' she said, haltingly. 'I'm sorry. I shouldn't say.' She looked up at him from a downcast face. This was another of her mother's useful lessons.

'You're safe on this boat,' said Caister. 'And you're safe on the *Dazzle*.'

'Thank you,' she said. 'I worry that I come across as odd. I really have had quite a sheltered life! I don't know what you think of me, a single girl, travelling with Grey. It's just—'

'I'm not as innocent as all that, Miss Rosefield. And you're not, either. You're playing a dangerous game.'

'Oh,' she said. Caister was wearing brown slacks and a white cable-knit sweater with a thick blue border around its V-neck. His eyes were pale grey without being pale. The white shock of his hair was distracting even after several days. She turned away from him, looked over towards the Captain, who had been lowered from his keelboat again and was earnestly fiddling with a mackerel, the sun flashing off it as it twitched.

If Caister could see through her, she had to change her tactics. When she first went to the asylum, she had tried to seduce Dr Morgan into letting her leave without telling her parents. He had understood exactly what she was doing. She had then become meek and pliable.

Henny's mother said that if you trick a man, you can have him for a day. If you turn yourself into what he wants, you can have him for life.

This dictum was not exactly germane. Caister could see she was being manipulative. Henny had to persuade him that a good person might act as she was doing through no fault of her own. And so she asked, very quiet, 'How do I stop? What would you do if you'd only ever had to choose between things you didn't want? Do you know what that is like? When is it a game and when is it not?'

Caister didn't answer immediately. Then he said, 'I don't know.'

Henny said, 'Nor do I.' She looked into his eyes, holding the right side of her top lip in her teeth. Caister's face was blank, scrutinising. Then she broke his look and said, 'This is all very serious!'

'Sorry,' Caister said.

'There's nothing to be sorry for,' she said. 'I've never left America before. Maybe I am in a peculiar mood. Because, well—'

'Because of Grey?'

'Yes. It's my own fault. I've been a fool.'

'No one here will make you do anything you don't want to do.'

'That's easy for you to say,' she said.

'Yes, I suppose it is. I'm sorry.'

'Please stop being sorry! I'm very happy to be here.' After some minutes, Caister went to talk to Grey. Henny stayed where she was.

Her fellow travellers circled the deck, little conversations, deep thoughts, writing, drinking, waiting for the fish that never came.

Miss Scarlet brought Henny some coffee. She leaned on the rail next to her. 'You're a cold one,' she said. 'We've had cold ones before. Are you going to fuck Johnny?' Henny didn't react. 'It won't work.'

'What won't work?' Henny asked.

'You won't get him. Everyone's tried.'

'Caro got him. Anyway, I'm not trying.'

'So you say,' said Miss Scarlett. 'What do you think of Martha? She's also "not trying".'

'I don't know her, I'm afraid.'

'Don't be dull. She's very young, you know. I think she might be younger than you, because I think you're a little older than you say. Twenty-five?' Henny said nothing. 'Well, let's assume so.' Miss Scarlett looked at her nails. They were scarlet. 'Martha spent years with one of those awful bloody frogs, who's fine if you know what they're like, but she assumed he'd leave his wife for her. I don't think you would ever be so innocent, darling.'

'You're wrong,' said Henny. Miss Scarlett sipped her coffee and stared at her from giant blue eyes until Henny continued: 'I know what it looks like, me and Grey, but I wasn't always like this. I was— I was a very late developer.'

'Oh, darling, not sex! What a ghastly bourgeois view of innocence you have to be sure. We all think sex is nothing nowadays, as if we were jackals or newts – it's practically the law.'

'What do you mean then?'

'You know very well what I mean,' said Miss Scarlett. 'You're out to get what you can. I don't blame you, the world can be bloody, but don't do it on my boat and don't upset Johnny.' A trawler sounded its horn some distance to landward and Miss Scarlett rushed to the cockpit while Grey gathered in his tackle.

Caister sat down on the same bench as Martha, sun in their faces, smiling, entitled. Henny turned away. When she turned back, they were still smiling. Caister had been watching her, though. She would be practically in silhouette. She stretched her shoulders, turned sideways and breathed deeply. Then she went to Miss Scarlett in the cockpit.

'I'm sorry if I seemed rude,' Henny said. 'I was surprised.'

'You apologising to me is rather suspicious, darling. I was the rude one.'

'But I do apologise. I'm a defensive person. I make a lot of mistakes.' She let her voice trail away and glanced, as if subconsciously, at Grey.

'Is he a mistake?' said Miss Scarlett.

'Yes! He's over sixty!' Miss Scarlett held her gaze. 'Oh,' Henny said. 'Oh.'

'Dido – Miss Pink – is fifty-six.'

'Zane is nothing like Miss Pink.'

'He really isn't,' said Miss Scarlett. 'Why are you with him? He's lost all his money, Mike says.'

'It's not about the money,' said Henny.

'You don't like him, though. It's obvious. So what? It's not sex?' Henny was quiet. 'Oh God. He wasn't your first?'

'He's amazing.'

'How would you bloody know? When I said you weren't inno- cent— I didn't mean. Sex is nothing. No, it's not nothing.' Miss Scarlett was red. 'I blush all the time, darling, ignore it, but no, look, you don't like him, do you? Not outside the bedroom?'

'Does that matter?'

'Good grief! Miss Pink is marvellous when— Well, she's bloody marvellous, but that's not the thing— It's not the be-all and end-all. I've had plenty of— Well, I think I understand what you're saying, when someone is so bloody marvellous that you feel like you're going to die every time, and you get in a flap that if you leave them you'll never feel that way again and your body will never forgive you, because that's what the stupid bloody thing is *for*. But it isn't. The body's there to carry you around, and to get you away from these vampires.'

Just once during this speech Miss Scarlett scanned the sea between *Harlequin* and the land. Other yachts from the harbour were dotted in the near distance, including *Berania*. Henny thought for a moment, and asked, 'Was it Joe Carstairs?'

Miss Scarlett reddened again. 'Aren't you the little clever toes,' she said. Then she leaned away from the wheel and into the sun. 'Does anyone else need a gin?' she called.

'I'll get them,' Caister called back.

Miss Scarlett turned back to Henny. 'I had a blue period. Joe was part of all that, and so was bloody awful Kim Waring. My husband didn't help.'

'You're married?'

'I was eighteen when I married. Dido and Johnny rescued me from it. Not from it, actually. From what came after.'

'From Joe?'

'Not really. A bit. But it was really this.' She pulled up her sleeve. Her forearm was badly scarred. Henny kept her face neutral. 'You don't know what it is, do you? It's Kiki and her bloody syringe, darling, egged on by Kim. I was bored and a child. I spent three years doing all those bloody things, the usual sort of story, and Joe didn't help, but it wasn't her fault. She's a selfish so-and-so anywhere outside a bed, but she's not really a bad weasel.'

'Who is Kim?'

'You met him in London?'

'I saw him. We barely spoke.'

'He has Caro round his finger, you know. She writes poison about anyone who upsets him, and everyone knows it, so they don't. He seduced me, and then he and Kiki showed me drugs, and then I went to their parties and I slept with anything that moved, mostly women. Pink was one of them, thank God. She says it was in Kenya, though it might have been any-bloody-where, and she saw something worth something in me – who knows why – and she got Johnny's help and they locked me up for a week while I had fits, and here we are now, usual sort of story.'

'Are you still married?' asked Henny.

'God, no. That was the next nightmare. My husband thought I'd come to my senses, which I had, but my senses were all about Pink. He went barmy, said he wouldn't have the world know he'd been turned over for an invert. Johnny said he'd be the man, if man were needed, and so the deed was done, usual sort of story. Oh, hello, Mr Grey.'

Grey was impatient. 'Get us over there,' he said, pointing at a distant trawler. 'Why aren't they calling for us?'

'It's probably—'

'Take us there! There are gulls.'

'Aye aye, sir,' said Miss Scarlett.

The trawler hadn't signalled because it was surrounded by blowfish. They rolled their slate-grey lengths – thirty feet or more – up through the surface, sinuous as snakes. One spouted yards from the *Harlequin*. The smell was foul and Henny stepped back. Mike laughed that these were tiddlers. One couldn't really say one had seen a blowfish until one had witnessed the battle royal between sperm whale and giant squid. Or a humpback calf brought down by whale-killers. He had witnessed many such battles, of course.

Time passed.

Martha approached Henny with a determined face. 'You spoke with Miss Scarlett for a long time,' she said. 'What about?'

'Usual sort of story.'

Martha laughed, then stopped herself. 'Yes, that's what she told me too. It's extraordinary, isn't it, what we can think is normal?' Then she asked, in a very serious voice, 'What's your normal, Miss Rosefield?'

'Why do you want to know?' asked Henny.

'I'm nosy, I guess. And also I— Well, maybe it's just that, in the end. Rather inglorious, if so.'

'There really is nothing interesting about me,' said Henny, and waited.

'All right then,' said Martha eventually. Then she took off her white sweater and arched her back, gave a little shudder. Henny wasn't sure whether it would be sensible to try to make friends with her, so she said nothing. 'Miss Pink and Miss Scarlett,' Martha said, 'and Carstairs and Kim and dukes and racing drivers and this boat – don't you find everything moving at a hundred times the speed of life elsewhere, as if you were a dragonfly?'

'A little.'

'Yes. But I can't decide whether it's all too fast because we're these poor, wandering lumps of blood and bone in a world of speedboats and telephones, or because we're civilised, pampered creatures thrust back into a fairy forest where it's all sex and death and every woman for herself.'

'That's interesting.'

'Isn't it? We're not in our natural reality, either way, don't you think?'

'I don't know,' said Henny.

Later, Henny waited until Caister and the others were listening, and told Grey crisply that she would never share a cabin with him again.

Henny sat down for dinner at Johnny's right hand. Martha sat opposite, with Grey next to her. Mike and Miss Scarlett flanked Miss Pink at the shortened table's other end.

Martha, burnt by the sun, was wearing another of Schiaparelli's creations. It was green and clung to her, however she moved, even when it seemed inevitable that it must gape wide. After watching it covertly for some minutes, Henny said, 'That's a wonderful dress. I can hardly understand how it works.'

'Me neither, believe me!' said Martha. 'You realise they're not mine?'

'They're not?'

'Oh, my word! They cost the earth and several seas just to look at. I'm tall is all, and no one knows or cares who I am, so I'm a useful sort of perambulating clothes horse.'

'Well,' said Henny, 'it suits you.'

'Thank you.' Martha spoke genuinely. She was open-hearted and well-mannered. She was, however, still suspicious of Henny and determined to follow up her suspicions. 'I don't choose my clothes,' she said. 'You choose yours, and you look marvellous. Where did you learn to dress?'

Henny didn't answer. She smoothed the silk over her knee, turned to Johnny and said, 'Everything's easy for you, isn't it? You don't have to think.'

Caister was taken aback for a moment, and then he said, 'Oh, you mean in terms of clothes?'

'Of course, Lord Caister.'

'Call me "Johnny", please,' he said. 'Well, *in terms of clothes*, you couldn't be more wrong. Single-breasted or double? Lapel shot with midnight-green? How starched the front? How voluminous the tie? When the differences are dainty, old fruitbat, every difference makes a difference.'

'If people are watching you closely,' said Henny.

'Yes, well, they are, aren't they?' He held her eye.

Henny saw Martha itching to speak, but unable to think of anything to say. Luckily, Mike barrelled in. 'Never bothered much with the rags, myself,' he said. 'Got this made before the war and it hasn't fallen apart yet. Proper tailor. Armenian chap. Only had one hand. Never had to think about it again. Best approach, eh, Grey?'

'Hmph,' said Grey. 'Only decadents and inverts care about clothes.'

'I don't agree at all,' said Martha. 'Not at all! What we wear is part of who we are.'

'Only the weak-minded judge by appearance,' said Grey.

'It's what we all do!' said Martha sitting forward. 'Clothes are terribly important, they're how we speak to the world. We use them to say what we're like, what we think looks nice. For bundles of people without much money or much luck, it's the only aesthetic decision they get to make.'

'They couldn't wear that gown,' said Henny.

'No, they could not, poor things. Life's not fair. But don't tell me clothes don't matter, and don't tell them either, just because they can't buy Schiaparelli, and don't tell me that this gown isn't art. Anything made more beautiful than it has to be is art, and art makes us human.'

'Oh,' said Henny in her most earnest voice. 'That's very profound. I've never thought of it like that.' Martha flashed pleasure and then caught herself, was suspicious again.

'There is nothing profound about clothes,' said Grey. 'If you want profundity, you need to hunt and kill. That is what connects you to the spirit of your ancestors, Miss Gellhorn. I don't worry what I'm wearing when I stand on the banks of the Rogue casting for steelhead. Have you fished for steelhead, Earl Caister?'

'"Johnny", please,' said Johnny. 'No, I haven't. They're trout, yes? Better than Taupo?'

'No, but, wait— Have you fished Taupo?'

'Indeed I have,' said Johnny.

'Ah, well, yes then, the trout in the Rogue are infinitely better than Taupo's. And they don't care what you wear. That's what nature's about. That's survival.'

'Well,' said Johnny, 'you're not trying to mate with the fish. Most women care what you wear, I find. And I prefer women who look nice. Wanting to attract a mate is pretty natural, don't you think?'

'You don't agree with this, do you?' Grey asked Mike.

'Don't try and put me between a girl and a nice dress,' Mike replied. 'Too old a hand for that. Will say, though, these girls are all trying to look as good as they can, trying to bag a man. Or a girl,' he nodded to Miss Pink, 'for which I don't bloody blame 'em, girls being much prettier than men. Lucky for some of us that some of 'em can't see it.'

'What's your point?' said Grey.

'Point?' said Mike. 'Well. Mating is a deadly serious business, and a girl in a dress is pulling out whatever stops nature and Mammon have given her. But when we're throwing flies at a trout, it's just a bloody game to us. Real hunting is about getting the fish any way you can, because you need to eat it or your kiddies will starve. Dynamite the bastards if you need to. If it's "nature" you care about.'

'Yes, Zane!' said Henny, giving her voice the faintest edge of hysteria. 'You just play at nature! You use all your clever knots and futuristic machines, and then, when you've captured some poor innocent creature and have it all trussed up, you say that what you're doing is *natural*. It isn't nature, it's a fetish!'

Grey looked at her almost with fear.

'Don't be too hard on him,' said Johnny warily. 'To be a human these days is not a very natural state. I think that's what Martha was saying about clothes – we are each our own work of artifice.'

'Yes!' exclaimed Mike, suddenly enthused. 'That's damned right!

We dress up because we know that the only thing that counts is what other chaps think of us. That is who we really are!'

'No!' Martha was shocked. 'That's not your truest self, surely?'

'You don't know what's in my head, do you?'

'No, but—'

'Then what does it matter?'

Henny said, 'Do you say that because so many people think you're a fraud?'

An intake of breath. After a few long seconds Mike said, 'Yes. Hands up. I've made some mistakes. I'll make more too, young feller, but I won't stop chasing windmills and I won't apologise for writing down stories that do me credit. I haven't got a pot of cash and I don't want to do a proper job.'

'It doesn't matter that you've never really found a lost tribe, or Atlantis, or whatever it is you say?'

'Not a jot.'

'I didn't expect you to be so candid.'

'Who are you going to tell?' said Mike. He looked around the table. 'Caister knows I'm a humbug, but he also knows I'm not a wrong 'un. He knows he doesn't have to worry about me.'

'Don't you feel responsible to the truth at all?'

'I feel responsible to myself, because no one else is. You only get one ride on the cow. Sorry, don't mean to sound shocking. Bloody good wine, this.'

'Johnny!' said Martha. 'Tell him he's wrong!'

'I don't know that he is wrong.'

Martha looked crestfallen.

Grey said. 'He's is wrong. You're both wrong. Other people don't tell you who you are.'

'Well—' starts Johnny.

'No! That's just an excuse, a way to evade responsibility. You are the mover. You create the world around you. You choose who you want to be.'

'I don't think we *can* choose,' said Johnny, 'not in the end. The world is too— Well, the world is real and it's too strong for us to control.'

Henny said, 'Lord Caister – Johnny – I think I understand. Do you mean that people believe that they know what you are like and, over time, however much you resist, however much you try to choose who you are, you are shaped by their belief?'

Johnny looked at her smartly. 'That is part of what I mean,' he said.

Grey glared at Johnny. He turned and put his hand deliberately on Martha's. 'You've never hunted, have you?' he asked.

'No.'

'You'll understand what I'm saying when you have, when you catch a fish. You only care about clothes because you've never touched nature as it really is. Man should glory in the wilderness, but instead we're destroying it – there's nothing left almost – look at the herring boats sucking every tiny fish from the sea – where will the tuna be in five years' time? At least I saw the West when it was empty, before civilisation came to carve it up.'

'I don't know,' Martha replied. 'It's terribly attractive to burble about wandering under the stars, and I'm sure it *is* in our deepest nature to hunt, but we have to move beyond that, don't we? We have to live in the world like it is. There are all these millions of people and we can't all eat wild rabbits. Agriculture and cities are how we survive. We have to divide our labour to conquer. That's how we can progress. Isn't that the reality of now?'

'If it is,' said Grey, 'I don't want it.'

'I've seen the West, remember,' said Martha. 'I saw the dustbowl.'

'I'm sorry for the farmers,' said Grey. 'But that was what we deserved for raping the land. It's not farming country, it's hunting country. The Red Indian knew it, and we despoiled it and now it is gone, and what do we do now?'

'That's the question,' said Johnny. 'Do you think we can dismantle civilisation? Look at what it's given us.'

'Fools,' said Grey, 'think the highest pleasures come from civilisation.' He glowered for a fraction of a second at Henny, and then spoke directly to Martha. 'You might not understand what I mean at first,' he said, 'but let me tell you something: a decadent guide will never dare take you as far as you'll go willingly on an innocent adventure. I promise you that.'

'Well,' said Johnny. 'What larks! Shall we repair to the saloon?'

Grey retreated to his cabin. Miss Pink took Mitchell-Hedges to her room to continue their backgammon tournament and Miss Scarlett pantomimed a fit of the vapours and declared herself ready for bed or suicide. Soon after, Johnny stood and said, 'Well, neither of you will leave me alone with the other, so I'm taking myself off. Sleep well, my darlings.'

Henny and Martha waited for each other to speak. Eventually Martha said, 'What do you think about it all?'

'I think I'm real, if that's what you mean.'

Martha said, 'What is going on with you and Grey? Why did he hold my hand? Was he trying to make you jealous?'

'Probably. Were you trying to make Johnny jealous?'

'What?' said Martha.

'You left your hand in Zane's.'

'I didn't want to be rude,' said Martha.

'Hm.' Then Henny said, 'You're wondering what he meant about "innocent adventure", aren't you?'

'No,' said Martha. 'A bit, maybe.'

'Well, I don't know if innocent adventure is what I'd call it, but Zane does take you further in that way, he honestly does.' Martha was surprised. Or incredulous, maybe. 'You won't believe me, but he does.'

'Are you telling me I should go to his bed—'

'No,' said Henny quickly, as if she wished she hadn't spoken. 'I just meant— It's nothing.'

They went to their cabins. Shortly afterwards Grey knocked on Henny's door again. She ignored him. Much later, she thought she heard an engine outside the yacht, and some muffled effort, and then soft feet on the deck, but it all took place in the state between deep sleep and wakefulness, and by morning it had been relegated to a dream.

Saturday 25th August–Saturday 1st September

Zane and Dolly Grey – Altadena / Scarborough

East Mariposa Street
August 25th

Dear Doc,

You say your precious Henny wanted to see me in New York! I made myself free the entire day we shared the city, and she, if you recall, was 'ill'. Excuse me if I laugh!

And because I must not laugh too much, I will not relay my reaction to how much you have always 'longed to battle Mitchell-Henry', or remind you of your previous feelings on England. You will find London appalling, I suppose, older and sootier than New York, which at least has vigor. I liked London, of course.

If Ledger is paying and you have a moment of time before you race off to harry your poor tuna, you must go to a restaurant called 'Rules' (or maybe 'The Rules'), and you must eat a partridge there. You must also take tea at the Savoy or the Ritz. One of these is incomparably more the thing than the other. I was told which when I was there, in no uncertain terms, but I cannot remember. Presumably the Earl of Caister will be able to help you.

I hope you are well, Doc, but I cannot help worrying. Brownie wrote me about your Henny, and although Brownie is jealous and angry, she confirmed that Henny sounds exactly the kind of designing creature who would play on your hopes. I repeat for the umpteenth time that no innocent girl would have found you where she did and said the things she said, if Brownie is to be believed, and in this I do believe her, because we have been here before.

The desperate irony, my dear, is that *you* are the innocent. It is your charm that your eye can still attune itself so readily to its freshest, most unguarded state and dream that there is no more to the iceberg than its gleaming visible cusp. It is the best of you, the thing that makes you a great artist when you want to be. The kind of tale you tell, the wonder and the openness with which you describe emotions and passion, is truly special. It is only when you are disillusioned that the wonder gets diluted. If you are fresh and clean in spirit, you must write immediately, all you can! Use this moment!

It is left to us poor hardened cynics to protect you. You say the girl cannot be after your money, but you do not know where she is from and how little might satisfy her. You have always had the girls, and your boatmen, and even to an extent me, as a retinue to buffer you against the world, against your critics and the kind of swells who will never understand you, who have not fought like lions for every inch of ground they ever won. Well, now you are in England and you are among just such a collection of swells, and your only buffer is this new girl who I do not know or trust.

And I do not either, by any means, trust Caister. I was almost surprised that you had heard of him, but I suppose that even you do not live in a cave all the time. In case your only knowledge of him is gleaned from the perspicacious pages of *Fish, Fishing and Fishmen*, then it might be well for you to be aware that he is the most famous rake in the British Empire, as well as a modern Croesus. Think about that second fact. Most of these nobles in their castles can barely pay for firewood – it's why they marry Americans; but the Caisters have stuck to their fortune like glue. The man pretends to be a dissolute, but he cannot be. What is he hiding?

You have not read his wife's books, have you? He tormented her with his women until she could no longer bear it. Not openly and honestly like you, my dear Doc, but hurtfully, sneakily and constantly protesting his fidelity. He is old blood and he is cold blood, and he is grasping. If Henny is half what you say, he will want her. If she's half what Dot and Brownie say, then she will want him straight back.

Did you take in the sentence about his wealth? He was wealthier beyond your dreams even when you were wealthy beyond the dreams of normal people. Do not measure your plans against his *Dazzle*, or you will destroy yourself. And how many times must I tell you: piece of paper or no piece of paper, Hemingway will not fish with you. Write about him or do not, but do not base your decision on impossible hopes.

You are touching about our love, but I prefer it when you talk of friendship. I don't think I could bear it if you fell in love with me again. The shock would stop my heart.

Do not think about me. *Soul of the Marlin* is a wonderful title, but it means nothing until you have written a wonderful book. Get the story down while your mind is clear, and catch a giant fish. These things will cleanse your being more dependably than anything else. If Henny is clearing your thoughts enough to help you do them, then I suppose I should be grateful to her, but what is below the water's surface, Doc, my darling? Please think about that.

I do love you, old bear,

Dolly

The yacht *Dazzle*
August 31st

Dear Dolly,

Your letter kindled a dark rage, which lasted nearly an hour. Then I told myself: you do not know Henny.

You fear I am too innocent to see through Lord Caister! What kind of a booby must I be to you? He and his parasite friends are what I expected they would be – bloated, boastful and pansified. He pets a pair of invert girls and lets them play ship's captain, and he keeps a nigger for his butler, and you only can imagine what else.

I am finally on board *Dazzle*. My cabin is large and that is all you can say for it. It has no soul. My fellow travelers have gone to bed in preparation for an 'early start' tomorrow, although 5.30 a.m. can hardly be called early! They have 'drifters' here, and some of the English swear by fishing alongside them, but these aren't the pretty little drifters we know – they are great, heavy tubs with miles of nets, which like as not swallow all the tuna themselves. We will go out with the day squadron of herring trawlers instead.

I am not tired – as well you know, I have more vitality than most men half my age after the few hours I am able to snatch every night – but I insisted to Henny that she take this evening to rest away from me. There are bunks on Caister's motor launch in which she could recover tomorrow, if she wanted, but I insisted, as I say. I sent her away so I could write to you.

Caister's fishing launch, *Harlequin*, is satisfactory, although the plans I originally made with the yard in Fort Myers have been vulgarized and she is not the boat that even the *Frangipani* would be, had we not been cheated of my fortune. Her engines, fighting seats and general equipment are 'first-rate', but, like *Dazzle*, she is entirely without grace. When I think of the line and grandeur of the dear old *Fisherman*, my heart still soars. No human heart could soar on seeing the *Dazzle*. Without masts, a ship is a mean, utilitarian thing. She is named for her paint – the willynillacious stripes we gaped at on the convoy ships in Halifax. *Harlequin* is similarly attired. One of the other yachts in the harbor, *Nahlin*, is as pretty as anything you ever saw in your life and I covet her more than I covet *Dazzle*. Perhaps I should not worry about grandeur – beauty, after all, is as sincere a virtue.

London, as you supposed, was exquisite torture for me. The sunrise, what I could see of it above the filthy roofs, which the hotel manager informed me through his snaggled teeth and rancid breath were a 'wonderful skyline view', snuck like a thief through the fetid air, and I watched for fully an hour as it crept a counterfeit of daylight over the rotten city. This is what passes in London for 'a beautiful summer's day'.

I was led mid-morning through a timid park, named after some long-dead king, I presume, with a sad line of trees and girls covering the grass and smoking and shrieking at each other. This 'network of green', said Caister, makes London special, gives its city-dwellers a sight and feel of nature. I do not suppose I have ever felt so alien as I did at that moment. But then Henny said, 'Isn't it awful?' and I remembered that it was all a trial to be endured on my way to a greater prize.

The evening we spent in London was abominable. Caister insisted on our dining in an underground hole peopled by pansies and viragos. They pawed and clawed at each other, driven by vicious jealousies it was beyond my dignity to untangle. I have said many times, and Mike agreed with me on the basis of his explorations in Central America, that the simple older life, where an enemy will declare himself and stab you in the chest, is incomparably preferable to this rank, civilized stew, whose poisons mix and permeate to create an ever fouler mixture.

I was glad to escape. Caister's former wife was drunk and she wounded Henny deeply, although Henny pretended to be brave. Another American girl was there, a journalist called Gellhorn, very young and wearing a dress of surpassing immodesty. I didn't know how she fitted into the party, but Mike has taken her as his secretary. I am not sure whether this means the obvious thing.

It is the evening of September 1st. I have decided that I shall deny Henny my bed for a second consecutive night. You will think me cruel, but it will teach her a lesson – her head has temporarily been turned by this yacht and its spurious luxuries. Please do not think that this is because she is like an 'iceberg' – it is very much the opposite. She is so simple and pure that she can hide nothing, and she is confused by Caister's showy wealth and excess. You were right about him. He clearly designs her seduction, but she will resist. She is too good to be long led astray.

I explained the peculiar situation on *Dazzle* to Miss Gellhorn in a new and interesting way. She informed me that she first met Caister two weeks ago at a country mansion devoted to the training of enormous dogs, and now she is on the grandest boat in Christendom hunting for whales. After pointing out the differences between tuna and whales, I told her that this place can be described as a kind of 'Fairyland', a wildwood from a storybook where the normal rules do not apply.

I am extremely satisfied with this insight. It so perfectly describes the enchanted world that you and I have built ourselves, a simpler, nobler world where our true natures are unfettered by the clutter of convention.

Caister has built a very different private world, and so have several others on these yachts. Ours is about being true to our selves, but these worlds here are about turning the pure, simple animal self into something distorted and gross, about surfeiting it on technology and chemicals out of a sheer boredom with life. Another of the harbor's yachts is called the *Berania*. Its mistress is 'Joe' Carstairs, a celebrated invert who is, naturally, a friend of our host's. I am told that she runs a decadent court of dope and perversion.

I should hardly be surprised, given my eternal, infernal ill luck, that I caught no fish today. At least Mitchell-Henry failed too. He has offended every angler in England and sails from a neighboring town called Whitby. I have not been there, but it can hardly be as awful and grey as Scarborough. I suppose it is like Wedgeport to Scarborough's Halifax.

I am using my own tackle, although Caister has everything one could desire, and new. He bought it from Hardy, of course. Hardy is not here, but I imagine he will arrive once he scents me. He'll not get a penny.

We must do conversation with Mitchell-Henry every evening as part of the rules of our contest. I am not sure why we arranged this to be so on days when nothing has happened, when my body is strung taut with the need for solitude or kamibbling, but we did. In Scarborough, as we went ashore to make our way to the meeting, I had to endure the sight of two splendid tuna shining silver in the evening sun being stared at by huge crowds of children and shopgirls.

I also must endure the loud encouragement of every local angling man. I have grown so used to the jealous silence of my fellow Americans, who refuse to accord me any respect simply because they cannot bear that I proved them wrong and told them so, that I forget that my achievements merit acclaim. Here they are not jealous, and keenly wish me to succeed over Mitchell-Henry, whose constant belittling of his fellows they rightly reprehend.

The acclaim is tiresome, nonetheless. I have repeatedly been exhorted to explain the difference between fishing for tuna, which I cannot call 'tunny' however often the locals say it, and hunting marlin. The 'hero-worship' drains me and yet I find the story I wish to tell grows clearer every day – that is the nature of Fairyland, as I explained to Gellhorn – everything is clearer here.

She is an interesting young woman. She and Caister have clearly been intimate, but they are not now, so what has he led her here for? You were right. I do not trust him. The forest always holds a wolf.

An infamous dinner. The others remain in the saloon. I could not suffer their company a moment longer.

As we entered the dining room, Henny praised Martha Gellhorn's dress and this led instantly into the most tedious imaginable chatter concerning clothes. I tried to return the discussion to some level of general interest by relating my experiences casting fly on the Rogue, but Earl Caister started making idiotic comparison between hunting and fashion, and the pursuit of a fish and the pursuit of a mate, and this dragged the girls into a frivolous whirlpool.

I tried to explain how every man must create his own fate, but Caister was too far gone to understand what I meant. Words mean nothing to him, I realize. He will use them to get whatever he wants. They do not, as they do for me, have an eternal and sacred power. He is twisting them to ensnare Henny, whose very simplicity makes her vulnerable. I watched him whisper his poison in her ear, my rage increasing, my soul burning white.

Caister is soft and bored. He talks of the chase, but he will never understand the true hunter, the man who will conquer and revenge, the natural man, the man of justice. He thinks to master me, to take my woman. It will not be so. It is I who understand the soul, the passions of an honest nature. He cannot even admit such things exist. He says the world is a chaos, he belittles me, because he is too lost to understand that a man must create his own story.

When I put my hand on Martha's and asked her whether she truly thought hunting was like seduction, Caister was immediately on alert. Such men as he are always jealous of their conquests, forever, however much they hide it. I touched him deeply, but he is so 'civilized' that he does not even understand what he feels.

I felt Henny's eyes were hot on my cheek. She too had to feel the searing knife of jealousy. It must have shocked her to realize that this boat is not her private playground, that any wandering will have bitter consequences.

I heard her return to her room a few minutes ago. She has learned her lesson, I am sure. I shall take the air and investigate whether she is ready to see sense.

In the cold evening air, I decided that I will not relent. Henny must stew for one more night. Maybe, indeed, I shall use Martha Gellhorn to further work on her jealousy, that deepest, most primal passion. If a lesson is to be taught, it must be taught well.

Saturday 1st September

John Fastolf, Earl of Caister –
The North Sea

Apart from the absence of tunny, Johnny is pleased with his first day on the *Harlequin*. She's every bit as trim as Andy and Saul said she was, and they think they can take her to thirty-five knots.

Andy is disappointed that Miss Scarlett is piloting the fishing trips, but Miss Scarlett is easier company, especially for the girls. Also, she makes better coffee than Andy.

Johnny doesn't know what to do about the girls. Martha Gellhorn is the kind of person who makes rash, spur-of-the-moment decisions, which she will then analyse and understand with great clarity in the cold light of day, but she will still have made them and Johnny could do without the consequences. Henny Rosefield is different, but he is not sure how. He cannot afford the uncertainty, not while all his plans are coming to a head, not with things so finely in the balance.

And so, cautiously, he tries to ascertain what Henny wants. When she responds with flirtation, he asks her to stop whatever game she is playing and she halts him in his tracks by asking where games end and reality begins.

Johnny's plans are not a game. He intends to put an end to Kim Waring's secret 'career' and all the subtle, hidden damage it has done. To that end, he has invited Kim and Caro to dinner on Wednesday. Joe Carstairs and her party will be there too. It will be tricky, but you don't avoid things just because they are hard or because you don't know exactly how they will turn out. At some point you have to act, clear out the machine gun, kill the man-eating lion, whatever it is. If it doesn't kill you, it might make you stronger. If it does kill you, well, that's an end to it at least. There are worse things than dying.

Henny regards him stilly, interested that she has touched a nerve. He shouldn't be stung. Why should he care that she thinks his life is a game? It is what everyone else thinks, after all, and what he often says himself. He is in a funny mood.

Later, Henny announces to Grey that he will never enter her cabin again. It is calculated, cruel and rash, and again Johnny does not know what it means. Perhaps, in order to give the girl something to focus on, he will have to sleep with her. With Grey on the boat it would be ill-mannered, but Grey is being an idiot and Johnny has more than one reputation to maintain. It might be the most sensible option.

He is aware that this thought would sound funny if he vocalised it. She is a very pretty girl.

In the evening, after dinner, after everyone has gone safely back to their cabins, Johnny dresses in loose black trousers and a black jersey, unpolished shoes with crêpe soles and a black woollen hat. He creeps from his stateroom and makes his way towards the *Dazzle*'s stern.

There's someone else moving on the deck. It is Grey, approaching Henny's door. Grey knocks softly. Johnny is surprised, after the way she humiliated him this afternoon and after she ignored him at dinner. The thought crosses his mind that this might all be a charade the pair of them perform to spice up their relationship, but minutes pass and there is no response. Grey's knocks get insistent, but he doesn't make them loud enough to raise embarrassing attention. He returns to his cabin, looking confused. Looking old, in fact.

Henny is definitely a problem.

When he reaches the stern, Miss Scarlett, also in black, glances significantly at her watch. 'Grey was out and about,' he says. 'He didn't see me.' She has already prepared the little skiff. Its Elto engine has been modified and muffled by Andy and a firm of engineers in Venice who specialise in this kind of discreet vessel, but Johnny still rows away from the *Dazzle* before firing it up and heading out to sea to rendezvous with the *Verloren Hoop*. He passed over instructions for the meeting when he picked up the bait this morning.

He and Miss Scarlett don't talk much on the journey out. They take it in turns to nap. They collect the cocaine from Meneer van Cleef and hand over an attaché case full of cash. Van Cleef passes Johnny a letter. Its wax seal is intact.

Johnny is not the Sphinx. The Sphinx is his enemy.

It is grotesque that Johnny should have become a drug-smuggler. His personal stand on drugs is not a pose, and God knows he doesn't need the money.

Blame Miss Pink. She was a spy during the war, or something like a spy. She got the chance to do something interesting with her life, something important, but as soon as the Show was over, a chap who wouldn't have been able to track down a fox if you tied it to his winkle patted her on the head and told her to find a husband. She wasn't having that.

It took her a while to set things up, but Miss Pink was patient and she had a knack for finding lost souls, people like Johnny, people who were unfit for society. There are some dogs that you can't keep in the city, basically, and Miss Pink offered them the hunt. It never felt innocent, but he never imagined— Each decision seemed sensible at the time, each one shut a door behind itself, and now he is here and it's as if he sleepwalked into it. He's responsible for it all, but it's not what he wanted.

That's why he snapped at Grey during dinner. You don't 'create the world around you'. The world is a mess and every choice you make gets you more tangled up. Johnny can affect how other people see him, up to a point, but he can't make anything real for himself.

Johnny slits open the seal, reads the letter. Van Cleef watches, agitated. The Dutchman doesn't know what it says, but he's heard things. He's heard that the Sphinx has finally worked out who he's up against, that he's getting ready to move against Johnny, that he might be moving already. Van Cleef is worried what this will mean for him and the *Verloren Hoop*. He didn't sign up for this, he says.

Johnny says that he's stuck now. Van Cleef thumps his hat against his thigh and says he has a family. He demands to know how Johnny plans to deal with the Sphinx, but Johnny says that he's got everything under control and climbs back into the skiff. Van Cleef isn't pleased.

'It was a reasonable question,' says Miss Scarlett. He doesn't reply. 'I'd be worried if I were him.'

'Are you worried?'

'Yes, of course.'

'The Sphinx' is supposed to be a mysterious Chinaman preying on white girls and forcing them to do his vile bidding. He is the plot of a cheap novelette, a story of sexual slavery and bestial cruelty, of a wicked and widespread web woven with fiendish complexity, and as such he is an easily understood villain for the press, the public and most of the police to fixate on. What lies behind this smoke and mirrors is a perfectly normal and sordid sort of dope ring. There's a collection of low opium dens exactly where you would expect to find them, and these are the guts of the business. Then there are Molly's girls, who are there to give society a whiff of sulphurous depths. And then there are a very few more prominent fiends – Kim Waring and Kiki Preston, for instance – to sparkle their way through the same society as the gossip writers. Somehow the impression is given, and gleefully passed on, that dope is everywhere. It is cleverly done, but it isn't the product of 'The Most Dangerous Mind in the East'. Johnny particularly admires the choice of 'Sphinx'. An Egyptian soubriquet for a Chinese villain perfectly encapsulates the heated and unthinking brand of melodrama that seems to bypass his fellow Englishmen's critical faculties.

Moreover, the Sphinx's dubious celebrity has been useful for Johnny. If the police blame everything on the Sphinx, then they also assume that this Sphinx has no competition. The Sphinx knows otherwise, of course, and wants to find out who the competition is. The Sphinx has even let it be known, very carefully, that a partnership would be preferable to a protracted and bloody battle. It is to manage this situation that Johnny sleeps with Molly Parker.

Kim's blackmail is a sideline, as far as the Sphinx is concerned.

Not every policeman is seduced by the story of the Sphinx. Specifically, there is a red-haired, innocent-faced inspector called Raskell. He has looked at the number of dope-fiends and not assumed they are the nose of a hippo. From this, he has worked out, more or less accurately, how large – or small – the business must be. He is rightly suspicious of the way in which, every time the police seem to close in on something concrete, there is a lurid revelation of sex, slaughter and nymphs in Chinatown, often accompanied by a body and a note stamped with the Sphinx's seal. Raskell thinks that the Sphinx is not a mysterious Chinaman, but rather a proper, nasty, murderous bastard who is having fun playing at being Moriarty. Inspector Raskell doesn't like this at all. What Raskell doesn't understand is how the Sphinx got to be so successful so quickly. He smells serious organisation at some level.

Johnny and Miss Pink have considered taking over the Sphinx's operation, but keeping the Sphinx's name. Raskell would make that awkward.

The note van Cleef passed on to Johnny is from one of Miss Pink's favourite spies, who has been doing a little digging in the Low Countries. It confirms, as expected, the last remaining details of the Sphinx's operation, where the drugs come from and by which route.

'Now what?' asks Miss Scarlett. He doesn't answer because he doesn't know. The fish has to be played to the boat, of course, but what then? Defeating the Sphinx will be the end of two years' planning, and Johnny looks forward to destroying Kim Waring, but after the kill? Following it all through, dealing with the detail, that's where the real fruits of victory lie, but it will be an administrative exercise. It will require concentration and organisation – the weapons of civilisation – and he doesn't have the substance for it, the bottom. He is bottomless. He is bored. Maybe he is getting careless because he doesn't care.

He knows that Miss Pink is worried about him. Will she suggest another hunt? She's as restless as he is. Does he want that? He thinks he does not. That is what his secret dream is all about. Maybe there is a way to get away clean.

Does the Sphinx ever think like this? Does the Sphinx ever think: 'I could have had a quieter, easier, less exciting life, but now I am here, and what else can I do? This is who I am now!'

Miss Scarlett is irritated that Johnny hasn't answered her. She is also uncertain as to what will happen when the Sphinx is defeated. Her uncertainty manifests itself in the posing of reasonable and awkward questions. 'Why are you sure that Caro isn't involved?' she asks.

'It's not her style.'

'Pardon me for saying, darling, but you're not the best judge of Caro.'

'Stop it,' he says. 'Just stop.' It's dark, but he knows she is blushing.

They motor for another twenty minutes. As the *Dazzle* comes into view, Miss Scarlett says, 'Once you push everyone away, you won't be real any more. You can't do this alone. Dealing with van Cleef in daylight this morning was crazy. People aren't stupid.'

'There are other van Cleefs.'

'What if the Sphinx gets to him before this is over? You won't know until you turn up, and then you'll be dead. You don't need to take the risk. When are you going to stop making the drops yourself?'

'I have to do something.' It's the honest answer, but it doesn't make Miss Scarlett wrong. Miss Scarlett also doesn't like that he plans to entertain Caro and Waring on the *Dazzle*. She knows full well why he keeps taking the risks.

'And what about Henny?' she asks. 'Are you going to fuck her?' He doesn't reply. 'It'll make her a target for Kim.'

'Have you taken a liking to her?' says Johnny.

'I told her about me and Kim, and what you and Pink did to get me away from it all. She'd be bloody surprised if she knew what we were doing now.' Miss Scarlett plays at being indiscreet, but she is seldom indiscreet. If she said something to Henny, she had a reason.

'I don't dislike her,' says Miss Scarlett, 'and given that she's a lying bitch who's after you, I should. Either she's an evil genius or there's something screwy going on, and it could be both. If she's not an evil genius, I'd rather Kim didn't get hold of her. If she is one, you should put the pair of them in a bag with some snakes.'

'Yes,' says Johnny.

'None of which answers my question. Are you going to fuck her?'

'Maybe. To keep her quiet. Keep her out of harm's way.'

'Oh boy,' says Miss Scarlett.

Sunday 2nd September

Martha Gellhorn – The North Sea

Letter to G. Campbell Beckett, ctd.

It's Sunday and I'm back on the jolly old *Harlequin*. I suppose we pay no attention to the Sabbath because the Lord loves fishermen. He has an odd way of showing it, in our case.

Ten minutes ago we sped past the *Spurwing*, which is the Captain's keelboat. I can now inform you that a 'keel' or 'keelboat' is the larger sort of vessel carrying out our rival tunny-fishers and their rowboats. The lesser ones without any shelter on the decks are 'cobles'. Both types of boat are apparently very distinctive and traditional, but they look nondescript and I'm glad as all get-out that I'm not on one. The Captain insists his way is best, though, and so there he is all day, most of it in the rowboat, alone but for a hearty local to ply the oars.

The Captain's feud with Grey is nothing out of the ordinary for him, it seems. He's based in Whitby because of some ancient quarrel with Scarborough's 'Tunny Club' – I think that's its proper name, but you know what I mean if it isn't. The 'Tunny Club' sounds grand and important, but it's a crooked little house down a crooked little alley, and it is *verboten* to our party. The comic-opera nature of this enterprise does not dissipate with the passing of the hours.

We've arrived and Grey is setting out his rod. More importantly, breakfast is ready. Patterson made us the most spectacular thing yesterday morning called *Huevos rancheros*, a Mexican egg-and-spices affair, which you simply must discover. I mention it because it smells as if history is repeating itself in that department, and my mouth is watering. Yesterday Patterson spent the rest of the day perched near the prow reading mystery stories. He has a lordly disdain for the whole fishing process.

*

Two hours have passed in the usual fever of activity.

Still no tunny. And lunch is some way away.

Johnny has gone downstairs to sleep, or maybe to escape Henny's fluttering eyelashes.

Scarborough is rather like Send, or at least it is if you spend your time on the yachts. One might be forgiven for wondering if the entire money-disaster was a bad dream. *Dazzle* is the grandest thing in the harbor at night, but there are four more big ones at the moment, and others come and go all summer, apparently. There's *Vita II* (if I were building a massive yacht I would give the darling its own name, wouldn't you?), *St George* (Mitchell-Henry's great enemy, Colonel Peel – I shouldn't be drawn in, but I find myself on the side of Grey against Mitchell-Henry for nationalistic reasons I am rather surprised by, and on the side of Mitchell-Henry against anyone else), *Nahlin* (if there is a more beautiful yacht on the sea I haven't seen it; it belongs to hearty Lady Yule, who I met at Send talking about family-friendly movies with her fellow do-gooding ignorami) and *Berania* (the floating home of the aforementioned Joe Carstairs and her menagerie of gorgeous actresses, debs, and so forth).

So it's all frivols and flutteries, and no one does a day's work or has seen the trouble I've seen, and then suddenly someone will say, like Miss Scarlett ten minutes ago, for instance, 'Yes, and then I told Boffo, that was my brother – both of my brothers died in the war, you know . . .' and you suddenly remember that 'Colonel' and 'Captain' and so forth aren't honorifics, though I'd still rather people didn't use them. You remember how shattering it was to read Caro's first book, with the death of another chum on every second page? When you start thinking about that here, among these people, you start to see how they were all terribly, terribly touched by it all. Absolutely everyone in their forties seems to have lost half of their family and childhood friends, and none of them makes a thing of it.

I write as if they are gloomy. They are not, that's the point. But they are not all champagne and organdie. I spoke to Miss Scarlett after breakfast, and she mentioned dead Boffo because that's how she met Johnny. He was Boffo's CO and ferried his effects home after the war. Miss Scarlett was very young, and Johnny took care of her and her mother. He didn't have any of his own friends left to look after. As Miss S. put it, 'the bitch Caro wasn't completely wrong,' and the war was utterly awful for Johnny, worse than it was for most of them. He lost absolutely everyone. Then she said, 'We all talk like we're made of tin tacks, but we're human beings, you know. He seems tough, but one day he'll go feet over toppers again and if that person ever— Well, I'll bloody kill her, that's all.' She was looking at Henny, so it seems that I am not alone in perceiving a crisis. I'm rather shaking as I scribble it down.

What I mean to say, I suppose, is that when Miss Scarlett talks like this, I see at once how benighted it would be to say her life hasn't been real, just because she currently resides in Number One, Fairyland.

Johnny and Miss Scarlett are so clear and direct that they make my clever friends in Paris sound like they're chasing rats around in a dark room. Maybe it is because they are being clever in my mother tongue, but I think it's something else. I think it's because they say what they think, even if it doesn't produce a pretty argument or a satisfying answer, because they accept that the world is a hopeless muddle. B— and the others are always getting into contortions trying to make the world coherent, but the world is not.

Except— Oh, I don't know. I want things to make more sense than they do, I suppose. Last night Mike said that the only thing that's real about us, so far as the world is concerned, is what other people think of us, and Johnny agreed. I can't get this out of my head. It sounds very apropos, and I am sure it encapsulates a sort of limited truth, but surely there are more fundamental ones to be found? I refuse to believe it is what Johnny thinks deep down – maybe he just said it last night in a rush? I must find out.

Grey makes lackluster efforts to entrance me whenever he thinks Henny is watching him. I have felt more flattered in my life.

I'm going to stretch my legs.

Sunday 2nd September

Henny Rosefield – The North Sea

They'd been fishing for several hours when Johnny emerged from his cabin. Almost immediately it started to drizzle, and then rain. Patterson and Miss Scarlett were in the cockpit. Everyone else headed for the cabin. They were motoring between trawlers, so Grey could join them. As she entered, Martha said over her shoulder, 'I'm glad you're awake, Johnny. I have a question for you.'

Mike stopped. 'Danger ahoy!' he hissed to Henny, 'I don't need another soliloquy on the meaning of life!' He went to the cockpit.

Harlequin's cabin was furnished in pale oak. A couch – padded bench may be a better description – formed a U-shape around a small table, and there were two surprisingly comfortable foldaway chairs either side of the door that led through to the sleeping quarters, galley and head. The foldaway chairs were almost invisible when closed. When they were needed they did not simply flap open, but rather emerged and protruded via a complex set of levers, and were upholstered and carved to represent the opening mouths of a pair of Chinese-dragon-like creatures.

Martha sat in one of the dragon's mouths, fixed her bright gaze on Johnny and said, 'I've been thinking. I don't believe you meant what you said last night. It must matter who you really are.'

'Who is that, though?' said Johnny. In spite of his sleep he looked tired. He was trying to sound light.

Martha said, 'You must know that, at least! Everything else might be a terrible morass, but surely you know who you are?'

'Not everyone does,' said Grey.

'How can any of us know?' said Henny. 'Johnny's right. We're all just atoms bouncing around.'

'Of course we're atoms!' Grey was angry now. 'Of course the world is a "morass". Do you think I'm a fool?' He was petulant as well as angry. 'Sometimes things don't happen for any good reason, but what good is that to anybody? The only way to make any sense of your life is to pick and choose, and when you do that, you're telling yourself the story of who you are. If you can't tell it, then you're nobody. That's what life is, it's choosing who you are, and some people never do it.' There was a moment's silence, and then Grey turned to Martha and added, 'Reality is the thing that makes you feel. A fairy tale is as true as the morass any day, remember that.' Martha stared at Grey as if she had listened to him for the first time.

Johnny seemed uncertain too. That might be important.

Harlequin's motor died. Grey stood, looking taller, and returned to deck.

Sunday 2nd September

Martha Gellhorn – The North Sea

Letter to G. Campbell Beckett, ctd.

That was interesting. One day, I suppose, I shall be less of a fool than I am now. It will be worth waiting for.

First, the fishing news: there is no news. A trawler tooted its horn half an hour ago, but some white-moustached geezer was practically next to it already and he has already hauled in a fish, which I shouldn't find funny, but the look on Grey's face!

In his dudgeon, he insisted on setting sail – or engine, or whatever you say – for the most distant herring boat we could see. Again, it was hard not to laugh at him.

Then it started raining and so we trooped inside. The cabin is rather cramped after the *Dazzle*, but everything is just so and very clever. To pass the time, I asked Johnny to explain what he had meant last night, and he started, but then Grey interrupted.

Grey said that 'of course' the world is an impossible mess. That is the point. That is why we have to make our own reality by choosing possibilities out of the muddle. Whatever we choose, *that* is the only way of making anything real for us. If we can't say clearly who we are, he said, then we are nobody.

This is a terribly egotistical point of view, and as I write it down I am realizing that the problem most of us have is that we want to create a picture where other things are just as real and important as we are, but it certainly makes a kind of sense, doesn't it? It is interesting, anyway.

Also, isn't it exactly the sort of thing a novelist might think? Maybe the fact that there is something about it that I dislike, deep down, means that I am not supposed to be a novelist!

Johnny had no reply. In fact, he seemed more discombobulated than he has at any point in our long acquaintanceship and I thought: Perhaps he is starting to realize that it is a true psychical problem for him that he cannot make any kind of sensible picture of his life? I can't either, of course, but at least I am trying.

I have just glanced at him again. He looks as if he is adrift, while Henny looks as calm as the moon. I don't know what to do.

Because, G. Campbell, what I am truly fretting about is what happened after we emerged from the cabin. While we were all scuttling about, Grey took another chance to flirt with me.

First, in tones of great portent, he said that the reason I am finding things unreal is that this expedition is like a journey into a fairyland. He said this with a straight face as if he were not repeating something I said to him yesterday. He is truly preposterous, and you can see everything he wants and is trying to do and is feeling, just as if he were a child. Thus, at present, you can see how confused and upset he is about Henny.

He kept looking at her and Johnny, and I did too. I also let him get close to me, to speak with every appearance of intimacy, and I laughed becomingly. And then the next thing he said was, 'You like Caister, but you can't have him, and then suddenly this girl comes along and she doesn't seem any different from you, no better, and there they are, and it doesn't feel right. You're talking to me because you want to make him jealous.'

Well! It is an utterly surprising thing when someone you are reading like an open book reads you like an open book. He didn't speak meanly, he was very straightforward.

Then he said, 'You're wrong about Henny. You and she are very different girls. She is an iceberg, perilous and jagged and hidden. I have always understood that about her, but Caister does not.' While I stood gaping at this lucid and revealing piece of insight, he said, 'There's no justice in nature, and no reason. There's only what you win and build and buy for yourself,' and it was hokey, but I saw for the first time what all the string of girls might see in him. He's old, but he has a tanned, fine face and sharp, clear eyes. He doesn't move like an old man.

I am not in the least falling for him, darling, but he is not a trivial human being, and it was cheap-spirited of me not to understand that. It was typical of a young person, I dare say. I must learn to understand the world if I am to describe it. I must learn generosity of soul.

'Talking won't make him jealous enough for your purposes,' he said meaningfully. I did not reply.

Now I am sat here in a tizzy. When Grey said that Henny was an iceberg, it crystallized what I have feared ever since I first saw her in London. She might not be evil, but she is set on some implacable course of her own and if Johnny is drifting towards her, then it is imperative that he see her for what she is.

He is standing alone. I am sure he doesn't want me to speak to him, but I have to. It is like a magnetic force. I can't do nothing!

Wish me luck.

Oh, what a fool I am! I came here dreaming that Johnny might change his mind, that I might be his salvation. I suppose this has been as obvious to you as it is to everybody else here. I am in a state of such mortification that it is all I can do not to heave myself upon the devouring deep.

I told Johnny what Grey said about perils and icebergs and he looked at me with – well, he was not cruel, but he was terribly stern – and he said, 'Do not interfere.'

I said that I only wanted to help, because I was worried about Henny.

He said, 'I asked you not to come. You cannot rescue me, and do not try. Do you understand? It will be enough if you can look after yourself.'

I believe I nodded to him and said, 'Very well.' If I did, it was the greatest act of bravery you ever saw. Using every scraped-together scrap of my courage, I dragged myself back to my seat.

Oh, what am I to do? I have not wholly been fibbing to you. Johnny was clear about the situation from the outset and I am sure this has cauterized the wound. When I see him and Henny, I do not feel my chest is cracking open. It is not for my sake that I am in this state, but for his. I fear that she is part of his story and I am not. I fear that the collision has already occurred somewhere deep beneath the waterline. I fear that when he says I cannot rescue him, it means he has given up hope in some way. I wish—

Well, it doesn't matter what I wish. He has told me not to interfere. He has been very patient and I must not become some pining albatross.

Maybe I should go to Grey's bed. I would not be doing it to make Johnny jealous, but simply to show him that he is free of me. I think it would be a kindness to Grey, as well. My father always said that men need women, that they suffer terribly when they cannot have one. In the past, I have used this as an excuse for giving myself to men I wanted to give myself to. But Grey *does* need a woman. He seems lost without.

Also, last night Henny told me privately that Grey was remarkable when *à deux*. Why did she say this to me? What did she mean by it, even? I've noticed that she seems well able to resist him.

I came to Scarborough by a series of odd events and I am bouncing along at a great rate of knots in this very strange place, and, of course, yes, I am soft on Johnny. I do not feel in control of my destiny is what I am fumbling to say, I am constantly a supplicant. And I always rather was that with B—, whatever games he played about following me when it was convenient to him. But with Grey, the matter would be on my terms. That would be a small thing, but I rather relish the thought of it. It would also be a symbol to myself that I have avoided being swept into a new vortex.

Writing like this, it seems I have made up my mind, or nearly. I am as cold as any fish.

It is absurd to be discussing all this as if it were some abstract algebraic problem, and you will quite probably be assuming I have lost my mind at last – or as usual – but I can only repeat that there is nothing else to think of and *Dazzle* is its own little world. If these dark woods are only a comedy, then it will be appropriate if I awake with Bottom.

Oh, at last! The rods are being collected and we are heading for home. I've learned nothing new about fishing today, so there are no notes in this letter for me to copy up. I shall throw it at a postbox this evening so that, when I start an identical letter tomorrow, marooned on this empty sea, at least I won't have the physical evidence before my eyes that I am repeating myself sentence by straining sentence. Console yourself at least with this: if I had not been scribbling away all day I should most certainly have thrown someone overboard, simply to change the scene.

Bless and keep you,

Marty

Sunday 2nd September

John Fastolf, Earl of Caister –
The North Sea / Scarborough

It is mid-morning and Johnny is desperately tired after last night's flit. He wants a spell in the cabin, but he doesn't want to show weakness.

'Why?' he thinks. 'Who to?'

He goes to his bunk.

When he wakes, certain things have settled in his mind, feel clearer.

For a start, Miss Scarlett was right last night – they should have sent someone else to the *Verloren Hoop*. The risks were part of what hooked Johnny in the first place, but he doesn't want Miss Scarlett to be killed because he has a death-wish, if that's what it is. Apart from anything else, Miss Pink's ghost would hound him through the seven hells.

The coup that he and Miss Pink are trying to pull off has cost a lot of lives. Whatever qualms he has about its morality are irrelevant by this point – he owes it to the dead to follow through to the end. The Sphinx will be destroyed and Kim Waring's secret career will be done with – that's the real prize. If Johnny can't escape himself, well, that's the deal he made.

So, clarity, he has a job to do and he cannot be distracted. Therefore he will not sleep with Henny Rosefield and he doesn't know why he even considered it. She can think whatever she wants about him. She is no immediate danger to anyone except Grey and, perhaps, herself. She cannot be his concern. He will not sleep with her.

In the cabin, while it rains, Martha will not shut up about reality. He wishes he had escaped to the cockpit with Mike.

What Grey says brings Johnny up short, just for a moment, forces him to consider. It is true that Johnny cannot tell a simple story about who he is. Is all this talk of chaos an excuse for what he has become?

No, the truth is complicated and there it is. He is not really a drug-peddler, he is not the sum of the awful things he has done.

Grey has a clear view of himself, but that doesn't make Grey 'somebody' in a world of 'nobodies'. It makes Grey a cartoon character in a cartoon landscape of his own puerile imagining.

When they emerge on deck – it's late morning now – Johnny talks timings with Miss Scarlett. From the cockpit he sees Grey resetting his rods and talking with Martha. She is trying to make Johnny jealous.

Time passes. They are off the port side of a dirty trawler called *Danielle Jordan*. Martha is writing her daily letters. Grey is staring at the sea. Henny is reading. So are Mike and Patterson. Maybe he should read too, to stop himself thinking.

Martha keeps looking at him. He can see her gathering her thoughts. She stands. There is nothing he can do to escape her.

'Please,' she says to him. 'I have something important to say.'

'Yes?'

'Be careful of Henny.' He doesn't reply. She says, 'At Send, when you and I were together – I'm not trying to ensnare you, truly I'm not – but the things you said, I've been thinking of them.'

'Don't.'

'Johnny! It seems to me that you would never have talked about smashed hearts and trusting people, and so on, if the whole business wasn't on your mind for some reason, if you didn't think you might have made a mistake.'

'Don't do this,' says Johnny. 'Do not interfere with things you do not understand.'

'But I think you might be ready to trust someone again—'

'You're wrong.'

'Please let me finish, I have to! I was talking to Zane just now, and he said that Henny is like an iceberg, all jagged beneath the surface, and I thought, "That's exactly right!" Zane crashed into her and now she is floating on to the next thing, and if you are looking for someone to trust, then she is exactly the most dangerous sort of—'

'I asked you not to come here, and you ignored me. You cannot rescue me, and I don't want you to try. The best way you can help me is by looking after yourself, do you understand?'

Martha goes crimson. She nods, she says, 'Very well', and she returns to her letter, carrying herself with some pluck. He doesn't at all dislike her, but she needed to be told. She must stay out of his way for her own protection.

Henny watched this conversation from where she has been leaning against the stern rail. Now, calmly, she crosses the deck to join him. 'Hello,' she says.

'Hello.'

Grey calls after her. She ignores him and faces the sea, self-contained.

'What are you doing?' Johnny asks. 'The way you've treated him isn't kind.'

'He doesn't need my kindness,' she says. 'He doesn't deserve it anyway. You've seen him.'

'Kindness is a good thing,' he says absurdly.

'Why did you let Martha onto your yacht? That wasn't "kind" if you're not going to do something about it.'

'I told her what the situation was and she chose to come. I didn't want to embarrass her, and I didn't want to cause a scene with Mike.'

'Pretty rackety reasons,' says Henny.

In the distance someone is onto a fish. 'It's bloody Ashton again,' shouts Mike. Colonel Ashton caught two tunny yesterday, both small. After twenty minutes Ashton loses his fish. The *Harlequin* is pleased.

Henny hasn't moved. Johnny is used to confident women, but he is not sure if Henny is that, exactly. Something indefinable about her calm and closeness makes him, for a moment, almost panic. Not visibly, of course.

He says, 'Grey and Gellhorn are adults. They're responsible for themselves. Whatever they think about us isn't our fault.'

'That isn't really true,' Henny says.

'No,' he replies. 'I suppose not. Why did you come here with him?'

'Isn't it obvious?'

There is nothing aggressive about how she says this. Johnny thinks she sounds sad. Her eyes are steady, but he imagines, just for a moment, that he caught an appeal. He repeats, 'Why him?'

'I'm pretty and I'm young, and that's all I've got. He was successful, but he's old and fading and so, just for a moment, we were balanced.'

'It's that simple?'

'Animals want to procreate with the worthiest mate. Once upon a time it was size, or speed, or who was the cleverest hunter. Well, we have pretty dresses now, as Martha said, and we've got other criteria. There's fame, and money. There's royalty—'

'Royalty's nothing.'

'That's beneath you, my lord,' says Henny. 'You were born attractive.'

'Not everyone does the same calculus.'

'There are some eternal verities. You don't know what it is like to have no options.'

Johnny is stung. He doesn't have options now, but once he did. He was blessed and he wasted his blessings. 'So,' he says eventually, 'what changed?'

'I decided that I could do better.'

'Indeed?' he says. 'I hope you don't mean me.'

'No, not for more than a night. If you're out of Martha's reach, then you're a long way out of mine. After all,' she gazes at him levelly, 'Martha's the thing I'm pretending to be.'

Is she offering herself for a night? Johnny can't tell. He says, 'A number of girls have played the game by saying they weren't interested in me.'

'I can imagine. I can also imagine that, as a result, you sometimes see it when it isn't there.'

'Perhaps,' he nods. He told himself earlier that he didn't have time to help this girl, but out here on the fishing grounds he has nothing but time. And so he says, 'You have more options than you think. You don't have to humiliate Grey. It's unnecessary.'

'You don't know the whole story of me and Grey.'

'What is the whole story?' She doesn't reply. 'What if you're wrong about being able to do better?' he goes on. 'What if you get stuck in England alone? You're taking a risk.'

'Do I seem like a risk-taker to you?'

She does and she does not. She's calm and sardonic, but she's in a place only a risk-taker would be. She seems to know what she wants, but Johnny would bet his boats that she has no idea how she got here. He recognises this combination of traits, obviously. Or maybe he is projecting them.

Long ago there was another calm, sardonic-seeming girl, and Johnny persuaded himself that what she truly wanted was him. It's a false parallel – Henny is not Caro. More particularly, Zane Grey is not Kim Waring.

'I don't know if you're risk-taker or not,' he says at long last. 'Sometimes one ends up taking risks because one thinks one has no choice, not because one is a risk-taker.'

'Is it always bad to take a risk?'

'No,' says Johnny. 'No. Risk-takers are important to the breed, I dare say. Presumably we need them, if we are to progress.'

'Interesting,' Henny says. 'So I might be carrying a useful sort of inheritance? If I have children, they might find El Dorado or make a new kind of bomb?'

'Yes,' says Johnny. 'If they survive long enough.'

'I'll just leave them on a hillside. A puny little risk-taker would be a terrible burden to society.'

He laughs. Genuinely, he laughs. He asks, 'So, in your world of few options, what will you do next?'

'I don't know,' she says. 'Maybe I'll find someone at your party on Wednesday evening.'

The party! The judders in sympathy with Johnny's gut. Henny must not try anything on Wednesday evening. It could ruin his plans and it would not be safe for her. Not that it is his job to keep Henny safe, of course.

He kicks himself for having started to relax. He thinks furiously. Here is this girl who is pretending to have no options. But she is pretty and bright, and she seems sensible. The only explanations are either that she is an extremely clever adventuress or that she has been so badly damaged that she can only imagine a very limited range of futures. Either way, she is prepared to take serious risks, and this might jeopardise who knows how many months of careful planning. He was right yesterday. He will have to sleep with her.

He hopes she is an adventuress. If so, he will occupy her hopes for two days and keep her from causing trouble, and then she will go on her way. If she is damaged, then he might break her. Martha understands nothing. He is the iceberg.

And there is another thing. However he dresses it up, he has wanted the girl since he saw her in London.

Johnny only sleeps with people he wants, except *in extremis*. The fact that there is sometimes another, more practical reason is by the by. If he only has practical reasons, then he can almost always find another solution to the problem. It's not exactly chivalry, but then an earl is an older, cruder thing than a knight. Blood of the Saxons, et cetera. There were a lot of risk-taking Fastolfs.

Is that true? His father is not a risk-taker. And one risk-taker could have lost the whole fortune. Or maybe there were risk-takers, but they got lucky, like Grandfather with his mine. After all, there haven't been that many earls. Any coin can come up heads ten times, but there's always a tail in the end.

The risk-taker faced the enemy and brought home the food. He was honoured and he had children. If his wife were honest.

'You don't know me,' she says.

'I'd like to,' he says.

The day passes on leaden feet. Martha maintains good form despite her obvious hurt. It's her fault for coming, but she wishes he hadn't had to to be so callous. She has style.

As they speed back to Scarborough, Johnny reclarifies the upcoming schedule with Miss Scarlett, and she tells him that Miss Pink has just radioed to confirm that his various guests will arrive in time for Wednesday's dinner. Hopefully, they will prove enough of a distraction for Kim and Caro. While he drives the others to Robin Hood's Bay to meet the Captain, Patterson and Miss Scarlett will make some deliveries.

By dinner time Johnny and Henny have caught and held each other's eyes several more times, and everything feels as if it is running along a predetermined track. Conversation is stilted, partly because Martha and Grey are watching powerless from their parallel rail. Mike, Miss Pink and Miss Scarlett are at the other end of the table, feigning disinterest.

Miss Scarlett and Miss Pink hate what Johnny is doing. Be that as it may.

After dinner, in the saloon, he and Henny sip their whiskies with equal impatience. It would have been impolite simply to duck out of company. Everyone knows what is going to happen, though, and the atmosphere is fragile.

Mike says, almost certainly apropos of nothing, 'Why the stickleback?'

Johnny looks at the brave little fish, lost in a sea of wall. Underneath it is a label: *Stickleback (Gasterosteus aculeatus), 3 oz, Caister New Ponds, 1916.*

'It's just a joke,' Johnny says. 'Don't you think it's funny?'

'I do,' says Henny.

'It's eerie,' says Mike.

'Yes,' says Martha. 'It's eerie. It's a sort of observer. If it were some huge trophy, then you would be showing off, but that's not what you're doing. The joke says something about you, doesn't it?'

'Not really,' says Johnny.

'I understand it,' says Grey, moving to Martha's side. 'You're saying that this little fish has as great a soul as any marlin. It's us who want big fish, but every fish is equally a fish.'

Martha says, 'Yes, we are all just fish!'

'Yes, Miss Gellhorn,' Grey says. 'That's what he's saying, and it's a lie. The stickleback thinks he is as important as the marlin, but the marlin is greater. Only small men think everyone is equal. You don't think it, sir, not in your heart.'

'Maybe—' Martha says, and halts. She nearly stops herself there, but in a rush she adds, 'Maybe he's saying that every fish can be hooked, just like every ship can be sunk by an iceberg!' She flushes.

Johnny finishes his whisky. Henny does too. They say goodnight and leave without pretence.

In his cabin, her body fits itself bonelessly into his. She is skilful. There is no reason for him to be surprised by this, simply because Caro was not.

She insists on his wearing a prophylactic. He always does this anyway, but he always waits to see which girls insist. It is a useful way to judge character.

Johnny's judgement is clouded by this girl, and any ball he drops this week could turn out to be a grenade. He needs to find a way through to her, past the defences. 'What do you make of this?' he asks.

'Of what we've just done?'

'Yes.'

'Morally?'

'No,' he says. 'Not qualitatively, either, if you don't mind.'

'What then? In my capacity as an anthropological observer?'

'Is that what you are?'

'Have I revealed myself?'

'I don't know,' says Johnny. 'Have you?'

'No,' she says. 'It was just a joke.' The phrase rings a bell. 'As for the physical act,' Henny carries on quickly, 'we're human beings. We need to do it, I suppose.'

'As a species or as individuals?'

'Is there a difference? If the species needs the act, then we must be bred to need it too. That's all it is, in the end.'

Johnny does not believe that Henny is being glib. He thinks she has considered this matter with a clear and clinical mind and she is presenting her conclusion. She is not an anthropologist, but the joke was not entirely random. 'Am I an experiment?' he asks.

'No. Please don't—'

'Why don't you want to talk about yourself?'

'Why don't you?' she replies. 'Please, this isn't going anywhere. I'm not secretly a duchess or a millionaire. I'm not dreaming of a future with you. What is between us is just the act, so let's talk about that. What do you think of it?'

She speaks very calmly. Behind the front, Johnny sees an emptiness. He feels she is ready to open up if he can just keep her talking. And so he replies. 'We didn't evolve to wear clothes,' he says. 'We didn't evolve to fly in aeroplanes or play the piano. Maybe this – the thing we do together when we're naked and alone – is a precious moment of nature in an unnatural world. What do you think of that?'

'I think that it is exactly what Zane says about hunting,' she says. 'And it's what Martha says about dressing up. Maybe it's something we always tell ourselves about the things we like. Eating. Dancing. Laughing. I don't know.'

'Nobody knows,' says Johnny. 'But what do you think?'

'I think that every time I have made a confident assertion about sexual matters, I have later found out that it was based on my ignorance and been mortified.'

'We've all found that,' says Johnny.

'All right,' she says. 'All right.' She sits up, purses her lips and folds her hands primly. 'I believe that the ecstasy of congress is *sui generis*. I assumed, before I met Grey if I may be frank, that it was merely immensely satisfying, an expression of triumph and unity of purpose, a fulfilment of bestial self.'

'And now?'

'I know better.'

'Better or more?'

She does not dignify this with a response. But she drops her shoulders and the tight voice. 'It's odd, though – it seems odd to me, as a scientist of no training – the animal urge for satisfaction was enough to convince me that I understood the whole business. And for men the satisfaction and ecstasy are the same thing. But for women the ecstasy is this separate matter, which seems to serve no purpose.'

'A gift from God?' asks Johnny.

'Do you believe in God?'

'No.' What Henny said about ecstasy is interesting. It is something he'd never considered before and that doesn't happen to him very often. Also, and this is what he had hoped for, the girl is revealing herself.

'Have you ever believed in God?' she asks.

'I don't know,' he says. 'My parents don't, so I never really got the chance.'

'Did you think about it in the war? Or do people never ask about the war? I don't know the protocol about that.'

'No, people don't ask,' he says. 'But that's fine. We all thought about God in the trenches.'

'So?'

'We make gods because we need them. We haven't all got time to invent our own moral systems. We need some organising principle to take up the slack, to save us from having to work everything out for ourselves. I rather like our God, for what it's worth, because I rather like us.'

'Even after the war? And all the other wars?'

'We have mostly made him better over time. I think that's what I approve of. We've done some beastly things, but we're trying to be better. Some of us are, anyway. I wish I were more— I would be a better person if I followed a few more Christian precepts, and I'm glad some people do.' Johnny really does believe this, he realises, just as he also realises he has a funny way of showing it. He wanted her to speak, but he has ended up speaking. 'What about you?' he asks.

'Much the same,' says Henny. She is still sitting up. He is lying next to her on his back, with his head resting on his hands, looking at the ceiling. 'Is this what you're always like?' she asks. 'You play the playboy, but you really want to philosophise?'

'Yes,' he laughs. 'That's it, exactly.'

Johnny feels decidedly odd. It's not just that he likes this girl, it's— He likes this girl! He's not in love with her, he's not insensate with passion, but he definitely likes her and wants her to like him. What has he become that it has taken him till this point to consider this possibility, let alone accept that it might be true? Furthermore, what does it mean?

Henny says, quietly, 'You didn't like what Martha said about the fish.'

'The stickleback?' he says. 'What's that got to do with the price of eggs?'

'I don't know. But I'd guess that everything they said made you a bit uncomfortable, because jokes *are* revealing. Like my regrettable joke about anthropology. We make them too quickly and like them too much to be careful.'

'So?' he says. 'What does my stickleback say?'

'For a start,' she says, 'it's a very public sort of joke. It feels like a revelation you have to make in code, something terribly important and personal that you're hiding up there in plain sight.'

'My goodness,' he says. He can't really tell her to stop.

'You probably *are* saying that hunting for big fish is rather arbitrary and all fish are their own little heroes. You probably *are* aware that there is something human in the way we look at bigger fish and value them more, and that this is an impulse worth querying. I wonder if there isn't some part of you that self-identifies as a big fish that others want as a trophy, but would like to be a small fish.'

'Or that I think I truly am a small fish and yet other people still want me as a trophy, all of which makes me particularly aware of the arbitrary nature of trophies.'

'You don't think you are a small fish. But I could imagine you telling yourself that was part of the reason.'

'These,' he says, 'are not particularly glorious motivations for my joke.'

'Jokes are often inglorious. But how about this: you are aware of the arbitrary nature of trophies, given the similar nature of souls – you fought in the war alongside every size of fish – and you want to honour the fish who are not sufficiently honoured. Is that better?'

'Yes,' he says. 'I prefer that. What do you think is true?'

'I don't think any of them are true, precisely. I think you made a joke because it's funny – which it is – and that it came from somewhere in your subconscious.'

'So, one of these explanations is true, but you can't know which without further analysis?'

'Perhaps,' she replies after a moment. 'Or all of them are a bit true. All told, I would guess that your motives were not self-aggrandising or self-pitying.'

'Thank you.'

'The most revealing thing is what you think about the trophy at any given point. And you would have to trust someone very deeply to tell them that.'

'I honestly don't know what I think,' he lies. 'The simplest is that it is a joke about the arbitrary nature of trophies that I find funny because I am a trophy. In fact,' he lies again, 'I'm sure that's what it is.'

Another thing he suddenly thinks: the stickleback is unchangeable. It is a fixed moment from a time before he became whatever he is now. He's never considered it like that. Miss Pink would say that he should let Henny think the usual things about him. It would be for the best – or, at least, it would be for the simplest – but he likes her.

He kisses her again, and again it is unusually good. Afterwards she lies with her cheek on his chest. Her ear is cold, oddly. 'How did you get like this?' she asks. Then, almost immediately, she adds, 'No, sorry, I didn't mean it. Forget what I said.'

Johnny knows from experience that intimacy is seductive. Women have told him some extremely personal things in bed. They have had no one else to talk to, and in this most private of moments they have equated 'private' with 'confidential'. Johnny has kept their secrets, unless they were secrets he was actively soliciting.

When she talked about the stickleback it was clear that Henny understands him better than anyone since Caro, but, unlike Caro, Henny sees him generously. Maybe Caro was generous in the beginning. It was so long ago.

He wants to tell Henny his story, or some of it at least. Enough for her to understand why— Enough for her to understand some things.

Was Martha right? Is he just looking for someone to trust? Or does he simply want to take a risk?

What would the risk be, anyway? If he cannot trust Henny, what will he lose? And if he can, maybe she is a lifeboat and not an iceberg. Talking to her, he feels something. It is worth at least reaching out a hand, and once he has shown that he trusts her, then she will be able to trust him. That's what he wants. He wants her to reveal herself to him so that he can help her. Maybe, if things go as Johnny hopes they might, they will be able to help each other afterwards.

'I'm going to tell you something I've not told anyone for—'

'Stop,' says Henny.

'I trust you,' he says. 'I want you to trust me.'

'I haven't asked for your confidence,' she says.

Johnny barely registers what she says. He does not say it exactly like this, but this is the story he tells.

When I met Caroline, I was green and fashionably liberal for my class and sex, and I was rich as all get-out, and blessed. I suppose these things remain true, except for the greenness.

Caro set her cap at me. It was during the war, of course, and we all had rather exciting times during the war; one did when one thought things might all be over the next minute. She was cynical about the war in a way I adored. I can't think why now. I certainly did not like her cynical friends. Perhaps it was that Caroline was cynical, but she took it seriously. Her friends did not. They just treated it as a joke, a joke on other people. Whatever else, Caro is not silly.

After the war, I pursued her as she had pursued me, but by then she had fallen for Kim Waring, and there is the comedy in a nutshell. Her friends despised me for having fought. I knew the whole show had been a set of appalling blunders, a catastrophe planned by fools and knaves – much more the former than the latter, on our side at least – but I knew my duty. I was a Caister. If one side was in the right, it was ours. If.

Caro has written, very often, that I was broken by the war. There were times when I believed her. The trenches were awful enough that you came out of them rather doubtful of yourself.

She has also written that we were betrothed in secret in 1915, but then we chose not to marry because we wanted to flout convention. This is not true. When, much later, I told people it wasn't true, she wrote in the newspapers that I had trespassed on her privacy with my comments and that it had all been perfectly well understood at the time. It had not been. Caro refused my hand many times.

She wrote that she eventually succumbed to my need for respectability. This also was not true. I said I would live with her on any wretched terms, and she said that it must be marriage. Of course, this was after Kim had married Mary Gandamack, for money of course. Caro had no money. She realised that marrying me and carrying on with Kim would be as happy as any other beastly option.

Eventually, many years later, I wriggled loose. Ever since then I have believed that there can only be one great love for every person. It is not because only one creature in the whole world is worthy of one's love – the mathematics don't stack up – but rather that one only has one heart. I smashed mine when I was too young to understand what I was doing. If that's the only sadness of my life, then it's hardly a spot of dust in the cosmic scheme.

And anyway, Johnny concludes, taking his own breath away, even if the pure thing only happens once, one can perhaps eventually recover and love someone in a different way.

'So,' he says. 'Now it's your turn.'

'No,' she says.

'How can I trust you if you don't?'

'What do I care whether you trust me?'

Johnny is shocked by this, actually shocked. He feels like he has been slapped in the face. His first ridiculous reaction: is there any way the Sphinx could have placed Henny with Grey?

No. When Henny met Grey, no one could have realised they would end up in Scarborough. It is conceivable that someone could have got to her since then, but he dismisses the thought. The truth, Johnny knows full well, is that he has suffered a blow to his *amour propre*.

Well, that's fine. His *amour propre* is nothing. He says, 'You don't have to tell me, but you should tell someone you do trust. You should tell them in case what you're doing is ridiculous and wrong. It's always worth checking.'

Her ear is still cool on his chest. She says, very quietly, 'Do you know what *you* want?'

Again, he thinks she sounds sad. He says, 'Be careful, Henny. It's very easy to withdraw from the world. And if you do that, then . . .' He isn't sure how to say it.

'Yes?' she asks.

'Martha thinks you're like an iceberg.'

'I'm not!'

'I know,' he says. Henny's response was instant. He wants to find out what has happened to this girl and rescue her. He's not in danger from her. In fact, more likely the opposite is true. If he can help her, then – in a furtive, private place – he will know that his older, better self has not been entirely lost.

Can he be redeemed by such an act? By saving one person? No. All acts have consequences. The war had consequences. Caro had consequences. Miss Pink had consequences. Caro lied to the world about what hollowed Johnny out, but that doesn't mean he isn't hollow. The dark star he followed has come to define him. The occasional good deeds are all so much sentimentality.

But a sentimental act can turn out well. If he were to keep Henny from being preyed on by Kim Waring, from becoming Kiki Preston, then her life will be better, and that isn't nothing. And Johnny would be doing it for simple liking of her, as any normal, honourable man might do. Also, possibly, he could keep her from damaging a lot of other people.

If Johnny weren't doing the things he does, then his place would be taken by someone else, and that other person would almost certainly be a nastier cup of tea than him and Miss Pink. As he follows through with this thought, his mind frames Henny replying: *Pretty rackety reasons.*

He says, 'Listen carefully. I'm fine, and I don't need anyone's pity, but my life would be very different, I think it would have been better, if when I was your age I had fixed my path by a more sensible star.' She will think he means Caro, but the advice is sound anyway. 'If you go down the wrong path – if you go too far down it – then you can't go back.'

'Well,' she says. 'I don't know whether to vault into a new circle of reality or read a book of fairy tales or buy a telescope and pick stars.'

'You forgot the iceberg.'

'No, I didn't.'

The way she says it makes Johnny want to hold her. He is certain that she is starting to listen.

Also, he realises, he must be more careful of metaphors. If he thinks of Henny as a 'ball who might be a grenade', or as an 'iceberg', or even as a 'lifeboat', then he's already looking at her in a particular way. He wants to see the whole of her.

'I'm sorry,' he says. 'It's become quite the linguistic tangle, but please do believe me. The thing about fixing your path by the wrong star is that at some point, in the end, you're going to be asked to follow through, all the way, even if it destroys you. Think about what you're doing now, while you still can.'

'If I still can.'

'You still can.'

'Who else have *you* favoured with all this?' she says. 'It doesn't sound like you're discussing Caroline. What is your dark star?'

'It's just Caro.'

'Hm,' she says. 'Just in case it isn't, you should perhaps talk it through with someone, in case you're being ridiculous and wrong.'

She's right. It's a simple thing, but it's absolutely right. He is mesmerised by her. There have been some splendid girls, but he has never thought one could help him before this evening.

What if his heart isn't smashed? He's grown comfortable with the idea over the years. It explains so many of the widely spoken love clichés. But what if he is wrong? What if the heart really does mend, as per certain other, less convincing, more fly-by-night clichés? What if he has retarded his own healing by clinging to a delusion? What if his precious theory has been a decade-long self-indulgence and excuse for behaving as he has behaved. If he's been wrong, he'll *feel* like a ninny, but it's much worse than a ninny that he's been, a far, far less happy creature.

And that's the bottom of it. He is what he is and he can't ever tell her. All he can say is, 'Trust me. I will try to keep you safe.'

Henny doesn't react.

Even this tiny resistance sends the blood urgently to Johnny's chest, constricting him. He needs her to respond. He says, 'I talked to you. I never talk to anyone.'

She says, 'You didn't tell me everything, did you?'

He says, 'If you talk to me, I will talk to you.'

She says, 'I'll think about it.' Shortly afterwards she returns to her cabin. Johnny is certain that he's almost through the shell.

He should be facing the worst of his demons and yet he feels, unaccountably, relaxed. He thinks about that fact for a long time, and he sleeps well.

Monday 3rd September

Martha Gellhorn – The North Sea

Monday 3rd September 1934
Harlequin
Somewhere off Scarborough

G. Campbell, Behold Me –

– for I am the Great White Huntress!

It is nine-thirty in the morning and a tunny that I heaved from the depths with my own poor bleeding hands is trussed up on the deck of the *Harlequin*!

It is the handsomest thing you ever saw outside a mirror and I keep going to peer at it. It is not a giant – Grey sniffed '400 lbs or so' in such a manner that a less-sanguine angler than I might have de-boated him for it – but it is a noticeable trifle larger than the one that Henny caught, and which is sitting plumply next to it.

Yesterday, Grey's disdain would have been merely rude. Given that I spent last night in his bed, it was astonishing. I find myself more amused than distressed by it, which is instructive.

It was a remarkable experience, in a purely physical sense. My back and shoulders are burning with a virtuous, deep glow and I was— Ow! Gosh, that was—

A brief delay – not that brief actually, two hours – to deal with violent cramps in my hand and wrist.

Harlequin has returned to its traditional inactivity, but everything is different after last night, and after these fish.

Last night— No. The fish first.

On Mike's suggestion and over Grey's violent objections, Johnny let Henny and me take the rods until the Captain arrived. He said it would show us how the anticipation is different when any fish caught will be your fish.

It was extremely cold, and I was wrapped in the usual seventy layers. Before we were strapped into our seats, I had to take off a large proportion of these, which I was informed would grow unbearably hot if I had to fight a tunny. I almost gave up right then, and only the sight of Henny disrobing as gleefully for Johnny as I dare say she did last night – yes, you read that correctly, it's all happened for good or ill – steeled me to the numbing dawn. Then we took our seats and buckled in.

Grey sulked that we were wasting our time – if ever a sea was devoid of fish, then it was this sea at this moment. I was inclined to agree. We cast our mackerel upon the arid waters and instantly, like a species of miracle, two tunny grabbed our hooks simultaneously. In direct contravention of Grey's barked commands and traditional good practice, we both played the darlings and we both brought them to the boat. The physical effort, dearie, is like nothing I have experienced in my life.

After yesterday's massive missive – assuming the letters are not arriving in one large and asynchronous heap – you are presumably not reading this and will never in your life read another word that I write. Well, I don't write for you, I write for me, so there! I wish I could remember what I said, though.

Did I say anything clever about tunny being a metaphor, like Moby-Dick? I know I thought something along those lines, but perhaps I didn't scribble it down. This fishing for giants must be a symbol for something, but I can't work out precisely what it is, and I feel this even more strongly today, because Henny and I both caught tunny after spending our nights with the quarry we had hooked over dinner. Maybe the important thing is what they symbolize for me? I dare write that is what Grey would think.

I hardly know what to write about last night, except that if this is a fairy tale, I fear it may be the German variety, where it is doubtful that things will turn out well in the end. We sat to dine at the usual early hour. Henny continued her pursuit of Johnny. He was not unwilling. He was pursuing her, in fact. Honesty, Marty, honesty. Something about him seemed different, more engaged somehow, and he seems even further that way today. They are not behaving like newly-weds or anything – my God, far from it – but he looks at her in a fashion that I am not sure he can control, and which indicates he is not the icy creature Caro described.

Henny, if I watch her with a jealous eye, seems serene, awful and untouched. But perhaps I should be more generous – it is hardly her fault that Johnny wants her. She asked me earlier about Grey in a perfectly human fashion and I remembered that this whole business must be even stranger to her than it is to me. I still believe there is something perilous about her imperturbability, and I am nervous of the harm she might do Johnny if he trusts her, but he has been amply clear that he does not wish for my advice or interference. He made his choice and I made mine.

Which brings me to Grey! It was important that I did something active and I was intrigued by what Henny said about him, and by what Grey had said himself. Why should I not find out what he meant about innocent adventure? Maybe it is my curse that I do not take the carnal act seriously, that I will do it out of mere curiosity.

It was a supremely surprising experience! I do not particularly enjoy looking like a fool, and you have heard all my previous aver-rations with respect to the body, and my attempts to come to some kind of understanding of it, to find a rule I can finally follow and never have to reconsider. I don't want to address the matter ever again, but I must. I will be honest in this life if it is the only thing I am, and Zane Grey has opened my eyes *again*, and I cannot yet tell whether I am happy about it. I decided, after Johnny, that my physical responses must be related to a mental connection, that being with him reminded me of the earliest times with B—, before we— Well, before that matter became such a tortured and long-winded decline.

Grey did not do anything that— You shall have to use your imagination, darling, and it will do you no good unless you are a very lucky man. Simply it was— I cannot say any more about it. I do not think it is describable. He didn't do anything particularly shocking, but he somehow was able to— Now I'm trying to describe it. I can't. Describing it would cheapen it, make it absurd, reduce it to a matter that one could relate to one's previous experience, and it did not relate to my previous experience.

I have no mental connection with Grey and yet the physical pull I felt thirty seconds ago on seeing him looking at me was extreme. Again you are thinking – I hear your voice in my ears as I write, very much as if I were losing my mind – that I should not be trying to create a life philosophy on a boat when my very bones are tired and I spent last night in bewildered ecstasy.

To which all I can respond is: it's easy for you to say! What else am I supposed to think about?

I do not want to be a slave to my body. The first time was in the early days with B—, and look what happened there. And B— was infinitely more suitable than Grey.

But I am not afraid of being enslaved by Grey. In fact, perhaps, that may be the lesson of him. Last night established that the body and the mind are different matters entirely. The danger is perhaps when you start to confuse the two. That is what happened with B—.

I have, under normal circumstances, a modicum of good sense. If that disappears in the face of bodily urges, then it is imperative to quieten my body, to master it. That will stop me dragging myself around after the unattainable and crippled B—s and Johnnys of this world, and keep me away from the ludicrous Greys. I want to be my own master, G. Campbell. That is what it is, in the end.

We are chugging home. Another day of angry fishlessness for Grey and the Captain. We're heading into Scarborough to weigh my tuna and Henny's, and then we're off for a costumed dinner on board Joe Carstairs's *Berania*. We are to dress as cowboys and Indians, in Grey's honor, but Grey is in a fit of the grumps and has announced that he will not attend. For a tiny moment I thought to stay with him.

But only a tiny moment. He must remain a salutary lesson and nothing more.

Mike is in particularly fine form about the evening. He has already begun rehearsing a speech about woman-love amongst a tribe of Amazons he met while exploring the Amazon. Miss Scarlett lapped this up delightedly and added salacious details about how one might enforce procreation on unwilling males, which I have no doubt that Mike will incorporate later on. He will either be treated as a pet or thrown into the cold and greasy harbor. Each of these would be delightful.

No doubt, tomorrow, I shall have changed my mind about every subject imaginable, and so into the letter box this shall go as a record of my evolution.

Toodle-pip,

Marty

Monday 3rd September

Henny Rosefield – The North Sea

Henny greeted Johnny as if nothing had happened last night. He replied in kind. She asked if he had slept well. He said he had. They were both twinkling.

They ate breakfast. She thanked Patterson when he put her plate in front of her. She had never spoken to a Negro before this week.

Afterwards, Miss Scarlett handed out coffee. Henny took hers and went to the rail to stand with Johnny, the same piece of rail as yesterday afternoon. She felt with her thumb for the screw-head that it had rested on then.

She had something to say, but she was worried it would not be effective if she seemed eager. Her mother would say: if he thinks you're pursuing him, he'll run away. Her mother would say: toy with him, keep him in a state of uncertainty. Henny had resented these lessons, but they had proven successful time and again since the asylum.

She said, 'I've been thinking about your "dark star".'

'Don't ask about it,' he said. 'Please.'

'What have you done, Johnny?' For a fragment he looked nervous, or suspicious, or maybe angry, and then it was as if nothing had been said. She had discomfited him. She said, 'I didn't mean anything, I'm sorry. I'm in an odd mood.'

She could not think how to proceed and their silence grew awkward. Johnny went to the cockpit. Henny considered briefly and then crossed the deck. Martha braced visibly at her approach. Henny said, 'May I sit with you?'

Martha said, 'Yes.'

'This boat is a very peculiar place.'

'Yes,' Martha agreed.

Henny rolled her eyes towards Grey. Martha had no one else to talk to about last night and she would surely want to.

Martha shook her head in disbelief and whispered, 'Golly!'

Henny nodded.

Martha said, 'I don't know what to think about it.'

Henny said she didn't, either.

Martha was still not at ease, but she was a young person and open-hearted. It would be much better to have her as an ally, if possible. Henny was a young person too, of course.

When they reached the trawlers, Mike suggested that Henny and Martha take the fishing chairs.

For the forty minutes it took Henny to land her tuna, she obeyed orders quickly and directly. At first they came predominantly from Grey, but once it became clear that she and Martha were both going to fight their fish, over his clear instructions that 'Martha should – no, Henny should – no, wait, Martha should unhook', he went sulking into the cabin.

When the tuna were lashed inside the starboard rail, Grey emerged and strapped himself into the seat. Henny went to the cabin and lay down. She intended only to think, but slept for two hours.

When she woke, her mind felt clear enough to proceed. She emerged into the sun. She waited until Johnny was alone, and then she said, 'I am not playing a game. I'm sorry if I seem— It's just . . .'

'Yes?' he said.

She gathered herself, aware that she must look as if she were gathering herself. She told Johnny that she had originally come to England as part of a plan concerning Grey, which she didn't want to discuss in detail because it was ill-conceived from the outset. She said that she had lost faith in the plan, but she had nothing else to cling on to and so she had been following through with it until she arrived on the *Dazzle*, as far as she could. She understood how, under the circumstances, she must look like a vamp, but she wasn't following a dark star. She wasn't really following any star at all. And now she was going to change. She was going to be sensible. She didn't expect anything from Johnny, she wasn't a fool, but she was grateful that he had taken her seriously. She might have seemed defensive last night, but that was because she was trying to protect herself. Now – and she should surely have done this before – she was going to remodel her life on rational lines. She said that yes, there had been a great mess of metaphors thrown about, but the one she kept returning to was Gellhorn's Fairyland. She was treating these few days as a tramp through a mysterious wood, learning lessons that would help her understand herself. Nothing was promised, nothing expected. Everything was experience, and all would be well. She would emerge from the wood remade and renewed.

Henny spoke in a matter-of-fact fashion. She hoped this would be the most convincing way to make Johnny believe that she was teetering on her life's axis, that whatever tiny push he gave would have an effect. She was pretending that she wanted to absolve him of responsibility.

Johnny didn't say anything and his face was unreadable. It was the face of a man with his own concerns. As her mother said, the problem with speaking to anyone else is that they are so busy following their own story that it is very hard to get them to follow yours, even for a moment. Henny's mother was a hateful woman.

'Isn't this what you wanted?' she asked. 'For me to reconsider my path?'

'Yes. If you mean it.'

'I don't know how I'm supposed to prove it.'

'It's difficult, yes,' he said.

Hours later Henny was sitting near the two tunny when Patterson brought her a cup of tea. When she first arrived she had expected him to have a terribly deep voice, but it was normally pitched. He was tall and strongly built. His hair was cut tight to his head, and there were two short, straight scars on his right cheek. He had an accent she didn't recognise. She asked where he was from.

'Cape Town, Miss Rosefield. In South Africa.'

'Oh. Does that make you— I'm sorry. I've never talked to a Negro before this week. I'm afraid I've been rude somehow.'

'I am used to it,' said Patterson.

'You mean I *have* been rude.'

'I am a servant, and a black man. Some people see one, some people see the other. Most people see a combination.'

'No one reacts naturally to you?'

'What is natural, Miss Rosefield? Is natural how they are with Lord Caister? Or a pretty young woman?'

'Is it annoying?' she asked.

'Yes.'

All afternoon she kept catching Johnny's eyes on her. He said nothing to her until they were approaching Scarborough. Then he said, 'If you are what you say you are, I like you very much. If you're hunting for a star, please be careful tonight. Joe Carstairs's boat will glitter with starlike objects, but they will all be dark, including me. If you promise to be sensible, to reject the more lurid offers that will most certainly be made to you, then I will protect you.'

'What offers?'

'You're a bright girl, you'll know who's offering trouble. Stay out of it is all I am asking. Will you?'

'Yes.'

'Good. But remember, it is just for three days. Let's get safely out of the wood, and then we will see where we are. I hope I will be there, but in all probability I will not. If I am not, most important this: do not undervalue yourself. You'll look back in ten years and you won't be able to imagine the possibilities that lay before you. And don't listen to the advice of old cynics like me, except when we're right, which I am now.'

He ended his speech as the *Harlequin* drew gently to the jetty, and he leapt across to dry land.

Monday 3rd September

Mike Mitchell-Hedges – The North Sea

Sept. 3 Scarbie

Dear Jane,

Unless things have gone arse-over-knickers, you're still sweating your way north 'neath purple tropic skies. I'm a damned bad correspondent, but it's either this or slogging through more of *Anthony* bloody *Adverse* (that had better pay off or I'll find Hervey Allen and castrate the bastard). I shouldn't be complaining, though. Things have gone better than I could have expected – if I catch the big one, then they'll be perfect. Here's the dish:

1. Johnny Caister played ball magnificently on our arrival. He saw clean through me or I don't know a sharp pair of eyes, but he said straight away that since he'd built the *Harlequin* on Grey's pattern, it was an honour to have the master join him for her maiden voyage. He sounded so pleased that I almost wish I'd sent him that telegram for real!

2. The *Dazzle* is everything you've heard and twice that, without a vulgar note. You could entertain the King quite happily so long as you hid the skipper and her ravishing first officer, who share a cabin. It doesn't seem so peculiar when you're here.

3. The *Harlequin* is just as swank – two fishing chairs, two small cabins and a little saloon, huge twin engines, space for seven of us to rattle around decently. I'm on board her now. Sunny, good coffee, scribble-scribble while Grey clutches his rod like some hybrid of Job and the Ancient Mariner.

4. On board the *Dazzle*: Caister and crew, including nigger batman. The crew is a dangerous-looking collection. There's a

hulking chap called Saul who moves like a leopard, and a whippety sort of engineer called Andy who showed me suspiciously round the gleaming innards as if I were going to steal a propeller. There's also a very tidy piece called Audrey, who might be French, but I'm not sure. Whatever she is, she has no time for me. I wouldn't cross any of them. Apart from Andy, they all seem to join in with everything from cooking to laundry. It's an odd system, but it runs bloody well.

Then there's Grey and his girl, yours truly and a girl called Martha Gellhorn, who is my 'secretary'. She's a lanky American journalist without an ounce of humbug in her – very much the opposite, in fact. She wants to know 'the real truth' about everything, which makes her sound annoying, which she mostly isn't. I nearly queered my pitch bringing her along, which I only did because she's enraptured by Caister, and Caister wanted to avoid her. Where the perverse imp comes from I'll never understand. I was oiled, I suppose. She's turned out not to be an idiot, thank God. Good family, well connected, behaves very well. She's not caused Caister any trouble, or me. I'd tumble her if she wanted, but I don't think she does. It's been a quiet week. Wish you were here.

5. Scarborough: a pretty sort of place in a bleak way and obviously doesn't know what to do with the sudden influx of dandies and pot-hunters.

6. The Contest: M-Henry won't set foot in Scarborough – another bloody feud, the man has a talent for them – and operates out of Whitby. Grey refuses to enter enemy territory and so we've picked a rotten old hotel bar in Robin Hood's Bay as our base of ops. They must fish at least six hours per day and may fish any hours they choose after that, but must remain in sight of each other for catches to count. Every day at 5 p.m., unless attached to a fish or delayed by same, they are to meet at the neutral bar and reveal the weight of their catches. The contest to proceed for six days, this being the limit of Caister's availability.

7. The Fishing: this is Day 3, and they've caught nothing. Boats on all sides, gleefully aware of the contest, are hauling in tunny as

if they were going out of fashion, which they are palpably not. Particularly funny today because Caister let the girls take the rods before M-Henry arrived and they immediately bagged a brace of respectables.

8. Grey's girl: I said she was a rum one and I say it again, in spades, redoubled. Could still be that she's trying to learn The Way of the Humbug, could be a much odder fish. I wouldn't cross her and I wouldn't let her into my bed. After the first night on board, it was clear that she wasn't tumbling Grey, either. Damned interesting, I thought to myself. She's after nobler prey, as suspected in New York, and she's caught it! Wouldn't have believed it if I hadn't seen it, but she's played a deadly effective hand and the great Lothario is as fitful as a spring lamb around her. Last night he squired her from the cocktail lounge, leaving Grey and Gellhorn on the sofa sucking peppercorns. And then, damn me if Grey and Gellhorn didn't go off together as well!

9. Johnny Caister himself: very interesting cove. By no means the effete dilettante. Another one who's not a humbug, but again not sure what else to call him. When he lied about the telegram, if I hadn't known for a fact that the correspondence was a sham, I'd have sworn the man was straight. Good company, though. More careful than you'd expect. Something very cold about the way he took Grey's girl from under Grey's nose. She's done well to bed him, but judging by their conferences today, which I have seen but couldn't hear, he's told her it will go no further. She likes him, but she's trying to hide it. Not sure she'll take no for an answer. I doubt it will do her any good, but I didn't think he'd bed her in the first place, so what do I know? They're both rum. Interesting to sit and watch. Tears before bedtime or I'm a Dutchman.

10. Joe Carstairs: she's here too. *Sonia II* has been replaced. Her new ship's the *Berania* and it's even fancier, though nothing compared to the *Dazzle*, and we're dining tonight with her and her merry bunch of maenads. It's a costume party, cowboys and Indians. It's all the rage in London, young feller, and Caister told us to order whatever we wanted from his usual dresser. Packages arrived this morning,

everyone secretive. I shall be Great Chief Tomahawk, torso to the wind. Give them a flash of the old magic: How!

11. On the subject of maenads: Pink and Scarlett. These are the Captain (Scotch bulldyke) and first officer (prettier version of Jean Harlow). God knows where they picked those names. Pink could have come from anywhere – I choose to believe she's a fisherman's daughter who educated herself into a lady don – and Scarlett is an ex-deb if I've ever seen one. They and I sing songs round the piano. They know most of the usual ditties, taught me a couple of new ones and were entranced by the Harvey Houlson/Mitchell-Hedges version of 'Baltimore Whores'. I like them – I'm engaged in a ferocious backgammon tournament with Pink – but last night she asked some pretty rum questions. I was gaming the old bitch, pretending to be drunker than I was, and she asked how I made my money. It was ungentlemanly, but she's not a gentleman. Within a couple of prods about getting into and out of Caribbean ports, I was pretty certain she'd nailed me for a smuggler. She also asked how I'd planned this contest, how I'd hit upon Lord Caister, and so on. I think I answered carefully enough to give away that I was sober, and she dropped it. She still beat me at backgammon, though. Like I say, rum. I don't think she's the law, but I don't know what she is.

12. England, by the way: what she always was. Papers full of tunny, cricket and do-nothings, with a nostalgic side-order of dope-frenzy, which is almost word-for-word what you'll remember from the Twenties – a sinister Chinee called 'the Sphinx' has enslaved thousands of 'our women' with his sadistic tricks, and so on. If you've been on the other side of the humbug, you can tell at once that this is a collection of tired hacks telling excitable editors what they want to hear. If you ask me, it's not even a laundry-wallah at all – why would a real mastermind advertise himself? It's probably not a mastermind at all, just five dead girls, a lot of newspaper space to fill and a bunch of moralising hypocrites to sell it to.

Oh. Heading for home. More anon, young feller, more anon. It's not boring out here, but I could do with someone catching a big 'un.

Monday 3rd September

John Fastolf, Earl of Caister
– Scarborough

Johnny lands softly on the jetty, rope in hand, and makes fast the *Harlequin*. He feels light.

What is he doing? Why did he tell Henny that he might be there for her after all this? He shouldn't be giving her hope, if she's the one he's giving hope to. As for protecting her, it would be a good deed, something of his own, but what if she sees the wrong thing? What if she gets into trouble when he isn't there? If she is harmed, what then? He can't guarantee her safety.

The plan is too close to fruition. It's not just his own life he's playing with.

They weigh the fish and pose for photos. The girls glow and the local worthies cheer them. The Scarbies are in Grey's camp against the fractious Mitchell-Henry, but they have hardly warmed to the American, and they're increasingly jolly at the prospect that neither champion will make a catch. Hardy, indeed, shouts, 'No marlin, Mr Grey?' and everybody laughs.

While this palaver is going on, Johnny deals with business. The first piece is unexpected. A squat slab of a man in a butcher's apron approaches him defiantly. 'My lord,' he says.

'Yes.'

'I'm a republican, my lord.'

'Quite right,' says Johnny. 'Quite right.'

'Indeed aye, my lord. I'm Mattock. I've been sending your meat, if you don't know.'

'I didn't know. It's been very good meat.'

'Aye. I just thought you should know, there's been a policeman.'

'Oh, has there, indeed?' says Johnny. 'In a uniform?'

'No,' says Mattock. 'Red hair.'

'Tall?' asks Johnny.

'Tall and thin. Asking questions about your boat, sir. Who's on it? How much food? He asked all of us. Seemed sneaky. You're not sneaky, my lord.'

'No, no I'm not,' says Johnny. 'Thank you, Mattock.' He considers a tip, and decides Mattock would be offended. He says, 'It's very good meat.' They nod to each other. Mattock leaves.

Damn it. Johnny will deal with Raskell in the end, but not until after this part of the story. He makes a phone call and plays the card he has held against this eventuality. The police will learn the location of one of the Sphinx's two main bases, a shabby warehouse behind the Queen's Club in Kensington, and Raskell will have to take a train back to London.

And then it's time for his assignation with Molly Parker. He hardly has the belly for it. They meet in a tearoom behind the covered market and she cranes her glossy lips up to his, but he pushes her away. She looks furious.

'Sorry,' he says. 'Not here. It's not safe.'

'The Sphinx is a hundred miles away!'

'You don't know who he is.'

Molly sits back, pouting. 'You're just using me!'

'No,' he says. 'Are you here with the girls?'

'No. I've been given a holiday. I was told to enjoy myself. You don't think he suspects anything, do you?'

'No,' says Johnny.

'It's got to be Kim,' she says. 'I don't know why you think it isn't!'

'I need you to help me, Molly. I need you to get a message to the Sphinx. You can do that, can't you?'

'Yes,' she says eagerly. 'Does this mean it's nearly over, darling? And we can be together?'

'Yes. You were right, Molly. It is ridiculous that he and I have been competing with each other. We're wasting time and resources. We should be partners.'

'I knew it!' says Molly.

'I want to suggest a meeting, as soon as possible. I need you to get him a message that I will make a peace offering. A very generous peace offering. Can you do that?'

This meeting is the culmination of Johnny and Miss Pink's plan. They know all the details of the Sphinx's operation, they can take it over very easily, and all that is left is to do away with the Sphinx. There will be no partnership.

'Why don't you think it's Kim?' Molly repeats. 'It's so obvious! Couldn't you be wrong? Maybe you can't see clearly what he's like because of Caroline?'

'Maybe,' says Johnny. 'Thank you, Molly. You do realise I love you?' He feels queasy.

'I think you do, but sometimes I need proof.' She reaches out to hold his hand.

'Later,' he says. 'I promise. It'll be over soon.'

Molly is an awful, dangerous woman, but she has never fully considered the things that make her operation possible, and this makes her relatively easy to handle.

Johnny returns to the harbour, tracks down Mike and Grey, and off they head to Robin Hood's Bay to meet with the Captain. Grey is fidgety and irritable. The contest has been good cover, but Johnny could do without it right now.

They leave the girls with the newspapermen and Tunny Clubbers. Johnny worries that their presence would only inflame the meeting, but the meeting gets inflamed anyway. Mitchell-Henry has brought his American wife, Marion, still attractive in her forties. She is frustrated at having to cool her heels in Whitby.

Within minutes, Grey and Mitchell-Henry are at daggers drawn. Grey claims he has been tricked out to Scarborough at the end of the season. Mitchell-Henry points out that plenty of fish are being caught by other people.

Then Grey, glaring around for someone to blame, fixes his eye on Mike and calls him a Jonah. Mike bristles, but doesn't say anything. Johnny is rather impressed by this restraint. Grey, into the frosty silence, adds, 'You're a Mitchell. Mitchells have been Jonahs my entire life.'

This is fighting talk. You can't unsay a Jonah. It's hard to see how Mike will be allowed on board the *Harlequin* tomorrow. Mike replies quietly that he's never had trouble catching fish himself. Mitchell-Henry says that his boat can hardly be free of Mitchells, and he'd be honoured to have another aboard. Mike doesn't look overjoyed at the prospect of switching *Harlequin* for keel and row boat, but the die is cast.

Grey, annoyed that his outburst has been dealt with so briskly, repeats his refusal to attend tonight's party on the *Berania*. He has no idea why he agreed in the first place.

Marion asks, 'What party?'

Before he can stop himself, Johnny says, 'But of course you were invited!'

Marion is exasperated that her husband has rejected jollity just around the corner without even telling her. 'Come on, Laurie!' she says. 'It'll be fun. Like the old days.'

It's bad form to turn down a pleading wife in public, but the Captain won't have anything to do with the *Berania*. Marion has had enough – Whitby will do that to a spirited woman – and she turns to Johnny and says, 'I'd love to come.'

'Of course,' says Johnny, and he hesitates. He is almost never awkward, but Mitchell-Henry is a friend of his father, and to defy him—

'May I stay on the *Dazzle*?' Marion asks.

There is nothing Johnny can do. 'That would be splendid,' he replies. He explains that it is a costume ball and says that some dressing-up boxes arrived from London this morning and there is bound to be enough to go around. Marion professes herself delighted.

As they leave, Mike leans towards Johnny and mutters, 'Fruity amos!'

They've been away from Scarborough for not much over an hour, but there's already a telegram from his agent in London. It reads, simply: DONE.

Monday 3rd September

Mike Mitchell-Hedges – Scarborough

Letter to Jane, ctd.

Back on the *Dazzle*.

Exciting times, young feller. By the point we were seated round the table in Robin Hood's Bay, it was clear that Grey was gnawing out his soul at the thought of the girls and their fishes. It sent him doolally and he called me Jonah.

Bad juju, that. I fairly seethed, trying to look calm. However barmy Grey is, that was me chucked off *Harlequin*. Caister was embarrassed, but not much he could do. M-Henry stood up for me like a white man. Upshot is that tomorrow I'll be fishing from the Mucky Old Keel *Spurwing* and the Captain's bloody coracle. All for the best in terms of my book, I suppose, but I'll miss *Harlequin*'s grub!

As for the book, one of the buggers has to catch something, or I have to. It'll read better if the English gentleman defeats the American gunslinger and, after Grey's claptrap, I want to see him dished.

Tonight is the *Berania*. Grey and M-Henry are in their twin dudgeons and refusing to join the fun, but the Captain's wife is having none of her husband's hash and she's coming along. She's more spirited than you'd think – made me see the Captain in a new light.

Bell for cocktails. Will finish this on return and post tomorrow, incl. report on whether Carstairs is all she's cracked up to be.

This headdress is massive. Indian chiefs must have had bloody strong necks.

Back! Bit blotto, I shouldn't wonder.

Grey's girl, dressed as a peculiar flapper sort of Indian, very fetching, muttered something interesting on the *Harlequin* as we pottered over – probably didn't even understand what she was saying – that this must be like visiting an unknown tribe in the heart of darkest England.

Something in that. Don't suppose I could ever bloody publish it, but *Berania*'s crew and guests are *just* like a bloody tribe, and Carstairs is the Grand Poobah, everyone kowtowing like crazy. Something about her made me think of what Grey must have been like when he was rich enough to have a retinue prancing around him as if he were the centre of the world. I don't know where that collective sort of humbug fits into the scheme of things, but it's not uncommon. It makes me think of something. Think, Mike, think. Got it: Emperor's New Clothes. Clever thought? Probably not.

Anyway, I told some Amazon stories I'd ginned up for Pink and Scarlett, and the *Beranian* Uranians treated me as a sort of mascot, which I pretended to rail against, but with enough good humour not to get myself bitten in half. The Furies were dressed like a gang of pelicans who'd flown through a paint shop, the ones who were dressed at all.

Carstairs is loopy about a little bloody doll that has its own place at table. Caister and I were the only gents there.

Tricky moment when Carstairs said Henny looked like Caister's ex-wife and asked if she was f—ing his lordship, and then baited Caister with more talk of Caro. Caister hated this, from soup to nuts. He doesn't like anything to do with Caro or her friends.

One of said friends was present. A striking American bit called Kiki something, who was dressed in a silver affair of no conceivable relation to the Wild West. We met her in London when she was ganging along with Caro and 'Kimmy' Waring, a loathsome tick who's Caro's consort. Kiki spent a damned peculiar ten minutes quizzing me about my travels, as if she were some bloody detective. She also offered me cocaine and said I'd better grab my chance because I'd never get any on the *Dazzle*, the Earl is so f—ing strict, but he couldn't touch her here. She was jazzed up to her eyes, and she was speaking to Caister rather than me. Caister looked murderous and I wanted no part of it. Drink was flowing like water, anyway.

As soon as it was practicable, Caister said he had to go. He expected Henny to join him, but she knocked him back, cheered on by the harpies. God knows what she's up to. I'd swear she set out to hook him, she's done it, she's brought him right up to the bloody boat and suddenly here she was, letting the bugger waggle free. Either she's mad or she's one of the Carstairs/Pink/Scarlett sorority, but Miss Scarlett says no chance of that, more's the pity. Gellhorn and Mrs M-Henry stayed behind as well. Henny and Gellhorn have been looking warily at each other since Moment One, but there appears to have been some rapprochement. Mrs M-Henry was pretty far gone. Caister wanted to drag her off, but it would have been a scene, and even then I wouldn't have fancied his chances. I departed, brimful of cheerful bluster. Might have been fun to stay, might have been rent asunder with no easy exit. Anyway, I know which side my bread is buttered.

Oh. Clattering on the starboard bow. It's one o'clock. They only stayed an hour. Thought they'd be away longer than that. Poss something gone agley. We have to be up early, but they can always sleep on the *Harlequin*; bloody lovely boat, wish I wasn't roughing it tomorrow.

Bloody hell, I'm drunk. Going to get some fresh bloody air and watch which cabins the girls scurry back to. Not sure how warmly they'll be welcomed if they try anything on.

Bloody interesting, young feller, a tangled bloody web. I sneak out to keep *cave*. They scramble aboard, giggling like schoolgirls, and all three head to Grey's cabin. Knock on the door. Mrs M-Henry starts shaking her head, then the other two hold her and, as the door opens, they scurry off. Grey perplexed. Mrs M-H. straightens her back. A few words, and in she bloody goes! Girls are tittering at other end of corridor. Gellhorn's cabin is next to mine, Henny's is next to Grey's. Henny takes Gellhorn's hand and they trip off to Henny's cabin. Henny ushers Gellhorn in, turns round, looks straight at me, gives a little wave and follows Gellhorn in. Door closes.

I've no doubt the pair of them are drunk, at least, but if Gellhorn's an invert, I'll eat a tunny by myself, and I don't think Henny's one, either. It's wheels within bloody wheels, Jane, and it's capital bloody sport.

I've got to be up in four hours. Bloody hell.

Oh hell. Oh hell! On my way to bloody Whitby. The bloody sun is tearing my bloody eyeballs from their bloody sockets. Will take all my strength to address envelope. What a bloody day to be on a bloody little rowing boat with a bloody little prig.

Hope your head is better than mine, wherever the hell it is.

Bloody hell,

Your Chief

Monday 3rd September

Henny Rosefield – Scarborough

On returning to *Dazzle*, Henny bathed and then, dressed only in a towel, she began a contrite and long-overdue letter to Cecilia at Mount Hope. After a slow beginning, the words flowed quickly.

Henny donned her costume and went to the saloon. Martha was already there, dressed as a squaw. It was just the two of them. Henny said, 'Hello.'

Martha said, 'Hello.'

Patterson entered with two champagne cocktails. Henny sipped hers. 'Well,' she said.

'Indeed,' said Martha. There was a different atmosphere between them today. Partly it was the fish; mostly it was what they had done last night. Martha's mouth twitched. Henny was also on the edge of giggling. How far is hysteria over the edge of giggling?

Martha looked Henny up and down approvingly. When Johnny had returned from Robin Hood's Bay earlier, he had told Henny that Marion was coming to the party unexpectedly and she would need a costume. He said that Marion was more or less Henny's size and it might make Marion more comfortable to be professionally dressed. Did Henny think she could find an alternative outfit in Scarborough? Henny said the shops were closed. Johnny had the swishest pair open privately for her. She had selected her original costume to be unobtrusive, but now her 'squaw's' dress was sequinned, her 'moccasins' were silver and her new 'headdress' contained a peacock feather. 'You look perfect,' said Martha. 'It's as if you planned it. Don't worry, I know you didn't.' She scrutinised Henny closely again and said, 'You seem happier.'

Henny said, 'I am. I didn't expect to be. I'm happier.'

Martha didn't know how to reply.

The sun was bright but pale through the saloon window and the chartreuse carpet was lit the colour of straw. The polished wood looked bleached. The chrome was almost luminous. Henny wandered over to the stickleback.

'What do you really think about it?' Martha asked.

'I think it's just a joke.' She kept looking at it, at the neat little label. '1916, though. It's a very old joke, and jokes go stale. Still, he's rich enough to make any jokes he wants.'

'Yes,' said Martha.

Later, on the *Harlequin*, during the short passage between *Dazzle* and *Berania*, Johnny (dressed as a cowboy, very conventional) spoke intently to Marion (Henny's cowgirl costume suited Marion very well) and Mitchell-Hedges (hilarious face-paint). Then he went to confer with Miss Pink.

Marion and Mike joined them from the opposite rail. 'We who are about to die!' said Mike, eyebrows akimbo.

'They'll probably worship you as a god,' said Henny.

'Yes!' he said. Then, 'Why?'

'They're just another wandering tribe, separated by their customs from the civilised world. Who knows what superstitions they'll be prey to.'

'Damned right, young feller!' he said. 'That's damned good, they're like a damned tribe! I'll use that.'

'Do you never feel shame?'

'Can't remember it, if I do.'

The *Berania* was more opulent than the *Dazzle*. The deck saloon was a haze of sweet smoke. Joe was a sheriff. There was a beautifully fine young woman dressed in exactly the same hired costume as Martha. A heavily made-up redhead and an angry, slightly older brunette were both dressed, like Henny, as sequinned modern squaws. Henny was grateful not to stand out. The drinks were served by a giantess standing still as a statue, dressed only in a snake. She was tall and massive, not tall and thin. They were tall, massive drinks too. The giantess's tray was constantly refilled by two other girls, also naked, but gaudily painted to mimic Johnny's boats. 'Meet Dazzle and Harlequin,' said Joe. 'Aren't they divine!'

As soon as everyone was present, Joe toasted Henny and Martha for their mighty exploits with rod and reel, for triumphing over the puny males. She had prepared this speech to tease Grey, but she ploughed on gamely in his absence.

When Joe finished, Kiki Preston, shimmering silver with a platinum circlet about her brow, took Henny's elbow in her skinny fingers and said, 'I want first dibs on you, mystery girl, if you stay here tonight.'

'I'm sorry, but I'm not a—'

'That's what they all say, darling, and some of them aren't. But if you change your mind, I want first dibs.'

'Why?'

'I think you'll be divine in bed, darling, and it'll drive Johnny crazy, which is a good idea for you, if you want to make him jealous.'

'Why would I care about that?'

'I've got eyes, honey, you're his pet. It won't last.'

'I'm not his pet.'

'He's very clever,' said Kiki. 'Whatever he says, it's all just to string you along. Look at the horsey squaw galloping after him, and look what he did to poor Caro.'

'Why would he bother to pretend with me? I'm nobody.'

'Yes, darling, but you're the nobody he wants to fuck.'

The red-haired flapper-squaw was standing behind Kiki, listening to all this. She looked furious. Kiki turned and saw her too.

'Molly, darling! Have you met the luscious Henny? I think she's fucking Johnny, but she's desperately discreet. Henny, this is Molly Parker. If you're very nice, she'll let you whore for her. Molly, tell him what a pill Johnny is.'

'He's a pill,' said Molly.

'Anyway,' said Kiki. 'You deserve some fun, Henny honey.' She opened her clutch bag to show a syringe and a transparent compact filled with white powder. 'It'll help you through the evening. Joe has bagged you for dinner, and Joe is quite astonishingly boring. This stuff is the only way Ruthie makes it through the days.'

'Who's Ruthie?'

'The sour-faced bitch in green. Joe has others, but Ruthie's always here. God knows why. So?'

'No, thank you,' said Henny. 'I need some air.'

Molly Parker followed her out onto the gangway. '*Are* you fucking him?' she asked.

'Do you speak to your mother like that?' said Henny. Molly turned on her heels and left, although the effect was lessened by her feather falling off and her having to stumble back to snatch it from the floor.

Almost immediately Joe Carstairs appeared from the door. With her fresh, round face it was easy to see her as a stocky, vital little man. 'Henny, darling?' she said. 'I've sat you next to me. Be careful of dear Kiki. She's not kind.'

'Are *you* kind?'

'To my friends.' Joe looked her up and down, calculating. 'Ah well, I see you won't consider it. Don't worry. I'm just an ordinary sort of chap. I'm not an ogre.'

The conversation at dinner was breathtakingly coarse. Henny drank too much. So did everyone. Marion sat opposite her, increasingly flushed.

Mike was on Henny's right, with Kiki the other side of him. Kiki was surprisingly interested in Mike's travels.

During the fish – tunny, naturally – Johnny said something flippant about Joe's doll, a snub-nosed, button-eyed, mitten-handed little thing a foot high, by the name of Lord Tod Wadley. It, or he, was seated next to Martha.

Joe heard Johnny's remark and she stiffened. A moment later, she boomed, 'Rosefield!', even though Henny was right next to her. When Joe was sure everyone was listening, she fixed her eye on Henny, and said, 'You look just like Caro! Does Johnny use her name in bed?' General tittering, Joe at the centre of attention. She leaned over. 'We put up with Caro for Kimmy's sake,' she hissed loudly, 'though she's wet as lettuce, or me on a good night.' More tittering, but pained this time. 'They're coming to join us tomorrow or the next day. Did you know that, Johnny?'

Johnny frowned, but he said nothing and a few minutes later he left the cabin. Shortly after that, Henny followed him, assuming that he would be on the deck and that she would be able to kiss him. She stumbled slightly. She was being overconfident.

The lavatory was empty, as expected. The door onto the deck was ajar. Henny started to open it, but through the crack she saw— She stopped dead.

Johnny was locked against Molly. His hand was on her bottom and she was pressed ecstatically into him.

He didn't see her. Henny went back to the lavatory and splashed her face with cold water, and stood in front of the mirror until she was more composed, pinching herself furiously.

As she returned to the table, Martha caught her arm and asked, 'Are you all right?'

'Yes.'

'You look as if you've—'

'I'm all right.'

Not long afterwards Johnny stood to leave, clearly expecting Henny and the rest of the party to join him. Henny sat tight, her nails under the table digging into her thighs. Martha gave her a significant look, Henny looked significantly back, and Martha sat tight too. Marion made to stand but she saw Henny and Martha were staying and a flicker of indecision crossed her face, and then she stayed as well.

'So, Rosefield,' said Joe when he had gone. 'Now you can tell me. Are you fucking him?' Henny didn't reply. Joe pressed on. 'Caro says he's a desperate disappointment.' No reaction from Henny.

The girl next to Martha, the exquisite twenty-year-old who was wearing Martha's costume and who was called Lapwing, world-wearily declared, 'Men have no idea what to do, of course, poor darlings.'

'Some of them do, I think,' said Henny quietly. It was the voice she had used with Caro in London.

'You've no idea, darling,' said Joe, and Lapwing and a couple of others cackled.

'Girls know what to press,' Henny said, 'and it gets one there efficiently enough, but I find it a technical sort of exercise. I don't really want them in the end. Efficiency's not enough. In the end I want a cock in me.'

Silence.

Joe, 'I don't.'

Henny, 'That's fine.'

Joe, 'No man knows what to press!'

Henny, 'How many have you tried?' Joe didn't like that and the crowd sat forward. Henny went on: 'And sometimes someone with a cock can be astonishingly efficient, more efficient than any girl you've ever been with, and it *still* won't do. It's wonderful in its way, but you wake up and you'd rather be somewhere else. The joy is divorced from any good reason for the joy, and it's not enough, rather like cocaine. Isn't that right, Marty?'

Martha wanted no part of this conversation. She said, 'I've never tried cocaine.'

Kiki said, 'Well, darling, there I can—'

'I think not,' said Henny softly. Everyone was listening. 'Joe's food and drink are far too splendid to spoil with cocaine.' She looked directly at Joe and said. 'It's all absolutely marvellous.' Joe smiled back at her. Joe was like Grey – the last thing she heard was the only thing she remembered. It was tiring, but easy to manage. Henny raised her glass and said, 'In fact, may I propose a toast to the marvellous and handsome Herr Carstairs!' Carstairs puffed up like a pigeon. Kiki looked to raise her voice, but Henny forestalled her, 'And another toast, darlings. To Lord Tod Wadley, secret prince and demon lover!' Joe was enchanted. She was royalty, so you used a trowel. It really was that simple sometimes. Of course, Johnny Caister was genuine royalty, and . . .

Conversation settled closer to normality. Joe asked, 'Who *are* you, Rosefield? Where are you from?'

Henny went, 'I'm just a small-town girl. I'm completely out of my depth.'

Joe threw her head back and laughed. On Henny's other side, Kiki Preston regarded her with intense interest. Kiki asked how often she was in England, and when Henny said this was her first visit, Kiki seemed sceptical. 'You're older than you look,' Kiki said.

'Thank you,' Henny replied.

'You had everyone in your hand just there. It seemed very natural.'

'Did I?' said Henny. 'Did it? If I did, it was an accident.' Kiki shook her head.

The naked giant silently placed two bottles of port on the table. Dazzle and Harlequin cleared the plates. Martha was listening to an animated Lapwing. Marion was glazed and confused in the middle of a conversation between Molly and Ruth. Henny carried on playing her part. Joe continued to like her. Kiki continued to be unsure.

The atmosphere was febrile and grew febriler. Henny looked at Martha, who nodded back. They had made their point to Johnny. They stood up.

Joe, disappointed, embarked on a round of parting toasts, knowing that more would be made to her and Wadley. She called for bottles of Russian vodka, which arrived encased in blocks of ice. The departure took twenty minutes and four burning mouthfuls. As a result, Martha was unsteady as she boarded the *Harlequin*, which had returned for them, and Marion was very unsteady. Henny was being careful again and she was not unsteady, but she felt reckless.

As soon as *Harlequin* was moving – Patterson was piloting her tonight – Marion sat heavily. Her face flopped down and her Stetson fell into her lap, and then almost immediately she re-righted her head and looked at Henny. 'When you said— About a man knowing exactly what to do in, well, in that way— Did you mean Earl Caister? I'm sorry,' she muttered. 'I know I shouldn't have asked.'

'I didn't mean him,' said Henny.

'Oh,' said Marion. She was disappointed. She said she was sorry for assuming; it's just that Johnny had, well, he had such a lurid reputation. Although she personally had always found him a perfect gentleman and he was an old friend of her husband's, so presumably he was on his best behaviour around her, and she was ancient of course, and she loved her husband, it was just— Marion was clearly at her wits' end about something. Not about 'something'. About sex. 'I'm sorry,' she said. 'I'm being embarrassing.' Her eyes were glistening. She said, 'Laurie is— He is a very good man, but he's difficult. And we used to— And it was good, and I was satisfied, you know, most of the time, although it was never the wonderful thing people describe. But we barely do it any more. And I'm old, I suppose, but—' Henny had not planned for this and did not know what to say. Nor did Martha. Marion sat back. She was a very handsome woman. She rubbed her eyes. 'Laurie has got so dumb about these fish!' she said. 'And I sit at home, and my life is drifting away, and I don't want it to end without me ever knowing what that thing is like, what you said, with someone who— I would feel so stupid to have missed it. Sorry. Sorry. You must think me a terrible fool. I do love Laurie. And I do enjoy it, when— But. Sometimes I don't know for certain that I have *lived* and— Oh, bother it.'

Martha looked at Henny, willing her to do something. After a couple of moments Henny said, 'We weren't speaking about Johnny. We were speaking about Grey.' Marion looked at her in disbelief. 'He's— Well, he's exactly what I said to Joe. It's revelatory.'

'It is!' said Martha, animated and drunkenly precise. 'That's the word, he's "revelatory". It's not the most important species of revelation, but it is one.'

Marion was shocked.

'I'm his secretary,' said Henny. 'I'm sure you assumed—'

'It's me you're surprised about, isn't it?' Martha interrupted.

Marion tried to say she wasn't, deep pink and not knowing how not to embarrass either or both of the others, at which point all three of them started laughing.

Martha explained her theory about Fairyland. Henny said, 'It is like that on the *Dazzle*, it really is.' Marion said that 'unreal Fairyland' certainly described her brief experience with the party.

Then Henny said, 'You should go to Grey's cabin.' Martha glanced at her. Both of them knew that Marion should do nothing of the sort. However, they also knew that it was a solution to the problem she described, and one that would not be repeated, or have to be.

They were approaching the *Dazzle*. Henny went quickly into the *Harlequin*'s cabin and emerged with three more small tumblers of vodka. 'Alms for oblivion,' she said, eyes very bright.

Still glowing five minutes later, she and Martha chaperoned Marion to Grey's cabin. It was the work of a hot moment. They knocked. Marion said she shouldn't be here, but her feet didn't move. Henny said, 'Do you really want to leave?'

Marion said, 'No.'

Grey opened the door, and Henny and Martha scurried away. Henny heard Marion ask if she could come in and turned in time to see her enter, Grey looking around uncertainly.

Henny, not having planned this, either, took Martha to her cabin. When they were alone, Martha said, 'We shouldn't have done that.'

'I know,' said Henny. 'We could rescue her.'

'It might not be a mistake,' said Martha. 'It wasn't for me, I'm sure.'

'No.'

Martha unpinned her headdress and put it on the dressing table. As Henny did the same, she noticed her half-written letter to Cecilia on the table. There was nothing she could do about it. She sat on the bed. Martha did not. Then Martha asked if it was true, whether Grey was as efficient as a woman.

'I don't know,' said Henny.

'Oh,' said Martha. 'You sounded so— Oh well.' She looked disappointed. She stood up. She said, 'We could try?' and then quickly, 'I don't want to.'

'Nor do I,' said Henny.

'I don't even want to with Miss Scarlett, and she's incredibly beautiful,' said Martha. 'No offence.'

'None,' said Henny.

'Do you want me to go?'

Henny shook her head. She poured them each a whisky.

Martha said, 'Why would we do it with Grey and not Miss Scarlett? It makes no sense!' She kept pacing. 'I bet she'd be good at it, too.'

'Why?' asked Henny.

'No, you're right. Maybe you don't have to be, if you're that lovely.'

'I don't think there are any rules,' said Henny.

'Certainly not on this boat,' said Martha.

Henny felt tired. 'Marion's an adult,' she said. Martha nodded. Then she asked, 'What about you? Do you think you have lived?' Before Martha could formulate any form of sensible response, Henny said, 'I want to live. As myself.' It was a pathetic thing to say.

'What happened when you left the table? Why didn't we come back with Johnny?'

'I wanted to,' said Henny. 'But he doesn't want me.'

'I think he does.'

Henny shook her head. She lay down. She said, 'He doesn't. I thought he did, because I'm silly, but he doesn't. He is what we thought he was; he is just a better actor about it, that is all.'

'What happened?'

'I saw him kissing Molly. The red-haired girl.'

'Really?' Martha looked genuinely shocked. 'Are you sure?'

'Yes.'

'Oh,' said Martha. 'But isn't Molly— Are you sure she didn't just throw herself at him?'

'He doesn't want me,' repeated Henny. 'He doesn't want who I seem to be, and he certainly wouldn't want who I really am.'

'Who is that?' said Martha. 'Please tell me. I know everyone keeps asking.'

'I don't know any more,' said Henny, sitting down heavily. She kept her voice still, but she had to set her shoulders rigid to keep them from shaking. 'Will you be my friend?' she asked.

Martha's eyes widened. She said, 'Yes.' Then she apologised, but she had to go to the bathroom. As soon as she left, Henny leapt to her feet, tore up the letter to Cecilia and threw it in the bin, and returned to her bed.

Martha returned and lay down next to her, both of them staring at the ceiling. 'Honestly, and sorry again,' Martha said, 'but if you want me to be your friend, you have to tell me who you are.'

'I'm no one,' said Henny.

'Self-pity won't do,' said Martha sharply. 'Sorry, but it won't. You have been very deliberately mysterious. Of course we're all intrigued. What are you doing with Grey?'

'It's not your business.'

'No,' said Martha, 'it isn't. But I like you, rather to my startlement, and I want to know.' Then she said, 'I was afraid of you.'

'And you're not now?'

Martha stood again. She looked at the small painting above the drinks cabinet, an oil of a dinosaur standing placidly in a herd of cows. 'It's a funny picture,' she said.

'Yes.'

'Please tell me,' Martha asked.

Henny did not say it exactly like this, but this is the story she told.

My mother was beautiful and she hated Halifax on principle, simply because it was where she grew up. She set her cap at John Hartshorne, a rich man who had returned from working in Europe and America for several years. She thought he would take her away, even though he said he had come home for good.

I heard older Hartshornes whisper about how the engagement came about. I do not find it hard to believe that my mother was compliant and sly. Certainly, she always said, 'Never be too proud to do what you must.' Anyway, she and my father were married. Later she talked often about how he trapped her.

That was when she was old enough to realise that someone as beautiful as her could always have escaped Halifax. She could have left and found the kind of man she wanted. But by then she had made her bed.

I had a sister. She was two years older and she inherited my mother's looks. I am pretty enough, but my sister was beautiful. She was christened Victoria Regina, which tells you a few things about my mother. My mother's *idée fixe* was that her daughter would marry a duke. This sounds silly, but there were whole magazines devoted to the subject.

Victoria was also silly, but not in the same way. My mother wanted Vicky to be a duchess; Vicky just wanted to be loved. She fell for boys from the age of fourteen onwards, and she told me what they did together from before I could understand.

Our father spent most of his life in the library. He read to me. I wanted to be an explorer. I read books about dense jungles and primitive peoples. Later I pretended that I wanted to be an anthropologist, but I really wanted to be an explorer.

My father had been an engineer. My mother sent us to deportment classes and music lessons; he taught me about science. While my sister was still alive, and I was young and precocious, these books convinced me that all behaviour has a simple biological explanation, which is an attitude I have come to temper. My youthful analysis of Vicky was: she is an animal and has a strong urge for safety; she is childlike in her attitude and seeks short-term security in things she can see and touch; she sees protestations of affection and affectionate acts as synonymous with affection; thus, she falls in love rapidly because she wants to love something she can touch, rather than something theoretical. I still think this. Possibly this is what I think now and I didn't think it then. Probably the truth is somewhere in between.

Certainly, when I was fourteen I thought Vicky was very shorttermist in her thinking, and the books I was reading said this was a classic symptom of being childlike and primitive. I disapproved of her choices, and when she spoke to me about being 'in love' I did not take her seriously, since she said the same things about a succession of boys. I thought her choices would not have positive outcomes. She laughed at me and said I did not understand.

I did not value my sister as I should have, but what happened to her was not my fault.

In 1927 Vicky was seventeen. The whole town was excited about tuna. Famous people came to hunt them, and Grey was one of the most famous. My mother said it was the first time she had been happy to live in Halifax. My sister met Grey at a reception in his honour. She spoke to him, simpering breathily, I am sure. Later that evening he passed her a note. Two nights later she was in love. Two weeks later, having been to Wedgeport and caught the biggest tuna in the world, he left. Vicky was pregnant.

She told my parents. She thought, somehow, that they would make Grey divorce his wife and marry her. It was a typically ridiculous dream. My father explained this, but kindly. My sister declared that at least she would have Grey's baby to remember their love by, and that would be enough. My mother screamed that she would not let all the family's hopes be ruined by her ungrateful child's wilful stupidity.

And so my mother had Vicky taken to a hospital, an asylum, called Mount Hope. I do not know exactly what happened there, but part of it was that the child was lost.

Vicky said almost nothing when she emerged. I tried to talk to her, but she refused me. Three days later she threw herself over a cliff. She left a note saying that she hoped to be reincarnated as a tuna, caught by Grey and mounted on his wall. She had lost her mind.

For a while, my mother groomed me to take Vicky's place. I was late to develop, but I was fifteen now. She gave me lessons on how to fascinate a man, and how to recognise who in a room was looking for a wife and who was merely looking for a woman. I hated her, but I was young and there was little I could do to avoid these lessons.

Slowly, however, I stopped doing what she wanted. By the time I was eighteen, we barely talked. My mother had reached a state of almost permanent fury with the world. She shouted at me, at my father and at the servants. I wanted to go to university. She mocked me. I ran away. I was brought home by the police.

This gave my mother the excuse to have me incarcerated at Mount Hope. The asylum could be an awful place – for most of its inmates I'm sure it was – but after a few first weeks of rage and horror, those were the happiest days of my life. I was not the only person (young women in the main) who had been sent there for petty family reasons but Dr Morgan compelled his colleagues to admit that they understood the reasons for our committal, and to treat us as an unfortunate class of imprisoned student.

We considered whether the female brain, as the numbers of women in institutions seemed to indicate, was truly weaker than the male. We asked how such a difference might have developed to serve the species, or develop from something that *did* serve the species. We asked how much madness was the product of a natural brain having to interact with the unnatural world of civilisation.

Dr Morgan's studies in the wards showed that impulsiveness, unwillingness to plan and difficulties with complexity were indeed common issues among the insane. These were all problems my sister had, but she was not mad, merely foolish. Dr Morgan explained to me that foolish women were locked in asylums while foolish men were locked up in prisons, and many, many more fools wandered around and rubbed along as best they could. He also said that there was a continuum of behaviour that tied the mad and the criminal to the sane, with no clear dividing line that he could determine. I remain to this day uneasy about placing people on this continuum.

I spent five years outside the world. My father, who visited me every week, began to worry that this was unhealthy. So did Dr Morgan. It did not seem so terrible to me. I felt I was like a nun, and in Dr Morgan, a nurse called Cecilia and several of the incarcerated guests I had a greater fill of friendship than had ever been the case in Halifax.

My father died. Without my permission, Dr Morgan wrote to my mother and explained that I was an adult and well able to make my way in the world. My mother replied immediately that she could see he had allowed himself to be deceived, that she could afford doctors whose words would carry more weight than anyone's at Mount Hope, and that she had decided to have me placed in a 'safer, less-progressive' institution.

Dr Morgan was horrified. I persuaded him to write that I had suffered a decline and that it would be too shocking for me to leave in anything under three weeks. This would give me time to plan my escape.

What was I to do, once I had left Mount Hope? In a flash of inspiration I made the decision to revenge myself on Grey, the cause of my family's distress. Cecilia tried to dissuade me, but I was adamant and she helped me prepare as best she could.

I realise now that my goal was foolish and inappropriate. My real enemy was my mother, but I could not face her and wanted to escape Halifax, and so I picked Grey.

I still don't know what revenge I wanted to take. To kill him? Certainly not. To break his heart? I suppose I considered that. To steal from him? Yes, if I could. I did not think carefully enough about these things. Whenever they came to my mind, I told myself that when I was in a position to hurt him I would know how.

Vengeance is interesting. It seems to be universal. I have wondered about it often these past months. Does it have a biological basis or is it purely societal? Does the fear of revenge keep people from acting destructively towards one another, and so help the species as a whole? For this to be effective, it must be understood and it must, periodically, be enacted. It must, to a degree, be irrational, since it is frequently the case that no one benefits materially. Fear of revenge is rational; taking revenge is irrational; but the fact that it is often taken underpins the rational fear. I certainly felt irrationally vengeful at the outset. This feeling has dissipated to a large extent, leaving a goal that I never properly interrogated, and then for a long while avoided interrogating because working towards the goal became a habit. Johnny said last night that I was following a dark star and must turn back, if I am to be saved. I knew at once that he was right. One day is not long enough to come to terms with this.

Sorry, I digress.

It was early February and I had decided to pursue Grey. In the days remaining at Mount Hope, I learned some practical things about coitus. Cecilia was shocked that I went about it in such a brutal fashion, but it was sensible to do so, given my aims which, to repeat, I understand were not sensible. I labour that point because—— It is for obvious reasons. I am talking too much.

I snuck back to my family home, stole my mother's jewels and ran away. I did not hesitate to commit this crime. My mother would incarcerate me whatever I did, and I would need money. It was my father's money. He would have wanted me to have it.

I travelled to California. I learned everything I could about Grey.

I learned how easy it is to deceive people. At root, other things being equal, people assume that you are telling them the truth. From that, everything follows.

My plan was to re-create myself in the image of one of Grey's idealised heroines – the shuttered Easterner yearning to be freed by the wildness of the West. It was an easy role for me to play.

For practical reasons, I changed my name several times. It was a surprising experience. I escaped Canada with the name Mary Smith. I felt nondescript. It was not the name of a Grey heroine, for one thing. I was very pleased with my next, which I thought I would keep for the duration of this project: Alice Toogood. But it was a giddy name and it made me feel giddy. It might have suited the purpose of trapping Grey, but I believe I acted recklessly under its influence, as if it were a mask.

Henrietta Rosefield is better. It has some backbone. I expected to be called Hetty, if not Henrietta, but everyone has diminuted it to Henny. I wonder if I look like a Henny? It is an odd thought to someone with a scientific cast of mind that a name might affect one's behaviour, that one name might be more appropriate than another name, but all I can say is that it seems to be so.

Then Henny explained how she seduced Grey and ousted Brownella Baker, how she was shaken by the experience of sleeping with Grey, how she set about binding him to her, how she helped Mitchell-Hedges manufacture this fishing contest, how Ledger and Grey used their contacts to get her a passport when she had no documentation, simply on her word that she was estranged from her family, and how she arrived in England no wiser as to how she would achieve her ends or what those ends were.

'So, you see,' she said, 'if I'm mysterious it's because I am a sort of void. I don't know what I am doing and I'm not anybody at all.'

'Do you still hate Grey?' asked Martha. She'd asked other questions, but mostly she had listened.

'No.'

'When did you stop hating him?'

'I don't know,' said Henny. She rubbed the metallic material of her dress between her fingers. It was more like soft chainmail than fish scales. It was not particularly comfortable. The shop assistant had said it could have been made for her, and Johnny had agreed. She pinched her thigh again. She said, 'I find it hard to imagine hating him now, but when I arrived in England I was still— Well, what I was doing was *the shape* of revenge, but it had no content. I hadn't thought of anything else to do until— I don't know until when. Not long ago. Even when I stopped sleeping with him I told myself it was part of the plan.'

'Was it difficult to stop?' asked Martha.

'No. It should have been, shouldn't it?'

'I don't know,' said Martha. 'I don't want to do it again. Well— No, I don't. That's the miracle of it really, because I think Grey may actually be a rarer beast than Johnny.'

'And yet,' said Henny.

'Yes. Maybe Grey is too rare. And the rest of him is— He's so ridiculous. I'm very glad I did it, though.'

'Yes,' said Henny. They were, among other things, still trying vainly to reassure each other about Marion.

'Grey's the most childish man I've ever met,' said Martha. 'Where is he on the continuum?'

'Oh!' said Henny. 'Oh! I'd never thought of him like that. Of course, I should have done. I don't know. He's wilful and selfish. He wants to have what he can see, and he can be cruel. He was pretty ruthless to Brownie when I made it clear I wanted him to be. And whenever he has had money, he spent it all straight away. So he's impulsive and short-sighted, but he's not mad or anything. He's just never grown up.'

'Like Peter Pan?'

'Yes. Cruel and kind of merry, but in the end he'll do what he wants.'

'Like Greek Pan, in fact, if we're in a fairy forest.'

'Yes.'

Martha interlaced her fingers and said, 'Do you think you describe him as childish because of the things you learned at Mount Hope?'

'I see that I should have thought about it like this before, but honestly I never have. Do you think I've got it all wrong?'

'No,' said Martha. 'I think you're exactly right. I don't hate him, either.' Then she said, 'You know what happened to your sister wasn't all Grey's fault.'

'Yes, I know. He didn't think that much about her, but she never told him she was pregnant. I think now that he might have looked after her if she did. She pursued him as much as he pursued her, and she wasn't innocent, and she was very beautiful.'

'She was too young for him, though,' said Martha. 'And he wasn't careful.'

'No. But I don't hate him. I hate my mother.'

Martha looked around the cabin and said, 'What would your mother think about all this? It's what she dreamed of.'

'She never wanted it for us. She wanted it for herself. If Vicky had ever bagged a duke, my mother would have cursed her for it.'

'So, what now?' said Martha.

'Will Marion be all right?' said Henny. 'She won't be— I mean, I don't suppose she's used to this. I don't think her marriage is anything like Grey's.'

'No,' said Martha. 'Why does Grey's wife stay in it?'

'Habit? They don't see each other much. It seems to work, somehow.'

'For them,' said Martha.

Henny was desperately tired, back down from whatever high the drink had given her.

Martha hugged her knees for a moment. Then she lay back down. 'This will sound like nothing compared to what you've been through, but anyway. Last year – for the last few years actually – I couldn't marry someone, a Frenchman, because his wife wouldn't let him divorce. I mean, I *thought* that was the reason. Actually, he didn't want to marry me. He wanted a mistress and I never understood.'

'Did he say he wanted to marry you?'

'Yes,' said Martha. 'It was gallantry, though. It's just what they say.'

'Grey doesn't. Or Johnny.'

'It's what they say in France. You're supposed to understand.'

'I don't think the Captain would understand,' said Henny. She lifted her legs. The dress had pressed a series of ridges into her calves. 'It's late,' she said.

Martha jumped to her feet. 'Yes,' she said. 'Of course.' She picked up her headdress and started squeezing her feet into her moccasins. Then she gave up and said, 'I'm a size eight, who am I trying to kid?' Then she went up onto her toes, came back down again, turned to Henny and said, 'I'm sorry, but I have to say something.'

'Oh?' said Henny. 'Yes?'

'It's nothing bad,' said Martha. 'All right. I idolised Caro when I first read *The Lost Boys*, but do you know what I've started to think? I think it was the other way round. I think Johnny loved her.'

'Yes, he did. He told me.'

'Oh!' said Martha. She sounded hurt. 'What did he say?'

'He said that he loved Caro, but she loved Kim. That he only had one heart and it was smashed, but that one might eventually recover and love someone else in a different way.'

'He said that?'

'Yes.'

'Don't you think that sounds significant?'

Henny mumbled, 'I don't know. Like I said, I'm a sort of void. It was like speaking to himself, maybe.'

'Come on! It's obvious what he was saying.'

'I thought it might mean that. I thought—' Henny turned her big eyes up to Martha. 'But what about Molly?'

'I don't understand that,' Martha said. 'Are you sure you were right? Or that it means— I think – I've thought ever since I met him – that Johnny is vulnerable. That's why I was afraid of you.'

'You were afraid of me?'

'For his sake. I thought that everyone had misjudged him.'

'I thought that too,' said Henny. 'You and I, look at who we are, two young girls; we thought that the world was wrong about this decadent aristocrat. Do you think we look ridiculous?'

'Perhaps. Perhaps we do.' Martha considered. 'I still can't believe it! I'm sure there is something fine about him, and I'm sure you can help—'

'Why not you? You like him as much as I do.'

'I do. You're very direct. He doesn't want me, though. And I don't want him, not in my conscious mind. I lost three years of precious youth to Bertrand. I will not be sucked into another disaster.'

Henny laughed. 'But you think I should be sucked into a disaster?'

'It wouldn't be a disaster for you. He wants you.'

'No, he doesn't. He's in his high-walled circle of reality at the end of a broken path. With Molly.'

'You don't know what Molly was,' said Martha. 'And forget the silly tangle talk. This isn't a game, and there aren't rules. Grey was right, you know. If we choose what we want, we can all see our way out of the forest, even Johnny.'

'Yes,' said Henny.

'He opened up to you. Everything he says about stars and paths, I think it's because he wants to take back his choices, start again. Don't you think so?'

Henny was too tired to carry on. She repeated that they knew nothing about Johnny, that after tonight the most likely thing was that all the stories about him were true. At best, he regretted what he had done and was trying to change, but he was still in a pit and so was Henny. She was a certified madwoman on the run in a foreign country. She had some jewellery left that she might sell, but she had no way of earning a living and no friends.

'It sounds as if you're free,' said Martha. Then she said, 'I'm sorry, that sounded casual. I didn't mean it to. I will be your friend.'

Tuesday 4th September

Martha Gellborn – The North Sea

G. Campbell, my dearest darling old fruit,

I can no longer deny that I am writing a journal. Since I swore I should never do such a thing again, I insist that you burn these letters. And yet part of the incredible nature of this adventure is that I am compelled to scrawl it down on paper in order to believe it real. (Is writing another way to try to tame the confusion? Or is it just another distortion?) I hope you are feeling strong.

I have developed the saltiest of sea legs, and I am not retching in spite of a night of terrific excess and very little sleep. Perhaps I will shortly fall apart, but as we zip over the jade sea under a perfect dome of glittering blue, and as my hands quiver from the potency of Miss Scarlett's coffee, I feel almost light-headedly well.

Last night we dined on board the *Berania*. The Captain's wife Marion joined us, I believe largely out of irritation that her husband refuses to attend any social gathering because of his feud with the world and its mother. Grey remained on the *Dazzle* out of general pique and embarrassment at his failure to catch a fish. Really, he and the Captain deserve each other.

I am tolerably used to these parties by now, darling, but your eyes would have been on stalks. We were attired by London's fanciest costumiers, Johnny footing the bill and apologizing for the trouble we were being put to. I was a basic sort of squaw, in miserably the same getup as one of Joe's entourage, who was the dashingest slip of a creature you ever saw. Johnny was a 'boring' cowboy, and looked gallant with his hat on and comical without it. Joe was a sheriff, with real six-guns, which she shot into the air to welcome us, which was a hair-raising experience because she gave one almost precisely no confidence that she might not shoot off one's feet by accident.

Henny had to surrender her cowgirl costume to Marion. It was hardly a problem, because Johnny majestically had the toniest local boutiques throw themselves at her feet. Naturally, my fears about her having gotten to him were going ten to the dozen at this point, but that situation has rather evolved, as I will later explain – it's good stuff; make a pot of java.

Anyway, the swanky boutiques transformed Henny into an updated squaw in silver and peacock feathers. I was green with envy. Two other guests had the same idea, as it happens – there are only so many things you can dream up with cowboys and Indians. I should have gone as a horse.

Henny and I were toasted time and again for our piscatorial escapades. Joe Carstairs is a sad sort of grotesque, desperate to talk, but such a dictator in her little world that her entourage is too scared to engage with her. But if they do engage and she doesn't like it, then it's off with their heads. Her 'best friend' is a doll about two feet high, and if you think it would be creepy to be seated next to such a creature at dinner, you'd be just about right.

Mike was rather splendid amongst the Amazons, or Red Indians, or whatever is the appropriate tribal description. He is ludicrous, and his relationship with the truth is abominable, but he is so straightforward about it with us that I find it almost impossible to dislike him. While he japed around, Johnny was restrained and charming.

I was sat between the repulsive doll and my dashing costume-partner, who was called, I swear, Lapwing. It can't be her real name. Everyone around me talked of nothing but sex: who was 'fucking' who; who wanted to 'fuck' who? It was the coarsest and most extraordinary thing. I wouldn't like to do it every day, but it was spellbinding. Lapwing was in floods of tears because she had been fucking Tallulah Bankhead, but now Tallulah Bankhead was off to America and didn't want Lapwing to tag along and it was the end of Lapwing's life. Marion Mitchell-Henry was white, listening to all this, but you could see her screwing her courage to the sticking place and determining to endure.

Joe taunted Johnny about Caro, whom she has invited to Scarborough to bait him. She did so, I only at this very moment perceive, because when Johnny is around she cannot be top dog. I wish I had been this insightful last night. I'm such a slow spoon at times.

Anyway, as soon as polite, Johnny prepared to leave. I naturally assumed Henny would leap up and race back to his bed, but she stayed at her seat and glared at him. She had won her earl, but suddenly she was rejecting him! Nothing made sense in Fairyland. What could it mean?

Desperate to find out, I stayed too. Rather more surprisingly, so did Marion. I suppose the courage was too tightly screwed to the sticking place for her to get it off in a hurry.

Once the men were gone, the filth increased, which I scarcely believed possible. Joe was frightful; Henny dealt with her magnificently. First she batted the old terror down and then five minutes later had her eating out of her hand, simply by raising a toast to the doll.

But it was all rather gruesome, and so we left as soon as—

Oh! Shouting! The Captain's hooked a fish and he and Mike are scurrying around like anything on their potty little rowboat. Must watch. The readers of *The Illustrated Banana* expect . . .

Thrills and spills, G. Campbell! An hour later and the fish remains hooked, but at large. The general impression amongst us *vieux chiens de mer* is that the Captain is 'into a big one'. Mike is with the Captain because Grey called him a Jonah yesterday, which is apparently a Big Deal. As a result, Mike is grinning over at Grey whenever he gets the chance, his second-most-alarming pipe jutting furiously.

Grey is sat grimly by his rod, unable to cast off until his Nemesis brings the fish to boat. He is sulking and expounding various theories of supernatural misfortune. I went to console him, fool that I am, and he was so petulant – he still hasn't forgiven me for catching a fish – that I snapped and called him childish. I told him that Henny and I thought he was behaving like Peter Pan, and this is not becoming in a grown man.

He could barely be civil to me. He believes – or at least claims – that Mitchells have always been his bane. As well as M-Henry and now M-Hedges, he used to employ a skipper called Laurie Mitchell, unrelated to Laurie Mitchell-Henry, by whom Laurie Mitchell had nonetheless been previously employed. Grey fired this Laurie Mitchell in acrimonious circumstances over drink, money and, of course, the failure of Grey to catch as many giant fish as he should have. My head was spinning by this point, and he was being so ridiculous that I left him.

Johnny explained that the sacking of Laurie Mitchell was quite the scandal in fishing circles. Grey's claims hardly stack up, since Mitchell was Grey's skipper when he caught his record tuna, and many others. Anyway, the Laurie Mitchell story is a subsidiary component of Grey's feud with the Captain, because the Captain was a friend of his near-namesake and has accused Grey of mistreating him, saying that Grey only knows what a fish looks like because this other Mitchell showed him. Johnny thinks there might be an element of truth in this, but added that Laurie Mitchell is a soak, and his wife is a sharp cookie, and it's not beyond the realms that they had their hands in the till during the good times, and Grey's moolah must have gone somewhere. It's a labyrinth, to be sure.

We saw the feuding side of Grey in full force yesterday, actually, when Henny and I were being photographed with our fish as if we were a pair of preening society couples. The indefatigable Taylor, who clearly sees himself as spokesman for the Scarborough contingent, pumped our hands like a politician, followed swiftly by Hardy, who is a seller of fishing equipment that everyone uses but, to the best of my understanding, no one pays for. Hardy tried to shake Grey's hand too, but Grey shook him off, saying that he knew Hardy – that Hardy would use the picture to publicize his cheating company.

Grey shouted to the crowd that Hardy wouldn't take back unwanted tackle. Hardy laughed that Grey hadn't paid for it anyway, so let's call bygones bygones. Then Hardy ushered forward his photographer once more, and Johnny interposed himself and told Hardy that Grey was his guest and he wouldn't see him bothered. Hardy said that having a picture of Grey was hardly an advert these days, by the look of it, and the crowd tittered. Anyway, this is background color and I'll save it for *The Illustrated*.

Back to last night and our return from the *Berania*. We were sozzled as swans – God knows what Patterson thinks of us, but he was discretion incarnate – and Marion told us considerably more about her disappointments with the Captain than I wanted to know. We in our turn told her about Grey. You will not understand how it might have seemed logical to escort her to Grey's cabin on our return. All I can say is that it did. I am appalled by myself, largely, but I still hope it might not have been a mistake. Maybe the thing is that you have to use Fairyland, or what's the point of being here?

Anyway, we saw Marion into Grey's cabin from a safe distance, at which point I noticed Henny's hand in mine. Hers felt warm, small and delicate. Mine felt like the flipper of a particularly inelegant seal.

G. Campbell, my question is this: have I invented the notion of enchanted woods to justify all manner of ill behavior? I imagine you reading this, horrified at me, at my cavalier treatment of others. Grey is not cocaine, but many people – most people, probably – would consider taking Marion to him worse than introducing her to a drug. What then is the difference between us and Kiki Preston? Certainly Henny and I stood for a minute that seemed like an hour looking at the closed door, breathing very loudly, before Henny squeezed my hand. We went to her cabin. After all the tension between us and the oddness of the evening, it felt like a barrier was split open and we must have some matters into the air before it resealed.

Oh, my days! The Captain's fish has just jumped out of the water and it's a giant! What am I doing writing this tedious stuff?

Two hours more have passed. Everyone is drinking champagne, and by that I mean everyone except Grey. I missed the fish's first jump because of my solipsistic whining, but the gasps were enough to drag me to my feet.

The Captain has caught a monster! It jumped three times – something we tunny veterans associate more with smaller, more agile fish. I could tell it was much larger than my poor tuna, of which I am so inordinately proud, and so will you be when you see the pictures, but beyond that I am not qualified to say. As soon as Johnny saw it, though, he gave a whistle and said, 'Well, that's the record.' Miss Scarlett gabbled that it was over 1,000 lbs, definitely, well over, and this seemed like a magical figure, although Grey muttered, 'People always say that. Let's weigh it. If he catches it.'

Well, after its jumping about, the fish dived away again, but this seemed to tire it out, and from then on the Captain was in control. You will wonder how someone can watch a man tied to a seat with a straining rod and be enthralled for well over an hour and I can barely tell you, but enthralled I was. Henny and I watched arm-in-arm. How I can have been so daunted by her only yesterday I do not know.

Eventually the behemoth was wrested to its doom. Grey was staring eagle-eyed for any infraction of the arcane rules by which angling records are, or are not, allowed to stand. Johnny asked him very clearly if there were any technical problems he could foresee on that front, and added that if Grey didn't air objections now, then he, John Fastolf, 13th Earl of Caister, would make it his life's work to see this triumph ratified.

For triumph it clearly is. We pootled over to the *Spurwing* to get a clear view as it was being winched aboard. It is precisely the shape of a fish that a five-year-old child would draw, but completely otherworldly in its scale: two tall persons in length and as tubby as a banker. They should take it straight in to Whitby, but Grey insists that his opportunities must not be curtailed any longer than they have been already by all this fuss.

So we have more hours out here on the ocean wave. How overjoyed you must be to hear it! Let me see where I had got to . . .

Oh, there. I can see why I hastened so eagerly away to the battle of man against tunny.

I hardly know what to say about the rest. Together alone in Henny's room, after being on the wicked *Berania*, we could scarcely not have considered the possibilities open to us. I certainly did, this being a voyage of discovery. And I was emboldened and ashamed by what Marion was doing at our instigation, and perhaps there was a small part of me that wished to be similarly outrageous, simply so we could tell her today that it was a night of mutual madness. But also, since it is not a part of my experience, I truly wondered if Joe might be right about women. It seemed hard to believe that the thing could be done more skillfully than it was by Grey, but then I did not believe what Grey could do until he did it. One cannot describe color to a blind man. But I did not really want to try it, and nor did Henny. It was rather a relief.

I could contain myself no further. I asked her why she hadn't left with Johnny. It was because she saw him kissing another woman on the *Berania*!

I was shocked to the bone! The other woman – she is called Molly something – is a famous— What word should I use? Is 'Madam' the most appropriate expression for someone who does that kind of thing in high-society circles? What could it mean that Johnny was kissing her! We wondered whether we had been duped – he is Johnny Caister and he has all these women, and I am one of them – but he was not cavalier with me. This seemed so out of character.

And especially so because he opened his heart to Henny the night before. He told her that he had utterly loved Caroline – as I had so cleverly divined, G. Campbell – and that he had never told anyone about it. He was reaching out to her, I swear. I don't understand it.

I have just re-examined the pair of them for a minute, pencil drooping from my slack and weary fingers, trying to imagine how I would feel if it were not for our conversation last night. I would see Johnny unable to hide his agitation, and I would see Henny pristine and aloof, and I would continue to despise her for an icy little mink.

But she is not! In our revelatory state she told me about herself and how she found herself on board the *Dazzle*. I will not tell the details without her permission, but I understand her now. Or I understand her somewhat, at least. She appears this effortless, self-possessed creature, but she has had an extraordinary life. I hope I never pretend that I have endured true suffering or hard times, but she surely has.

I have decided, in my grandiose way, that she is a worthwhile person. I think that she is damaged, like Johnny is damaged, and I think they both believe they are stuck in their own little circles, and this means they are not properly trying to escape over the walls, rather as I didn't try in the period when I thought my life could not continue without B—, but if they did try, then perhaps they could do so and perhaps they could help each other. I explained this to Henny, at no doubt tedious length. Do not imagine I am being self-sacrificing, G. Campbell my love, it is merely that I will not be in thrall to anyone again.

Except I am still troubled by the idea of Johnny and Molly the Madam. What if we are being fools about him? Or maybe she also has a secret past and I am making another hasty judgment? Surely not everyone can have a heart of gold!

Whitby ahoy! It is smaller than Scarborough and rather pretty, in a workmanlike sort of way, at least from the sea. I will not send this until we have weighed the tuna. You must be chewing your knuckles with anticipation!

Tuesday 4th September

John Fastolf, Earl of Caister – Whitby

There is enormous excitement in Whitby as the Captain's fish is hoisted into the air. The locals see fewer tunny than their neighbours in Scarborough, but they still know she's special. Reporters and others have raced up the coast to see her. She's eleven feet long and her flank glints like watered steel.

Johnny edges alongside Henny. They have barely spoken today. She said she trusted him, but then she stayed on board *Berania* last night. Does she mean anything she says? Is she really an iceberg? Does she have a split personality?

He says, 'She's a beauty.'

Henny says, 'Yes.'

'I can't protect you, old thing, if you hang around on strange boats.'

'I release you from your obligation,' she says, and then silence. That seems to be that. He can't make any sense of it. And he doesn't have time.

The scales' operator, a one-footed man in an old navy jacket, looks nervous as he raises the fish so Johnny isn't too surprised at what happens next. The operator studies the dials, removes his cap and wrings it in his hands. He shamefacedly explains that his machinery is not up to the job. The scales are only good to half a ton. Anything else needs the shipyard or, for finer work, the railway station, but they're all shut up now, so it'll have to be the morning.

Even though this confirms that the tuna is a record, that it weighs more than 1,000 lbs, everyone is rather deflated. Grey says that if the fish isn't weighed now, the record can't count. Who knows what the Captain might do to it overnight! Maybe he will fill it with lead!

Johnny says he will attend the weigh-in tomorrow morning, with

Grey, and they will inspect the fish. He repeats his earlier vow that he will see justice done and Grey ridiculed, if Grey plays the fool. Grey accepts this with no grace at all, and Johnny leaves Patterson to organise the tunny's carriage to Mitchell-Henry's warehouse.

The Captain invites everyone to join him as and his wife, who is looking radiant in a rather frenetic way, for a celebratory champagne in the bar of the Royal Hotel. Grey's face is savage.

The locals clap Mitchell-Henry on the back all along the road and as he enters the bar. He is popular here or, more to the point, Scarborough is not popular. Everyone knows about the competition. Certain among the crowd, he feels, are hushed, excited, waiting for something. This makes Johnny uneasy.

The hotel's manager, who has been drawn from his lair by the excitement, sidles greasily through the throng and ushers Johnny to the wall. He hands over a copy of *Time & Tide*, his smooth thumb marking a page. The headline reads: *Is Zane Grey the Worst Author in the World?* The byline, naturally, is Caro's.

I am told that Mr Zane Grey is a great fisherman [it reads]. *I hope so, because he is a ghastly writer. In spite of his inconceivable sales, in fact, he is such a bad writer that I wonder if the word should be used of him at all. I would generously describe him as a pulp hack with execrable taste. One despairs for one's fellow creatures that they read his drivel in such numbers.*

Why did I suffer through one of his books this week? Well, as English newspaper readers know to their cost, it has been impossible to escape news of Mr Grey's tedious and unsuccessful fishing expedition with my former husband in Scarborough. Why does the press concern itself with such trivial nonsense when the world is a tinderbox awaiting the spark? I cannot say, but there it is, and I have always made it my business to know intimately anything that I have the temerity to criticise.

In literary salons, it has become fashionable to say that while Mr Grey may not be an 'artist', he is a wondrous 'storyteller' and his 'thrilling' books allow people to 'escape from the daily grind'.

Of course, none of the 'critics' in these salons has ever read his books. Out of curiosity, therefore, I purchased Riders of the Purple Sage, *his purported 'masterpiece'. I was curious to learn whether it did, indeed, contain some alchemical magic.*

It does not, and I also fear that Zane Grey, whatever his apologists say about 'storytelling', believes that he is perpetrating 'Art'. His pages are packed with lurid, overwritten sunsets, lizards of 'nameless color, but of exquisite beauty' and heroines who agonise 'sightless' and 'voiceless' like 'writhing, living flames'.

And while we are in the kingdom of the sightless, one of Mr Grey's heroes rides a blind horse. I am not inventing this and I am astonished that anyone else could have.

The heroes of Riders of the Purple Sage *are, naturally, the violent he-men that Mr Grey dreams of being. A complicated and melodramatic chain of events sees one woman victimised by Mormons while another escapes a life of outlawry with her father, who turns out not to be her father, but the former tormentor of her mother, who bore her to a deadly gunslinger who has ever since wandered the Western wastelands on some childish and murderous peregrination of revenge. All this is described in a peculiar, clumsy and archaic tone that symbolises Mr Grey's discomfort with modern reality.*

It is possible that Mr Grey embarked on his regrettable career armed at least with the romantic virtues, but without coordination or restraint they have passed into excess, lost proportion and ended in caricature. He writes for readers who want infantile mush, and because the public has been infantilised it is easy to make a fortune pandering to it.

I have heard people say that Mr Grey's type of story is wholesome, that he writes morality fables. Poppycock! These are tales of brutal men and pathetic women, which perpetrate outmoded ideas and instil ridiculous hopes in members of the moron class. An eye for an eye and a tooth for a tooth is the closest Mr Grey aspires to any form of morality! Look at where that has got the world!

Mr Grey, like my husband, is a hollow man. I once imagined that such unfortunate creatures were products of the Great War, but I was too generous. They are simply men whose luxuries and other advantages have forever debarred them from adulthood, who are frightened by seriousness, who refuse to engage with those things that make the world worthwhile.

I pity them, I fear the results of their vapid dreaming, and I gape in horror at a world which esteems them.

The article cannot be kept from Grey. As he reads it, his jaw locks and he flushes behind the bronze of his high cheeks. The atmosphere was already flattened by the unratified record and now it sours irreparably.

It is interesting that Grey does not seem crushed. He seems angry, as if this is another link in the same conspiracy that has seen the Captain catch his monster. Johnny is relieved. He's already dealing with a resentful Grey and he thinks a depressed one would be worse.

They are about to return to *Harlequin* when Grey demands to see where the tuna is being warehoused. It is an odd request and oddly sudden, but there is no obvious reason to deny him. The Captain and Johnny lead the way. Johnny feels certain that something is going on behind him, but he doesn't know what it is.

He is very tired – maybe he is starting to see things that aren't there. What has he imagined Henny into, for instance? Why does he want her to be more than an adventuress?

They complete the pointless inspection – Mitchell-Henry's warehouse is shipshape and secure, and the tunny lies on a bed of straw wrapped in wet blankets, several of which are further wrapped around blocks of ice – and make to leave for *Harlequin* again. Again Grey stops them.

'I need to send a letter home,' he says.

'Now?' Johnny is irritated.

'Now. It must be in a postbox tonight.'

Before Johnny can object, Henny announces that she will spend tonight with the Captain and his wife in Whitby. 'I fancy a change of scene,' she says. Johnny looks across at Grey, who shrugs back as if to say that Henny is not his problem any more. Grey's shrug is not convincing.

Johnny's innards shift. What can this mean? Henny cannot possibly be connected with the Sphinx, but— Oh! This thought gives him the solution. Molly Parker must have said something to her last night. Molly was presumably trying to be subtle and she underestimated Henny's powers of comprehension, and now Henny thinks that he and Molly are some kind of item, and Henny is angry.

It accounts for everything so neatly that he should have realised earlier today. He wants to grab Henny alone, to explain that Molly says a lot of things that aren't exactly true, that Molly doesn't understand the nature of her relationship with Johnny, but to do this would be unforgivably reckless. What if Henny bumps into Molly again and said something?

It is a salutary reminder that there are many things outside Johnny's control. He will try to protect Henny, he gave his word, but he cannot tell her the truth about himself, not yet.

Henny departs with the Mitchell-Henrys and the rest of the party returns with Grey to the hotel.

Johnny wants to walk alone, but Martha won't let him. 'Caro is awful, but isn't she right?' she says. 'Aren't we rather fiddling while Rome burns?'

'I suppose we are.'

'I was at the economic conference, you know.'

'You said.'

'Did I? Well, I ended up writing about the audience's hats because I couldn't concentrate on all the numbers. I can't presume to lecture anyone.'

'What did your French friends think of it all?' asks Johnny.

'France thought she had escaped the financial disaster, and now that she discovers she hasn't she's in a horrible mood. Everyone in Paris is looking for someone to blame.'

'Yes, well,' says Johnny. 'It's easy to be generous when you're not suffering. What are you like in the crisis?'

'Don't you think all the suffering and confusion might be an opportunity, though? Everything's gone to pot so that we can remake a better world, and so forth? You know? We can choose who we want to be, like Zane said?'

'We don't have that much choice.'

'I suppose, but the more I have thought about it, the less silly it sounds. You see—'

'We don't remake ourselves in a vacuum,' says Johnny.

'The past is always part of the egg basket, you mean? And other people, and what they want?'

That is exactly what Johnny meant, but he doesn't need this conversation. He says, 'You have to be careful with people when they're remaking themselves or they might go rotten.'

'Should we all be nice to the Germans, then? Or should we have been nicer before, and now it is too late?'

'I don't know,' says Johnny. He walks faster.

When they get back to the hotel, Grey goes inside to write his letter, Martha follows him and Johnny slips away to the terrace by himself.

The Sphinx has sent a message suggesting a summit tomorrow night, on the *Berania*, during Johnny's party. It's what he's been planning for. He must not be distracted.

Tuesday 4th September

Martha Gellhorn – Whitby

Letter to G. Campbell Beckett, ctd.

Well, darling, such frustration you never saw! I'm now on dry land, but we have not been able to weigh the Captain's tunny. The local scales are only accurate below 1,000 lbs, and the bigger ones at the railway station will only be manned in the morning.

I'm scratching this down in the lobby of the rather beautiful Royal Hotel in Whitby, at least partly as a way of escaping the poisonous atmosphere in the lounge. (Whitby is the country cousin, by the way, very neatly turned out, but not so brash and glamorous as Scarborough. I prefer it.)

Grey was furious from the moment he saw the Captain's fish, but matters got even worse and more awkward when we arrived here an hour ago to discover that the dreadful Caro has written about his books in *Time & Tide* (which I should perhaps note is a prestigious literary and cultural journal and not a set of numerical tables devoted to the restless ocean). She calls him a hack writer with bad taste who writes infantile books for infantile readers. It's awfully persuasive, and one feels in one's bones that she is right.

But, as we know, Caro is capable of persuading one of things that turn out to be untrue. I utterly believed what she wrote and implied about Johnny, for instance. How do you know who is grinding an ax and who is writing down reality as close as they can? All I can say, darling, is that I am trying to do the latter.

Anyway, even though Caro wrote her review to embarrass Johnny, what she said about Grey feels to me as if it might be a desperately ungenerous version of the truth, but true nonetheless.

Mike didn't help matters by bellowing that he wasn't a Jonah now, was he? Grey said that it was he, and he alone, who is jinxed by Mitchells. The Captain puffed himself up and said it was nothing to do with Mike, or Mitchells, or anyone else – it was just fishing. Grey was practically frothing. It was horrible and Johnny hurried matters to a close, saying that we'd return at seven tomorrow morning to see the tuna weighed. Grey complained that he would miss the first hour's fishing. Johnny asked if he would accept anyone else's assurances with respect to the tuna's weight, and Grey said, 'No.' In the Wild West that would be shooting talk, I imagine, but Johnny let it pass.

It was salutary to glance through the magazines in the lobby, darling, and the newspapers. We are fussing over these fish as if they are the only things in the world, and the papers write about them because they are jolly, but one looks at *The Times* and *The Sketch* and *Time & Tide* and one remembers that there was a life before this week, and one spent it in earnest discussion of gold and Herr Hitler. These are the realest and most important things. But one can't do anything about them, so is there any point in worrying? I don't know.

The more I look at Johnny through the glass doors, the more distant he seems from this fishing business. He has wider concerns and I don't know what they are. He's talking to Grey, and he is getting impatient. Now everyone is putting on their jackets. I suppose we are off to the *Dazzle*.

Still not on the *Dazzle*. I have copied anything that might be useful to *The Illustrated Thing* into my notebook and I will drop this letter into the box momentarily, but we have been on a quick and peculiar excursion and I have a few minutes to describe it while Grey pens a missive home, which, all of a sudden, cannot wait.

He thinks the world is against him and I feel sorry for him, I truly do. He's staring around while he scribbles, almost as if he expects someone to snatch his letter away from him. He's like a wild beast, wounded and alone. Does that sound absurd? I thought it might as

I was writing it down, but then I looked at him again and I stand by it.

The fuss earlier was that Grey had insisted on seeing the fish again. We trooped off, confused. On the way, Grey spoke to Marion. I don't know what he said, but Marion went white. Then Marion pulled Henny aside.

The upshot, my darling, is that mystery piles on intrigue. Grey is sending his packet home as a matter of absolute urgency and Henny is to stay with the Mitchell-Henrys in Whitby tonight. She claims to want a change of scene. There is clearly more to it, but I don't know what. She whispered at me not to worry, but I do. Perhaps she cannot bear to be around Johnny after seeing him with the other woman last night, but it didn't feel like that. She departed with her new hosts, and the rest of us walked back to the hotel.

I asked Johnny what he thought about the big things in the world, and whether we are fiddling while Rome burns, and he said that we probably are. He also said something good about how we remake ourselves in crises. The whole world is up against the wall, and different countries are doing different things about it. The French were very smug for a long time, but now that they are suffering, they are lashing out. And the last time they suffered, of course, during the war, they were utterly beastly afterwards. If A is beastly to B when B is suffering, what does that do to B?

Now I consider it, I am not sure whether Johnny was talking of France or of himself and, if he was talking of himself, was he talking about Caro or Henny? He is strung very tight.

Oh. Grey has finished wrapping his packet. The porter has stamped it, but Grey won't let it be posted by any hand other than his own, and so we're off to the box right now.

I am so tired that I doubt I am making sense,

Your Marty

Tuesday 4th–Wednesday 5th September

Henny Rosefield – Whitby

When Mitchell-Henry's tuna outweighed the scales at 1,000 lbs, Grey's face was savage. Martha whispered to Henny that bringing Grey to England to witness this day might almost class as sufficient revenge!

Walking to Mitchell-Henry's fishing shed, Henny watched Grey hiss at Marion, and Marion go pale. Grey showed Marion something from his satchel.

While the others reworshipped the leviathan, Marion whispered to Henny. Apparently Grey has a secret camera and he takes pictures of himself and his conquests in bed: did Henny know about this? Henny shook her head. Marion said Grey was going to post the film home right now, so as to protect his proof. If she didn't persuade her husband to say his fish was falsely caught, Grey would send the Captain copies of the photographs.

'Do you believe him?' asked Marion.

'Yes,' said Henny.

'Yes,' said Marion. 'So do I. There's no way I can persuade Laurie without telling him the truth. He'll protect my name, but it will be the end of the marriage.'

'I'm very sorry,' Henny said.

'It's not your fault,' said Marion after a tiny hesitation. 'There's nothing I can do, is there?'

Henny said, 'There's one thing, maybe, I think.'

Mitchell-Henry was surprised to be sharing his dinner table with Henny, but Marion explained that she and Henny had enjoyed each other's company last night and Henny was tiring of the *Dazzle*, and especially of Grey's attentions.

'Can't have been unexpected,' said Mitchell-Henry.

'It was, sir. I realise that sounds foolish, but I had a very sheltered upbringing.'

'Hm,' said Mitchell-Henry.

He talked about his fish, but not for very long. He talked about Johnny. He said the man was born lucky to a lucky family, but he'd made his own luck over the years – credit to him – and whatever you might say about him and his women, he'd never heard a good man say Caister wasn't straight-up. He asked whether the Gellhorn girl had set her cap at him.

Henny said she thought not. She said she thought Gellhorn a fine person, but restless and too concerned with an ideal of herself to be happy with a man she could not dominate, and too proud to accept a man she could.

'Deep stuff for the dinner table,' said Mitchell-Henry. 'This how you Americans always talk when you get together?'

'No, sir. I think I have been rather discombobulated by the atmosphere on the *Dazzle*. Gellhorn calls it a fairyland. I think there's something in that.'

'Yes,' said Marion.

'Hm. Even gladder I didn't come to Carstairs's bally dinner.'

'You would have liked it, darling,' said Marion. 'It was like the old days.'

'Hm. Don't suppose you believe her, Miss Rosefield, but I was rather fast when I was younger. Not as fast as Carstairs, of course.'

'Not quite that fast,' said Marion. 'But fast enough for me.'

'Hm. Things getting mushy. If there were another man, we'd run off to our cigars and talk cricket.'

'But you're trapped, darling.'

'Hm,' he said. 'Yes. Worse things happen at sea.' Suddenly he beamed. 'Big 'un, that fish,' he said.

Earlier, as they walked to the little house before dinner, Henny told Marion that they must arrange to spend the night in the same room. Marion said nothing could be easier. There was only one guest bedroom, with two beds, and Marion often left the Captain alone to snore. When she arrived in her nightdress at about eleven-thirty, Henny asked if she might borrow some old clothes, in case something happened to hers. Marion fetched a dark outfit, drew Henny a map in pencil and gave her Mitchell-Henry's keys. It was midnight.

Whitby was soft and grey. Henny saw hardly a light in the town. The shed-yard was shadowed only by the moon, all silver, no gold, but Henny found her way easily to the door and the lock snicked open smoothly. Earlier she had noted where the lamps were and she lit two of them.

She took the largest saw from the rack and cut the tuna's head off, just below the gills. The bed of hay was not as damp from the fish as she had feared, but there was nothing she could do to shift the wet towels from under it. She hacked them away as far as possible. She found the tins of oil and soaked the carcass and such other pieces of cloth as she could find. She did not know how long it would take to cook the fish to destruction. She left it smoking horribly while she gaffed its head, dragged it with difficulty down to the harbour and kicked it over the edge into the black water, softly lapping.

She returned to bed at five-thirty. Marion was beside herself. 'I thought you weren't coming back, I haven't slept!' she said. It was the second night she hadn't slept. Henny could hardly answer her. She was covered in soot and oil. Marion bundled up the clothes and said she would run a bath. It took Henny some time to get clean.

Wednesday 5th September

Martha Gellhorn – Whitby/Scarborough

Sept. 5th
Harlequin

G. Campbell,

The news, the news! It's a quarter to six in the morning and I am scribbling in the five minutes it will take us to reach the dock at Whitby. We anchored here last night ready for the great weighing, dined in a dazed mood and made plans to sleep until the unimaginably luxurious hour of 6.30 a.m., but twenty minutes ago the radio buzzed frantically to tell us that the Captain's warehouse has burned to the ground, tunny and all!

This explains last night's mysteries. By which, for clarity, I mean that it doesn't explain them, but it is surely connected to them in some way I do not yet understand. The fire must be related to Henny, but from the story she told me two nights ago, she favors the Captain over Grey. I'm certain she was telling me the truth. I hope she has not done something awful. I hope she is all right.

Oh, G. Campbell, I am here! I am here! It is a hellish scene, and it reeks. It is quite warm out of the breeze and I am seated on the floor, back against wall, sun on face, watching a small crowd scurry back and forth with serious mouths, even though everyone knows that nothing can be done. Yesterday this was a prim, fussy place – imagine a small New Hampshire barn from the hazy days of our disappearing youth, walls crammed with inexplicable pieces of cane and metal in meticulous order. The tunny was resting on a bed of hay under copious damp towels.

The shed, or barn, or whatever it is, has not in fact burned down – it is wrecked rather than destroyed. Everything is coated with unctuous grime. The tunny is ruined. Her size is still evident, but a fish must be whole to be weighed officially and her head is gone. It is surprisingly shocking. The towels around her are scorched to tatters. Apparently petrol or similar was used. Grey is overjoyed. He is trying to look otherwise, but he cannot dissemble.

The Captain is being rather impressive. He is the victim of fantastic malice, but he is not raving in the way I imagine Grey (or I!) would do under these circumstances. His first reaction, naturally, was to question Henny, but she has an alibi. The Captain snores so clamorously that Marion often spends her nights in the guest room, which she did last night, along with Henny. She barely slept and swears Henny never woke. The Captain trusts Marion absolutely.

The next suspect was Grey, obviously, but one of *Dazzle*'s crew is on watch at all times and no one left the yacht.

And so the Captain is left with his enemies in Scarborough. I'm looking at him now, bustling around. He is brisk and businesslike with the locals who have gathered to his aid. None of them saw anything, but they are all trying to think who in Whitby might have been awake and alert enough to notice anything, and what route an interloper might have taken, and which of the toffs might have put who up to it.

I took listless notes on the Captain's various feuds. This will all be marvelous color in *The Illustrated Whatsit* – 'The Fish That Never Was', and so forth – but I feel empty.

'Could Grey have paid someone to do it?' one said.

Johnny said he'd stake his reputation that Grey hadn't. Grey was barely out of his sight yesterday. It was inconceivable that he had been able to arrange such a thing.

The Captain accepted this too. Oh, wait, Johnny is coming over to me.

Johnny says the Captain has reacted so nobly because, deep in his soul, he believes the world is against him. Thus his reaction is one part stoicism, but also one part determination to go down fighting. He was born to huge riches, which his profligate father threw away, and although he is still in a comfortable and privileged position he has not had anything like the ease he might have expected, and despite his clear abilities and achievements he has nothing like the respect of his fellow men, either. The Captain can't see that he himself is to blame for this. (Grey also claims that the world is against him, of course, but in his case it is all on a silly and cosmic level, because in truth he has been incredibly lucky. The Captain's feelings are more understandable.)

Johnny is now talking to Henny, who is standing straight as a ballerina, perfectly calm. Johnny is calm too. The perfection of their mutual calm could light a fire, G. Campbell, if that is not, in the circumstances, an unfortunate image. He knows she is involved in this somehow, and he is livid. Maybe he even thinks that she is working for Grey, that she has been all this time, that she has deceived him. I cannot believe this is so, darling. I have to find out what has happened.

Ugh! A wave of stench hits me, reminding me that it is only a slightly stronger wave in a general miasma and that this is a depressing scene. I am going down to the waterside.

So, the whole awful affair is clear now. Henny found me on the front and explained everything. I shall scratch it down while it is fresh in my mind, before my righteous indignation twists it into something even worse.

(I have now come to Scarborough, by the way, where I will spend a brief period before heading to the *Dazzle*, where I shall ransack Grey's room. The others have embarked on a curtailed day of tunny-hunting.)

Yesterday Grey was already furious by the time we reached Whitby and Caro's article sent him over the edge. This does not forgive what happened next.

When he led us off to see the Captain's fish, it was to give himself the opportunity to speak to Marion. The famous satchel does indeed contain notebooks, as he says, but his protectiveness is not as funny as we thought. Instead of purple cowboy prose, the notebooks describe his women in intimate detail, and along with them is a packet of secretly taken photographs. Marion saw only one page and a couple of pictures, but these convinced her that Grey had taken photos of her as well. Marion realised that this explained his insistence on bright lights and the way he was so keen that certain acts took place in certain places. Henny and I both recognised this description uneasily and felt rather foolish at having had not the slightest suspicion. And we felt other things, as well, of course, though there is scarcely time for all that.

Pictures of Marion (along with ones of me and Henny, presumably) are on three camera films he showed her, which also travel in his bag.

Grey sent these films home last night – hence his determination to remain in plain sight until his precious package was safely on its way. He explained to Marion his terms for not sending copies to the Captain: Marion must convince her husband to withdraw any claim on his record, to say the fish was caught outside the rules, that he was assisted by Mike, or some such. Marion said this would be impossible. Grey said she must do so or else the Captain would learn the truth tomorrow, from Grey's mouth, before the weighing, and he would surely withdraw his claim then. Grey was giving Marion a chance to find another way, as a kindness to her.

Marion was desperate. She asked Henny whether she believed Grey would do it. Henny did. We managed to perceive that Grey was Pan-like, but we underestimated, as people do, that Pan is not just a merry boy. Grey cannot bear to be crossed in any way, and although he does not always have the power to do anything about it, Henny thinks he would be utterly cruel and destructive if he did have that power and it suited his ends.

Marion told Henny that there was no way to persuade her husband short of telling him the truth. The Captain would protect Marion's honor publicly and withdraw his claim, but the Captain lives his life in black and white and it would be the end of their marriage. Marion asked Henny if she could think of any escape.

Henny realised at once that the fish must be destroyed.

She told me this matter-of-factly, but she was looking out to sea, not at my face. She was angry and ashamed. She has ruined a decent, if difficult man's prize and pride. Marion is distraught, of course. It had to be done – a marriage is more important than a fish – but it was a wretched thing.

Maybe the marriage could have survived the revelation? Oh, darling, there is no point thinking like this. The fish is gone now. Perhaps the Captain could have overcome a night's infidelity, but surely not with Grey.

Henny feels desperate and I feel desperate for her. She had begun to open herself to the world, and immediately she saw Johnny kissing that woman, and the next moment Grey did this. I fear she will withdraw from everything again.

Without revealing all the details of her life, I think it will help you to know that she originally pursued Grey in order to annihilate him, and then she decided not to, and now he has done this and she feels responsible, which of course she is not.

But what does 'annihilate' mean? She certainly did not intend to kill Grey. She thought of trying to break his heart, but he has a heart that will heal itself rapidly. While Henny was looking for some other way to punish him, she came to pity him. But if every time Grey is spared or pitied he does something appalling, then is the right course of action not to put him down like a wild animal that has gone rogue? It is not right to talk that way about a human being, darling, and it is not what I mean exactly. I apologize for constantly describing him as wild, animalistic and an embodiment of primeval nature, but once one has started thinking it, it dominates one's understanding of him.

I want my words to be pitiless and precise, like bullets, and to describe the very quiddity of things – Grey is a man, a tuna is a fish and so forth – but if my mind honestly perceives one as a wild beast and the other as a symbol of man's unquenchable need to challenge himself against nature, then how are these things not as 'real' as anything else I observe?

Grey is a man, and one cannot put him down like a dog. And the wrongs he does are so silly and childish that more sensible moralities hardly apply. Except, of course, he is not a child. He is a responsible moral actor. But would he understand punishment? Would it change him? If it would not, is one not taking a petty vengeance that will only lead him to do worse in the future?

This is exactly what I thought when I was speaking with Johnny about how we must try to treat each other kindly in a crisis. If you have been living in Europe you see very clearly how dangerous it is to revenge yourself on people just because they have been wicked.

The upshot, my dear, is that I barely know how to proceed. The Captain, once it was clear that nothing more would be achieved by staring at his fish, turned a brisk face to seaward and said it was time to stoop and pick up his worn-out tools – or some of Johnny's tools, if he may, since his own are blistered and caked in tunny-soot. He suggested that they set straight off to catch an even bigger fish. Johnny fell over himself to lend tackle, the best he had.

Grey tried to complain that all Johnny's tackle should be retained for his sole use. He didn't get very far. Next, Grey tried to forbid Mike from rowing out with the Captain, since he was obviously a Jonah in one boat and a rabbit's foot in the other. As I say, one watches Grey do things like this and finds him comic, and then one remembers again.

And so off they went. I said I wanted to speak to people in Scarborough for my article and couldn't face another day at sea. This, as you will have surmised, is a ruse. Henny and I have the beginnings of a plan.

Grey keeps his satchel with him at all times and we must learn what is in it, to see if we can find some material to employ against him. Henny will try to get hold of it today. While they are aboard the *Harlequin*, I shall squirm into Grey's cabin somehow. He takes such care of the satchel that one doubts there is anything incriminating left behind, but I might at least learn how he takes his photographs.

We simply *must* manufacture some grip over him. What if the

Captain were to catch another fish today? The whole business with Marion would be repeated in glorious Technicolor and it would be too unbearable for words. Grey might be impossible to punish effectively, but he will likely understand blackmail.

So where does all this leave me? For instance, it has not escaped me that the Captain's fish, because its official weight was never written down, has become suddenly unreal in some way. To write a thing can indeed make reality; to keep it from being written down can destroy it utterly.

Oh, G. Campbell! I do see how fantastical all this must seem to you. My life has become some form of high pathetical romance, as if I am being written by Edgar Wallace multiplied by John Buchan. All I can say, I suppose, is that such adventures are less incredible than I always imagined them being. One gets up in the morning and lives as if one were a dragonfly and by the time one has done so for a week, one has found oneself in a hundred implausible positions. A skillful psychological novelist has no need for all this flapping about, I am sure, and sees the world in a grain of sand, and can write all about the inner lives of humdrum sorts of farmers, but as it so happens, that is not the life of any of these people here, and nor is it the life I have led. I was the wife – in all but name – of Colette's Chéri, and I have been paraded by Schiap and courted by princes, and now I am in a gilded aquarium surrounded by magnates and dope-fiends whose lives make mine look like that of a dullish type of deep-sea squid. I feel in my pampered bones the need to write about the more usual sort of life, the struggle and the dirt of it, the battle to free one's forehead from the heel of one's birth-appointed oppressor, but I would desperately resent anyone who says my life isn't real. I am here. It is the only life I have. It is privileged, no doubt; it is different from most lives; but it is as real as all get-out.

An unbecoming whine with which to sign myself off. I am still half-in and half-out of Fairyland and that will never do. I must make a decision and grab hold of my story one way or the other. I shall plop this into a box and hail a horny-handed harborman to haste me to the *Dazzle*. I hope I do not disgrace myself as a criminal. I still, astonishingly, do not hate Grey, but I am so angry with him that I could scream.

Love, as always,

Desperate Marty McGraw

Wednesday 5th September

John Fastolf, Earl of Caister – Whitby

When Johnny sees the destruction in the shed-yard, he knows he has some time before they set off for the day's fishing. He sends Patterson to Scarborough to see if there are any messages.

The tuna was obviously Henny – he doesn't know how she suborned Marion – but it makes no sense. It can't possibly be related to anything Molly Parker told her. That would have made Henny want to revenge herself on him, not on Mitchell-Henry.

She said she had originally wanted to destroy Grey, but is she actually attached to him in some psychopathological fashion, and her whole performance towards Johnny has been about making Grey jealous? That only fits if she has a split personality. Do such maladies exist outside of books? Johnny doesn't think they do.

He doesn't have enough information. Suddenly, surprising himself, he clenches his fists.

Even in the face of what Henny has done, Johnny cannot get out of his head the idea that she is a fine girl who needs to be rescued. This is patronising and idiotic, and utterly out of keeping with the man Johnny has had to become. *Has* become. He didn't *have to* become anyone. But he became who he is, and there it is. He doesn't consider himself a bad man, but he has wandered terribly far from the flock.

And this is the thing: two nights ago, with Henny and then after she had gone back to her cabin, he honestly felt as if he might be capable of renewal. For a moment, even, he wondered if it might be possible to re-examine these past few years. He can't undo what he has done, but he is a very rich man. Maybe there is a way to make some restitution.

The same thought recurred yesterday when he spoke with Martha about using a crisis to rebuild. There is something in the idea that he wants to catch hold of and use, but his affairs are so encumbered, especially today, that he cannot get near enough to it.

It is clear that his crisis, if that is the right word, has been triggered, at least in part, by the girl. He likes her because— Well, he likes her very much. But, to repeat, this is the last feeling of all his feelings that he can trust—

He clenches his fists again. He has been deliberating about this irrelevancy for twenty minutes! Given what he must plan for this evening, this is all but suicidal. Henny cannot be his focus. She has made her choice and he washes his hands of her. She must go her own road to perdition.

Which evil acts are justified by good ends? Johnny no longer knows. He has let Miss Pink decide for both of them.

When Miss Pink was told there was no place for her in the post-war intelligence service, she did not accept the situation. She surprised Mansfield Cumming – not the easiest thing to do, incidentally – in a Lyons Tea Room on the Holloway Road in early 1920 and made him a proposal. She knew that his budget had been cut. What if she were able to recruit and fund a small unit, answerable only to Cumming, Kell and their parliamentary masters? This unit – she named Johnny at this point, whose money made the whole thing possible – would have certain advantages over its unacknowledged partners in the Service. It would be flexible, and deniable, and it would be able to operate in murky waters.

C, after some thought, agreed to a trial. It was just the kind of show that appealed to him. The trial was successful. Cumming's gone now, of course, but the new C was happy to keep the unit active. Johnny has been largely able to dissociate himself from its more morally ambiguous actions, until this operation.

For nearly two years now, he and Miss Pink have been running a dope ring. Innocent people, more or less, have been destroyed by the cocaine and heroin he has sold them. It has taken so long partly because the Sphinx's identity was well guarded, but mostly because they needed to untangle their enemy's operation entirely in order to eliminate it, right to the roots. It is almost done now. All that is left – almost all – is to draw the Sphinx into this meeting.

The coincidence of tonight's meeting and Johnny's party is not a coincidence. He knew perfectly well that a large shipment of dope would be delivered this evening. He hoped that if he winkled Joe away from the *Berania* the dope might be delivered there, and so it has transpired. It will be easier to deal with everything on a yacht than in some hotel full of bystanders. All the same, it must not appear as if Johnny foresaw the time and place, and so he sent a message to the Sphinx pretending that tonight would be inconvenient and asking if there might not be an alternative.

It is a complicated ploy to lure out a complicated villain. Not a superman, but a careful enemy. The multiple lives, the lies-on-lies, that Johnny has lived the past years have rotted him as surely as any smashed heart or the horrors of the front. If you're never who you are, you stop being anyone.

Patterson motors to a halt in a spray of grit. And here is the Sphinx's reply, on heavy, beige paper in a fine hand.

Lord Caister [it reads], *I am still prepared to treat with you, but the time and place are fixed. I imagine that you have by now heard of a minor misfortune that befell my Kensington factory. You may believe this means I shall be negotiating from a position of weakness. Be very assured that this is not the case. I do not negotiate from such positions.*

It shall be the Berania, and it shall be tonight. You will have to leave your guests to their own devices. We both know that you are not a gentleman.

I look forward to our meeting.

There is another message, this one in Molly Parker's loopy, excitable script:

Darling Johnny,

Something is happening! Kiki has just told me that we mustn't come to your party tomorrow night!! We must pretend to be sick (I will be sick with fear about what you are doing with that American girl!!) because we have to deal with <u>your meeting</u> on board the Berania, and only very few people can be trusted at the moment!! I am one of the Sphinx's most trusted people!!

<u>You Know Who</u> is <u>definitely</u> here <u>himself</u>!! The reason is there is going to be a dope delivery and he was going to be here anyway! Joe and Ruth (and stupid Lapwing) won't be coming back to the yacht after dinner because they are being motored down to London overnight to fly to Nice the next day. It is so clever. All the crew have been given the evening off except for one person to look after the boat, and Kiki says that the Berania's crew member is One Of Us. But how are you going to leave your party! Does this mean the meeting will be off??

Kim is here and the Sphinx is here. Coincidence?! You know what I think! I bet he doesn't come to your party for some suspicious reason! I am going to try to get into his room before I come back to the Berania tomorrow night. I can easily sneak around a hotel as you well know. I <u>will</u> find proof! If I can, this will all be over and we will be free to love!

Can you come? It is impossible, isn't it!

Desperate love,

Molly x

Before Johnny returns to the *Harlequin*, he writes Molly a note telling her to be careful, and not under any circumstances to enter Kim's rooms – it would be an unnecessary risk. He writes that he will do everything he can to be there tomorrow night, but that if he isn't, please will she play her part with the ultimate care? Be a good soldier. Follow orders. Report back to him afterwards. He writes to the Sphinx to say that, very well, he shall be on the *Berania*, somehow.

Then it's time to go fishing.

Wednesday 5th September

Mike Mitchell-Hedges – The North Sea

Sept. 5
Bloody Coracle

Dear Jane,

I know I posted one to you only yesterday morning. Don't worry, not losing my mind or getting sentimental. Scribbling to stay awake.

Hard to bloody believe it's only been a day. I'm tired as a dog. I'm writing this on the bloody old *Spurwing* as we steam out to the tunny-grounds at the unaccustomedly late hour of ten o'clock. Does this mean I have had a good night's sleep? Does it buggery!

I fished with the Captain yesterday, thanks to Grey's stupid bloody paranoia. Odd bunny, the Captain. Raised in fabulous wealth, which I didn't realise. Full of schemes, sounds like a crackpot, but actually quite practical – inventions and whatnot. Doesn't get where he should in life because he can't see that sometimes you have to take unfair things as they are. He's one of those chaps with a thin skin and an iron sense of justice, and he operates as if the world will somehow bend to righteousness in the end. It's as if he's never looked out of the window, read a newspaper or seen a war.

As we laboured out to sea, he described his various spats with Grey and the Wise Men of the Scarb. Tunny Club. It is clear that the Captain is generally, largely, in the right. But he's in the right about small things that aren't worth arguing about, and then when other perfectly decent men, who aren't in the wrong, try to mollify the situation, he goes after them too – he won't tell the little white inevitables that lubricate the daily round. He's frustrated with a world that's kicked him, but it's damned foolish. He hasn't fallen out with Caister only because their fathers were chums. The difference: Caister's father added pot after pot to his pots and pots; the Captain's threw all his pots down the crapper.

The litany got damned dull after an hour, and continued as we got a toot from a nearby herringer, beat the *Harlequin* to the roiling waters, climbed into the coracle and were lowered to the sea, and it didn't let up for the next forty minutes, at which point I was contemplating the prospect of another seven hours with horror. And then, wonderful to relate, the man finally hooked a fish. I'd started to think my book was in peril. Colonel Ashton and Vera Broughton have been hauling tunny out of the North Sea like goldfish from a pond, so we knew the beggars were out here, and when Lady Broughton latched on to another five minutes after she wet her line, the Captain was almost fit to burst, but a jiffy later his own reel started squealing.

I've not got time or energy to describe the derring-do right now, but I'll write it up into a struggle to beat them all, and I'll barely have to sugar the tea to do it. Three hours it took, and the damned creature even breached a couple of times to show us what a monster it was. As soon as we clapped eyes, we knew it was the record and it wasn't close. The Captain's face went grim, and even I started taking the thing deadly seriously. Apart from anything else, it was one in Grey's eye! Call me a Jonah, will you? I'll have fun with that!

We got Leviathan boatside, with the Captain shouting out rules and regulations like a demented parrot lest any transgression cost him his prize, then hung around for hours while Grey failed to emulate us, and ferried the fish in triumph back to Whitby, where the scales couldn't handle it, so we arranged to return this morning to the bigger ones at the railway. The girl Henny stayed on shore with the Captain and his wife, which seemed rum last night and seems rummer now. Caister was suspicious straight off. First she wanted him, then she cast him off, now this. Unknown forces were bashing each other around somewhere under the surface, and I thought to myself that I didn't trust Miss Rosefield a fragment more than I had in New York.

I was bloody right, because this morning was all panic, palaver, hide in the halls, for the wolves have grown wings! We were rent from our slumbers with the news that the Captain's fishing shed had been torched and his tunny was ruined. Grey was on the *Dazzle* all night. Marion says she was in Henny's room because the Captain was snoring and she swears the girl never moved. God knows what the pair of them got up to together, but the Captain has taken his wife's word for it like a gentleman. Dread to imagine what he'd think if he knew about her and Grey. He blames the Scarborough lot, and he might be right at that.

The Captain was impressive, I have to admit. He didn't rant or rave. He's a fool to himself for not letting the small injustices pass when it would do him some good to, but he didn't trudge to bed and weep. As soon as it was clear there was nothing to be done, he hired some local boys to clean up and said we'd missed enough fishing time already. So here I am again, in the bloody coracle. It's a bright day. Ten more minutes of this and we'll let the keel take us back over to—

Another fish for the Captain! Respectable, but not a giant and only took forty-five minutes. Fish deposited with *Spurwing*.

Vera Broughton and Colonel Ashton have each hooked big 'uns today, by the way. They've been scornful of our poor efforts, given all the ballyhoo, but they changed their tune yesterday. Now they shout over that they were horrified to hear about the fire, and I think they're telling the truth.

The Captain, every time you name a Scarborough notable who might be involved in the sabotage, refuses to believe it of a fellow angler. The only one he's prepared to entertain any suspicion of is Hardy, whom he hates as a competitor in his damned tackle business. All's fair in love and commerce.

Bloody Hardy appears every time you turn a corner, incidentally. Never met a bugger so keen to be paid for stuff he's sold you. Luckily, Grey owes him a pile more than I do. Hardy keeps asking Grey if he's caught a marlin. Shouldn't find it funny.

Staring at the *Harlequin* all day is enough to drive a fellow mad. You never know which way she's going.

Enough for now.

Further thrills, young feller! I don't know whether to be delighted or enraged.

Couple of hours ago the Captain needed a widdle and offered me twenty minutes on the rod. He didn't really want to, but he knew it was the decent thing. The decent thing on my part would have been to refuse. Fat chance of that.

(Grey never let me touch a line on the *Harlequin*.)

Well, for the second time in three days, our party hooked twice in a minute. First, Grey got on to a fish, God rot him! Almost immediately my own rod thumped into life. The tunny is a strong brute, a more dead-weight, bruising kind of fighter than a marlin. He dived and strove, and I damn near had him to the boat-side when he charged off towards the *Harlequin*, which was a couple of hundred yards to windward. He'd breached and I could see he was fair-sized, but no better. Still, I wanted his picture for the flyleaf, didn't I just!

As he charged, Grey's fish, which he had been playing to the other side of the *Harlequin*, circled towards us at a furious rate. There was all kinds of shouting from him for me to unhook, but I was damned if I would. It happened fast, but also with a ghastly inevitability. The fish crossed each other, dragged for a moment, and then both lines sheared away.

There was nothing to be done. Sometimes two forces collide, and there's nothing exactly evil about them, but the results are hideous and all that's left is to apportion blame. I should have been the one to unhook, since he was on first, but the rules on the open water are hardly bloody clear and the thing happened too quickly for sea-lawyering. And I'm not a bloody saint, as well you know. The Captain, punctilious as he is, didn't tell me to unhook, either. Nobody's perfect. God, I'm tired.

It's five. We're in the hotel in Whitby again. Caister and the Captain are off somewhere ensuring that today's fish doesn't get damaged. Grey hasn't joined them and he's glaring at me from the other end of the room. We are by no means on speakers. He doesn't even want to let me board the *Harlequin* back to Scarborough. Caister's having none of that, thank God. Only one day's fishing to go now, and we've had enough fish to make the book, so anything else is gravy. I'm pretty sure Grey's lost fish today was smaller than the Captain's, which weighed in at 670 lbs, which was more than I expected. Grey's pretending I cost him a giant, predictably.

He's also saying we tricked him by making him fish from the *Harlequin*. All around him people are catching tunny from rowing boats, so that's obviously the only way to do it in these waters, he says. Caister points out: a) that's what everyone told Grey, and what he came to England to prove wrong, isn't it? And b) didn't Grey just claim he caught a 'giant' from *Harlequin* today? Caister is losing patience with Grey, but Grey is long past hearing sense. He insists that tomorrow he will also fish from a rowing boat. Caister offered the Captain the use of the *Harlequin*, if Grey wasn't using it. Grey cried foul. The Captain said he didn't mind, he was happy in his coracle. Grey's a bloody child.

None of the local lads, or the police, have come up with any information re the fire. It has to be something to do with Henny and, the more I think of it, it has to be something to do with Grey. I'm just too exhausted to work it out. I've got to get ready for the ridiculous bloody party tonight.

Did I write about the ridiculous bloody party already? Probably did, but have no memory of it or any other bloody thing, so here goes again:

The night we arrived in London and Caister jumped feet-first into this shindig – God knows what we'd have done without him because tunny-hunting is a dashed expensive business – we ran across Caister's vicious little bitch of a wife and her slippery-voiced companion, a bad 'un called Waring. He's the sort of thing civilisation can't help throwing up now and again, which is why the whole show will probably fall apart, and good riddance. Caro Fastolf is a beauty, and she might have been shown a better way if she'd been caught young, but Caister was too soft to do it. By which I mean, since he's not soft, he was too good or too besotted. He wouldn't treat her like she needed treating, but would have slain anyone who threatened her honour. He's well rid of her, if he is rid of her, and she's welcome to Waring. The pair of them don't show up on the humbug scale, young feller, they're curdled milk.

They've come up to Scarborough to cause trouble, I assume. Caister is giving a dinner for Carstairs and her crew – always repay in kind if you're a gentleman – and Caro and Waring will be there too, which has sent Grey into his latest batch of conniptions, because Caro wrote a bloody funny dissection of his florid oeuvre in some London mag. He says he won't leave his cabin while she's on the boat. He seriously thought this might persuade Caister to disinvite them. Grey is the most ludicrous optimist. In fact, I wonder if that isn't his defining characteristic.

Caister returns. He's outside in the sun. He's spent the week looking unnaturally fresh, but he doesn't now. He looks dead drawn. Could be about tonight. Could be about the Captain's burnt fish. He stood umpire and there's been dark-dealing, and he doesn't like it. He especially doesn't like that Henny is hard to exonerate. Bet he wishes he hadn't tumbled her.

Looking at him again, actually, something's up. Must go. Thank you for keeping me awake. Not for the first time.

Wednesday 5th September

Henny Rosefield – Whitby / The North Sea / Robin Hood's Bay

Henny took a last look at the burnt, decapitated fish and then she, Johnny and Grey walked, together and not together, down to the *Harlequin*.

As they headed out into the morning sun, Miss Scarlett brought her a mug of coffee. She looked worried. She asked if Henny was all right. Henny said, 'Not really.'

'You didn't want to burn her, did you?' said Miss Scarlett. 'How did he make you do it?' Henny said nothing. 'I'm sure it wasn't your fault, but don't be a fathead today. We can fix it when this other stupid thing is finished.'

'The competition?' Henny asked.

A fraction of silence and then Miss Scarlett said, 'Yes, the competition.'

Despite the coffee, Henny could hardly stay awake long enough to get down to the bunk in the cabin, where she stayed for two hours. She was woken by a commotion on deck and she emerged to see *Spurwing* take possession of a fish from the Captain.

Grey said that this was the last straw; that they had raced away from that precise fishing spot moments before the Captain hooked; that Johnny was conspiring with Mitchell-Henry, and this was the proof. He said, 'I decide where we fish from now on.'

Johnny said, 'You have decided where we fish since the start of the contest. If you do not improve your behaviour, this will change.'

Grey bemoaned his luck again, and said he had been doomed as soon as Johnny filled his boat with women. Everyone knew women were bad medicine. Johnny told him to calm down. It was Grey who had brought Henny and who had fished with women for years; and Vera Broughton over there was pulling her umpteenth tunny of the week from the cold, dark sea. Grey opened his mouth to protest, and Johnny said, 'Grow up.'

Before Grey could object again, his rod twitched. As he grabbed it, it bucked. He let off a whoop and tightened his buckles. His satchel was stuffed underneath his coat below the chair.

Moments later there was a similar whoop from Mitchell-Henry's boat. Mitchell-Hedges was also onto a fish. They were only a couple of hundred yards away. 'Tell him to cut loose,' said Grey. 'Tell him.'

'Mr Grey thinks you should cut loose, Mike!' called Johnny.

'Bugger him!' was Mitchell-Hedges's reply.

'Tell him!' grunted Grey, straining at his rod.

'I told him,' said Johnny and sat down to talk with Patterson. Grey was furious. Henny, for a moment, was unscrutinised. She snagged the satchel's strap with her toe, slipped it stealthily towards her and snuck it downstairs.

The satchel was locked. She cut through its strap with a sharp knife from the tackle-box by the door. It contained a folder and two black notebooks. She took these to the lavatory and bolted herself in.

The folder contained some thirty pictures. A few were of her. They had been taken in America. She wasn't always blindfolded, not in the ones in Grey's lodge. She did not know how Grey had taken them, what arrangement he had. Maybe even an assistant. None of the photographs were from this trip, none were of Gellhorn and Marion. It would have been impossible for Grey to have had pictures like these developed by someone he did not know.

She did not find the pictures exciting. Several women, including Brownie and herself, were posed by Grey in exactly the same way, for a fixed camera. The pictures looked mechanical, which was surprising. There had seemed nothing mechanical about the experience.

She turned to the notebooks. She looked for her name. The first time she went to Grey's room, he had written, 'HR after dinner !! Type 3, pinker than average. Size normal. Grip disappointing. Warmth average. Smell stronger than average, but not unpleasant. Hair less than average. 2x. 2nd much better, poss relaxation. No pictures. Kifoozled 1x. HR is eager and naturally able. Expect quick improvement. Expect kifoozling will lead to kamibbling.'

The next entry he said 'Grip' was improved and there was 'kamibbling', as expected. Her kamibbling was 'poor', but 'probably result of inexperience'. Her 'eagerness/curiosity' were 'extremly promising'. By the time they were aboard the *Majestic* she was 'v improved, nearly in the Ackerman class, and not yet jaded/complacent. Quite unlike BB. Delightful. Almost resonant of LA, but needs less direction. Responds more fully. (Noise average.)'

Then, a few days ago: 'On Dazzle. HR refuses me.' Then, the next night, 'HR refuses me again. In enemy country. Has this has all been a trap? Possible HR may be in cahoots with Caister, who is OLD FRIEND OF M-HENRY! Explains speed of her improvement (was deceiving me at first!), explains eagerness for me to reject BB, who has always been the girl I truly love. Also explains infernal luck on this trip. Will I never stop being too trusting?'

Then Gellhorn. He wrote she had 'superb grip' (she was a 'Type 2', whatever that meant). She was 'excellent taught' and an 'outstanding kamibbler'. She was also the 'hardest kifoozle that ever I had'. This was 'surprising' in light of kamibble as 'almost impossible to give adeptly if you do not know how to take. Peculiar girl. Needs further experimentation. Interested to see face in pictures. (Continue pleased with operation of typewriter case.)'

Grey's notes on Marion were written in closer to longhand. 'Very intriguing and unexpected. My motive = dislike of M-Henry. Presume hers also. Have not experimented with female older than 30 for two decades (DG apart). Skin feels different. Had not considered this and do not notice it with DG. (Familiarity? Other explanation?) Presume my skin must be similar. Drier and more fragile. Less rubbery. Type 3, I think, but age has effect and makes me uncertain. Grip satisfactory, smell almost non-existent. Eagerness to be satisfied extreme, and extremely satisfying, especially in kifoozling. Almost silent and think this not just because of boat. Eagerness to satisfy in return felt dutiful at first, but extremely skilful + sensitive to response, surprising given presumed fidelity to M-Henry. If this level with little practice, then imagine would quickly reach Ackerman class and perhaps long-suspected new class. Atmosphere very different to that with younger girls. Subject of M-Henry raised by me, and set aside emphatically by her. Not raised by me again. But conversation not stilted. Relaxing. Partly result of drink, presumably. Overall experience: found self less focused on moving through schedule, and more focused on enjoying whole. Unlike prev. night with Gellhorn, did not insist on sleep in preparation for morning. Could not resist continuing. Unsure as to why, unless novelty (?). In morning, unusually, do not regret this. Originally allowed her into my cabin with intent of telling M-Henry. Will not do so. This may be new dawn for me/moment of maturation. True Love? Will winning her from M-Henry be my real competition?! New country triumphs over old!!'

Henny flicked back through the pages to look for Brownella Baker.

There was a heavy knock on the door. 'It's Caister. Grey says you have his satchel. Give it back.'

'Do you know what's in it?'

'I don't care. He's my guest. I haven't time for this.' She hesitated, then took a page to rip it out.

Caister broke down the door. Henny snapped the diary shut, clutched it to herself.

'Give it to me,' he said. 'Right now.' She sat, holding it. 'What is it?' he asked.

'I can't tell you.' He reached to take it, she crossed her arms over it. 'You can't read it,' she said.

'What's happening, Henny?'

'I can't tell you.'

For the time it took to take in a breath, his body rippled stiff and then back to soft, and the veins on the back of his roll-sleeved arm pulsed. Then, steadily, he said, 'Give it to me, and stop this, whatever you're doing. I offered you my protection, you didn't take it; that's your choice, but you will stay out of my way. I don't have the time to look after you people. Caro is here tonight, with the rest of them. That is all I can deal with. Do you understand me?'

'Yes.'

'No, you don't. But give me the bloody satchel.' He took it and walked straight back onto the deck.

At least Grey lost his fish.

They headed back to Whitby in near-silence. Grey knew now that Henny was his enemy and hugged the satchel close. Miss Scarlett wanted to talk to Henny, to find out what was happening, but Johnny was so clearly furious with Henny that Miss Scarlett couldn't do it. Patterson quietly finished his book and started another.

On shore, Grey went to the hotel while Johnny and the Captain weighed today's fish and locked it up securely. Patterson and Miss Scarlett sped off in Johnny's roadster. Marion Mitchell-Henry was waiting for them by the scales and took a step towards Henny, but Henny gave a tiny shake of her head. Marion understood. She looked worried and joined her husband.

The police had no idea who might have torched yesterday's fish.

Mike and Henny wandered to the hotel bar to wait for Johnny and the others. Mike joked about the apocalyptic potential of the coming evening's festivities. Henny didn't want to talk and so she left Mike with Grey – it was an uncomfortable atmosphere even though they were twenty yards apart – and went back outside. She braced herself against the wind, her hands on the white-painted railings, looking out to sea with the sun on her back.

Johnny took a long while to arrive. When he did, it was a quarter to seven and she was cold. He walked in a near-facsimile of his normal elastic cadence, but there was something disconnected and vacant, as if he had been replaced with an astonishingly skilful marionette. He was ashen.

She ran over to him and Mike hurried out of the door. Something in Johnny attempted to smile and— What? Whatever calm impression he wished to convey cracked before it got anywhere. He caught the crack before it split his face entirely and he said, 'Well. Yes. Ah.' He had to gather himself. 'Sorry to say— I'm sorry. Car crash. Miss Scarlett and Patterson, er, well, they're— They've been— Well, you know. Both of them, just like that, "Oh Death, where is thy sting" and all that sort of picnic. Should be used to it by now. But, ah— I should be used to it. Well, anyway. Bit of a shock.'

Henny stepped towards him and he recoiled.

'No, no,' he said. 'That won't do. Not at all. We'd better get back to the boat and dress for dinner, what?'

Henny looked at Mike. He didn't know what to make of it, either.

Wednesday 5th September

Martha Gellhorn – Scarborough

September 5th, 1934
Dazzle

G. Campbell, dearest,

I should make a terrible burglar, you will be delighted to hear, and I am back in my cabin empty-handed.

When I arrived, Miss Pink demanded the full story of the Captain's disaster. I told her only the publicly accepted version. She knew that I was being circumspect and gave me a look implying that I was a favored but grievously disappointing niece. This would have been catastrophically effective in my youth, but I have disappointed so many good people in the last five years that I have grown a skin that would shame a crocodile. I felt like a horror all the same.

I removed myself on the pretext of needing a rest and twenty minutes later I was in Grey's cabin. His secret camera is attached to the inside of his typewriter case. It was on the obvious shelf, given how he positioned me at various points. I feel such a chump.

There is a small hole for the lens, and in the case is a coil of wire which runs to a rubber bulb that can be operated at a distance. A small lever can be poked through a slit in the outside of the case and attached to the camera itself – I am almost certain that this is a winding mechanism that can be pulled quickly whilst a blindfolded or otherwise distracted subject is unaware.

There were no films in the case. I considered throwing the thing overboard, but there is no sense in putting Grey on his guard until we have definitely gathered material with which to blackmail him, if we need to.

My next target was Grey's portable writing desk, which is very fine. It can rest on a table, but also on the knees of a sitting man or on the belly of a reposing one. I rather covet it. I contains two unfinished letters.

I felt like a sneaking rat reading these, but sneaking and ratting were what I was there for, after all. The first letter was to the girl he cast aside for Henny. Her name is Brownie Baker.

The Old, Dead World
September 4th

Dear Brownie, Dearer to Me than Life,

No doubt you realize by now that I fled from you because the love we share was so feverish and strong, so elemental and furious, that I feared it might unmoor me. As you understood, and as you warned me, this fear made me vulnerable to the clever tongue of a quiet, spiteful girl who seemed to offer me safe harbor and calm waters.

But the world's waters are not calm, and I should anyway have remembered that I have ever been more at home in the tempest. You are young, you are a Being of the Modern World, which is a world I cannot hide from. Just as I would be able to chart you a course through peril and maelstrom anywhere in the five oceans, so you can guide me through this maelstrom that is Modernity, this seascape of shifting shoals and hidden banks, no less treacherous in this rancid little country with its phony antiquity than it was in Manhattan.

I need you. I am beset from every side by half-humans whose very souls have corroded and been remanufactured into snaggled things with no constancy or natural impetus. You, although your heart is an organ of pure and unfettered impulse, would be able to understand them. You are pagan and yet you are sophisticated, you are the thing I have waited my life for, and it has taken my very self to be scarified on the world's edge to understand that great verity.

I feared you for your modernity, but I was wrong. Someone young who is not modern cannot be honest in their heart. I need you as a dying man needs water, as no man ever needed a woman to complete him in his wandering and his loneliness.

You know me so truly. You know that this is the outpouring of my deepest well of truth in the words that best fit those feelings. I cannot help the way I see the world, that I think a man is different from a woman, that I think right is a different thing from wrong, and that I am prepared to say so clearly, to describe the endless battle between them, and that I write in grand old-fashioned words because they seem to me the most real and I do not see why I should not, when millions have thrilled to read them.

I have only two more days of this torment to survive, and then I will return. My dreams are all of kifoozling you, and they are such dreams as I will dream in Elysium . . .

The letter is the most dreadful, undignified guff you ever heard and if Miss Brownie Baker can stand it, then she deserves him. I understood absolutely what Caro wrote about how concerned you can feel for your fellow human beings when you encounter something this inane and remind yourself that it appears to be what the public demands. The public does not read Grey's mooning self-pity, of course, but the thought that the writer who produced it has sold more books to the American public than any twenty people you can name drives one to despair.

Because of my foolishness the letter is still in Grey's cabin, but certain passages are carven into my brain, and I wish they weren't. He says that he only left Brownie and America because he was frightened of the strength of his feelings, because she was sophisticated and pagan, where all his life he had found himself making love to the delicate and refined. Only now does he understand that hers is the love he has been building toward all his life, that his poor words shall never be able to catch a fraction of his strange and splendid passion. Also, he dreams of 'kifoozling' her. He really does. I can imagine what this means and I am very glad he never used the word in my presence. Perhaps, as one of the delicate and refined ones, he thought I would be shocked at such racy language.

He proceeds in this fashion for a page or two, and is clearly driving toward a final passage wherein he will beg her forgiveness.

The other letter was more interesting. It is to his wife. He started it just after we got back from storing the Captain's giant tuna in its shed yesterday. Reading what he wrote, knowing that he had secretly engineered the fish's destruction, made me furious, G. Campbell, beyond almost any fury I have ever felt.

Scarborough
September 4th

Dearest Dolly,

I am sorry for the hasty end to the last, long letter, posted safely an hour ago with its precious and dangerous package. Keep it safe for me, and never ask me why, or what it is.

I must swallow my pride and admit that you and Brownie were right and I have been deceived by Henny. My openness was my downfall, as has so often been the case. What I have only come to realize out here, out on the edge of the world, is that I was vulnerable to Henny because I was running away from my feelings for BB. Brownie is so different from all the others, so modern and daring, and my feelings for her were (and are) so furious and frightening that I listened to Henny's voice simply because it seemed quiet, old-fashioned and safe.

However, if there is one thing I have learned in England, it is that there is no lie like something (or someone!) that pretends to be old. We all live in the present day. These earls and dukes with their castles and coronets are no different, not one tiny iota, from our own oil kings and cattle barons. They have the same decayed minds and spend the same decayed energy on the same quests for ever-more-sordid frontiers of novelty. In this grim and grasping world, a truly *antique soul, a wild soul like mine, needs a guide who can*

*navigate the novelty, and Brownie is that guide. You must persuade
her to be waiting for me on my return.*

*The coils of privilege are trying to snake their way around my legs
over here, but they will never drag me down. Today, M-Henry,
abetted by his lucky charm and name-sake, caught a tuna. As I have
mentioned, I should not be at all surprised to learn that M-Hedges
was a secret agent of the Catalina Tuna Club working in concert with
M-Henry, sent by them to New York to force me into this Stygian
labyrinth. Anyway, M-Henry caught a tuna. All the local villains are
colluding in the pretence that it is some giant, simply because it took
the wheezy villain three hours to bring to boat and then a decrepit set
of scales in Whitby 'failed to register a reading'. I have little doubt
this was some stunt concocted in order that M-Henry or one of his
compatriots may doctor the scales tonight while we sleep, but I have
my ways of fighting back at this cabal, and I shall not be surprised to
hear news tomorrow that M-Henry has weighed it and found it lighter
than everybody seemed to think, or that he admits it was not fair-
caught. I have a 'sense' that this will happen.*

*Even the men surrounding me who once seemed fair I know now
to be foul. And that goes doubly for the women, who are without
exception degenerate. Henny connived her way into Caister's bed,
and I have cut her dead since then. Gellhorn was my revenge on the
Earl. I did it for honest vengeance – never jealousy, as you know,
never jealousy – which is positive proof of how little I now feel for
Henny. And Caister's ex-wife (how little these people care for the
permanence of marriage) has at his behest penned a shrill, sly
excoriation of my work for one of the London newspapers. She says
that 'anyone' can have a million readers. I wonder why she has not?
She says I am how I am because I grew up in luxury. What does she
know about me? What inspires such savagery? It is jealousy, of course.*

*I have told you how I explained to Gellhorn the various ways in
which this boat and these people are like a fairyland. Well, I also
reminded her that in the forest there is Pan, spirit of eternal youth!
He is untouched by the woods, and he is perilous to the unwary
who taunt him in his realm. So am I perilous. I cannot explain more*

to you for various reasons, concerning which you must never press me, but M-Henry will not so readily attack me again, I think.

There are two ways in which I plan to best my accursed luck, to triumph in its despite. First, I shall beat M-Henry in this twisted contest if I have to pluck a tuna from the sea with my teeth to do it, and second, Soul of the Marlin shall be a great book. It shall, Dolly.

I see now that when my hero escapes the land for the pure hardness of the ocean, his stowaway must not be some innocent but will instead be a modern girl, a pagan who like him has had her fill of civilization, who like him needs to be free, who is by him refreshed and renewed, as he is by her. I have not decided whether or not he will catch the fish of his dreams. Perhaps the truth is that we never do, or do I only think that because of my ill luck?

Why do I feel, why do I always feel, that there has never been an angler with the same brand of misfortune as haunts me? Maybe this tormenting mental aberration is common to all anglers, but I cannot in my heart believe it. And yet, as I watched M-Henry fight his fish today, the thought came upon me: tragedy and comedy in fishing are practically synonyms. It depends who is looking and who is doing.

Will that be the voice of the book I will write about this adventure? How will I display the wisdom I have wrung from a bitter and unlistening world? A wanderer has greater joys, but also suffers greater griefs than other men. We know we will never return to all the places we have been, to the dappled-evening Rogue River, to the Rainbow Bridge with Dot, to the first night you and I shared on the warm grass, tickling and laughing in an ecstasy never paralleled. And the wanderer also has the grief, a grief not known to men who close their eyes to the wideness of the world, of all the many places he has never been, of the torture that there are places he has missed. I do not know which of these griefs is the more poignant.

I have been lucky in one thing. I wandered long and freely in our country when it still was young, before its riches were gutted and sold, before the teeming millions raped its reaches for their selfish ends. When I see the patches of prisoned field that pass for open land in this sordid little country, and I watch the fleets of dirty, *noisy, greedy boats hauling tons upon tons of herring from the wailing ocean, I know in my heart that this will all be ravaged, that this bounty will be destroyed as the passenger pigeon was destroyed, as all our bounty will be destroyed.*

I need Brownie. I need hope and youth to replenish myself, to make it possible for me to go on. You will do it, won't you?

I had some hint of Grey's marriage arrangements, but he is open with her in ways I find hard to imagine.

He whines – there is no other word for it – about how he has been deceived by Henny, and claims that what he felt for her was never real, merely the result of his running away from his much more powerful and honest feelings for Brownie.

He mentions me, in passing, as further evidence of the nothingness of how he felt for Henny. I am not flattered by this.

He also – and this is so bare-faced I laughed out loud – repeats his claim to have originated and explained *to me* the idea that the *Dazzle* is a fairyland and that he is like Pan! It's interesting that he recognizes the latter and embraces rather than repudiates it, wouldn't you say?

The most enjoyable passages see him blaming Mike, Johnny and a more general conspiracy of his enemies in Scarborough, probably acting in concert with malign forces back in America, for his lack of success. He lies bare-facedly that the Captain's tuna was 'decent-sized' and says the weighing machine was 'broken' and it was 'almost certainly brought to boat under dubious circumstances'! He'll tell his wife about his women, but he won't tell her that he schemed to have the Captain's tunny annulled. You have to call that interesting.

And yet. Grey is not altogether a fool. There are moments when he suddenly flashes with self-knowledge. He understands rather clearly that he is a dreamer who needs novelty for sustenance, but to realize such a thing and feel no need to change it demands a strength of will that is, as Johnny says, 'not negligible'. I detest Grey, but I can't deny there is something about him that is— 'Appealing' is the only word I can really think of. He is such a selfish child, but his optimism is, in its twisted way, heroic.

None of this is blackmail material, but it would have been worthwhile to have carried it off to my cabin, and I should have done so before I read it. We criminals suffer from *esprit d'escalier* too, you know.

But just as I had finishing reading and was slowly working out where I might hunt for more salacious material, there was a brisk rapping at the cabin door. I stood stock-still. The rapping was repeated, not unkindly, and Miss Pink called my name.

I opened the door. Miss Pink looked at the papers on the desk, and she looked at the open typewriter case, with its camera clearly visible. This put her instantly on alert. 'Who is he? What does he take pictures of? Is he really Zane Grey?' It was a very odd moment and over almost as soon as it had begun. Her face set, and she thought for what cannot have been a minute but felt like ten. 'Of course he's Zane Grey. So what is this? He takes pictures of his women, yes?' I nodded. 'Of course. He took pictures of the Mitchell-Henry woman and threatened to expose her. That's what the fish is about, isn't it?' In an instant, she had woven her way through the entire plot. But Miss Pink spoke in a relieved way as if she had feared some other thing. She said that she would say nothing to Grey, and that I had better leave everything as I had found it. Then she strode off along the gangway and I followed like a naughty schoolgirl.

I wondered as I walked whether her rooms would reveal strange and peculiar things about her character – frills and flounces, perhaps, or leather and yellow velvet – but her lounge is in keeping with the rest of the *Dazzle*, modern without being gimcrack or oppressive. She mixed Martinis from a cabinet housed in a globe – something I have always coveted in general and now covet in specific having seen hers, which has been beautifully built by some surrealistic cabinet-maker. The style is antique and 'Here Be Dragonnes', and you don't notice anything peculiar about it for a moment, and then you realize that the continental shapes are familiar, but the world has been shifted on its axis. The countries and borders are all invented and the colors pull off some extraordinary trick of being vivid without screeching for attention. Does it seem as if I examined the globe rather than meeting Miss Pink's eye? It should.

She said she would not tell Grey about my snooping, on the condition that I was honest with her. I thought she would ask for details about the destroyed fish, but instead she asked me, with no preamble, to tell her everything that I knew about Johnny. I didn't know what to say. And then she said something like, 'Has he revealed anything private to you about what he is doing? I need to know, so I can help him.'

Miss Pink didn't seem to be thinking about Caro and the smashed heart, and so forth. She seemed to be asking about more concrete revelations, which I presumed must mean Henny. Because I was such a dithering chicken, she pressed on. She asked me if Henny is who she says she is. Might Henny be lying? Did I have any ideas about that? It was like her asking whether Grey is really Grey. Of course Henny is not who she says she is, but it is odd of Miss Pink to ask these questions. She wanted to know what is going on between Henny and Johnny: what are his intentions, in my opinion? I replied that surely she knows him better than I do. She said, 'Just answer the question.' There was something very disquieting about the clippy way she said this, G. Campbell.

I told her that I really didn't know what Johnny's intentions were, and that I found this whole conversation baffling.

At which Miss Pink sighed, as if she were very weary, and said that the business with the pictures and the fish explained how I was behaving, and it also explained why Henny stayed on land last night, and that was the main thing. I asked why it was the main thing, and she said it didn't matter. She told me not to be frightened, but she was trying to keep Johnny safe. I am to remember that tonight's guests are not just unpleasant, but perilous, and if I am sensible I will keep as far away from things as possible. And so it is business as usual – everyone is trying to protect everyone else.

I asked her why Johnny is having the party. She said that good manners render it inevitable. If Kim and Caro are in town, he simply has to entertain them. This explanation has never rung true, darling, and I'd finally had enough of it. I asked her why, even if he did have to see them, could he not simply host a dinner in Scarborough, where he could escape from them whenever he chose?

Miss Pink said that the Earl has standards that are higher than other men's, and that he is utterly scrupulous with respect to Caro. I didn't believe this. I asked if he was still in love with her.

When I said this, Miss Pink looked at me sharply and said, 'So that's what he told you, is it? He talked to you about Caro!'

'He told Henny,' I said.

'Oh yes. Of course.' With this news, Miss Pink relaxed, as if she had still been worried I might be up to something else. Then she said, 'I suspect that the Earl is trying to provoke a crisis. You would do well to keep out of his way.'

When she said that, the reason Johnny is so keen to carry on with tonight's party momentarily fell into place. He has told me and Henny that he isn't exactly free, and that we 'remake ourselves' in crises, and this must be what he is trying to do! I am not quite sure how Caro fits in, if he no longer loves her. Maybe it is because she still dogs his footsteps, either from jealousy or dull obsession. If so, then maybe his 'perfect manners' dictate that she must let him go before he may follow his heart.

But could this be right? It fits better than anything else with all that he has said, and with what Miss Pink said as well, but surely no one cares so much about manners as this? Johnny is an earl, though.

I have no illusions that any following of his heart might lead him to me, although I hope I may have helped start him thinking along these lines. I do not wish, let me repeat, ever to be trapped again. But I truly believe that Henny may make some kind of comrade for him if she can get past him kissing Molly, and he can get past what she did last night. Or do I think all this simply because they are both here, and I am here, and the human brain wants to make neat patterns out of whatever it sees?

You and I have spoken often about how people settle with one another sometimes because they have found the right person, but often because they have found a suitable person at the time they are ready. Johnny may be ready to exchange his present reality for a new one, and he needs the crisis to give him the excuse. He does not need me scurrying around his boat getting in the way and ruining it. I don't know how I would do so, but that must be what Miss Pink fears.

She dismissed me and I returned here. I have scribbled away while all was fresh, and now, my darling, I shall doze. I wish to be alert for the evening.

Miss Scarlett and Patterson are dead. There was a motor crash. I scarcely know what to say. My hand is shaking. I believe I am only writing to keep myself from going mad.

The anglers came back rather late, so we assumed they must have caught something. The Captain did, in point of fact, but it doesn't matter.

When the *Harlequin* returned, there was a freakish silence while Johnny leapt aboard and went to Miss Pink and whispered to her, holding her hands. By the time he reached her, she could see Miss Scarlett was not along with him. She didn't flinch while Johnny whispered. Apparently, while the fish was being weighed, Patterson and Miss Scarlett were running errands for Johnny and they simply crashed. No sense, no explanation.

The party tonight is going ahead! It is the most horrible and inexplicable thing. I thought Miss Pink would put a stop to it, but she nodded and the rest of the crew calmly proceeded with their preparations. Johnny told them, 'Life must go on, that's our duty', or some such. I suppose he got hardened in the war, and I dare say most people on board did as well, but this is not a war. Johnny's voice was metallic when he said it, shiny and hard. He will not deviate from the course he has set.

It seems utterly irrelevant now to say that Henny did not steal anything from Grey, and she failed in such a way as to ruin our chances of future success. She took Grey's satchel to the *Harlequin*'s bathroom while Grey fought a tunny (he lost it to an accident involving Mike, the details of which are unclear and I simply do not care about). Grey's notebook is full of his private adventures, with everything detailed. Henny said it was like reading a gruesome teenage diary, which made me think of my letters to you, G. Campbell, which is something I am embarrassed to admit thinking, given how small a thing it is and how great are today's tragedies. I am also embarrassed to admit that I blushed when I realized that Henny must have read what Grey wrote about me. Am I the selfishest of God's creatures? Anyway, Johnny broke down the door of the bathroom and returned the satchel to Grey. He was frightening, said Henny. He told her that he could not afford distractions and told her to stay out of his way. It is as if he has lost his mind.

I relayed my conversation with Miss Pink, and said that I had been given a very similar set of instructions. I added that I think the tempest around the party must be something to do with Johnny freeing himself from Caro, and that maybe this has become his *idée fixe*, and because of this he cannot give it up. It seemed half-plausible earlier on in the day, but it didn't seem plausible as I was saying it to Henny and it doesn't seem plausible now. I simply cannot understand Miss Pink's reaction to Miss Scarlett's death. I cannot understand why things are proceeding.

I suddenly recalled: Kim Waring said Johnny would eat my heart for another hour of living. I do not think this is true, but I cannot believe he is being so selfish.

I must paint my face and don the last of my Schiaps. I am afraid of Caro, I am afraid of Kim Waring and Joe Carstairs, and I am afraid of Johnny. I am afraid of him and for him. If Johnny is trying to provoke a crisis with Caro, it is unfortunate that these other disasters should be distracting him from it, but it is unforgivable of him to worry about his own situation – a thing he could do any time, however much he has had to steel himself to it – when other things are desperately more important. If I were Miss Pink, I should hate him for it.

It is nearly time, my darling. Once more unto the breach. It is all horrible.

Wednesday 5th September

John Fastolf, Earl of Caister
– Scarborough

Dazzle flashes in the evening sun as Johnny pilots *Harlequin* between *Nahlin* and *St George*. He is taking the short journey at appropriately funereal pace, reviewing all his decisions of the last few days, berating himself for the self-regarding hours he has spent worrying about Henny. What should he have done differently? What did he miss? Is he still missing it? Miss Pink and Patterson and Miss Scarlett were the three he could trust, and now there is only Miss Pink.

He has already received a message from the Sphinx. It assures him that the killings were an unfortunate error, an overzealous underling trying to make his name, a miscommunication. The Sphinx hopes and expects that this error will not jeopardise the meeting.

Miss Pink will not blame him. The planning has been hers as much as his, more so even. But he blames himself. He assumed that tonight's summit and the consignment of dope would be enough to keep the Sphinx's hands full, but he was wrong, and Miss Scarlett and Patterson have paid, and Miss Pink. And now, because this is not personal, because they answer to a higher authority, they have to follow through with the plan, whatever the shocked faces of Henny, Grey and Mike, and of Marion and the rest of them back on shore. It will be worse on the boat. Martha will have no idea how to react.

He swings up to *Dazzle* in eerie silence. While Saul and Audrey secure the gangway, he strides quickly to Miss Pink. She knows. 'How?' she asks.

'I'm not sure. It looks like a car crash, but obviously—'

'Yes.'

'I'm so sorry, Dido,' he whispers. 'I—'

'I understand. The show must go on.' He can tell nothing from her voice, nothing at all.

He makes his announcement. He insists that no one is to mention the tragedy this evening, tonight's guests are not to be made uncomfortable. Martha is dumbfounded. Henny crosses to speak to her. Shortly afterwards, he knocks on Miss Pink's door.

She hasn't changed for the evening. She hasn't been crying. He thinks he would have cried. 'I'll stay here,' she says. 'No one will miss me, I think. Dicky tummy or something. Not suspicious, is it?'

'No, Dido. Not suspicious.'

'It wasn't a mistake, was it?'

'No. The Sphinx knows it was me who tipped off the police about Kensington, and this was a show of strength. I'm sorry.'

'No time for that,' says Miss Pink. She forces herself to think. 'It was disproportionate, wouldn't you say? It's not a sign they know what we're really up to?'

'I don't think so. I think they're just rattled. What do you think?'

'The same. I was just checking. We're supposed to know who it was, and why, and swallow it. Price of doing business.'

'Too high a price.'

'Johnny!' Miss Pink's face is flint, her eyes steady. 'We finish this or it's been for nothing.'

Miss Pink is desperately upset, but she is thinking of the bigger picture. Is that unnatural? Or is it a way of honouring the dead? She has been distorted by this secret life, but that doesn't mean she is wrong, or bad, or cold.

'I know,' he says. There is nothing else to do. And it's the right thing to do, of course. Except— He is very tired. It is the right thing to do, but these are bad seas he's sailing in.

'There are other people still involved,' says Miss Pink. 'There are people who are depending on us not to lose our stomach. You cannot stop now. You understand that?'

'Yes,' he repeats. 'I understand.'

'This meeting could be an ambush. Saul and Andy should go across first and then send back a signal.'

'I'm going,' he says.

'Johnny—'

'I'm going.'

Then he tells her about Henny playing silly buggers with Grey's satchel. He says he didn't get to see whatever is in it, because he took it on deck without thinking and Grey demanded its return. He asks if Martha did anything unusual today, if she revealed anything new about Henny or about what happened to the fish. Any clue as to whether they are what they claim?

'No,' says Miss Pink. 'She did nothing. Forget these girls, and forget the satchel. Martha spent the whole afternoon in her room. Don't be distracted by her, or by Henny. This is not about them. We finish this tonight.'

Wednesday 5th September

Zane Grey – Scarborough

Letter to Dolly Grey, ctd.

It is a madhouse here. I have locked myself in my cabin, and nothing on this spinning earth will induce me to open the door before dawn.

Caister, to torment me, has invited his wife to dinner. The fact that he did not rescind this invitation after her jealous and cowardly attack on me yesterday is proof positive that the attack was at his behest. The man has no concept of manners. I saw her arrive from my cabin window, and soon they will sit and dine from golden forks in spite of the fact that the *Dazzle*'s first officer and Caister's Negro butler were killed in a motor smash not three hours ago. Nothing affects these people. They are not human.

The rest of tonight's party is made up of London socialites and the *Berania*'s perverts. They boarded a quarter-hour ago in various states of undress (I saw them briefly as I hastened to my cabin) and they were subdued, in honor of the dead, for maybe five minutes. Then the music started.

It has been another cursed day at sea, although it started gloriously: we woke to the news that M-Henry's fish had been mysteriously hacked apart and burnt! I was not surprised by this, certain in my heart that my enemy would manufacture some spurious excuse for its weighing much less than yesterday's wild claims. Accordingly, everyone now pretends that the fire destroyed a tuna weighing 1,000 lbs. As you well know, such stories attend every unratified or illicit fish.

Who knows who did the deed! Could it be M-Henry himself, knowing the truth? Could it be his wife, wanting to protect him from his shame and keep him in fatuous ignorance? Could there be another explanation? I do not know, but this I say: do not taunt Pan in his lair!

You will be keen to know about my own angling. When we finally reached the tuna grounds, M-Henry's tame captains blew their horns deceitfully and we followed wherever they called. Of course, we were never near a fish, while M-Henry somehow stumbled on another. It was no great size, but I finally lost my patience and demanded of Caister that I choose where we cast our bait.

Accordingly, an hour later I was onto a truly enormous tuna! The Herculean power in its smooth mass was beyond anything I have ever felt, beyond anything I ever believed could exist outside the world of steam and steel. The *Harlequin* cannot be towed, but if we had been in a rowboat the tuna would have taken us to the Pole before she tired.

You already realize that this tale must end in cataclysm. M-Henry, in his arrogance or lack of durability, had given M-Hedges a spell in the fighting harness. M-Hedges struck a fish. We were too close to each other. His fish was small and it was second-hooked. Of course he had to cut it free! But no, he did not! The Englishmen conspired against me once again, and M-Hedges guided his biddable fish, a fish as mean as mine was grand, toward the *Harlequin*, and in the inevitable tangle my tuna, the first thousand-pounder ever to face a man he could not best, was lost in the ocean vastness.

No other fish were hooked today.

My only consolation is that no good comes of evil deeds. It must be clear to the most simple-minded baby that Caister is part of the cabal that sent M-Hedges to New York to ensnare my participation in this charade. But Caister's triumph has turned to ashes! I have bested him in that other arena, the truest arena where men are measured. First, I took Gellhorn from him. And then, last night, Henny stayed in Whitby with M-Henry and his wife. The coincidence of this and the burnt fish torments Caister, and perhaps it had something to do with someone taunting Pan, who knows!

As I always realized, bringing Henny with me, even though she and I were never well suited, has proven to be masterstroke. She has ensorcelled Caister. You should not be surprised. If she could enmesh me in her web, even as briefly as she did, then a coddled English lordling will have been small work for her, especially after what she has learned at my feet.

The pair of them argued bitterly while I fought my fish. Afterwards Caister asked her outright whether she had anything to do with the destruction of M-Henry's tuna, whether she was still secretly in my employ. Joy! He knows he cannot trust her! It is a desperate canker for this man, whose name has brought him so many slavish disciples, to be spurned! He can think of nothing else but her!

The English have had some days of success, but the race is not yet run and I have ever been stronger at the battle's end than at its beginning, have ever trusted my vision, my endurance and my strong right arm. Any man can start, but very few can finish. Caister's wife is a fool, and the rest of them are fools. They think I set out to write 'best-sellers' because that is what my books became? There were no books like mine before me! If I wanted to write a 'best-seller', I would write another *Flaming Youth*! It is the easiest thing in the world to be 'sensational'! You write about depraved youth and jazz and dope, it is the safest way to success and yet the parrots call it 'daring'. What is hard, what is desperately hard, but the only path to art, is to write what you truly believe in, what you dream of writing, what no man has written before you, and to write it in the wilderness with no support, save yours, dear Dolly. If I succeeded, if I sold a million books, it was not because I wrote what I thought some fool would buy. I wrote from the depths of my own soul and so shall I always write or die.

It is not late, but I am alone, more alone than a man ever was in such a throng of people. Tell me that Brownie will be waiting for me. I know you will.

Tomorrow, I will have my final triumph.

Wednesday 5th September

Henny Rosefield – Scarborough

Henny dressed slowly and carefully.

A champagne cocktail arrived at the usual time, Audrey carrying the tray in Patterson's place. Audrey acted as if nothing had happened. Henny went on deck shortly after seven-thirty.

The *Harlequin* arrived from the shore carrying Marion, Caro Fastolf and Kim Waring. There were three others: a bearded Falstaff of a man, a shingled girl in a Chinese dress and the shingled girl's uncle, who was an editor of some kind. Martha was in the saloon. She and Henny were staying distant from each other, as if that would make them less complicit. It was quieter on deck, a better place to explain things to Marion, and Henny took the older woman aside.

Marion said, 'Johnny said that I'm not to tell the others about poor Miss Scarlett and I haven't. My problems seem like rather small things now, don't they?'

'Well—'

'Of course they do. And they are. It's awful. Why is the dinner going on?'

'I don't know.'

'Sometimes,' said Marion, 'you can be so shocked by something that you just carry on. You can't make a decision to change course. It must be that, mustn't it?'

'I suppose so.'

'Or it's the damned war. They all got used to carrying on, and so we must too.' Kim and Caro had gone into the saloon with Johnny. Henny couldn't hear what they were saying. The evening was chilly. Henny said, 'Martha and I both tried, and we know how he takes the pictures now, but we didn't get anything. And he knows we tried. I'm sorry.'

'Well,' said Marion. 'As I said. It seems rather small.'

'Yes,' said Henny.

'All the same, we'd better hope that Laurie doesn't catch anything big tomorrow. Who knows what I'll have to do if Grey does it again.'

'Yes.'

'I need a drink,' said Marion, and went inside to join Martha under the stickleback. Henny stayed outside to watch *Berania*'s launch skid to a stop alongside the *Dazzle*. Carstairs was piloting the launch. Ruth and Lapwing were leaning over the side. Johnny emerged to greet them.

'Johnny!' said Carstairs, as she climbed up the ladder in her gleaming white captain's uniform and jumped down beside her host. 'Sorry no Kiki and Molly – they've got some tummy bug and are vomiting black bile.' Ruth was glassy-eyed, clearly under some influence or other. Lapwing skipped into the saloon and grabbed a drink. Henny followed her inside.

Lapwing kissed Martha and Marion, and then darted back to Henny. 'Darling,' she said, hugging Henny deeply. 'You were too marvellous the other night, really too marvellous! Oh, it's Pippin!' and she pulled Henny over to the Chinese-dressed girl who, looking wry, introduced her to the two men. The bearded man was 'Jim' and Pippin's uncle, Roger, was the editor who had hired Martha to write about tunny. He seemed to enjoy his magazine being described as *The Illustrated Doodah*. Pippin whispered with gamine weariness that the old puffin was altogether too soft to survive in magazines. He wouldn't spill the beans about anything that happened tonight. He wouldn't even be very scandalised by it. Pippin sighed at how difficult it was getting to shock the older generation. Bearded Jim had met Martha at Send Manor. *Everyone* went to Send, said Pippin.

Caro joined them, dangling her champagne glass, diaphanous in indigo threaded with gold, and golden slippers, and a golden torc around her slender neck. She was loose-limbed and girlish, but the corners of her eyes were starting to cut with lines. She knew everyone. After the hellos, Caro theatrically noticed the stickleback. 'Oh, darling, *that* old thing!' she said.

A moment's collective caution, and then Pippin asked dutifully, 'What is it?'

'A *memento mori*, my darlings. *Et in Arcadia* Johnny's ego *est*. Typical sentimental Johnny, all symbols and no substance. I caught the poor little chap the day we met. Johnny was used to having whatever he wanted; I was a tiny, fresh little thing who dreamed of art and freedom. It was a match made in hell and we sealed it in blood by sneaking away to the river and taking an innocent life. Johnny thought it was funny to mount it, and he still does, but it's not the fish he stuffed, my darlings, it's me.'

Silence.

'I drove Straight's Maserati down to Dartington,' said Jim. 'Terrifying bloody thing, but fast. It's red, like Johnny's.'

Caro ignored him. She asked Pippin where she had managed to find such an interesting dress. Pippin held her own with defiant politeness.

Jim looked Martha, Henny and Lapwing up and down, and selected Lapwing. 'Another drink, my dear?' He put his shovel hand on her bare back and led her over to Audrey at the bar. Pippin and Uncle Roger joined them gratefully. As Henny followed, Lapwing turned to her, rolled her eyes towards Jim and grinned.

Sliding alongside, Waring caught Henny's hand, as if playful. He was wearing an exquisite dinner jacket, which, under these lights, was insolently purple. 'So,' he said. 'Swapping hot glances with the ravishing Lapwing. You'll have competition, but if you get her pissed enough she'll probably fuck you. Get me a drink, Caro.' Caro hesitated and went.

'You seem nervous,' said Henny.

'No, I don't, but nice try,' said Waring. 'Johnny's invited the beautiful, silly, promiscuous Lapwing. What can it mean?'

'It means Lapwing is my cousin,' said Johnny, whose arrival was as noiseless as Kim's.

'Of course. I forget the ancestral thrill of incest. Where's your little cowboy?'

'In his cabin.'

'He's not joining us? Because of Caro's review? Poor lamb!' Caro returned with two glasses. 'You venomous viper, you,' he said. 'Grey won't come to dinner.'

'Poor lamb!' said Caro.

'That's what I said. One forgets how sensitive these artist chaps are.' Then he said, 'Caroline?'

'Yes?'

'Take Johnny over there. Talk to him about money.' Waring waited until she was almost certainly out of earshot and said, 'She's a jealous bitch, but Caister's made her very rich. Marvellous boat. Never been allowed on board before.'

'Surprisingly.'

'Beneath you, darling; even Martha could have come up with that. I presume by now you've fucked him?'

'I—'

'Thought so. Don't be angry with me. I've got an unfortunate manner, but I could see when we met in London that you're worth five of Earl Caister.'

'What does that mean?'

'It means I'll fuck you, if you want, and it would be fun. I wouldn't promise you anything, or pretend I was "protecting you" when we didn't fuck again.' He watched her carefully while he said this. 'Again yes. He probably said it to Gellhorn too.'

'He isn't—'

'Caister's a poison swamp, darling. He plays the damaged cavalier, but he's William of the Wisp. You'll follow him in and you'll never come out.'

'A bit baroque, Mr Waring.'

'Defensive formality? Is that the best you can manage? You were impressive in London, but this is very disappointing. Maybe you're tired.' Caro rejoined them. Waring didn't seem pleased. He said, 'We were talking about Henny and your husband.'

'Yes,' said Henny. 'Mr Waring gets very exercised about Johnny, doesn't he!'

'I—'

'His imagery is all over the place – I can't work out whether Johnny's supposed to be leading me into a swamp, or whether he's the swamp itself.'

'Oh,' Waring said. 'Better.'

There was a seating plan, but Waring and Caro ignored it – Caro laughed as she threw Henny's name-card on the floor. Gellhorn was stuck opposite Henny between Joe Carstairs and Ruth. The lovers bickered over her head. Henny was next to Waring, inevitably, and to her right was Jim, who boomed away at Lapwing on his other side. To Kim's left was lugubrious Uncle Roger. He had drawn the short straw, because to his left, at the head of the table, was the doll Tod Wadley, and then Marion, and then it was Joe. Caro was opposite but one, to Ruth's left, and she was pretending to ignore Henny, but it was difficult, because she didn't want to turn left and speak with Pippin, who was chatting blithely with Mike and Johnny at the table's foot.

Kim acted as if Caro weren't there. He didn't touch Henny, but she leaned backwards all the same. He ignored Roger.

The hors d'oeuvre was *foie gras*. Joe had three helpings. The champagne was excellent. Lapwing said, 'I wonder what *foie gras* tastes like when you're not potted?' Then clear turtle soup, then devilled sole. Conversation around the table didn't flow, but it was maintained, with much of the weight borne by the shore party. They hadn't been told about Patterson and Miss Scarlett, but they could see something was wrong. Henny looked around. There was a sense, not from everybody, of waiting for something. Caro watched Waring, and so did Caister. The sole was followed by quail.

Joe was bored. She asked Caro, three to her left, what she was going to do about Kim and Johnny, now that they were fighting over Henny rather than her. 'There's always a berth on the *Berania*, in case you finally want to learn what a good time is really like. You look like you've never had one.'

'You're wasting your time,' Kim said across the table. 'She likes cock, cock and nothing but cock. And, the terrible irony, she doesn't have the first clue what to do with one.'

'It's my tragedy,' Caro managed to say. Her face was a mask and her voice was steady and bright. 'At least I practise hard. And I think the fact that I am trying to please you pleases you.'

'Oh Lordy!' laughed Waring, and half the table laughed with him. Huge Jim said, 'Steady on, Waring.'

Waring did not steady on. 'After Caister, she finds my honesty bracing, don't you?' Caro nodded. 'And we're not married, Jim. And we don't pretend, like you and Lily Ppynrryn. We just fuck when I can't find anyone better.'

Jim was furious, but Lapwing put her hand on his. Quiet for a while. Then Joe, Marion and Martha tried to start a separate conversation, and for a moment a small, uncomfortable hum returned. Ruth whispered to Henny across the table, quite audibly, 'They do this whenever they're around Johnny. God knows how he never rises to it.'

But Caister did rise to it. He did not lift his voice, but the table silenced as he said, 'I'm sorry, Caro. I have to ask: are you all right?'

Waring was delighted. 'A bit late, wouldn't you say, my lord?'

'I'm not speaking to you.' Johnny stood up, jerkily. In a still voice he said, 'Is this really what you want, Caroline?'

He said it very tenderly. It was a voice that had love in it. Maybe old love, but love. Caro said, eyes on Waring, that yes, it fucking was. It was what she had always fucking wanted.

Waring said that it was hardly his fault – it's not like he needed Caro hanging around his neck – but whereas Johnny was a glorified estate-manager pretending to be a dissolute modern gentleman, he was the real potato. It's just one of those things a chap can't help, he said.

Silence again. Johnny looked at Caro, then at Waring. It appeared that he wanted to sit down, but was unsure how he could achieve this without looking ridiculous. Then he said, 'Medicine's too strong for me. Don't stand up. Think I'll head off early.'

Carstairs, Waring and Caro were surprised and excited by his departure. Joe gave a thrilled 'Wooooo!' The other guests were embarrassed. 'Twice in three days!' Joe added. 'He's losing it!'

Waring told Audrey, serving his end of the table, to bring him a couple of bottles of champagne and then bugger off. He was sick of constantly waiting. He'd deal with the drink himself. When the bottles arrived, he fiddled with them and kept them on the floor by his seat. He filled glasses for Henny and Marion, and topped them up. Henny was careful of this to start with, but stopped worrying after half a glass. Waring continued to ignore Uncle Roger.

The shore-party departed as soon as they could. Martha stood and said she was going to bed. She asked Henny if she would as well.

Henny finished her champagne. 'Yes, I'm going to bed,' she said. She slurred. She hadn't drunk that much. She didn't rise. Marion was very flushed.

Martha asked, 'Are you coming?'

'She's fine, darling,' said Waring. 'Don't you worry.'

Henny started to speak, but the words wouldn't form properly. She wasn't ready for bed anyway. Kim Waring was very handsome. Martha, awkwardly, left.

Caro pointed at Henny and Marion and said, 'Kimmy?' Waring nodded and waggled the bottle in his hand.

Joe said, 'What have you done?'

Waring said, 'Nothing to you.'

Joe said, 'You shouldn't have done it. Johnny won't like it.'

'Fuck off, Joe.'

Very soon afterwards Joe, Ruth and Lapwing headed for the shore, Joe's Daimler and London. 'It's perfect use of time for us, you see,' said Joe, 'because I can sleep anywhere.' Ruth said bitterly that she couldn't. Lapwing said there was bound to be someone still around, if they got to town quickly enough. It would only be four or so.

Joe wanted Kim and Caro to come with her. She said they would get into trouble if they stayed. They ignored her.

Henny, Marion, Kim and Caro were now at one end of the table, with Mike at the other. Kim said, 'Bedtime for you, Mike?'

Mike said, 'Do you know, I think it is. Good evening.'

Henny was very hot. Waring poured her another glass of his champagne. 'Drink it,' he said firmly. She drank it. He laughed. She stood up, lurched, sat down. 'I'm dizzy,' she said. Caro giggled. Marion's hair was dank on her forehead.

Waring led the women to the saloon. It was 9.50 p.m.

Wednesday 5th September

Martha Gellhorn – Scarborough

Letter to G. Campbell Beckett, ctd.

It is still horrible! Oh my dear, I do not know what to do. The dinner is carrying on in the dining saloon, but after my galumphing departure I do not know how to return.

I was supposed to be sat next to Marion and Johnny, but Waring ignored the place-names and then everything was higgledy-piggledy. Johnny didn't bat an eyelid. He said we were all friends. There were twelve of us for dinner, I think, maybe more. I'm trying to picture it. Lapwing's here with Joe and Ruth. For my benefit, Johnny also invited Pippin and Uncle Doodah, who turn out to be tenuous cousins of his, who were tickled pink to get the call, but must have had a dreadful evening. They brought big Jim from Send, who is a sort of chum of Johnny's and was instantly infatuated by Lapwing and downed three cocktails in five minutes at her instigation, which made him louder and then much quieter. Pippin and Lapwing, darling, are two of those porcelain English girls who make me feel so brutal. I don't suppose it contributed to my galumph, but I don't suppose it helped.

Waring was vile throughout the meal, whispering about our host to Henny just loudly enough for the rest of us to catch his flow.

Johnny sat quietly through the starter and into the main course, and then Joe Carstairs, upset that she wasn't the center of affairs, asked Caro what she was going to do now that Waring and Johnny were locking their horns over Henny and not her.

Kim was awful, and he started speaking in the hideous, hideous way that these people speak, and Johnny suddenly couldn't bear it anymore. When he left, he looked like he'd been defeated, but I would swear that there was something else. I'm not sure I'd call it a sense of purpose, but I think this was the crisis he wanted. But what was he going to do with it, if he wasn't in the room? Something still doesn't fit.

Anyway, the atmosphere was dreadful. Pippin took her poor uncle back to *terra firma* – he edits *The Whotsit*, so he knows how the world works and he seemed entirely unfazed by the whole business. Jim wanted to stay with Lapwing, but she shoved him onto the landbound *Harlequin* too. She has to drive to London tonight with Joe and Ruth because they're flying to some party in Nice tomorrow. Poor Henny was still trapped with Kim and he was trying to make her drunk, so I stood up and said we should go. I was sure she would want to escape, but she didn't. Either she is drunk already or I am still wrong about her, or Kim is a mesmerist, which is sometimes how he seems. My departure was a triumph of awkwardness, even by my standards.

I went to Johnny's cabin to see if he was all right. I thought I might tell him to go and rescue Henny. I'm not even sure Henny is who he wants anymore. His light was out. I could not believe he had gone straight to sleep. I went around the yacht trying to find him, but nothing.

And so here I am. I want to know what is happening in the saloon, but I would feel a chump returning after such a decided exit. Oh, G. Campbell, it is possible that I will read all this tomorrow and everything will suddenly make perfect sense, but I truly think something is going on that I will never learn about if I stay hidden in here like a frightened little rabbit. Of all the many things to be scared about, the least is to look like a chump. That horse, surely, is far over the horizon.

Wish me luck.

Wednesday 5th September

John Fastolf, Earl of Caister – Scarborough

Outside the saloon, Johnny drops his awkward pose. He walks quickly to his cabin and changes into his blacks. Saul and Andy will have packed the skiff with unnecessary firepower. They are good men, but they are not Patterson and Miss Scarlett. He cannot think about that now. He holsters his Luger, slips out quickly and along to the *Dazzle*'s stern. It would be annoying to be seen, but he reckons his surprising departure will have given him five minutes' grace and he hasn't taken three.

As soon as he drops into the skiff, Andy starts rowing, and a few minutes after that they power up the Elto. Saul and Andy don't say anything.

Johnny is almost certain that the Sphinx is honest about wanting a partnership, and if that is the case he might be able to extract some final pieces of useful information before revealing himself. But an ambush is a real possibility. If so, he might die and Miss Pink will have to wind up the Sphinx's operation. He has willed her enough money to keep the unit going. Has nothing changed this week – would he still be happy to die? No, it's not that, it's just that he'd rather die than see Saul killed, or Andy.

He tells Saul and Andy who the Sphinx really is and explains that he will go up *Berania*'s side first, to make sure all is well. They are spoiling for a fight. Andy says he should go up first because— Well, Andy says it because he knows he's expendable. Johnny says no.

Berania is out to sea for the rendezvous and it is twenty minutes before he kills the Elto. Saul takes the oars this time. He served under Johnny in France. So did Patterson and a couple of the others. The rest came via Miss Pink. You learned what people were capable of during the war. Johnny and Miss Pink have abused that knowledge, and they found other wandering souls like Audrey, and— There it all is, anyway.

Caro told his guests about the stickleback. It was stupid of him to leave it there, even if it is not as easy to read as Caro thinks. He shouldn't be annoyed that Caro thinks she understands him; his whole life is about giving people that impression.

Maybe Caro does understand him. 'A contract sealed in blood,' she said. What irritates him is that Caro told Henny, and that Henny might have drawn the wrong conclusions, might have thought that the contract still held, on some primeval level.

It is interesting that out here on the ink-dark sea, urgently needing to focus on the job in hand, trying to work out if he is prepared to die, he has a sudden moment of clarity about the girl: she is not his one true love – there is no such thing – but that doesn't make her unimportant. Life is not all or nothing, and she is the first person he has seriously considered a future with since— Well, for a very long time. It is a rare situation, to be given due consideration, not to be treated lightly. That is why his subconscious has not been able to let her go.

The corollary being that if he *does* like her, truly like her and want what is best for her, then he should not drag her into his orbit. In that case, what he has done this week – pushing her away, ultimately – has been, in its fumbling way, more or less the right thing. The right thing is at odds with what he wants. Nothing new in that.

Well, the 'right thing' now is to send Andy up the side of the *Berania*. It will make Johnny feel guilty and a coward, but he should do it all the same. The operation is much more likely to succeed if Johnny lives. He has the stomach to die, Miss Pink knew that, but what he needs is the stomach to do the right thing.

And so he tells Andy he has changed his mind. Andy is happy

to take the lead, but surprised. Andy and Saul are disappointed in him, he thinks.

He takes a short, heavy pole with a cloth-covered end and fends off the *Berania*. They have silenced the side of the skiff with a padded apron, and they lash her tight under the ladder.

Johnny left the saloon at 8.54. It is now 9.36.

Andy climbs the ladder, black against the blackness. He disappears over the rails. The moment is unbearable. Death is the ultimate reality. The world might be chaos, but every death is a fixed point. It's the cliff at the end of the path.

After a few long seconds Andy's head reappears and he knocks the signal that all is well. Johnny and Saul clamber up to join him. They slip noiselessly to the bow and then work their way aft. The *Berania* is silent, absent their soft footfalls.

After an empty saloon, empty wheelhouse (odd), empty galley and two empty cabins, it is shocking to open the third cabin and find Kiki Preston tied to a chair, head lolling. She's alive, but she's been drugged. Almost certainly. It could be a trap. Johnny leaves Andy with her, just in case.

Johnny and Saul move on carefully.

More empty rooms, including Molly's, which contains Molly's large trunk, which is almost empty. Then Joe's cabin, which smells rank somehow. They descend into the guts of the yacht. Two small, empty rooms, barely more than cupboards, full of fishing gear and deck games. It is hard to imagine Joe flinging quoits.

Then the closed door to the main hold. A light is shining from under it. Johnny shifts the gun in his hand. He crouches down low and nods to Saul, who quickly opens it, and Johnny, still in his crouch, slides into the doorway. No shots ring above his head.

At the far end of the room, twisted over a pile of rope, is Molly. Her throat has been cut.

'Hello, Johnny,' says Miss Pink.

It is 9.57.

Wednesday 5th September

Martha Gellhorn – Scarborough

Letter to G. Campbell Beckett, ctd.

What is this, G. Campbell, flapping about between my stupid gawky legs? Yes, indeed, it is my tail.

They'd left the dining saloon by the time I got there, and Carstairs's launch was weaving off toward dry land. I crept to the saloon and peered through the window. The gramophone was playing loudly and Henny and Marion, Kim and Caro were on one of the corner sofas, all melted together somehow and laughing hysterically, but it didn't seem to be forced. I hoped that Henny was putting it on, but I honestly believe she was not. Caro saw me and nudged Kim.

Kim called me in. He said that it was kind of me to snoop, but I was no longer required. This was a night for big boys and girls and I should go to my cabin. That wasn't the expression he used.

Henny started to protest and Kim didn't try to contradict her, but simply repeated himself. She subsided. I left.

I have only been out of my cabin for five minutes. I thought I understood Henny. I thought that what she and Marion did to the tunny was out of necessity. But maybe she has tricked me as well as everyone else. What kind of a bozo must you be to know that someone has fooled everyone else and assume that she hasn't fooled you?

It is not terribly late, but I am tired. We are all tired. I am too excited to sleep, but I am too frightened to leave the cabin. Peculiarly, writing this has made me feel calmer. It is an exorcism.

I'm going to have a bath, G. Campbell.

*

Oh, darling! I lay in the bath like an idiotic whale, assuming things would slip into quietness, and of course what happened is that my slow brain finally started to understand Marion's silly grinning face, and Henny's. It must be dope! Johnny warned us about Kim, and dope seems to be everywhere we go, and I still didn't make the connection. Has Kim made her take it or has Henny been a dope-fiend all along? It must be the former; I only write the other down because I have been wrong about everything else, and I don't want to be a fool anymore.

I believe everyone who says Kim is dangerous, but I am not going to hide here. If you hide in Fairyland, you just get eaten by the wolf. No, that's not right. What happens is that someone else gets eaten by the wolf, and you could have tried to stop it and then you can't live with yourself. I know I said all this before and then I rabbited straight back, but this time I won't.

Wednesday 5th September

Henny Rosefield – Scarborough

Kim Waring turned on the gramophone and sat between Henny and Marion on one side of the L-shaped sofa. Caro hovered around the sofa's corner.

'You should leave,' Henny slurred.

'You really are a tough one,' Waring said. 'So, what I was thinking is that we should put Marion to bed and then go fuck.'

'Do you really want to?' said Caro.

'I'd rather she was that brutish Jim Justice, but beggars can't be choosers.' Caro laughed, but the sound fractured and she grabbed her mouth. Kim said, 'God, Caro! Stop being so abject.'

'Yes,' Caro said. 'We should hurry, though.'

Henny's head jerked. She said, 'I'm tired.'

'Not exactly, darling,' said Waring.

'What about the fish?' Caro said. 'She'll tell you everything now.'

'Of course! You can be a semi-useful secretary at times.' He turned to Henny. 'Henrietta!' Henny's eyes opened. 'Mitchell-Henry's giant fish.'

'Giant.'

'Yes, a veritable titan. And you destroyed it, yes?' Henny's eyes widened. 'It had to be you, darling.'

Henny gripped her knees. She said, 'Marion was with me all night.'

'Bet she had a good time,' said Waring. Then he said, 'You don't fool me. She must have been in on it too. Why?' Henny's head drooped again. Marion's cheek was resting on Waring's shoulder, her eyes staring at the conversation. Waring turned to her and said, 'Come on, darling! I can smell it was you. Why? Is your hubby a beast?'

'I love him,' Marion mumbled.

'You will tell me, old things,' said Waring. He waved the bottle. 'Special bottle. Full of secret goodness. Should feel guilty but I'm a bad egg, you see, made that way. But I'm not evil, just a little naughty. No real harm will come. Tell me why you did it.' Henny shook her head. 'You will. Don't leave out anything about Johnny.' Henny shook her head again. Marion giggled for some reason. Henny giggled too. She couldn't stop giggling, in fact, but she didn't answer Warning's question.

'All right,' said Waring. He turned to Marion. 'You'll tell me, won't you?' He put on a gentle voice, held her hand and said, 'As you know, I'm your friend. If you tell me why you destroyed the fish, you will feel much better about it.'

'Will I?'

'Yes.'

'But you're bad.'

'No, no, no. I *pretend* to be bad, but I'm good. When you tell me, everyone will feel better.'

'Will they?'

'I promise.'

So she told Waring what had happened, and after a moment Henny didn't protest. He encouraged them softly throughout, grinning at Caroline. At the end he said, 'Well, darlings, what a fascinating, tawdry tale it is! I'm going to help you out with nasty Mr Grey. First we—'

Caro nudged Waring and pointed at the window. Gellhorn was staring in. Waring gestured for her to enter. He said, 'You ran away to bed, little sneak. You don't get to play with the big boys and girls now. Go to your bed, or knock fruitlessly on Johnny's door, or fuck off in some other way, but fuck off.' His voice was still soft. Henny started to rise. Waring gripped her arm and kept her from standing. He said, 'I'm helping you, aren't I, Henny?' Henny nodded. For a moment Gellhorn didn't leave. Then she did.

Waring said, 'Check on her.'

Caro went to the door and looked outside. 'She's gone.'

'Excellent.' Waring took Marion's hands in his and said, 'I, my darling, am your knight in shining armour. That Mr Grey has been horrible to you, and he's still a threat, isn't he?'

'Yes,' said Marion.

'You would like me to do something about him, wouldn't you?'

'Yes.'

'All right. After tonight, he won't ever cause you trouble again. Do you trust me?' Again Marion said yes. 'Do you want to help her, Henny? Because this is ultimately all your fault.' Henny said yes, very quietly. 'Good. This is what we are going to do.'

Marion and Henny had another glass of Waring's champagne while he explained. They could hardly stand. Then they had some cocaine. Waring said it would wake them up.

With Caro and Waring out of sight, they knocked on Grey's door. When he saw Marion he said, 'I thought it might be you—' He saw Henny and stopped.

'I need you,' Henny said. 'We both need you.' Marion giggled. Before Grey could properly react, Henny kissed him and pushed past into his cabin. Marion grabbed his hand and pulled him with her.

They both kissed him. They took off his pyjamas and their dresses. Henny asked where his cuffs were. He got them and told her to lie down. 'Not tonight,' she said. 'You tonight. You deserve it.' Marion giggled again. They cuffed him, and then went to the door to let in Kim and Caro.

Kim was holding a knife. He said, 'If you make a noise, I'll cut it in half.' He declared himself impressed by the hidden camera. He said he had been horrified to hear how Grey had blackmailed Marion, and they were going to take some pictures they could use to prevent him doing it again. They took these. Marion and Henny did whatever he told them to do. He was in a hurry. It was 10.36.

He put on a gramophone record, 'just in case there is some accidental noise'.

Then Kim and Caro tied up Marion and Henny. Then he gagged them, and Grey. Then he said, 'That was easy.' He sat down and crossed his legs, the knife-hand resting on his knee. He announced that he was going to kill the girls.

'Kim!' said Caro.

'Oh, shut up, darling!' said Kim. Obviously, he went on, he was not doing this to help some old fisherman's wife. He was not a knight-errant sort of chap, he left that kind of posing to Johnny.

Who, incidentally, he hated. And who, incidentally, was fabulously, unfairly rich. The pictures, combined with two corpses, would make a wonderful scandal, which Johnny would pay almost anything to avoid. 'Isn't that delicious?' he asked Caro. She nodded, but she was green. Kim said that Grey would live, since he was rather too famous to disappear, but he would never say anything for fear of the photographs. Mitchell-Henry would say nothing either, not when he knew about the pictures of Marion and Grey. And the girl had no one. It was perfect.

The time was 10.47.

Wednesday 5th September

Zane Grey – Scarborough

Letter to Dolly Grey, ctd.

I cannot sleep. People are stamping around the boat as if it were New York City. The music is deafening. Caister deliberately placed me next to the saloon to keep me from resting, I see that now as clearly as I see this pen in my hand.

What I do not understand is why, wherever I go, I must be the eye of the storm, the focus of every drama. I conceive there is a natural power, a collision of spiritual forces, which means that others may live peaceful lives nearby, while I am tossed and turned, battered and bruised. Mine is the name that was used by my rival to sell this tawdry contest; mine was the risk in coming to this godforsaken backwater; mine was the reputation trashed in the popular press; mine was the great fish broken away from the tip of my rod by the actions of my jealous fellow fishermen; mine is the sleep that is being denied. And yet, like Job, it seems there is more for me to endure, for mine is the door that someone is battering on. Let them. I shall endure, I shall endure.

I— The knocking will not stop! I will tell them what I think.

Wednesday 5th September

John Fastolf, Earl of Caister – Scarborough

It is 9.57 p.m.

Miss Pink is sitting at a rough table. Her gun is pointed at Joe Carstairs's giant mute, who is wearing clothes this time. Between them is a ledger, stained with blood. 'Sorry, Johnny,' she says.

'Why?' he asks.

'I didn't trust you to be careful enough. And I wanted to be here. I wanted to see the Sphinx's eyes. I wanted to murder her for— Well. It was a stupid thing to do. We could both have been killed.'

'What happened?'

'I've only been here ten minutes,' says Miss Pink. 'Empty boat, apart from Kiki. I crept in here to find the mute standing over Molly, knife in hand. Molly was holding the ledger.'

Miss Pink speaks calmly, but the gun is quivering. She wants to fire. The light in the hold is soft and gentle. The smell of ropes and old metal is comforting.

'What is the ledger?' Johnny asks.

'The Sphinx's whole business, it would seem. Account numbers, aliases, everything. The ledger lays it all out, says it's all Kim Waring.'

'Oh,' says Johnny. 'What do we think has happened here, then? Molly stole the ledger from Kim – the Sphinx – and the mute is in his employ and was taking it back?'

'That is certainly what it looks like,' says Miss Pink. Saul, who is no fool, says nothing.

'Except there's something wrong with the picture, isn't there?'

Johnny says. 'Because I am here to meet the Sphinx. So why is Kim not here?'

'Because he knows about you,' says the mute, who is not a mute. 'Because he found out Molly was a traitor. Guess what he's doing now!'

Johnny's blood is suddenly noisy.

'Yes, my lord, that's right. He's on your yacht, having fun. He planned for you to come here. You're ruined. He'll have taken pictures. If he shows them to the police, they'll never leave you alone.' The giant speaks in a monotonous voice, not accented, but with an accented rhythm, if that makes any sense.

'What's he doing?'

'I'm not sure, but I imagine he's killing people, don't you?'

Saul is already moving to the door. Johnny wants to sprint back to the skiff, but he and Miss Pink can't leave *Berania* without finishing what they have started. 'We know you're the Sphinx, Molly,' he says.

Silence.

Death is the ultimate reality, but Molly is not dead. Her throat is cut very carefully, very shallowly, just for show, and now her eyes snap open. The giant jumps at Johnny, and falls under a bullet from Saul. Molly brings a little automatic up from behind her and Johnny shoots the forearm holding it. He was firing anywhere in her direction. Disarming her was luck.

Molly doubles over her arm. 'Damn,' she says. 'Damn it, that's sore!' She looks at Johnny. 'How long have you known?'

'Before we slept together.'

'Annoying. Damn it. Ow!'

'How long have you known I'm with the police?' says Johnny.

'Not long,' says Molly. While they're talking, Johnny is wrapping up Molly's arm, stopping the blood.

'The giant's dead,' says Miss Pink. 'We've got to go.'

Johnny believes that Kim is wreaking hovoc, but he can't leave Molly here and he won't kill her in cold blood. He wrenches her arms behind her, ties them hastily and tries to bundle her out of the hold. She won't stand or help him. Saul picks her up to carry her.

It isn't easy. Johnny knocks her on the head. He doesn't put her out cold, but she's stunned.

It would be quicker to take the skiff on his own, but Molly might have a crew coming to pick her up. Everyone is moving as fast as they can.

They don't row on the way back to *Dazzle*, but the journey still feels unbearably slow. At some point Johnny wasn't careful enough, and Molly found out or guessed that he was only playing at being a villain. She realised that he must at least be close to identifying her as the Sphinx. Thus she needed a scapegoat and she decided to frame Kim, so she put together tonight's little tableau. Johnny was supposed to run back to the *Dazzle* leaving her 'corpse', after which Molly would have disappeared. Presumably the mute was a willing sacrifice, or was blackmailed, or would be very well rewarded. Whichever it was, Molly would never have been seen again, not under that name. She'd probably have called herself 'the Phoenix' next time. She has a lurid imagination.

Molly knew Johnny was after her and she had Patterson and Miss Scarlett killed, and she set Kim to do mayhem on his yacht, without any compunction. Johnny looks at her. She's alert now and staring at him.

'You're cracking up,' she says.

'Shut up, Molly.'

'If you've known who I am for months, then it's not me you're after. You're after my suppliers. They're the real villains. I'm nothing. It suited me to play the oriental, and now it will suit them that I turn out to be a pretty flapper girl. It's all them, darling. I'm nothing.'

'You're not nothing.'

'No, but I'm not the whole thing, am I?'

'You're enough.'

'I'm never going to court, am I?'

'Yes, you are.'

'But then—' She's quick. She says, 'But if I go to court, your cover is blown. That's what you want! You want out, Johnny darling.'

'Shut up, Molly.'

Molly is right. Court has been his secret dream, his furtive hope. He wanted this to be his last operation, however things turned out. If he died, he died. If he didn't die, if he captured Molly, then he'd have to come into the sunlight and that would make him useless to C. He had begun to fear he couldn't see right from wrong and that would never do.

'Why do you want to stop?' says Molly. 'Is it because you like the girl?'

'No,' he says. It is possible that Henny is dead. He has to be prepared for that.

'We're both dished, Johnny. Even if you save the girl, you're not the Galahad she wants. You should have just joined me. You still could, you know. You on one side of the fence, me on the other, playing—'

'Shut up.'

'You can't blame me for trying,' she says quietly.

'Patterson and Miss Scarlett – was that Kim?'

'Of course. He thought it was rather extreme, but he enjoyed the idea of it too much to ask questions. I hoped it would make you too furious to think straight, but you're a cold fish.'

'This is a bloody mess,' says Johnny, 'but there's a right side and a wrong side. A child would know which is which.'

'Right and wrong!' says Molly. 'Oh, darling!'

He slews the skiff alongside the *Harlequin*'s ladder. Leaving Miss Pink with Molly, he races up, Saul at his heels. As his feet hit the deck, Martha shouts from the darkness to his right, 'There you are!' Mike is behind her in his dressing gown. 'Hurry, they're in Grey's room!'

He pelts along the gangway. The gramophone in Grey's room starts up as they reach the cabin. Johnny listens for the briefest moment, steps away, nods to Saul and to Audrey, who has joined them as they run, and breaks down the door. Kim says, 'Darling Johnny, how dashing you are!'

Johnny says, 'Drop the knife.'

Kim does and says, 'Self-protection, old thing. You never know who you'll meet at an orgy. I thought you were off the boat. I wasn't doing anything very bad.' Grey shouts through his gag. Marion and Henny are alive, but barely moving. 'Don't listen to Grey,' Kim says. 'Grey will say anything. We're taking pictures to blackmail him, you see, because he took pictures of Marion, which meant she had to destroy her husband's lovely fish. What a wicked man he is! He sent Henny to help her do it.'

'Shut up, Kim.'

'She's a bad fruit, Johnny! I hope she hasn't got her hooks into you.'

'You don't care about Grey.'

'I care about everything, darling. The girls, I admit, seem rather tipsy.'

'They're drugged,' Johnny says.

'Really? What dissolutes you let on your boat, to be sure.'

Caister searches Waring. He finds another knife and a small revolver. Saul unties the others. Grey starts to speak, but Waring says, 'Why don't you shut up? Won't it be better if no one knows about this?'

Mike and Martha put Henny and Marion to bed, walking them like zombies. Grey refuses to speak. Johnny exposes the film in Grey's cameras. He sends Caro to an unused cabin and puts Audrey outside her door. He doesn't tell Kim that he knows about Molly. He's not sure what Kim knows. He ties Kim up himself in the last unoccupied stateroom.

'How delicious,' says Kim. 'Be as rough as you like.' But Kim's heart isn't really in it.

Thursday 6th September

Mike Mitchell-Hedges – The North Sea

Letter to Jane Harvey Houlson, ctd.

Sept. 6: Jane, young feller, do I have a tale to tell you, and it's a tale that's going to make me rich, at long bloody last! Remember how I planned to puff about Scarbie being a wild and wanton outpost, deadlier than the darkest jungle? Well, it bloody is! Miss Scarlett and the nigger butler died in a motor crash and Caister said the show must go on. Accidents happen, but it was damn cool, if you ask me.

Dinner was every bit the ghastly show you'd imagine. Banshees and hellions, venom and vendetta. I like a good bit of spite, but there wasn't much sport in the room, if you wanted to keep your eyes. Spoke with Caroline Fastolf for a few minutes early on. Rather a triumph. Asked what she thought of *Adverse*, let her prose on for long enough to determine that she hadn't read it and then asked if Anthony had done the right thing going to Havana. Girl next to me, dashed pretty in a Chinese dress, saw what I'd done. Made the whole bloody thing worthwhile, because Caro's a snake, but I got a warning look from Kim Waring and I didn't need another. Even your deadly darling savage boyfriend would have thought twice about getting between that one and the last sandwich.

Lucky seat at dinner between Caister and one of Carstairs's houris, name of Lapwing (I doubt that's what her parents call her). We chatted away, but in a watchful sort of mode, as per a herd of antelope who can see some lions getting fretful in the near-distance. Waring and Caro Fastolf were disgraceful, and they baited Caister, and he went off early – suspiciously bloody early in fact, but I was too busy drinking and staying out of trouble to realise it at the time. But the atmos stayed frosty and I didn't hang around very long myself, and nor did Caister's friends from the shore, and even Joe Carstairs and her gang scarpered pretty quickly. By the time I made myself scarce, Waring and Caro were getting Marion Mitchell-Henry – what she was doing there I only learned later – and little Henny drunker than skunks, except Waring was feeding them more than just drink. Everything's always so bloody obvious, looking back. Martha was down our end of the table and was well out of it. She left. I left. A quick, bad dinner.

I took a bottle of rum with me. Had a bath. Started reading Fred Walker's book. Capital stuff. Doubt anyone will remember much of it in a few years' time, if you know what I mean.

And then, God knows what time it was, there was a fearful battering at my door. Enter Martha Gellhorn, in a state of wild panic.

Waring and Caro have Marion and Henny in Grey's cabin, she says. Good luck to them, I say. (Nothing surprises your Chief any more.)

No! She wails. It's a trick. Waring drugged the girls, then he sent them in first, they let him him in and he has a knife. A big knife.

I say, It's Caister's boat, get him. She says, I tried him first, of course! Bit hurtful, but I let it pass. Apparently Caister's nowhere to be found. *Dazzle*'s practically deserted. *Harlequin*'s not back from the shore.

We're on deck by now. She's trying to drag me to Grey's cabin. Internally your Chief is applauding the girl's moxie, but Waring's a vicious bugger and he has a knife. I say, We need a weapon. I spy a light in the wheelhouse. I ask who's in there. Martha doesn't know. It's the girl, Audrey.

She's not happy to see us. We ask where Caister is. She says Caister is off the boat. We say Waring has the girls in Grey's cabin, with a knife, and we need a weapon fast.

She knows this is serious, but right then we hear a little engine ploughing up to the side of the boat and we dash down to see Caister and another crewman, all in black, swarming up the ladder with tommy guns over their shoulders. It's like a bloody movie. There's no delay and into the Valley of Death they charge, except they're fine, of course, because they've got guns and Waring is just a society parasite with a knife. It's a very nasty knife, by the way. The girls and Grey are tied up. No one's hurt. The girls don't know which way is Wednesday.

Caro and Waring get swiftly and separately incarcerated. It seems they were taking photographs to blackmail Grey. He had taken photographs of himself and Marion to blackmail Mitchell-Henry with, and that is why the Captain's fish was burnt.

That's the official story. There's clearly more to it. Why does Waring care a tinker's cuss about Mitchell-Henry? Why were the girls tied up? I told you that Waring's a wrong 'un.

Also, why was that red-haired girl heaved on board, and what happened to her? Some things are not meant to be known.

Anyway, off we go to our cabins for some well-earned rest that I assume we are all too jangled to take, and fifteen minutes later I am summoned to the saloon.

I pass Grey, looking sick, and Martha is still in the saloon with Caister, who is on a stool by the bar. I say, What ho! There are no cheerful greetings in return. Caister nods and Martha leaves. He says, Thank you, Marty, and means it. Then it's me and him.

Grey's not going to write about this, he says. Nor is Martha, and I'll make sure the Captain doesn't, either. I've covered their expenses. So?

It's a tricky thing to be asked your price by the richest man in the Empire. I don't have an answer ready. He says, Stop thinking, Mike. Here's what I propose. You're a crook and I don't trust you. You'll publish this the moment you think the ups outweigh the downs and, who knows, I might die tomorrow. I don't want any of this printed, ever, so here is what we'll do. I will pay you a thousand pounds, right now, as a sign of my good offices. Then I will put you on an income, sufficient to pay your way. If ever you are tempted to print, you will come to me first, and I might increase that income, or alternatively I might have you killed. If you print, I will have you killed. My executors will pay you until you die, if it comes to that, and they'll know all the conditions. They're competent chaps. You do not, of course, know whether to believe me. On the other hand, I'm offering you a decent living wage – it will be that – for doing nothing.

It didn't sound like humbug. I shook his hand and went to bloody bed.

So that was last night! And where are we now, do you think?

We're fishing!

It's the next morning and we're bloody fishing! We didn't want the Captain to know that anything had happened. We didn't want the locals to get a sniff. So out we came, and here we bally are.

I'm on the *Harlequin*, thank God. The Captain wanted me on his coracle, but no bloody dice when I didn't have to! He's being lugged around by his usual local worthy. Grey's rowing boat – he has decided that only rowing boats can land these peculiar English tunny, on the basis of his own failures – is being rowed by Johnny Caister himself, who insisted on taking the job. He also insisted that they take Waring with them. He said he wanted Waring under his eye, and he wanted him where he couldn't speak to anyone – he was too dangerous. It was bloody rum and Waring kicked up a stink, but Caister didn't listen. He told Waring his choice was tied or untied. Waring said tied. Caister bound him hand and foot. Waring said Caister couldn't take a joke. Caister said he didn't often make jokes and gagged him.

The money will be bloody welcome, security is what it's always been about, but it would have been a good bloody book, young feller, and more or less true. I could have held my head high again.

Huevos rancheros, Miss Scarlett's coffee and a good gin-fizz— Gellhorn and I agree that it is the breakfast of kings. I like Gellhorn. She's been scratching away as well.

Thursday 6th September

Henny Rosefield – Scarborough

Henny woke. Her wrists were sore. Someone was rapping at the door.

'Come in,' she called, but the words were thick.

Audrey entered. She was carrying a raw egg yolk in one glass and a measure of something brownish-red in the other. Henny sat up. Audrey dropped the yolk into the red-brown mix and said, 'Drink it, quick.'

Henny did. She nearly gagged.

'Don't know if it helps,' said Audrey, 'but it looks so bloody awful that you sort of think it has to. Do you know what happened last night?'

'No.'

'No. Mrs Captain doesn't, either. Saul's taking her home. Kim bloody Waring drugged you. He was going to kill you. Johnny saved you.' Henny's eyes were wide. Audrey stared evenly into them. She said, 'There's more to it, obviously, but that's basically what happened. I think Johnny likes you. What are you going to do about it?'

'I don't know.'

'If you don't know, don't do anything. Go away. It's not your fault. Don't dare stay out of gratitude. Get dressed.' She left.

Wednesday 5th–Thursday 6th
September

Martha Gellhorn – The North Sea

Letter to G. Campbell Beckett, ctd.

Oh, my dearest darling G. Campbell, oh! At least no one has died. I am too stunned to write anything. I will finish this tomorrow.

It's Thursday morning and I'm on *Harlequin* again. We're heading out to the tunny-grounds as if nothing has happened, which is what we are pretending to the outside world for some secretive reason, and we're towing a rowboat for Grey to fish from. Waring is in the cabin, gagged. Johnny is sat outside it. He won't let anyone else go near.

This may seem baroque, and it is, I suppose, but last night was terrible, much worse than I thought even when I was scribbling to you, when at least one half of me suspected I was being overdramatic and it was all a fuss about nothing. I felt silly about my cowardice and wanted to know what was happening, but I didn't believe anyone was in actual peril. I snuck into the corridor and was just in time to see Kim Waring lead Marion and Henny to Grey's cabin and follow a few minutes after with Caro. As Waring went in, he pulled a wicked-looking knife from a sheath hidden somewhere above his ankle. My heart almost stopped!

I ran to hunt for Johnny again, and now I was practically out of my mind. I still couldn't find him. Eventually I roused Mike. He was not the bravest thing you ever saw, but he saw a light in the wheel-house and – well, I don't know what to tell you about it all. I have been sworn to secrecy. Later I might be clearer, but for now let me say that Johnny arrived back like the cavalry and broke down Grey's door. Marion and Henny were tied up, eyes rolling with drugs. They don't remember a thing between them. Grey was tied up, and says Waring was about to kill them. Waring says he was helping the girls take revenge on Grey, and what he was doing was no crueller than what Grey had done. He sounded very plausible.

Johnny believed none of it. He was something like a minor god of war, quite irresistible. He tied Waring up, left him with his burly crewmen and took me and Grey to the saloon. He told Grey that if he ever wrote about these events, Johnny would break his name forever. He asked me if I would be prepared to publish nothing about it – he would square things with *The Illustrated Doodah*. I said that was fine. I was dazed.

As soon as Grey was gone, I asked him about Molly, and told him that Henny saw him kissing her on board the *Berania*.

He said, 'Oh, that was it!' His relief to have found a reason for Henny's sudden coldness was utterly convincing. He said that he couldn't explain the situation with Molly, except to say that Henny had misinterpreted it and Molly was nothing to him. Then he said, 'I'm very sorry I can't tell you more than this, but trust me that I am trying to be on the side of the angels.'

Then Mike arrived and Johnny asked that they be allowed to speak privately.

Now that I have slept some small amount, I think I should feel resentful that I agreed to being muzzled, that this adventure has been a big story, which, like the Captain's tuna, will never be recorded. But I do not.

Henny has been standing like an automaton by the starboard rail, but a moment ago she turned round and she looks completely lost. Johnny rose from his seat by the cabin. She took a step toward him and then turned away. I'm going to speak to her.

She doesn't know what to think about last night. I told her that when Johnny heard she was in danger, he ran like a tiger, didn't waste a breath at Grey's door. She said that he didn't do it for her. All he cared about was stopping Kim.

I said this was nonsense. I said she mustn't be embarrassed or prideful, if these emotions are only going to ruin something she doesn't want to ruin. I said she mustn't run away from Johnny, just in case the true situation is that she likes someone who happens to like her back. I said she must at least give him the chance to say that. Where I developed this unusually wise collection of advice I do not know – I wonder if I shall be able to draw on it in my own case, or is wisdom only ever available for use second-hand?

Henny looked doubtful, in spite of the wisdom. She asked where Johnny had been last night. She heard he arrived with a gun, from who knows where. I'd somehow lost sight of that in all the fuss. When you've been asked to believe six impossible things before breakfast, sometimes the seventh slips past you unawares.

Well, I don't know where he came from. Johnny might be the most desperate smuggler known to man, but I don't think he is. I can't say what took place last night, not really, but I want to believe what he said about being on the side of the angels, and I think I do. That's what I told Henny.

Then she asked, 'What about Molly?'

I told her what Johnny told me. It sounded less reassuring from my mouth.

Oh, darling, I have clearly not understood a tenth part of whatever has been happening around me this week, but for all my short-sightedness I am adamant that Henny and Johnny have collided at a vital moment.

One sees how completely one could get absorbed in such personal dramas if one spent one's life among these people. That is what I must resist. Whatever extraordinary things have been happening behind the curtain, they have all been to do with a world of pointless excess and private malice, and I simply refuse to make that world my primary concern. I want to speak for the masses of people who will be ignored if no one speaks for them. I want to make myself something useful, and work on the hardest parts of life – the guts of it.

Maybe I can visit Fairyland from time to time, but it must only be a vacation. I must not imprison myself in a field of peacocks while half the world is starving and the other half burns.

We've breakfasted now. Mike has also, in his words, 'been silenced'. He asked me what Johnny's paying me! He saw that I was offended and changed the subject. He asked why Johnny demanded to be Grey's boatman for the day, and why he's taken Waring out with them as if Waring were a virus. He asked me if I knew what Waring had done. It was obviously personal between Johnny and him.

I said I didn't know.

Mike said that Waring was the sort of bad ox that only a butcher could make anything out of. I do not know if I believe in evil of that kind, but Waring makes my flesh crawl.

Oh, Grey's onto a fish! It seems so anticlimactic, somehow. I dare say it might make the papers, but it will never be the thrilling closing chapter of Mike's book, since Mike is not allowed to write same. That was Mike's first thought on hearing the shouts, and he sounded almost wistful when he voiced it. I asked him if it could be true that he cared less about Johnny's money than about writing something that people would admire at last. He told me I was being 'bloody stupid'.

My God, G. Campbell! Waring's dead! He stood up while Grey was fighting his fish, and the boat jerked and he was thrown into the water. Johnny tried to make Grey let the fish go, but Grey didn't want to. Johnny cut the harness free and the tuna took the rod, but as they turned back to Waring, somehow the line tangled him up and he was snatched into the depths.

We searched for him for an hour. Grey kept saying that this was yesterday's giant fish, stolen from him for a second time, but Johnny told him to shut up. Eventually we saw a tangle of gear and Waring bobbing up from underneath it. Johnny and Mike went down to pick him from the sea – the harness had caught up in the rod, they said, and hooked around Waring's foot.

Thursday 6th September

John Fastolf, Earl of Caister –
Scarborough / The North Sea

Johnny, rather surprisingly, sleeps well.

Miss Pink rouses him with the news that Molly is dead.

In the seconds between waking and hearing this, he works his way all but instantaneously through the following guilty train of thought: Patterson has woken him, when necessary, for the last fifteen years; who would wake him in Patterson's absence was one of the many things Johnny did not have time to consider yesterday; in fact, the loss of Patterson and Miss Scarlett is a much greater one than capturing Molly Parker is a gain; the loss to him is profound, but nothing like so profound as the loss to Miss Pink, and yet here is Miss Pink waking him; he will have to find someone to replace Patterson; Saul and Andy are good, but not good enough. He certainly doesn't want someone chosen by the Service. Perhaps Miss Pink will know of someone else, but of course that cannot be what she is thinking about now.

'I'm very sorry,' he says.

'I know.'

They go to Molly's cabin. She had a poison capsule in her tooth. She's written a note:

I'm sorry, Johnny, there's nothing you could have done to stop this. If you were hoping to have your day in court, well, tough luck. This is the best thing for me. The worst that could happen is that one of my lot gets to me in prison. I've been told what they'd do to me then – and I told others, and I meant it too, and I had it done once

— and nothing's worth that. I've had a good run. It's better to die clean.

It's just a bloody game, you know that. That's what you meant about doing it for the thrill. You can't pretend that the papers weren't funny about the Sphinx.

Kim Waring's as good as dead as well. You may think you can protect him until a trial and get out of this, but you can't. You will only let my side know who you really are, and if you do that you're dead. Telling you all this is my good deed for the day. My suppliers still think you're a criminal — I worked the truth out for myself and I didn't tell them. They wanted me to learn everything I could and get you onside, because they think they can use you. They might even offer to make you the new Sphinx, who knows? They'll want you even more now that you've beaten me, because it'll save them the trouble of building a new operation. It's not as if you don't already supply dope. It's not as if we're all that different deep down. It's not as if you can really stop the trade. If they learn the truth, you're dead, and you'll wish you'd never been born.

You could quietly give up, pretend you'd lost your taste for it. They might let you. Probably not, though.

Anyway, I've had a good run. Or an exciting one, anyway. I know there's nothing the other side of the curtain.

I hope you weren't faking everything. I wasn't. You can be quite fun,

Molly, aka the Sphinx

('Molly'! I chose it because at first I was pretending to be a moll. Stupid name to pick. Well, that's that.)

Johnny is not shocked. He thought Molly might kill herself if he left her alone, and he didn't do anything to stop it. It is good that she is dead. He hates the tone of her letter, as if they were somehow compadres. There is a real difference between them, and this is not a game, and she was not a lovable rogue.

Calling it a game – this thing that has killed people and keeps killing them – is disrespectful, trivialising. It represents an amoral cast of mind. The rules of a game are amoral. The laws of a society should be moral.

That, ultimately, is what frightens Johnny about working outside the law. He believes that the state should take responsibility, that justice should be publicly done. Molly would surely have been executed, but she would have been judged as anyone else is judged.

If the judgement is put in Johnny's hands and in the hands of Miss Pink, then what is to stop them exacting private vengeance? Last night, Johnny tried to kill Molly. He may have been firing in self-defence, he probably was, but he wanted her to die.

Molly's claim that she was a pawn of some shadowy group of bosses is disingenuous in the extreme. Her network wasn't a thousand fiendish Chinamen subverting half of London, but it was a significant criminal enterprise, and catching her will have crippled it. She was not a tool of her suppliers; they were partners running complementary organisations. It was Molly acting on her own initiative who ordered Patterson's death and Miss Scarlett's.

It's no use dreaming. Molly is dead, and she is dead in secret. That leaves Kim. Maybe his masters would kill him before he came to trial, but maybe they wouldn't. If Johnny has to testify, then Johnny could still escape.

Is this selfishness? He has done some mean and grubby things these last ten years, but if these things have protected more people than they have harmed, then is it mimsy for him to stop? He has learned that there are some enemies who cannot be fought in the open.

And finally, just like that, he understands why Grey was wrong about picking a story out of the chaos to explain who you are. Grey is constantly rewriting the world in such a way as to fit it around his own immutable and infantile self. That is not Johnny. He is prepared to rewrite himself.

But what does this mean? He must not pretend he has a clean slate. He has done things in the past that he does not disavow, and he has responsibilities to the future that he must not shirk. He is an instrument of the state. He thinks it is a good state, as states go, but faith in a state is a very precarious faith and he must constantly be wary lest he become one of its mistakes. If he carries on as he has been doing these last few years, he will become a gun. You cannot trust a gun. He must always think before he shoots. It must always be a choice.

That is why he can trust Miss Pink. She wanted to kill Molly Parker last night, but she could not do it in cold blood. She has not lost her moral sense.

How can Henny fit into this, if he even wants her to? Maybe it is this: unless Johnny makes some connection to the world, unless he cares about something in it, his moral sense will atrophy. Maybe, if it weren't for the fluke of her appearance with Grey, he wouldn't be thinking any of this. It's impossible to know.

What if she rejects him? That is secondary. She is his first chance since Caro, and it has been so long that she may possibly be the last chance he will get. If he reaches out and is rebuffed, what has he lost? He was drowning anyway.

He has a choice now. He looks at Waring.

Grey's rod yelps and Grey starts barking instructions.

When Johnny is done with the first batch of rowing and Grey has settled down for a bout of grim tunny-holding, Johnny ungags Waring and they have a little chat.

Thursday 6th–Friday 7th September

Mike Mitchell-Hedges –
The North Sea / London

Letter to Jane Harvey Houlson, ctd.

Well, young feller, the vicious web's last strand is tangled! Grey hooked a fish – a big one, I think. I mumbled to Gellhorn about how it would have made a fine last chapter for the book, especially in the States, and she piped back with some guff about how I secretly preferred art to money. Well, you can talk to her about that, sometime!

I took the glasses for a gander, see if I could judge the strain on Grey's rod. Caister was rowing. Then he stopped and I was about to put down the glasses while Grey clung onto his fish for a while, but I saw Caister ungag Waring. Waring was grinning. They talked. Then Caister bent down and did something, at which point Waring stumbled to his feet and started to shout. Martha asked me what was going on – without the glasses, all the others knew was that Waring was standing. I said I didn't know. She demanded the glasses. I kept 'em. This all happened in the blink of an eye, and the next thing was that Caister had dug in an oar and pitched Waring overboard. Very neatly done. Now Caister turned to Grey, who looked at him in fury, but before he had a chance to unhitch the fish, Johnny had grabbed the rod and struggled for it and thrown it into the water, and off the tunny went. 'Somehow', we hear, it tangled Kim's ropes and took him to Davy's locker. Well, *I know how*, young feller. While he was struggling for the rod, Caister was looping a cord around around the reel, and if that cord wasn't tied to Waring, I'll eat the *Dazzle*.

If I'd thought of doing Caister the dirty over the pension he's giving me, that was enough to keep me honest. Waring needed putting down, but it was coldly done.

We found him soon after. The tunny tore the line and reel off the rod, and the latter bobbed like a float. Johnny said he'd go down and pick the body out of the water. I said I'd join him, he'd want a witness. He looked at me queerly, and I told him I'd seen what happened and he had nothing to fear from me. The story would be better coming from both of us, I said. I was trying to make myself valuable to him, but I might have made myself dangerous. Wouldn't want him thinking like that, but it's done now. I'm pretty sure he's straight. He has a bloody funny way of showing it, though.

Sept. 7: Plus one day. Back in London.

Police took statements, 'terrible accident, could have happened to anyone', and so on. Caister has sway and he stood guarantee for us. We were free after a couple of hours. Gossip papers flocked about, Caister took the lead and we gave them a dull-as-ditchwater version. They'll print Caro's shrieks of 'Murder', though, and I don't suppose Caister will sue.

Grey was glum and ran away to Liverpool, or was packed off, more likely. Caister drove Martha, Henny and me down to town at a fearful speed and dined us late at the Savoy. All very formal, polite and unclear. I tried to hang around afterwards to see if Caister went off with Henny, but Martha dragged me away. I asked what was going on. She said it was none of my bloody business. She gave me a goodbye tumble as a reward for being a good boy. Splendid girl, but very serious deep down. Troubled. Anyway, water under the hull.

Caister's been as good as gold. Surprised note from my bank first thing this morning re deposit of £1,000. Must be an angle I could play, some ruse that would bump up the amount, but I think I'll just let it come and spend it quietly. Must be getting old. Keep thinking of Caister turning up like that, dressed in black, guns. Sometimes you've got to know when there's a bigger duck in your pond and keep out of its way, if it'll let you.

So, no book, no head high, have to rattle together some other way to rebuild the old credit. I'll think of something. Whatever Gellhorn says, what people think about you is what you really are, and they're going to bloody remember me.

The things we do to stay alive! I'll send this now. It's been a bloody tiring week. I'll be in New York about three boats after this arrives.

Fiercely,

Your Chief

Thursday 6th September

Henny Rosefield – Scarborough

Henny watched Waring die. She spoke to the police and confirmed what everyone else had said. Then she sat in a quiet corner of the hotel's restaurant.

Caro had to be sedated, and she was given a room upstairs. Later, while the interviews were being conducted, she emerged and found Henny before anyone could stop her. Her eyes were red and she was slurring. 'He murdered Kim. You know he did.'

'Are you seriously expecting me to help you?' said Henny. Caro didn't know what she was talking about. Henny gave her a moment. Caro still did not understand. 'Kim was going to kill me,' said Henny. Caro said nothing. 'Has he done it before?'

'No,' said Caro. 'He wouldn't have done anything. It was a joke. He wanted to frighten you.' She didn't believe herself. She looked past Henny's shoulder. Johnny was approaching. Her mouth twisted at Henny. 'You know Johnny doesn't really want you,' she hissed, once he was within earshot. 'He just sees you as a younger me.'

'Younger, yes,' said Henny. Caro hated that.

Johnny said, 'She's nothing like you, Caroline. Come, Henny.' A few steps away Johnny said, 'I do, up to a point, feel sorry for her.'

They spoke to Mitchell-Henry and his wife. Johnny said, 'I'm sorry, sir. You won, but it doesn't seem right to make a thing of it.' Mitchell-Henry wanted to contradict him, but Johnny was firm. 'Not the done thing,' he said. 'My father would agree. He would like to see you again, I think. It's a long time since you were in Norfolk.'

Mitchell-Henry's face contorted. 'At least we know I beat the blighter,' he said.

'Yes,' said Johnny. 'I'm sorry for everything.' Marion took her husband's hand and led him away.

Grey's tormentors in Scarborough were, under the circumstances, muted. Hardy circled, but Johnny got rid of him and promised to deal with Grey's debts. The fuss over Waring's death was swiftly overtaken when an excited little boy arrived at the quayside having caught a 600-pounder. Briefly forgotten, Johnny left with the remainder of his party.

Johnny informed Grey that Saul had taken Grey's luggage to the train station, that tickets and some money for his expenses were arranged, that he was to go immediately to Liverpool and was not to consider returning, and that the rest had better be silence, was that clear? Grey didn't answer. Johnny repeated, 'Is that clear?' Grey nodded, petulant. 'Your train leaves in an hour. We're going to London. Goodbye.' He didn't wait for a reply. Grey ignored Henny throughout this.

There was not much to do. It was seven, and the police were happy to let them leave. Miss Pink had charge of the boats. Johnny offered Henny, Mike and Martha space in the Hispano-Suiza, if they wanted to get out of Scarborough. He'd have their bags follow them, he said.

And so they walked to where the car was garaged. They began in a gaggle. Then Henny put herself between Johnny and Martha, and walked slightly faster. Martha, after a moment, started speaking to Mike and dropped behind.

'Thank you for last night,' Henny said.

'You don't even remember it,' said Johnny.

'I've been told.' Scarborough was grey. The wind was rising. It was chilly. 'Who was Waring?'

'A baddie.'

'What happened today. When you—'

'I killed him.'

'Yes. It wasn't about your wife, was it?'

'No.'

'It wasn't about me, either?'

'No.'

'I didn't think so,' said Henny. 'Good. Is it dope?'

'Partly.'

A few steps, and then: 'Sorry, but what about Molly?'

'Ah. Martha says you saw me and her. That was— I'm sorry you saw it. I will explain it one day, if you let me, but not today. You'll not see her again. I didn't kill her. But she's dead.'

'Oh. Whatever it is, it's not over, is it?'

'No,' he said. Then, 'Yes and no. It's never over.'

'Which side are you— You're not exactly the police, are you?'

'That's it,' said Caister. 'I'm not exactly the police.'

'Natural justice?' said Henny.

'There's the rub. I don't trust natural justice because no two of us pygmies think it's the same thing. That's why we have laws. Vengeance is too satisfying. That's why we should leave it to the Lord.'

'So?'

'So I'm in a paradoxical position, and there it is. But I do try to do my best.'

They were still walking. Martha laughed at something Mike had told her. The conversation with Henny had only taken forty yards. Henny asked, 'If it's not over, what's going to happen now?'

Johnny said, 'I never know. What I do is dangerous.'

'I've got nothing. No one.'

'You realise that I'm fond of you?' said Johnny. He could have been explaining that he didn't want to see her again. He could have been saying the opposite.

'I'm fond of you, too.'

'But we don't really know each other.'

'No, we don't,' said Henny. She hesitated. She thought of something to say, but it would be the wrong thing. So, surprising herself, she reached out and touched his arm.

He looked at her sharply.

'Sorry,' she said.

'No,' said Johnny. 'You're right. We don't know each other, but one never does at the start.'

'Do you know what to do next?' she asked.

'No,' said Johnny. 'It's tricky. I've been very low, for a long time.'

Friday 7th September

Martha Gellhorn – London

Letter to G. Campbell Beckett, ctd.

Well, darling, it's all over and I am coming home, home, home at last.

It's Friday morning and I am at the beautiful Savoy, at Johnny's expense. Yesterday was so astonishing, after the night before, that we were desperate to escape Scarborough. Johnny said he had business in London and would drive us. He said he would not be hard to find, if the authorities wanted him.

We all spoke to the police, of course, and Caroline screamed murder, but Grey was in the rowboat and he insists that nothing happened untoward – he would have to, since he wanted to keep fishing and not even pick Waring up! And Mike says he saw the whole ghastly accident through his glasses, and it was all Waring's fault – typical idiot landlubber. As if you could trust Mike. The police do not, of course.

Do I think that nothing happened untoward? It was terribly odd that Johnny took Waring out to sea, and terribly convenient that he died. What I am saying, I suppose, is that I rather believe Johnny killed him, and I should mind that desperately, but I do not.

I slept all the way to London. We arrived late, but the Savoy was expecting us. Henny and I arrived downstairs before the men, and I asked her what she was going to do. She said that depended on what Johnny is. Well, exactly!

What do I think? What we saw, or believe we saw, does not put him on the angels' side, but I think he is. Or rather, I hope he is. That's what I told Henny. She said she felt the same. Then she added, 'He said he was fond of me.'

I said, 'What! Really!' or some such. I've been in England long enough to recognize a passionate statement of intent when I hear one. Henny has not. Johnny told her he hoped she might stay in England, but she worries that he was just being polite. Good grief! I asked her if she doubted, honestly, in her heart, what he meant? She said she didn't, after seeing my reaction. But she is nervous about what Johnny is.

She asked what I planned to do now. I blurted out the fruits of all my mental labors. I said that I have been calling this week a fairyland as if that was something desperately unusual, but it is just the latest of my ventures in European fairylands. I said that I rather adored them, but I must always remember that I am just visiting. All the different circles might be 'real', but some are more real than others, and this one is not real enough to make me feel worthwhile. I will not live in a cage.

She said she didn't think Johnny would cage someone. There was something defiant about how she said it and I dare say she's right, but I would feel like I was caged and I can't let that happen again, whatever it costs me. I will choose my life, and of course I will be part of other people's stories, but I must focus on my own. If other people think I am living with my toes in different oceans, that will be their damned business and I can't help it.

Grey, by the way, is gone. Johnny packed him off to Liverpool, or one of his men did at any rate. Johnny's paying for everything, covering what Stoat Ledger won't. It's easy to be a millionaire. I'll work out what I feel about Grey too in the end. I've no idea now.

It was not a comfortable meal. Afterwards, Mike desperately wanted to spy on Henny and Johnny, and see where they went. I did too, but it was not our business anymore and so I dragged Mike away. He said he didn't want to know about any funny business, was just interested in his shipmates, nothing wrong in that. We went to our own beds, but only after a while. He deserved that at least, absurd creature that he is.

This morning, I called Henny's room so that we might breakfast together. She was gone. Johnny didn't stay at his club last night. I didn't know who else to call, and then I didn't call anyone. It seemed an appropriate end to the whole farrago. I suppose I will see them again, assuming they aren't simply elves who have melted back into the forest, and assuming that I really have been away for a week and not for a hundred years.

In retrospect, as I sit here and try to puzzle out whatever has been going on this week, I can't help thinking about something Mike said yesterday. I asked if he was disappointed that he lost the fish he hooked and he said, 'It was just an accident and there was nothing to be done.' But that's not right, is it! From what I understand, Mike should have let his fish go and he didn't only because of who he is. The Captain only let him fight it, and Johnny only didn't call across to stop Mike, because Grey was on the other tunny and everyone had turned against Grey by this point. The collision was an 'accident' in that it wasn't intentional, but it only happened because of who everyone was and because of precisely when it took place. One thing I do know, darling, and that is that I have had enough of egotistical fishermen to last me a lifetime.

A few short days after this letter finds you, so shall I, and you shall make me tea and we shall laugh about it all, and I shall apologize for the miserable agonizing hours I have put you through since I left Bertrand. Splashing it all onto a page has been all that's kept me sane. So thank you, as always, my darling old thing.

Your devoted,

Marty

Thursday 6th September

John Fastolf, Earl of Caister – The North Sea / Scarborough

Waring is happy to be ungagged at last. 'Need some intelligent conversation?' he smiles.

'No,' says Johnny. He speaks quietly. Grey, concentrating on the fish, will not be able to hear. He asks, 'Answer me honestly, Waring. What do you know about me?'

'You're rotten. Caro hollowed you out, and you went bad.'

'What does Caro know about you – about what you really do?'

'Nothing, poor darling. Very useful to have an innocent playing the innocent.'

'What did Molly tell you about me?'

'Poor Molly!' says Waring. 'I think she went a bit barmy at the end, old thing. Forced me to kill the pretty invert and your nigger. I told her it wouldn't help, if she wanted a partnership. She said it was a show of strength. Nothing I could do, darling. I'm just a humble spear-carrier.'

'Why do you think I haven't killed you?' asks Johnny.

'It has been on my mind, I have to admit. I almost believe I've been right all along and you cannot bear to have Caro hate you. But all in all I think it's because you realise how useful I can be to you. I was useful to Molly, after all. No one expects me to be a good chap – gives me some leeway.' He is very nearly the usual sparkling Kim Waring and his gaze appears cool, but that is the third time he has licked his lips, and the pupils flick to Johnny too often. He saw that Johnny didn't want Grey to hear their conversation, and he is keeping his voice low. That is not like Waring. He doesn't want to die and this is his desperate final pitch. 'I can make you a lot of money,' he whispers.

Johnny laughs.

'Of course,' Waring acknowledges bitterly. 'Stupid gelt, what am I thinking of, isn't it all so dull when you have it in gallons? But I can help you become the only player in this game. I presume that's what it is for you, though it's hardly the way I expected you to spoil. The excitement, I suppose? Savaging a society that savaged you, that sort of thing? And it's a good, hard game, red in tooth and claw. Back to nature, instead of all the folderol?'

'You never knew me,' says Johnny. 'And I'm not playing games. I am the law.'

A beat.

'You're the law?'

'I'm the law.'

'Oh, darling!' grins Waring. Another beat. 'So I am safe after all? Oh, Johnny! Prison will be jolly!'

'I know who you really are.' Grey has started to wind his reel furiously behind Johnny, oblivious. 'Who you *really* are,' Johnny repeats. 'I know everything.'

Kim Waring is a Russian agent. If all this had just been about a dope ring, C would never have called on Johnny and Miss Pink.

Affairs with Russia have got dirtier these past few years. The Soviets' objective with this particular operation was to give Kim Waring the chance to blackmail prominent Britons. Molly Parker built up the ring oblivious to the fact that she was nurtured, and her path smoothed, by Russian suppliers. It sounds like a giant network of evil, but it was not. It was a small, capable, committed team with a lot of money who picked a bright girl – Molly was their fourth attempt, incidentally – who was able to build a successful operation involving thirty people and two warehouses. It's not as if they were running an army, and they had a government's resources.

Waring did it for the money. He had married wealth and spent it all, and he didn't care what he did to get more.

The Russian operation was successful for a time, and then three years ago Kim misjudged a blackmailee, and that blackmailee knew someone in the Service.

Johnny and Miss Pink took their time to close the Sphinx's ring down, for several reasons. First, they wanted to root out as much of the supply chain as possible. They would have wanted to do this if they were the police, but it was even more important to infiltrate and disable a network with political connections.

Second, they wanted their operation to look as if it was nothing to do with Russia. They wanted it to look as if dope-dealing Johnny had acted against his competitor, the Sphinx.

Third, they had fed Russia various false informations via Kim Waring. In the wake of what happened at Send Manor – where Kim had poisoned the dope in order to create a scene that would have compromised Rudderick Drake even more completely than Johnny had planned for – Kim had contacted Drake and made his terms clear. Drake had passed on a folder carefully prepared by C. It was their sixth successful handover, their luck had held well, but now it was time to cash in their chips.

Keeping Kim from going to trial is not just a matter of Johnny's cover. If the Russians don't know what has really happened, then the misinformation will continue to do its work and the rest of the things Miss Pink and Johnny have learned will continue to be useful.

'Molly was my handler,' says Kim.

'No, she wasn't. We know who your handler is. We'll leave him alone for now.'

'Was Ruddy one of yours?'

'Yes. You underestimated Molly too, by the way. She worked out I was police. The "show of strength" was her trying to set you up.'

'Oh. Obvious now. Well played, Molly.' Kim is sweating heavily. 'Look, Caister. I can still be bloody useful to you. I can turn turtle, all chums behind the curtain, passing on false gen and whatnot. Double agent, you know?'

'Answer one question. Your side wanted me to join the Sphinx. Did they ever suspect I wasn't a crook?' If the Russians have any idea, then Johnny is blown. There will be no point keeping Kim out of court.

'It never crossed their minds, Johnny darling, I swear. I gave them chapter and verse about what a rancid aristo you were. They lapped it up.' He is bending close to Johnny, imploring. 'They haven't a clue, I swear.'

Johnny knows he will be weighed in a fine balance, that his will never be an easy shape to see, but he is made of the decisions he has made.

Driving back to London, while the girls sleep, Johnny talks to Mike. He likes Mike, likes the tightrope he walks between all his different personae, likes particularly the lack of self-pity and the willingness to carry on telling his preposterous stories. Mike will keep his side of the bargain. He's the sort of chap who might even be useful, further down the line.

Red-haired Inspector Raskell had returned to Scarborough in time for *Dazzle*'s landing. He took Johnny aside and said, 'I've been told what's going on, sir, very privately indeed. I don't know what I think about it.'

'Nor do I,' Johnny had said. He told Raskell what had happened to Kim, and why. He said that the alternatives were almost certainly worse, that Kim in court would be utterly unreliable and that his evidence would be designed to be destructive rather than useful. He was prepared to face the music, if their masters disagreed.

Raskell had assimilated this information and said, 'I don't think they'll mind, sir.'

'No,' Johnny had said. 'I think I'd prefer it if they did, though. I'm sorry you've been wasting your time chasing after me. You did very well, I think. That sounds patronising. I don't mean it to.'

'No, I suppose not,' Raskell had said. 'So, now I know, and I cannot un-know apparently, so now I am one of you. Do you know where we go from here?'

'Not exactly, no.'

Thursday 6th September

Zane Grey – Liverpool

Letter to Dolly Grey, ctd.

Everything is lost, Dolly.

This place, these people, everything is so close and crowded, and it has choked me and I am coming home. I cannot bear ever to write about it, not for Ledger and not for myself. When I told Caister this, he begged me to put pen to paper, to tell the whole truth. When I refused, he said he would pay me whatever Ledger promised as recompense for my suffering, which you may take as proof that he has been thwarting me all this trip and feels ashamed.

Nothing interesting happened last night at the party. I heard nothing. The knock on my door was a servant with some cocoa.

I do not know if the newspapers will have reported a trivial incident that took place today. An Englishman was killed while fishing with me, that is all. It was an accident. He fell overboard and tangled in my gear as Caister fumbled it overboard. It was not a murder. If anyone asks you, be very clear about that.

I am certain that today's fish – for such is the nature of my twisted fate – was yesterday's giant returned to taunt me, my own white whale. As I let him free, as the Englishman's face paled away from our little boat and into the green, mysterious depths, I never felt such a powerful sense of my own ill-fortune.

From that moment, all I wanted was to be traveling home. The police were impertinent, the gaggle of tourists in Scarborough even more so. I sent Hardy on his way for good and all, I refused to travel back to London and I set off immediately for Liverpool. Caister was relieved, of course. He knows I could have persuaded Henny to join me if I had chosen to forgive her, but I did not so choose. I am not leaving my hotel room until it is time to join my ship.

This will reach you very little before I do, I am sure. I send it tonight, and tomorrow evening I sail myself. I will then go straightway from New York to Altadena. Pray leave a message for me in NY that Brownie will be waiting. I do not think I will ever write my story of Catalina. It would be a great work, but my soul could not bear the strain. Fishing is too sacred for fiction. Please, therefore, confirm whether you have had a concrete response from Hemingway.

I will consider Australia.*

Your,

Doc

* Grey went to Australia the next year.

Thursday 6th September

Henny Rosefield – London

Henny and Johnny barely acknowledged each other during dinner at the Savoy. Afterwards Martha took Mitchell-Hedges away. He did not protest too much.

Johnny led Henny into the bar. 'I am not sure what I can offer,' he said. 'As I told you, we do not know each other very well. And I have a quite informally arranged life.'

'That all sounds irresistible.'

'Yes,' said Johnny. 'I imagine it would.' It was a public bar. Covertly, almost everyone was watching them. 'You get used to that,' said Johnny. 'You'd rather not have to, but you do.'

There was a band. Johnny asked her to dance. He danced beautifully, of course. They sat down again.

'Shall we give it a try?' he said.

'And you prefer to leave dangling whether this is a personal invitation or an opportunity to join the not-exactly-the-police?'

'No, I prefer not to leave that dangling, actually, for the sake of my poor smashed heart. If you want in, it's all in. No promises that anything will come of it, and no hard feelings if not, but I'm entering the raffle to win the whole pig.'

'I haven't got anything else to do, I suppose. I learn quickly.'

'Well, that's useful.'

'OK, then. I'm in.'

'Yes. Well, good-oh. I'm pleased. I thought you would say yes, but you never know. Been a while since I cared about the answer.' The edges of his mouth twitched. 'At this stage better tell you, before you know what's what – and this is not in the personal matters, but in the other ones – when I say "Jump!" you have to jump, all right? You won't always know why.'

'I understand,' said Henny.

He walked her to the stairs, kissed her once and said, 'You need to sleep. I'll see you tomorrow.'

'Would you like to come upstairs?'

Johnny checked his watch. 'Very much, but I'd better not,' he said.

'Would the hotel be shocked?'

'No. It's just that I have a couple of things to clear up.'

'I hope this doesn't become a habit.'

'I wouldn't bet on that, certainly. I'm extremely glad you said yes.'

This time, Henny finished her letter to Cecilia. Who knew how the other girl would react.

She woke at three in the morning. Someone was knocking at the door. It was Caister, still in dinner dress. His left arm was dangling uselessly. He grinned, started packing her clothes and said, 'Jump!'

Acknowledgements

Thanks you to my unfailingly supportive agent, Louise Greenberg; to my excellent publishers at Jonathan Cape and Vintage; to all the archivists and librarians who have helped me around the world; to my friends and family, who have heard a lot about fish for a long time; to Stephen Brown as usual; to my hockey teams, cricket teams, Tall Tales and The Mighty Fin; and, most, by miles, to Jane.

Historical Note

I thought long and hard about whether to use real names in *The Dazzle*. As explained in the foreword, I decided that I would enjoy reading the story more if it contained real people, even if I knew that their biographies had been tweaked. I cannot fully explain why this is, because I am evangelical about proper history, but it is probably something to do with the feeling that many modern readers will find it easier to believe that this kind of thing went on in the thirties if there are some Gellhorns and Greys to give them an anchor.

If you think what happens in *The Dazzle* is unlikely, you should read James Fox's brilliant *White Mischief*, the true story of a 1940 murder in Kenya. Biographies of Golden Age movie stars are eye-opening (*Tallulah*, by Joel Lobenthal, for example), and there are also some super books by smaller presses. I particularly enjoyed *The Danes of Send Manor*, by Robert Heal, *What's the Bleeding Time?*, a biography of James Robertson Justice by James Hogg, and Charles Sweeny's autobiography, *Sweeny*. Send, Robertson Justice and Sweeny all appear briefly in *The Dazzle* – Sweeny's wife, Maggie, did eventually marry a duke and remains infamous because of a very rude polaroid.

There are many excellent books which give an insight into the morals and mores of the inter-war fast set, and the literary moderns who were determined to do away with fusty old forms. I'm particularly indebted to Katie Roiphe's *Uncommon Arrangements* and Kate Summerscale's *The Queen of Whale Cay*.

The latter is about Joe Carstairs. Making fictional characters out of Carstairs, and also the Greys, Gellhorn, Mitchell-Hedges and Mitchell-Henry, inevitably involved choices. Not every decision I made was the most likely one, but I don't think I wandered that far from the path.

Zane and Dolly Grey, for instance, maintained an extraordinary open relationship, maybe not quite as open as portrayed here but very similar, and many of the things they say in this book about men and women are drawn closely from their letters to each other. Grey did indeed keep coded private journals about his extra-marital relationships. I have imagined what they might say, based on my reading of him from his letters, journals and books as a sort of ageing, wilful teenager. I strongly recommend Thomas H. Pauly's 2005 biography. As for the secret photographs – I made that bit up. I think Grey might have taken naughty pictures, but I doubt he took them furtively.

Mitchell-Hedges is a very interesting character. He has a lingering fame as the 'discoverer' of the most perfect of the crystal skulls beloved by a certain kind of credulous person (he is name-checked in the fourth *Indiana Jones* movie). He later claimed to have found this skull in Honduras, but he actually bought it at Sotheby's. He was a tremendous fibber and a very decent prose stylist. I have chosen to make him an open-hearted rogue, self-aware and unrepentant. His 'Girl-Friday', Jane, wrote a book of her adventures called *Blue Blaze* which is as gung-ho as Mitchell-Hedges's books of giant fish and features a memorable passage about silk underwear.

Mitchell-Henry was a difficult man who was, indeed, born to great wealth which his father lost on trying to improve his Irish land. He bickered and invented, he was English and eccentric. I know almost nothing about his wife, but I have read about her family and visited their church in New York and I think it's likely that they had a dashing and metropolitan younger period.

Martha Gellhorn is the most 'famous' of my characters. The tortuous entanglement she had just emerged from was with Bernard de Jouvenal, who in his youth had been *that* lover of Colette. She was in Paris at a major international economics conference, where she wrote about hats. She did have some funny ideas about sex, partly as a result of Bertrand, partly via her father, partly via analysis. She was at this time very involved in trying to work out what she was going to do. I heighten here and tighten there as I move her about, but I think mine is a reasonable version of her state of mind. Basically, the Hemingway connection made her inclusion irresistible once I learned that she was in England and that she had just written to G. Campbell about her love for an 'impossible earl'.

As for Johnny, Kim and Caro. I cobbled them together from bits and pieces of real people – a bit of Lord Erroll here, a touch of Vera Brittain there.

As for the rest, I read the standard histories of the early intelligence services – Christopher Andrew is always excellent – and books about inter-war crime. Marek Kohn's *Dope Girls* had a big influence. It was probably a more reliable source than *Murder Must Advertise* by Dorothy L. Sayers, but I can't pretend that the latter didn't help set me on my way.

Kiki Preston is a minor character in almost every one of these books, as she is in mine. The real Kiki was not part of a big dope ring, but she was at least as extraordinary as my version.

A Note on the Type

The Dazzle is set in Goudy Old Style, and not because the font has a jazzy italic 'z' and diamond-shaped full-stops like the signage on the Tube. Or even because of the sharply-canted hyphen. It is simply a charismatic but unfussy font of the book's period.

Frederic Goudy spelled 'Gowdy' until his father learned the old Scots spelling didn't design a font until he was forty. Then, from 1908 onwards, inspired by William Morris and the Arts and Crafts movement, he created more than a hundred. He is famous in certain circles for the typographical witticism, 'Any man who would letter-space blackletter would shag sheep.'

www.vintage-books.co.uk

ALSO BY ROBERT HUDSON

The Kilburn Social Club